# THE RESPLENDENT THRONE

## A LITRPG ADVENTURE

### THE TRANSCENDENT GREEN
### BOOK THREE

## MATI OCHA

Robot Dinosaur Press
robotdinosaurpress.com

*Dha na daoine a tha ga cumail beò.*

*For the people keeping her alive.*

# CHAPTER
## ONE

G hilla felt the intrusion like a barnacle between his shoulder blades.

He was not used to having a corporeal form, but the sensation transcended the spirit-formed flesh, the sinews, the bones. Throughout aeons, he had never felt the need for a physical metaphor—until now. He wanted to scream.

This was not supposed to happen. All of the work he had painstakingly done—building his body from scratch, drawing deeply upon the triune threads of spirit and pathos and will, the focus, the strength—now teetered on the precipice of unravelling like so much wool.

That freshly built body now ached with the overextension of spirit. Spirit exhaustion hurt on a cellular level—no, a *molecular* level. It drained one's energy to the point that electrons moved as slowly as if they'd been frozen. It left his body prickling with the sensation of a million infinitesimal needles rippling across his flesh.

With effort, he got to his feet, supporting himself against a large boulder splattered with blotches of multicoloured lichens like alternating pale green and rust-red filigree.

Ghilla had no idea how long he had been unconscious; he shuddered at the mere thought of being rendered insensible. Yet it had happened as he had tried—and failed—to harness a herd of deer, and though his strength returned, he felt the memory of that all-consuming, dreamless void like staring into a black hole.

And now that he had awoken once more, that gods-forsaken barnacle was still there.

The land around him veritably roiled with spirit. The first waves of ascension were always the most tumultuous, and this unrest would likely last for some time. Ghilla had only a vague awareness of how long it took this dismal, worthless rock to make a circuit of its star, but even that was enough to posit that the people here would be occupied long enough for his purposes.

He hadn't expected resistance.

Oh, Ghilla knew he would encounter aggression—that much was a given. But once his pathos passed from his powerful spirit into its new and unwilling host, that was supposed to be the end of it.

For most, it had been. His creatures sought out the biggest threats and left him trails. They couldn't help but manifest his will on this land.

Or so he had thought.

It had started with that human.

Not the first one, no. That one was consumed enough by his guilt that Ghilla had found steady purchase, and anyway, that first human had perished.

It was the second one.

Perhaps it was that the second one had been infected by the first and not Ghilla himself, but further evidence refuted that vain hope. Whilst he could still feel this second human's alignment with Ghilla's programming, it was this human who was a barnacle between Ghilla's shoulder blades.

Always present, sharp edges and stubbornness and a shrewdness that ought to have long since vanished into rage.

It hadn't stopped there.

Ghilla felt the corvids circling to the east. He had sent them north, and they had obeyed at first—until they didn't. Now, they lurked far enough away that Ghilla could not even act upon them.

He forced himself to look upon the land. It had been sparsely populated before the ascension and was sparsely populated now. This part of Earth was some sort of scenic park, he thought, full of lakes and rolling hills.

That information was virtually useless; Ghilla had no need of fresh water or inane viewpoints. The existing population was another matter, of course, but he could do nothing at all about that for now. That knowledge ate at him, worming under his new-made skin like burrowing larvae.

*Bide, Ghilla. Time is on your side.*

Ghilla drew a breath through his nostrils, feeling the cool air pass over the fine hairs upon his upper lip. When he breathed out once more, the air was warmed by his body.

There. That was better. He had come here as barely a wisp of consciousness, and in such a short time, he had built himself a form of his own.

He could and would surmount this obstacle too.

Brushing the remnants of disturbance from his consciousness, Ghilla began to form a plan.

His greatest threat was to the north.

It rang out like a beacon in his mind, a nascent danger. This being was not yet a true threat, but the whisper of it was there. That it existed at all was remarkable enough in this world that had yet to even drag itself out of the muck of scarcity and violence and squabbles. Ultimately, though, it mattered not; whoever this was lacked Ghilla's strengths, experience, will.

Nonetheless, Ghilla needed to ensure that he approached with caution. Compared to the people of this planet, he was a god, but he was a god who had, like them, begun once more at the lowest rung of the ladder.

Support was imperative.

The deer had been a miscalculation. Being as he was, Ghilla had no class and no helpful updates from the Ascended Alliance. All he had was his memories, his instincts, and his knowledge of spirit. He'd no way of knowing his limits until he hit them and either transcended them or was humbled.

Grudgingly, Ghilla admitted that he could not simply harness other avian species. Not now. Not yet. He needed to further build his strength, and that meant working with what he had, however inconvenient.

If he could not reach the corvids from here, he would go to them, and they would learn their folly.

Some part of him was aware that if they saw him coming, they would simply fly away, and Ghilla himself was not yet capable of flight. *Yet.*

Ghilla *was* capable of stealth.

They would never even see him coming.

None of them would ever see him coming.

He held onto that thought, ignoring his own irrationality, but still that horrid barnacle lingered in the centre of his back with sharp edges and tenacious obstinance.

Once Ghilla had handled the corvids, he would handle that, too.

And then he would turn his focus to the north.

# CHAPTER
# TWO

"Explain it to me like I'm five," I said, scrubbing my face with a towel to keep the sweat from running into my eyes.

Even with the wind coming in from the bay, I was roasting, and an overheated brain did not get on well with maths.

"Think of it like the Richter scale," Meeksy said patiently—or at least patiently compared to Ronald, who'd gotten so annoyed that he'd gone off to punch something for real instead of staying to spar.

"Right," I said. "Something-something a ten pointer is exponentially more powerful than a nine pointer. You're sure this is how it works?"

Meeksy had been about to say something else, but he closed his mouth again, the tightness at the corners of his mouth barely disguised by the neatly trimmed beard that covered most of his face. Maybe not so patient.

Rather than risk further cracks in his veneer of calm, I planted the butt of my staff on the tarmac, unable to resist giving it a jiggle to feel yet again how the crafters of Oban had made tarmac into something that wouldn't absolutely wreck us if we face-planted on it. Which we did often these days. Now, the formerly hard surface had a give to it, like rubber but more responsive to reciprocal force.

The physics nerds of Argyll were having a field day.

"I mean, no," Meeksy replied finally, exasperation creeping into his voice. "This is still conjecture, but it would explain why enemies only a couple levels above us have absolutely handed our arses to us."

"If it's right, though, wouldn't Bawbag have been unstoppable?" I squinted at my friend. "He was level thirty-seven compared to us in our teens. Unless the ascension's punishment really made him that vulnerable."

Meeksy nodded eagerly. "That's just the thing—it stripped him of his class bonuses, and it seems like at least to a degree, having those bonuses is partly what allows for the leap. Also, we've had our own perks helping us that he didn't."

I took a deep breath, leaning my head first to one side and then the other to stretch my neck. Part of me didn't really give a toss why we'd beaten Bawbag—we had killed the bastard, and that was what counted. But at the same time, there would likely be others like him.

Most games I'd played in the days pre-ascension made the experience gain stretch more and more between levels, which was true to an extent for us, but it still didn't account for Bawbag having twenty levels on us.

"You'd think if the power differential were so exponential, they'd make it harder to hit higher levels," I said absently, looking out over the harbour where a pair of fishing boats made their way into the sheltered bay between the arms of the isles of Lismore and Kerrera. The small spire of Hutcheson's Monument at the northernmost tip of Kerrera stood out even from this distance, pointing skyward.

"You say to explain to you like you're five and then you say that," Meeksy muttered, following my gaze.

"Not that deep, mate." I caught his eye and shrugged. "Just seems like they'd make us grind more if that were the case."

"Aye, that'd be my assumption." But Meeksy frowned, staring past me now.

"Then again, we're the outlier in every way," I said on sudden inspiration. "Sure, that power differential matters a lot when you've got people like Bawbag around, and to *us* it seems impossible that there'd be some place anywhere that didnae have his sort. But maybe it's usually moot."

The sweat was starting to dry on my face and neck, sending a chill through me that had nowt to do with the way Meeksy was suddenly looking like he'd swallowed a live rat.

"No, that—bugger." Meeksy let out an annoyed sigh. "I bet that *is* it. We've been working with a shite assumption that there was a paradox when maybe there just isn't one."

"The paradox being . . ."

"That their whole 'work together' schtick clashed with the way higher levels are able to crush lower levels like swatting an entire swarm of midgies in one swipe." Meeksy's exasperation washed away with the gust of salty air that came in from the waves. Excitement crept in to take its place, and his dark eyes veritably sparkled. "If they were only talking a big game about cooperation an' aw, that'd be one thing, but if the places that usually ascend are really starting from a point where they're not having slap fights over land and power, that would actually make sense."

I couldn't blame my friend for the relief in his voice—or the relief I felt. At first, it had seemed like murdering one's way through the populace was a tantalisingly efficient way to level up, and to an extent, that was true. But Bawbag and his flunkies had found out the hard way that brute force only went so far in an ascended world.

A grin started to tug at the corner of my mouth, and Meeksy mirrored it.

"We could make a proper go of this," he said.

The yearning in his voice wasn't lost on me. After years of pandemic and war and, well, humans slap-fighting over land and power, it felt like that brisk breeze flowing in from the Sound of Mull: fresh, clean air and a hope of change for the better.

Not far from where we stood, the mythic birlinn we'd built to cross Loch Awe weeks before floated in berth at the pier's wharf. Birlinn an t-Seann Ghiuthais was its name—it stood as a symbol of what an ascended people could create together.

I was just about to say something about it even as Meeksy loosened his shoulders to get back to sparring.

Naturally, that was when Oban's wards rang out with a deep, threatening *gong*.

Brac-Meanmna flared on my back where I'd placed the weapon —or rather where my living staff had grabbed hold of my armour—and the pulse of spirit from it did nothing to lessen the sudden dread.

Meeksy and I were off running, him panting beside me, heading to the north.

Clouds scudded across the sky, and I spotted rain in the distance up in Ardnamurchan, but it wouldn't reach us for a while yet. For now, we had dry pavements and the shock of our ever-changing ascended landscape.

As my legs pumped to propel me on the path to the breach, I

still couldn't help but goggle at the differences between the Oban I'd grew up in and the Oban we now called home.

All cars had been gathered and their materials repurposed; with ascension crafting, it was terrifyingly easy to strip them to components and make something new from the rubber and metal and glass. The rubber had gone into the sparring area on the north harbour; the metal into weapons and armour and tools.

What was left was streets that seemed far wider than they ever had, a silence in the wake of the vehicles and the air left cleaner with the absence of their exhaust. Beyond that, the bed and breakfasts, the hotels, all of the empty holiday lets owned by folk who didn't deign to spend more than a handful of weeks out of the year here—all of that? Community housing now.

It gave me a fierce sort of glee to see it. For so long, folk like me had been forced out of the Highlands and Islands because we couldn't outbid people who only wanted tourism money and never intended our houses to be homes. Now the landlords could go hang; we'd been here to defend this land when they hadn't. For maybe the first time in Scotland's history, the land belonged to the people who tended it.

People still poured into Oban from the outlying areas as word spread; in the month since we'd defeated Bawbag, the quiet had transformed into life.

And now, as Meeksy and I fell in with another band of higher-levelled fighters with a nod, we saw faces peering out windows at us, along with a few tentative waves.

"Anomalies?" One of the new additions to our sudden trail run asked the question of me.

"Dinnae ken," I said. "We were at the harbour sparring."

We passed Witchwood House with its stately stone and gables, not far south of the Dog Stone—and that was far as we needed to go.

Perched on the top of the stone itself and visible even from five hundred metres away was an enormous golden eagle.

Golden eagles were *already* enormous birds before the ascension, but now? Now they put Tolkien's to shame.

The raptors were a year-round presence in Scotland, elusive in their grandeur. Mull was often the best place to look for them, and if you were lucky enough to see one, you'd scarce doubt it. With a two-metre wingspan, if they came anywhere near you, it'd take your breath away to see them aloft.

This particular specimen was probably more than two metres—tall.

Its wingspan, if it were to spread those massive things, would easily be double that.

The bird made the tree growing out of the top of the Dog Stone look like a sapling.

"Holy shit," someone said behind me, and I had to agree.

As we got closer, I saw a the team of fighters on duty at this edge of the town border hanging back warily, necks craned to watch the eagle.

It was eating a grey seal.

Grey seals, if my fuzzy memory served me, weighed several hundred pounds.

A familiar head of auburn hair turned to look our direction. My heart gave a little patter at the sight of Eilidh MacIntosh, my heart's palpitations a phenomenon that still felt new after the last month.

As was the dopey grin that spread across my face, even more notable for the fact that she returned it with a wide smile every bit as dopey.

"Ah, gaol," Meeksy murmured between heaving breaths as our pace finally slowed.

His sighing about love didn't bother me in the slightest—he

was one to talk anyway, with him and Iain every bit as twitter-pated as freshers with their first crushes even after years together—but Meeksy had earned the right to take the piss. The other folks sniggering, on the other hand, got a sharp look and responded with a few gulps.

Eilidh came to meet us, glancing back once over her shoulder at the golden eagle before breaking into a trot.

"Hey," she said to me, her eyes still full of warmth I couldn't believe was for me. "It hasn't caused any trouble—except for the seal, I guess."

"Aye, that seal had a bad day," I agreed.

Unlike the goshawk, which had attacked us in the middle of the night, this eagle was clearly otherwise occupied. Clach a' Choin—the Gaelic name for the Dog Stone—was a decent place for a giant bird to eat uninterrupted.

Reflexively, I reached out to the golden eagle with Connection and a thread of Tàthadh. I wasn't really trying to create a bond with the bird, but I was curious.

She seemed to reciprocate that curiosity. With some amusement, the touch of her mind told me that she'd not just chosen Clach a' Choin for a luncheon spot for its height. We'd activated a different kind of stone not long after defeating Bawbag—the keystone that protected the town from invading forces—but we had wards in place too in case of more mundane threats.

The golden eagle, it seemed, could sense both.

*Safety-nest-home* was the predominant impression I got from her, along with a fierce admiration. People used "bird brain" to mean stupidity, but this creature's brain was easily five times the size of a human's and had clearly grown its intelligence right alongside its sheer volume of brain matter.

Somewhat cautiously, I returned the same impression she had given me. Safety, nest, home. Protection and community I added to it. Eagles were often solitary birds, but the respect she returned with my offered thought told me she saw the value in a flock.

Her stomach satisfied on seal meat, she paused in her — gruesome—lunch to lift her blood-covered beak. The eagle's head cocked to the side as she gazed at me.

To my utter surprise, the next thought that came to me from her mind was something I could only describe as asking for permission.

Like me, she wasn't looking for a bond, or at least not the type that Tàthadh offered.

What she wanted was what we had.

*Safety-nest-home?*

Flummoxed, I looked around at the others. I wasn't in charge here; we didn't have anyone who fit that description.

"She wants to know if she can live here," I said aloud, seeing a few startled heads turn in my direction. "The eagle. She admires us and wants to stay."

"What?" Meeksy turned on his heel to look at me. "You're *talking to birds now?*"

I shrugged. "She wants to stay."

Pausing, I listened, cracking a smile in the raptor's direction. She'd resumed eating, seemingly unbothered by the squawking of flightless humans—or, as was maybe more correct these days, elves—but despite her nonchalance, she was indeed invested in my answer.

The next thought that came through from her was another series of impressions, these ones of soaring high above the Minch to the west, beyond Mull and Eigg. The fish were changing there, big enough to sustain her, and she could be helpful to us without being a burden.

That *all* of that came through with little doing from me told me this eagle had grown in far, far more than simple wingspan alone.

"She says she won't hunt here and she won't hunt people," I said slowly. "She's offering to not just shelter here but to be part of our community."

"Every time I think I've seen the weirdest shit possible, this shit gets weirder," muttered a woman whose name I didn't know, quickly silenced by an elbow to the ribcage from another woman who looked like she had to be a sister. Pale cheeks flushed pink as they both caught me looking at them.

"Any objections to our feathered friend?" I asked dryly. "Aside from the weirdness quotient."

After a moment of hesitation, heads shook.

"If she can pick up a seal, do you reckon—" This came from a wide-eyed young lad, probably in his early twenties, and it was hushed just as quickly, this time by Meeksy.

Satisfied, I reached out to the eagle once more, extending our welcome.

The giant raptor straightened up from where she'd been eating again, and her feathers puffed up in pride.

With an ear-splitting screech of triumph, the golden eagle winged her way into the sky. Her feathers sent gusts of wind and dislodged leaves and dirt hurtling towards us where we stood in awe.

One enormous feather drifted downwards from her exit, and without a thought, I walked over to it. It was as long as my arm, heavy when I picked it up. I had the sudden absurd image of Eilidh sprawled languidly in a meadow with someone fanning her with this single giant feather.

"You know," Eilidh said thoughtfully, chasing the errant thought from my head as she stared after Oban's newest inhabitant, "I reckon she triggered the wards on purpose. She knew exactly what she wanted—and I think she knew who she wanted to talk to."

At that, every eye turned to me where I stood holding the feather in both hands as it caught the gust of wind blowing in from the sea. I hastily tucked it away into my inventory.

"My wren friend is going to be jealous" was all I could think to say in response.

CHAPTER

# THREE

With the wards a false alarm and no further incidence of anomalies corrupting the countryside, we quickly settled back into our still-young routine.

For me, that meant time with Brac-Meanmna and a *lot* of time crafting.

It felt like curiosity had infected the entire town. Maybe it was that most people's jobs had vanished overnight; maybe it was purely that magic was suddenly real and accessible to *everyone*. But it felt like that first month had ignited a fire under everyone's arse to explore what this ascension had made possible.

People poured in from the rest of Argyll, but people also trickled out—many wanted to search for family and friends who had stayed outwith Argyll. Others went to establish lines of communication, which wasn't going nearly as quickly as anyone had hoped. While we had communication crystals gu leòr now *and* the promise of instantaneous travel, the communication crystals at this level only worked over a few miles, and until another community was able to establish itself, the whole teleportation thing was moot.

Even so, lines of connection inched outwards from the town, and within Oban itself, people made miracles.

The first thing had been sanitation. One thing you learn *really* bloody quick in an apocalypse is just how fast you start caring about plumbing and sewage. All the little things we'd taken for granted living in the twenty-first century meant there was an immediate fervour in favour of, well, fixing shit.

Literally.

Or maybe fixing shitters.

Plumbers and mages worked together on drainage and wastewater and simply making sure the people of our community had running clean water. With what we'd learnt from my woodworking and Ealasaid's further experimentation, it was less a matter of "how" and more a matter of "how quickly can we get round to every occupied home?" From there, boilers quickly got disconnected from gas lines and reconnected to enchantments and glyphs.

The collective cry of ecstatic relief when hot showers returned? Aye, that was memorable.

As for me, though, aside from helping out with those things where they just needed a deft use of spirit or someone to convince a family of ascension-enlarged mice to go about their mousey business elsewhere, I focused on my own strengths.

And I was finding, after several weeks of this, that my strengths leaned heavily towards the arcane levels of crafting.

It wasn't much of a surprise, not with my affinities and my connection with trees, but even so, it filled me with a certain amount of awe. Sure, working in IT had sometimes felt like I was toying with occult forces beyond my ken, but getting to see the work of my hands on fishing boats, on storefronts, in people's own paws, in armour and tools and trimmings?

It made me feel like I was contributing to the community

with more than just being in the right—or wrong—place at the right time.

The other wonder of this was the experience.

With the constant threat of Bawbag and never knowing what else would attack us, we hadn't had the time to understand or appreciate this aspect of the system. But once we were safe and the town secure?

It became obvious just how much of a fool Bawbag had been.

Before the ascension, he'd already been the type of person to believe in some sort of divine right of those born into wealth to take whatever they wanted from the rest of us. He'd dived into the world of magic only looking for what he could take, had figured out quickly that killing humans raised his level, and he'd taken every impulse to control, to subjugate, and to plunder.

At first, I'd thought the Ascended Alliance must have committed a grave oversight in just how fast Bawbag had managed to level—but that was only until we killed him and discovered for ourselves why we'd even been able to touch him.

Because as strong as he'd been, for all the experience he'd drained from the lives of other people, if this had been a normal ascension and not a fluke? If Earth's people had been prepared for it, had passed all of the required tests and met all of the necessary requirements?

Bawbag would have been squashed before he even began.

This was what occupied my thoughts as I made my way through Oban. The town was the same—and it was also worlds different. A mere month and the street lamps glowed with magic at night, fuelled by the sun. They could shift colours with a burst of spirit, and the fairy lights strung between them could do the same. No more LEDs or filaments. Just simple glass globes hung by crafters.

Eilidh was waiting for me near the old CalMac ferry terminal where one Oban landmark remained in full steam— literally. The seafood stall bustled with people now that the fishing boats were able to venture out again. The only difference was that nobody used money.

It was a strange, utopian sensation to watch folks simply wander up to the stall and take their mussels and langoustines. Everyone seemed like they had let out an impossibly full breath.

Everyone except Eilidh.

She had a half-eaten piece in her hand, her shoulders straight and tense like a cord pulled taut, about to snap with a twang.

Her gaze focused on the nearby Isle of Kerrera, one of the two arms of land that guarded Oban harbour from the winds and weather blowing in through the Sound of Mull from the Minch beyond.

I tasted salt on the air as I made my way over to her.

When she glanced at me, sensing my approach before her eyes and ears told her I was near, some of that tension faded. A slightly bewildered smile tugged at her lips, and her shoulders crept downwards from where they'd been nudging up towards her jaw.

"Shin thu," I said fondly, closing the distance between us.

"Shin thu fhèin." Her smile went from bewildered to tentative, but the light in her eyes was what drew me.

I gave her a brief hug, smelling the salt air on her hair and the lingering scent of heather and raspberries from her soap. Eilidh returned the hug as she always did, tightly despite its brevity, as if she were determined to prove to herself I was really here.

We'd been taking things at a glacial pace, which didn't bother me.

Something in me relaxed around her, with her presence. It felt like the time I'd gone guisin' at Hallowe'en and wore a polyurethane mask, smothering me all night when I didn't think I could get away with taking it off. When I'd finally removed it, damp and smelling of rubber, it had been like emerging from a cocoon.

That's how it was with Eilidh these days. No mask. No smothering. Just clean sea air and the scent of home.

"You all right?" I asked her in English.

Her blue eyes were nearly the colour of the sea, framed by auburn lashes she hadn't darkened with mascara. The delicate —and new—points to her ears poked up through her loose curls. I still couldn't get over how much they suited her.

"Just a strange feeling," she told me after a beat, her eyes reluctantly leaving mine to gaze back out over the harbour.

"Danger?"

"Chan eil fhios agam." She murmured that she didn't know in Gaelic, eyes turning pensive. Then she appeared to shake herself. "Are you ready to go see what Ronald's caught for us?"

Now it was my turn to turn pensive. "No," I said dryly. "I don't want to get anywhere near those anomalies again, but I'm not sure we have a choice."

Eilidh turned back to me, cracking a smile at that. "Aye, I know the feeling. Reckon that means we should get it over with."

"You are, as usual, correct," I said playfully. I caught her hand and kissed it, watching her eyes soften again at the gesture.

Without another word, we headed towards the Whyte house, where Sailean would be waiting.

I couldn't shake the feeling, though, that Eilidh could be right about her own strange premonition. A pulse of Connection returned nothing unexpected, but now that she'd said something, her apprehension had lodged in my mind. We'd had so many threats on land alone, none of us had really had to deal with danger from the deeps. The thought made me look out over the sea, but nothing disturbed the waters.

The house was empty when we got there, but for the Scottish wildcat kitten we sought.

For Sailean's part, she felt us coming and had her furry wee face practically plastered to the window in the lounge that looked out over the doorstep. A soundless mew accompanied her tiny mouth opening and closing. The kitten's presence in my mind was a ball of desperation and love.

Eilidh chuckled, shaking her head. "One of these days, she's no gonnae let us leave the house without her."

Cracking open the door, I snorted as I heard the telltale thump and scrabble of claws on the wood floor, followed by Sailean launching herself at my leg and climbing me like a rock wall.

I grimaced. "Nach tu tha biorach," I grumbled, wincing at the sharpness of her claws.

Sure, my skin would heal in a moment, but that didn't mean I rejoiced in puncture wounds. Sailean's answering purr made it worth it, though.

"She's got you wrapped around one of those tiny paws," Eilidh said with a grin, shrugging out of her jacket and making for the corridor to where her room lay.

Catrìona was out on the fishing boat for the day, and I didn't know where Iain and Meeksy were, but we'd a full house these days. Eilidh's room had been the office of Catrìona's late husband, who'd passed a few months before the ascension.

Sometimes I caught Catrìona staring at Dougie's door, her grief still palpable.

And sometimes I had to wonder—if he'd held on just a few more months, would the ascension have healed his cancer? It had healed others.

It was something none of us dared to voice aloud. We'd no power to change the past, only the choices of the present.

Sailean teetering on my shoulder with her tail curled around my neck for balance, I made my way up the stairs to my own room. It didn't take long to get myself kitted out—the literal kitten didn't count—in my armour. Brac-Meanmna, my living staff, hung on the wall beside the door.

Like with the the kitten, I felt a surge of excitement and affection from the thing, which was much more disconcerting from a glorified stick than it was from a small mammal.

Regardless, I couldn't help but return the affection.

I cast Keen Eye on it, not expecting it to show me anything beyond what it already had. If we'd been in a literal video game, I was certain it would have extolled the virtues of my glorified stick, but as it was, the ascension's system simply treated it like it was a person.

*Brac-Meanmna*

*Level 20 Living Staff*

*Affinities: Nature, Healing, Synthesis*

*Specialised Affinities: Wild, Coimhearsnachd*

*This staff was made by your hand and will be your lifelong companion, growing with you as well as teaching you.*

That was it. Nothing earth-shattering, no hints at how best to utilise it, nothing. Nada. Zilch.

But the one thing I had learnt myself was that the more I used it, the more I *communed* with it, the more natural my magic felt.

Displacing Sailean for the present—she was well-used to

the drill by now and sat primly on the edge of my bed—I quickly put on my armour. We didn't expect much trouble en route to where Ronald had holed up with his captured anomaly, but I wasn't about to take any risks.

Well. Any more risks than the existing folly of catching a corrupted, dangerous critter who could potentially infect others.

Safe as houses.

After the armour, I added an item I'd made myself, if clumsily. Working with wood was easier than working with leather, so Eilidh'd had to help me, but I was proud of the outcome.

Sailean was adamant about not being left behind again, and while she was growing quickly—too quickly, as kittens are wont to do—she was still a baby. Which meant we needed a way to both transport her and to keep her safe in case of battle.

Never in my life did I think I'd be trotting about Argyll with a living stick and a kitten in a magically warded bum bag, but strangely, I didn't think I'd trade it for the world.

The moment I'd secured the bum bag—it *was* a bum bag, let's be real—Sailean vaulted into it from the bed, turning around three times before settling with her paws on the small ledge around its edge.

That bit could be pulled over her like a convertible's soft top, and it was patently ridiculous and engraved with protective ogham, but magic rendered it virtually impenetrable.

Perfect for protecting a baby half of Oban'd probably die for.

"Deiseil is deònach?" I asked the kitten, who peered up at me and let out an answering mew.

Her accompanying surge of *yes* energy through our bond told me she was, indeed, ready and willing.

I gave her head a pat, hearing Eilidh downstairs.

"Right, ma-tà," I muttered. "Rachamaid is rollamaid."

Eilidh's burst of laughter at my "let's rock and roll" pun almost made me forget why we were leaving Oban today.

The image of the giant anomalous rabbit's rotting flesh helpfully emerged in my mind.

Almost forget. Not quite.

Ronald had holed up in Kilmelford, south of Oban. Most of the people from the village had migrated into Oban proper already, and it was still close enough for him to raise the alarm if something went terribly wrong. It was also far enough away that we'd have time to respond to said alarm.

After so many weeks of danger, even the following weeks of relative peace had left us all on edge. It was one thing to be in constant crisis-response mode, something else entirely to adjust to a new reality.

All of us except the youngest weans had experienced that once before with COVID, when the world changed overnight and hugging a friend became a potentially life-threatening behaviour. Having to do it all over again but with the full understanding that things would *never* return to normal again? Aye, that was enough to shake even the most stoic Highlanders.

As Eilidh and I made our way out of Oban at a brisk walk, people greeted us and waved as they went about their own business. That was something else to get used to. Sure, I knew what it was like to live in rural areas where you run into people you know all the time, but this was different. Before, it'd been a two-way street. If they knew me, I knew them too. Now, though? Now, most of the people who greeted us knew me and Eilidh on sight, but we didn't know them unless they were in the relatively smaller circle of folk we'd worked with or bled with on the battlefield.

Both Eilidh and I relaxed as we got out of Oban proper, keeping the sea on our right until we had to turn southward and cut overland until we reached Loch Feochan. The clouds covered the sky, letting through only diffuse light, but I wisnae worried about rain. Imagine it taking the end of the world to rid Scotland of brollies—the rain remained, aye, but with magic, we no longer had to end up soggy.

Just went to prove right that old saying: there's no such thing as bad weather, only the wrong clothing.

"What do you reckon he's found?" Eilidh asked me suddenly as indeed a light mist swept in from the sea.

"Not a clue. Hopefully some idea of how to reverse the corruption or at least contain it." I could hear the doubt in my own voice, and from my kitten carrier, I heard Sailean's answering disgruntled mew.

As was my usual strategy, I cast about with Connection, even knowing Eilidh was likely doing the same. It was the base spell of the Nature tree, and since it was tough to live in the Highlands of Scotland *without* gaining some sort of affinity for nature, just about everyone had it. Connection was also one of the most useful skills I'd learned. The number of times it had saved our collective arses was adding up to *a lot*. It didn't look like much on the surface, but the more you used it, the more you were able to see exactly how the flows of spirit in this ascended world worked upon each other, see how they interacted and shifted with the currents of people's actions and reactions.

Because it was my usual strategy, I didn't expect to find anything out of our new normal's ordinary.

I should have known better.

Nothing in this ascended world ever stayed the same for long.

My spell was higher levelled than Eilidh's for now, but she wasn't far behind. I barely had time to stop short in disbelief, my feet skidding on the tarmac of the A816, before Eilidh let out an exclamation of surprise.

"Thighearna, dè fon ghrèin—"

Her startled *what the hell* was cut off by a sound that made my skin ripple into gooseflesh. The noise was one that we both recognised instantly—it just didn't belong here. Not in Scotland.

An eerie song rose up through the hills off to the west on the outcropping of land that was home to several lodges and holiday parks, obviously now closed.

Then another voice joined the first—and another.

Never in my life would I have expected to hear the sound of a howling pack of wolves in Argyll.

"How can that—*what*?" I wasn't quite as articulate as Eilidh'd been.

It was an asinine question considering we'd battled a fuath, met a glaistig, pulverised a beithir, and I'd just made pals with a giant eagle. But wolves were a real creature, just one that had long since been hunted to extinction.

Their voices seemed to be moving away from us. Both Eilidh and I stared into the west in the direction they were headed. There wasn't much but burns and hills and eventual sea—the Sound of Kerrera and the Irish Sea beyond, Mull in the distance.

"Should we . . . follow them?" Eilidh asked uncertainly. "A pack of wolves could be a problem, especially ascended ones."

"I think we need to get to Ronald, but we should warn

Oban, just in case they didn't hear that howling." As I said it, I reached for my one bandolier that crossed my armour, where I'd tucked a communication crystal.

It didn't take long for me to alert Oban's patrols about the wolves, and even as I did, I heard the person on the other end make a startled sound.

"Looks like another report just came in from someone else," the bloke told me. "We'll send someone who can get close without being seen."

"Send Rhona," I said immediately. "She's good at risk assessment."

There was a moment of silence, but then I could almost hear the man's nod before he agreed verbally. "Got it."

"Let me know if anything else of note happens," I said. Placing the crystal back in its leather casing, I shook myself.

"Every time I think I am getting a handle on this, something else changes," Eilidh murmured, a shadow passing over her face.

"I know," I said. "But we're not alone in this anymore."

The shadow faded almost as soon as it had come, and the skin at the corner of Eilidh's blue eyes crinkled ever so slightly with her small answering smile.

"Aye, you're right," she said. "That's all anyone can ask for."

Without another word, she broke into a trot, and I hurried to keep up, wondering once again if there was a second conversation happening beneath whatever one I thought we'd been having.

The rest of the journey to Kilmelford passed without incident— at least in ascension terms. We encountered a few spirit-twisted critters, all easily dispatched, and soon we were skirting the edge of Loch nan Druimnean on the way into the village.

Another loch lay just to the east of Loch nan Druimnean, this one Loch a' Phearsain, which was where the wee bothy Ronald had commandeered sat, nestled between the water and the A816.

Smoke curled from the bothy's chimney, filling the air with the familiar smell of peat.

For all intents and purposes, the small, whitewashed shelter looked practically cosy.

It was anything but, if what it held was any indicator. There was little cosy about a creature mutated into a state of living decay, full of rage but not even undead, just continuing to exist.

I just hoped Ronald hadn't found, like, an adorable stoat or pine marten or something. Then again, I couldn't think of anything that would be *preferable* to see in such a state. An adder? A house spider?

The thought was enough to make me shudder.

"Ready for this?" Eilidh asked me as we approached, a wry smile tugging at her lips.

"Not really." I returned the smile just as wryly to her answering snort. "Something-something in the name of science, right?"

"Oh, naturally."

Our light back-and-forth was really just nerves. I could feel the shifts in spirit between us. Whatever connected me to this woman served like a string between two tins. What came through might not have always been perfectly intelligible, but it did give me the sense of tension.

I walked up to the door of the bothy, but before I could knock, it opened.

"Oh good, you're here," Ronald said without preamble, turning aside and leaving the door open.

"Hello, Ronald. Nice to see you." I stepped over the threshold, wincing at the smell. The peat smoke, instead of masking the odour of decay, merely added a layer to it, like the oaky flavour of an aged wine, but a million times grosser. "Less nice to smell this place."

"What?" Ronald turned on his heel as Eilidh followed me in.

She started to close the door behind her, then wrinkled her nose and seemed to think better of wasting the breeze of fresh air from outwith the bothy's pungent interior.

"The smell," I said to Ronald patiently. "It smells like week-old roadkill in here."

"Oh. You get used to it."

I wasn't sure that was a good thing.

"What *is* it, exactly?" Eilidh asked, peering at a rectangular crate nestled in the corner of the bothy's single room. A rough-woven burlap cloth had been flung over it, and it was eerily quiet within.

A tentative pulse of Connection disabused me of that illusion very quickly.

The silence broke immediately as if the anomalous rabbit inside sensed my spirit. Maybe it did.

Ronald walked over and removed the burlap, revealing the rabbit. Even with my spirit recognising it first, I wasn't prepared for the sight. Hell, Eilidh and I had fought literal hundreds of the things, but this one was somehow worse. Rotting goo oozed from its missing patches of fur, and similar to everything else we'd seen like it, it had an uncanny surreality to it, like turpentine poured over a photorealistic oil painting of a zombie bunny.

The thing was grotesque in every sense of the word, a picture of the macabre.

I couldn't possibly have explained it, but beyond the simple revulsion, the thing filled me with dread.

There were far too many questions. Where were these things coming from and why? Did those blokes down south just stumble upon the anomalies or did they have something to do with the creation? If it was contagious, how?

Ronald was saying something, and I was too lost in my head to have heard it.

"Sorry, what was that?" I asked when I noticed he was looking at me expectantly.

He gave an exasperated sigh.

"I said that whatever the corrupting influence is, it's stable. It doesn't seem to progress past a certain point." Ronald turned away from me, pointing at the unfortunate mammal. "I do think it is something that doesn't happen immediately, but once it begins, it climbs to the level you see here."

I thought of that bloke, Ezekiel Bosworth. Was he . . . like this now? The thought was unsettling to the extreme. I wouldn't wish that on anyone. Well. Maybe a few people, but only the ones responsible for making this island the absolute bin fire it was even before the ascension. Like Ezekiel's father. Instead, it seemed like the sins of the father skipped the perpetrator and visited themselves upon the son, who I almost hoped was as big a wanker as his da so he might deserve the fate this rabbit displayed.

On the bright side, at least the apocalypse inadvertently ended the energy crisis the elder Bosworth had practically created himself.

"Do you think there's any hope of reversing it?" Eilidh's blue eyes narrowed at the hapless creature in the cage, which simply sat there and quivered in response, loose rotting flesh jiggling with the movement of the tremors.

"No idea yet," Ronald said. "Alison is going to join me tomorrow for some experiments. While you're here, though, I could use your help. Maybe that ability of yours—what is it, Keen Eye?—could give us some sort of clue."

"B' fhiach an fheuchainn, co-dhiù," I muttered, more to myself than to anyone else.

"What?" Ronald said blankly.

"Worth a shot," Eilidh translated. "You know you can just use the clach-cànain, right?"

"Everyone speaks English." Ronald squinted at Eilidh as if she were suggesting he take up trapeze instead of walking from points A to B.

Eilidh and I exchanged a glance, and she—probably prudently—changed the subject, moving closer to the rabbit and asking Ronald about its feeding.

Speaking multiple languages for me was obviously second nature, but also there were so many studies that showed the cognitive benefits that I couldn't understand for the life of me why someone wouldn't take the chance if all they literally had to do was pick up a rock.

Then again, there was plenty I didn't understand about Ronald.

"It seems to still be able to survive on a herbivorous diet despite its eagerness for meat," Ronald was saying, which only served to reinforce my previous thought. "I'm not sure if it actually wants to eat meat or if it's just trying to kill, but the instinct is obviously unnatural for a herbivore."

"That's not entirely true," I said suddenly. "Rabbits sometimes eat their own young—that was true even before the ascension. It frequently has to do with whether they're territorial or protein deprived in some way, and it also sometimes happens when a kit is stillborn, but it's not unheard of or even that rare."

Both Eilidh and Ronald were staring at me, Eilidh with an unsurprised nod and Ronald with a look of horror on his face.

I shrugged.

Naturally, the rabbit took that moment to start to scream.

# CHAPTER
# FIVE

"What the fuck is happening?" I had to almost yell the words over the incessant screech from the anomalous rabbit.

It felt as if every hair on my body was standing at attention —or possibly trying to wriggle itself out of its follicles. The noise was like silverware on ceramics in the hand of a sadist. Worse than fingernails on a chalkboard could ever *dream* of being. It gave me the distinctly horrific sensation of having my eardrums shredded with a cheese grater.

Worse, the rabbit wasn't scrabbling at the cage or trying to escape. Oh, no. It was standing stock still in the centre of the cage, its mouth twisted agape in a terrifying rictus that exposed its long incisors and the necrotised flesh inside its mouth, puffy and bloated like a cottonmouth snake's.

Ronald muttered something inaudible over the ghastly din.

Connection told me nothing when I slammed spirit into it. Keen Eye was similarly unhelpful.

*Anomalous Rabbit*

*Caught in a wave of spirit upon Earth's ascension, this rabbit mutated far faster than can normally be expected for a creature of its complexity.*

*As you have already established, anomalous creatures are vulnerable to Purifire, but this creature is under the effects of an unknown power.*

It was my turn to mutter under my breath. Wincing against the impulse that struck next, I gritted my teeth as I did the one thing I *really* did not want to do.

I reached out to the anomalous rabbit with Tàthadh.

Like with the eagle, the goal was not to establish an actual bond with the creature—no bloody way in hell—but more to see if and how it would be different to another creature.

At first, I didn't think it was going to work at all. My tendrils of spirit seemed to slip right off the edges of the creature's mind like trying to grab a hot plate with buttered hands.

But then something reached for my spirit.

Or not reached.

*Grabbed.*

My feet rooted to the battered wooden floorboards of the bothy and a cord blazed into existence in my mind.

It wasn't the rabbit.

I didn't know much, but that alone was clear.

No, it was as if I were seeing *through* the rabbit like peering through an impossibly long telescope.

And something was staring right back at me.

Recoiling was pure instinct. I jerked my spirit away from the rabbit, my feet freeing themselves from the floor in a stumbling step away from the cage as if the movement could somehow evict the sensation of pure wrongness that had lodged itself in my core.

Both Ronald and Eilidh stared at me. I was dimly aware that the rabbit had stopped its horrifying screaming. Somehow, that was far worse.

The rabbit's eyes were locked onto me without blinking, its mouth still open soundlessly.

Without further thought, I lashed out with Purifire, incinerating the creature where it sat with a whip of pure, blue-green flame.

Despite my explanation, Ronald was perturbed at my murder of his subject.

Eilidh, however, had my back.

"The entire point of researching these creatures is to learn about them—not to paint a target on our heads," she said to the man, her tone so reasonable that he gave her a grudging nod. "If whatever is causing that corruption somehow saw through the rabbit's eyes, Calum absolutely did the right thing."

"It did," I said darkly. "It certainly, without a single doubt, one hundred percent did."

The rabbit had been reduced to cinders in the cage, but the putrid scent lingered, even though we'd thrown open all the windows in addition to the already-open door. What also lingered was the unnerving sense that I'd been perceived. Not just seen, but measured.

Measured and found to be a threat.

"We did learn something, at least," I added after a reluctant pause.

"And what is that, exactly?" Ronald had gone to lean up

against the worktop on the far edge of the bothy, an unhappy grimace still twisting his nearly nonexistent lips.

"A couple of things. One, don't use Tàthadh on them." I bared my teeth at that. A few other people had accessed that skill—not many, but enough that the warning was useful. "Two, the anomalies are indeed connected. Not just to each other, but to whatever created them. And whatever *that* is, it's an intelligent consciousness."

"That *is* useful information," Ronald said with a grumble. He gave me a nod, blowing out a breath. "And if it saw you, it probably won't hesitate to send more."

Eilidh's gaze was pensively glued to a knot in the wood floor. "Calum," she said suddenly, blue eyes moving to catch my own. "Remember how the rabbits we fought before seemed to come straight for us?"

"Aye," I said. "I wish I could forget."

"So it already knew we were here, at least peripherally."

"That sounds reasonable," I agreed. "But now it really knows we're here."

"Maybe that's a good thing," she said.

Ronald's long neck swivelled to turn his head so he could stare at Eilidh. "How could that possibly be good?"

But I was following. Himbo hamster or no, I wasn't a complete dunce.

"If it was just sending things off to look for us, that makes it harder for us to predict. But if we know it's coming for us . . ." I trailed off, giving Eilidh a crooked smile she returned just as lopsidedly.

"Then we can both prepare and react." She turned to regard Ronald. "You'll have to find another specimen to study."

"Yes, I had figured that out," he said dryly. "My last one is ashy paste."

"You may still be able to learn from that paste," Eilidh told him. "Get some scientists or alchemists out here, but be careful."

"Perhaps you ought to tell that to your man," Ronald retorted, eyeballing me.

Touché. I ignored the bite of his words in favour of the sudden heady glow of thinking of myself as Eilidh's man—we hadn't labelled ourselves as anything, really, but the bloke wisnae wrong.

"I solemnly swear to avoid serving the next one en flambé," I said, more flippantly than I meant to. "But really, mate, when it comes to these things, it's better safe than sorry."

"I'll get the team on it again."

Ronald's words were a clear dismissal, and with a shrug in Eilidh's direction, I made my way out of the bothy even as the beanpole of a former schoolteacher started talking into his communication crystal.

Both Eilidh and I remained somewhat pensive for the entirety of our return to Oban. Sailean, somehow unperturbed by the entire anomaly debacle—perhaps she just trusted I'd deal with it—woke up only as we reached the harbour.

"I'm going to go find out what I can about the wolves," Eilidh said to me, her brow creased with a mixture of bewilderment and concern. "If nothing else, more big predators are something to look out for. Though they might keep the deer population under control."

She came close enough to me to kiss my cheek, a soft brush of lips and a fond smile somehow a ghost and a promise at once. Sailean gave a mew from her carrier, and Eilidh reached in to give the kitten a wee scritch behind the ears. She seemed to hesitate for a moment, but then Eilidh withdrew her hand and gave me an uneven smile, which I returned, probably every inch as unevenly.

I nodded at her as she trotted away, hearing Ronald's words again. *Your man.*

Whether Eilidh thought of me like that or not, I couldn't see fault with it. It felt right, somehow.

From Sailean's tiny purr, I had the strangest feeling the kitten agreed.

With some effort, I made my way towards the CalMac pier, where sailors and dockhands were hard at work on *An t-Eilean Muileach*, or the *Isle of Mull*, the ferry that ran between Oban and Craignure and had been in port when the world ended. If we could get that working with magic, it would restore a major, major connection between us and the Hebrides.

The thought made a lump form in my throat, so I cleared it with a cough, turning my mind to what Eilidh had said before she departed.

Since Scotland had eradicated the European lynx, bears, and wolves, we'd had no large predators that could threaten the deer—or many things much smaller. The lack of predators meant that small mammals proliferated, which wasn't wholly a bad thing, but it also had consequences, like the absolute tick epidemic in South Uist that led to the island having the highest incidence of Lyme disease in most of the world. Something like eight percent of the ticks in Uist carried that nasty bug.

One of the bizarre positive side effects of the apocalypse was that our newly ascended world meant we could heal people of Lyme.

I shook my head in disbelief at the thought—never thought I'd be grateful for an apocalypse.

Beyond the work on the ferry, the pier and the cleared carparks beyond had become the site of our crafting emporium.

As I approached, the yells on the ferry gave way to the buzz of spirit on the air, punctuated every so often with chatter.

The mixture of people was encouraging to see—multiple generations worked together, from older woodworkers helping explain and give context to ascension-driven knowledge to adolescents plunked into an unschooling philosophy where they were learning by doing. Even a few younger weans were dotted in amid everyone else. Whether they were helping or not was anyone's guess, but it gave me hope.

They'd grow up in such a different world to the one they'd been born into. With a bit of effort, maybe it'd even be better.

My own purposes for coming here were pretty straightforward. Rectangular, actually.

The woodworking area had grown since my last visit, with new bundles of tools in a magic-hewed set of cubbies. My fingers itched to give them a go; while we *could* craft just fine without tools at all, the most exciting developments had come from master woodworkers pre-ascension. They'd learnt to hone their skills with ascension knowledge, and we were all profiting from it every day.

There was something I wanted to do to contribute.

Our other woodworkers could cover a wide range of things we *needed* in Oban. They were making staves, bows, tools, tables, just about anything we could think of, all of it with magical properties that would enhance our community. From the attributes we'd discovered on our trek here from Bawbag's manor, like increasing nutrition and purifying water, to new additions that prevented pest incursions and ensured structural longevity, we were learning that this new world would prepare us for the long haul.

They had all that well in hand. What they didn't have was something I did, and I thought I'd finally figured out what I wanted to do with perhaps the weirdest trophy I'd collected.

Bawbag's mahogany doors.

I wanted to do something that would utterly cheese the man off if he were still alive. Call it spite, call it cheek, call it whatever you want—it was clear those doors meant something to him. Probably something that came at others' expense. If I had anything to say about it, which I did, I was going to turn the wood into something that would *open* doors for others, not slam them in people's face.

And I thought I knew just what I wanted to do.

Oban wasn't monolingual, not by far. Beyond English, Gaelic, and Scots, we had Meeksy's Farsi along with Hindi, Mandarin, Cantonese, Thai, Swahili, Arabic, and many others.

What would it be like to live in a world where we could all speak to each other in everyone's native tongues? For those who might never see family again or who had come to Scotland as refugees? How much might it mean to them to know that anyone could pick up a stone, a precious Clach-Cànain, and be able to understand them?

I had no idea what that sort of world would be like; I only knew that I was dead set on finding out.

Finding an open workstation, I opened Sailean's carrier, letting my hip jut forwards so she could scramble onto the surface of the table. Her warm, furry presence in my mind surged with affection as she clambered onto the wooden surface, whiskers puffed forwards with curiosity and her little stick tail straight up. Her confidence was encouraging. Be she but tiny, she was ready to take on the world.

We humans could learn from her on that score.

Sailean, showing prudence beyond her years—or, more accurately, weeks—moved out of the way of the table's centre, scampering over to the long worktop that connected the various stations. There was a series of cubbies, all empty, and she promptly picked one and slunk straight in, turning around a few times before settling in a furry ball, blinking owlishly at me from her new cave. I gave her a fond grin, which she returned with a yawn that did psychic damage for the pure cuteness.

Her little whiskers peeled back, tiny teeth exposed, and her wee face practically split in two.

"Big yawn," I said appreciatively, out of pure obligation.

A low murmur arose when I pulled the doors out of my inventory, but people still gave me a wide berth, going about their business with little more than a glance over their shoulders at me.

I really wasn't sure what to do.

But humans have always been good at beating the odds.

Frustrated, I moved Brac-Meanmna from its place between my shoulder blades. The work bench where I was stationed had a place for staves, and I was grateful for that. My living weapon was a powerful focus, as I was learning, and its help with this project would be invaluable.

My staff's eagerness rose to meet my own spirit as I began to channel my magic. Before doing anything targeted, though, I sank my spirit into the doors themselves, much as I might with a living tree.

Wood was technically dead, but memory remained in its cells, its DNA, its atoms. Spirit allowed me access to all of those things.

For the second time that day, I recoiled.

A wave of revulsion rushed over me, like getting splashed with an ocean swell made of backwash from a fucking spittoon.

I fought the urge to retch.

It was as if just being in Bawbag's manor had infused the wood with his sickness. The way that the silicone ring in my mum's old Instant Pot would take on the smell of garlic and feed it back into anything sweet she tried to make after that, that was how this wood had taken on Bawbag's repugnant, malodorous stench. It was like accidentally sniffing his taint after he'd been on horseback all day.

Ugh.

That would not do. Not at all.

Despite my disgust, a smile quirked at my lips.

The first weapon I'd really used against the man would do here.

Drawing deep on my well of spirit, I wove a lattice of delicate, purifying flame.

# CHAPTER
# SIX

A hushed gasp, quickly muffled to silence, reached my ears as the web of Purifire cascaded across the exquisitely polished mahogany.

On the outside, the doors looked like the family heirlooms they were, passed from arsehole to arsehole over generations of bleeding the land dry. On the inside, well. "Spiritually crusty" might have been the best descriptor. I still wanted to shudder even as my magic seeped into the wood, filtering through the space between the particles that made it up. Purifire chased away all manner of sins, and Bawbag's were no exception.

An impulse rose, one that I didn't think was entirely mine. When I concentrated on it, a blooming sense of warmth and encouragement in my mind, I realised it was coming from Brac-Meanmna.

I'd reached a state of flow with the staff before in my training movements, but this was the first time I thought it had reached out to get my attention outside of combat.

Unsure what I was doing, I mentally felt along the connection I had to my staff, almost like a climber traversing a section of rock by feel alone.

The information that flooded my mind as I made contact came in a torrent of images and sensations and feelings more than words.

It pulled up how I had felt when I'd—quite by accident—crafted the staff itself. A sense of protection, connection, yearning.

The staff recalled what my mind had whispered about Curiosity, at our naming our creations after Earth's greatest virtues as we sent them into the unknown.

Brac-Meanmna recalled my stubbornness, a trait that had connected me to that old oak on the islet of Innis Chonnel, the very trait that had awakened the oak to my presence and earned its respect.

"Tapadh leat," I murmured aloud, my breath a sharp intake as I understood what to do. Thanking my living weapon felt like the right choice.

Purifire still threaded itself through the mahogany upon my work station. In her cubby, Sailean watched me through heavy-lidded eyes, slow blinking at me.

I thought of her trust, of *all* of our trust as we navigated this new world. We were doing something important here. And these doors would be a part of it. We would take Bawbag's bullshit and transmute it into something better. Screw alchemising lead into gold; we were starting with a turd. But it would become diamond.

Okay, maybe that wasn't the analogy I really wanted to run with.

Something was missing here; I knew it, and my staff knew it.

As I slowly withdrew the Purifire, content with the new sense of determination and compassion that radiated from the mahogany—along with an odd sense of relief I couldn't account for—I stood back on my heels, looking at it as if the doors themselves would provide the answer.

The doors, of course, did no such thing.

But after a moment, I felt a different presence coming my way and turned to see Eilidh picking through a small gaggle of Obanites who were comparing some wooden implements they'd created. A few of them turned to stare at her in awe, one going as far to gawp at her, openmouthed.

Eilidh, naturally, didn't even notice their attention.

I wasn't going to pull the "oh, she had no idea how beautiful she was" schtick as if low self-esteem was a good thing. To the contrary, Eilidh moved with confidence, quiet strength and the pervasive aura that she was at home in her body and knew exactly how it worked. Her beauty was as much because of that as anything else. She simply wasn't bothered by what anyone else thought of her; she knew who she was.

My heart gave a wee pang at that thought, a pang I didn't quite dare interrogate.

My smile became crooked all over again at the knowledge that I was the target she'd aimed herself at—she threaded her way over to me with a look of resolve upon her face that dissolved into something every bit as crooked as my own grin.

The thought entered my mind that, around Susanna and other exes, I'd always felt the need to put on a face, to—I don't know—"man up," be stoic and aloof. But with Eilidh, I had nothing to prove. It was strangely liberating.

"The wolves have gone off to the south," she said without preamble, though her voice held a note of relief and warmth that had nowt to do with the words.

"That sounds promising," I said, hearing a similar quality to my own voice.

"Some scouts are going to keep tracking them for now, and I

didn't want to get in their way." Eilidh nodded at the doors. "What are you making?"

"I'm not entirely sure yet. I started with chasing out the last of Bawbag's taint, as it were." I winced the second the words left my mouth, and sure enough, Eilidh wrinkled her nose.

"I really don't want to ever think of Bawbag's taint again," she said.

"You and me both."

Eilidh's face grew pensive. "Can I help?"

I blinked. "Of course!"

She stepped up beside me, her warmth blooming with the proximity. Her hands reached to the doors, running long fingers along the exquisitely crafted carvings. I couldn't fault the artisan who had made these doors; part of me felt guilty for being ready to destroy an antique just because of who had owned it last.

We batted ideas back and forth for a while, considering and tossing out everything from a bookshelf to a coracle. No, whatever we made from this needed to be to the benefit of as many as possible, something that could pour life into this town. A beacon of welcome and hope in the face of apocalypse.

No pressure.

The sky darkened as clouds rolled in from the Sound of Mull, and a break in them cast down fingers of golden light over Kerrera and Lismore. If we didn't want to work in a squall, we needed to think of something.

A small sound of delight reached my ears from not far away, and I looked over to see a young woman holding up a familiar stone in triumph.

"Tha Gàidhlig agam!" she crowed, hugging the Clach-Cànain to her chest.

"Ceud mìle fàilte ort," Eilidh called out in benediction, and the young woman's face broke into a shining grin that rivalled the golden sunlight on Kerrera's vibrant green slopes. A hundred thousand welcomes—not a usual turn of phrase with welcomes in Gaelic, but one I felt to my marrow.

"Eilidh," I murmured to her. "Beachd agam."

I had an idea.

Eilidh had produced a notebook from her inventory, and as I spoke my idea into being, she sketched furiously with a pencil.

As our plan took shape, a seed of giddiness germinated in me. This would be an act of love that would echo into future generations.

At least I hoped it would. If we could pull it off, it would be beautiful.

The inspiration that came to me wasn't without a certain sardonic flair—after all, such a thing had its roots deep in myth, legend, religion, and the collective consciousness.

The thing was, we were also building something entirely new. Earth had ascended, and we were going to prove to the Ascended Alliance that we could be worthy of such a boon. It didn't matter that we'd not earned it. It had landed on our heads, and we were going to find a way to survive.

Once the design was on paper, all flowing lines and graceful arcs, I felt to my core that it was the right thing to do.

Eilidh tore the leaf of paper out of the notebook and secured it to a clip on the edge of the cubbies, just above where Sailean was now snoozing. The kitten stirred at the movement in the air, whiskers twitching, but she didn't rouse.

Without a word, Eilidh began pulling other things from her inventory, things we'd collected together and things she'd found on her own. I recognised some of the petrified hearts, bits of wood and root, blackthorn, spirit-tanned leather, claws, all sorts of things.

I watched as she arranged them atop the doors, and I began to see a pattern.

Blackthorn was a powerful ward against hostile magic—a must, I thought somewhat wryly. Pine was nurturing; oak was stalwart. A few branches of rowan joined it, another potent protector, and with it, sprigs of holly and hazel for creativity and ceremony, inheritance and passion and heritage.

Digging into my woodworking knowledge, I dredged up what I knew of mahogany. It came with strong senses of fiery inspiration and grounding in earth, enhancing intuition and calling our attention to our potential.

*Yes.*

That seed of giddiness sent up a shoot that unfurled into a leafy feeling of hope.

It seemed contagious; when I looked over at Eilidh, her blue eyes were shining with the anticipation of creation. We'd both crafted things separately before, but we'd never tried to make anything more complex than armour *together*.

The doors now held a second pattern above their carvings, a layer of carefully chosen additions that would strengthen and fortify what it was we wanted this new structure to mean.

"Deiseil is deònach?" Eilidh asked lightly.

"Deiseil is deònach," I replied with a grin. Ready and willing.

This time, our smiles lacked any hint of uncertainty—to the contrary, mine felt assured, and Eilidh's exuded that same confidence with which she'd moved through the gathered crowd on her way over to me.

She took a few steps around the edge of the table to stand on the far side, directly opposite where I waited. With a glance at the drawing she'd made, she turned back to me, placing her hands on the edge of the doors.

The doors themselves were situated to take up the entirety of the worktable crosswise, so Eilidh had one hand on the top of each door, and I mirrored her at their bottom edges.

Slipping into spirit with her felt so natural.

Our fighting experience, though, was one thing.

Creation was something else entirely.

I heard Eilidh's slight gasp as her spirit met mine, threads of pathos and will reaching out to embrace my own.

Will, I thought, was both of our strongest secondary spirit resource, which made sense. We were both stubborn bastards in our way, and not for the first time, I was thankful we were on the same side—not that we'd ever been enemies for real.

Together, the threads of our spirit sank into the wood. The Purifire had been almost weblike, the way tempered glass would look after an impact that crumbled it but the moment before it shattered into pebbles. This time, it felt like a net, strategic and woven like a dance, each strand of spirit, pathos, and will reaching out from myself or from Eilidh to join with the others. A twist here, a change in direction there, like an Orcadian strip the willow, making its way down the line until every square inch of the doors was covered with magic.

And the wood began to flow.

As our magic sank into it, everything between me and Eilidh seemed to swirl into itself. It created a whirlpool of spirit and substance, but instead of the grains of wood dissolving, some of it remained visible. The intricate knot-work carved round the perimeter of the doors snaked around the edges of the whirlpool. The animals in relief seemed to come alive, moulding themselves to the images in our minds of the animals in life. A hare, a raven, a fox—all sprang forth from the wood together.

And then, from that cauldron of creation, something sprouted upwards.

Like that giddiness I'd experienced in anticipation of this act, it reached for the sky, unfurling as it climbed. And when it reached the height it desired, it unfurled like a firework, sprays of spark-like spirit released joyously into the air.

Connected as we were, I *felt* Eilidh's wonder, her own miraculous joy, and it created a feedback loop with my own. We poured that joy and excitement back into our creation, watching as it reached higher and as details began to emerge.

The raven found a roost; the hare a hollow.

The fox slunk around the edge, tail held high.

In the highest reaches, an eagle found a perch, proud and fierce.

In the lowest, a family of dormice, their fur in exquisite wood grain detail, peeked out from curves of our creation's base.

I felt something else then, a spark, a glimmer.

And around all of it, the doors' original knot-work threaded through our work, making a home amid everything else we'd made.

When we finally stepped back, both Eilidh and myself breathing hard with the exertion of working with spirit to that degree, I wasn't even surprised to hear the chime in my mind.

*You have created a living sculpture.*

# CHAPTER
# SEVEN

*You have created a living sculpture.*

    Across the workbench from me, I had to lean to see Eilidh around the result of our efforts, and when I did, I was greeted with a smile that lit the entire crafting space like she'd pulled down the sun from the heavens.

Between us was a tree.

It would surprise no one, really, that a tree was what we had aimed for, but the shocker of it was that we'd made something *alive*.

Brac-Meanmna, from its position nearby, exulted, quietly smug.

"Showoff," I muttered under my breath to my staff, but the smugness only increased.

Eilidh made her way back around the jutting peninsula of the worktable to come stand beside me, and her hand worked its way into mine. I interlaced our fingers and brought our conjoined hands up to my lips to kiss the back of hers.

"Abair gu bheil i brèagha," she said softly.

She was right; the tree *was* beautiful.

It rose atop the workbench, its roots splayed out to

stabilise it since we would absolutely have to move it some-where else. The deep reddish mahogany was swirled with paler yellows, and the animals that had made their home there looked as though they might blink or move at any second. The knot-work from the doors, the original crafting of the artisan who had sculpted them for Bawbag's family once upon a time, twisted through the tree's trunk from roots to branches.

And the branches—they reached out from the zenith of the trunk, falling almost like a willow's in graceful arcs that ended with delicate fronds we'd modelled for a very specific purpose.

Belatedly, I realised that a crowd had gathered. Crafters had put aside their work—or brought it with them, I noticed, when I saw someone with a half-finished bow dangling from one hand—and had come to stare. A small squeal of a delight pierced the air as a wee lad pointed at the dormice, exclaiming at how cute they were.

"Where's it going to go?" Someone called out the question from the middle of the crowd at the same time someone else yelled, "What's it for?"

Eilidh and I exchanged a small smile.

"For the first question of where it goes, that's for the town to decide," I said.

"And for the second, you'll have to wait and see." Eilidh's eyes crinkled with her widening grin. "If you want to find out sooner, maybe spread the word that we need a very public, very accessible place for something special."

"It's *alive*," someone blurted out, then jumped when she realised she'd said it aloud. It was the same young woman who'd been so excited about learning Gaelic. "Duilich, a Chaluim—chleachd mi Keen Eye."

I was slightly more startled by her apologising to me by name than by the second part of what she said, but a moment later, it hit me that I was thankfully not the only one with the Keen Eye skill.

"Na bi duilich," I told her reassuringly. There was no need for her to be sorry. Then I wondered if she still had that Clach-Cànain on her. After a brief pause, I just asked. "Eil a' Chlach agad fhathast, o 'n do dh'ionnsaich thu a' Ghàidhlig?"

"Tha!" She answered in the affirmative, wedging herself between a pair of men who were staring at the tree and made her way to me and Eilidh.

A moment later, she deposited the Clach-Cànain in my hand.

Blank looks painted faces in the crowd, and I gave them what I hoped was a mysterious smile.

"Find us a place to put this," Eilidh said after a beat. "Then we'll tell you what it's for."

Disgruntled murmurs rippled through the crowd, more of mild disappointment than actual irritation, and people started to disperse.

"Calum," Eilidh said to me under her breath. "Use Keen Eye on it, for fuck's sake."

A laugh burst from my throat before I could stop it, and I pulled on my still-recovering spirit to do as she said. I wanted to snort at the information that popped up since it was far and away beyond what my ability would tell me about my staff, but I decided I wouldn't look a gift living tree in the mouth. Or branches.

*Craobh an Òbain*
    *Level 1 Living Sculpture*
    *Affinities: Nature, Healing, Synthesis, Justice*
    *Specialised Affinities: Wild, Coimhearsnachd, Seer*

*This exquisite piece of living art was created by Eilidh MacIntosh and Calum Green working together.*

*Formed from purified mahogany and sacred woods and vines of the land of Argyll, Craobh an Òbain is both a symbol and a practical addition to the growing community of the town of Oban.*

*Because it is imbued with spirit and alive, once situated in its permanent place of residence, this tree will grow.*

*As the community thrives, so will the tree, and it will offer its fruits to all who come beneath its branches, so long as they seek to do no harm to the community.*

The implications of this were . . . staggering.

I immediately pushed the text to Eilidh, waiting for her to read it. My mind rolled through the knowledge that our affinities had manifested in this creation—*both* of our affinities. I hadn't realised she'd unlocked another specialised one. I'd have to ask her about Seer, because it brought to mind the way I'd found her earlier staring out at the sea.

Just then, though, wee Sailean seemed to realise she was missing something interesting. She nudged her way out of her cubby hole, stretching out her forepaws and digging them into the wooden worktop—or trying to dig them in, anyway. The wood was magically enforced even against kitten needle-feet. Undeterred, Sailean wiggled her little bum in the air with the stretch.

"Big stretch," Eilidh said solemnly, and I could only nod.

Sailean righted herself after a moment, padding onto the workstation where the tree sat. If it were on the ground, it would be just a bit taller than me and Eilidh stacked on top of each other, so it looked much bigger on its platform with its roots at the height of my waist.

The kitten, however, was much smaller than a full-grown human adult, and she walked up to the nearest root and sniffed it—and then she saw the dormice.

With a startled mew, she hopped backwards, her back arching and her still-scraggly kitten tail puffing out as much as felinely possible.

"They're not going to hurt you, you wee numpty," Eilidh said fondly.

Sailean had the grace to look abashed, and as if to prove her courage, she gave herself a shake and stalked back up to the intricately formed wooden dormice as if to say *A'm no feart.*

"God, it's good she's growing, because I am not sure I can take this level of cuteness for long," I muttered.

"You're telling me," Eilidh replied, shaking her head.

The familiar golden pulse in my vision was enough to distract me from kitten-watching.

One glance told me that Eilidh and I had gotten experience from what we'd done.

It was time to dig through the notifications.

In the weeks since the Battle of Ganavan, Blàr Ghaineamhain as the system referred to it with the Gaelic, my crafting had boosted my levels already from sixteen to twenty.

Now I'd just hit level twenty-one, which was exciting as much for the slow approach of my next class specialisation—at level twenty-seven—as for the pure joy of *numbers go up.*

*You have reached Level 21! You have two attribute points and four skill points to distribute.*

An extra skill point. Huh. I rummaged through the rest of the notifications, dismissing the ones for basic stat increases from use—I was glad to see that my meagre Constitution had taken a jump to thirty, at long last—but I really did not enjoy seeing the quest update that followed the more mundane messages. As it turned out, crafting the tree alone hadn't been responsible for the jump in experience. We'd completed the anomaly quest.

*Quest complete: A Quick Brown Fox . . .*

*Your attempt to probe the anomalous rabbit in Ronald's care led to the discovery that a powerful and intelligent force is behind these anomalies. You also suspect that you have discovered part of the reason why these anomalies seek you out specifically: they recognise you as a threat.*

*As this is an evolving quest, completing the first stage has unlocked the second.*

*Objectives:*

*-Utilise the petrified heart in crafting or improving an item (Eilidh or Calum) (Complete)*

*-Train others to use Connection and to improve their skill (Calum) (Complete)*

*-Unlock the Nature affinity and learn Connection (Rhona, Ronald) (Complete)*

*-Learn Connection (Eilidh) (Complete)*

*Rewards:*

*-Experience (commensurate with current level progression)*

*-1 skill point*

*-Increase Nature affinity*

*-Blueprint: Purification Cage*

That last quest reward made my blood feel sluggish in my veins.

When I mentally reached for the blueprint, I let out a disappointed breath.

*Purification Cage*
*This item allows for the safe containment of corrupted creatures where they cannot infect others in their vicinity.*

It wasn't that it was unwelcome, but for a moment, I'd allowed myself the hope that putting something in there would cleanse it of the corruption. I ought to have known it would never be that easy. It also brought up the unsettling knowledge that the cage Ronald had used for anomalous rabbit storage was *not* safe. He could have been corrupted at any time. A shudder went through me at the thought. Eilidh and I could have been corrupted when we visited, too. It bothered me that we didn't know how such corruption even spread. Bites like zombies? Touch? Droplets? It probably wasn't airborne like COVID had been, or Ronald would have been corrupted without a doubt.

Small comforts.

Part of me—a distant part—whispered that if the Ascended Alliance knew how to cleanse the anomalies of their corruption, they *would* share that information.

The implications of that were all sorts of confusing. Or maybe not confusing—maybe just unsettling.

They hadn't given us any such thing, that was certain, so

either they were withholding it, which seemed to go against their entire ethos, or they were as clueless as we were.

If we'd somehow stumped the universe's most advanced conglomerate of planets and peoples, well. Let's just say this was not the distinction of uniqueness I had hoped to cultivate for Earth.

I would much prefer we not be the anomalous special snowflakes of the universal community. Couldn't we just be unique for our pluck and can-do spirit? Not an unstoppable alien corruption that made the zombies in *28 Days Later* look friendly?

With a sigh, I braced myself for the next stage of the evolving quest and almost groaned when I saw the name. This was not encouraging or delightful.

*You have discovered a quest!*

*New quest: Blood From a Stone*

*With the attempt to connect to an anomalous rabbit using Tàthadh, you have discovered that the creator of these anomalies can use them as eyes and ears. This entity now knows you, and there is no doubt of a coming response.*

*This entity does not know where you are precisely, but it will send further scouts when it is able. You must be prepared.*

*Objectives:*

*-Create Purification Cages to house any captured anomalies*

*-Capture three different species of anomalous animals*

*-Explore further uses for Purifire*

*-Examine the remains of the conduit anomaly (Ronald)*

*Rewards:*

*-Experience (commensurate with current level progression)*

*-1 skill point*

*-1 item (ascension dependent)*

With a grumble, I dismissed the quest notification. Purification cages and more pyro experimentation, though that particular objective was as vague as all get out.

I now had four skill points to assign along with my attribute points. The attribute points were easy; at this point, I just put all of them into Mind since just about everything else I could increase organically. My physical exertions in training had increased my Strength, Stamina, Agility, and Dexterity fairly regularly, and while Constitution was a bit more nebulous—I wasn't about to go eating dodgy food to see what would happen—it had increased along with the others, suggesting that as an attribute, it responded somewhat holistically.

My skill points would wait for a bit, but I went ahead and put my attribute points into Mind. It boggled me to think of just how far I'd come in the past few weeks.

Name: Calum Green
    Age: 36
    Level: 21
    Class: Draoidh (Further class specialisation at: Level 27)
    Affinities: Nature (Level 13), Healing (Level 5), Synthesis (Level 9), Staves (Level 13)
    Specialised Affinities: Wild (Level 9), Coimhearsnachd (Level 5)
    Marks of Esteem: Life, Connection, Justice

Alteration:
    Strength: 28
    Dexterity: 40
    Agility: 43
    Mind: 89

Regeneration:
    Constitution: 30
    Stamina: 61

Manipulation:
    Spirit: 90
    Pathos: 43
    Will: 47

Boons:
    Blessings
    Làmh na Glaistige
    Glòir a' Ghiuthais
    Blàr Ghaineamhain

# EIGHT

Oban was abuzz when Eilidh and I finished going through our notifications. Word of the tree had spread through the town, and I wasn't surprised to see my best mate trundling towards us when we had just finished whinging to each other about the new anomaly quest.

"Oi, I leave for a day and you go off and create more living . . . whatever the fuck that is?"

Iain bellowed the words from a hundred metres away, and Sailean, who had been giving herself a dainty wee bath nestled between two of the tree's roots, stopped mid-lick and stared his way. Her irritation at the disruption was only slightly marred by her little pink tongue sticking out where she'd failed to retract it.

"Eilidh," I said quietly, "Sailean. Blep."

Eilidh's head swivelled so fast, I thought she might pull a muscle in her neck. "Oh, mo chreach."

Sailean looked at me indignantly, every inch of her kittenish self telling me she was now sticking her tongue out at me to be rude.

"Don't look at me, mate," I said to Iain, tearing my gaze

away from Sailean as she grumpily went back to licking her own chest. "Eilidh did it too."

"I swear, we leave you two alone for an hour and you become parents to a tree." Iain stumped up to us, squinting at the branches above our heads.

Eilidh choked, her crafted canteen only halfway lowered from her lips where she'd just taken a drink. "Parents?"

Iain looked back and forth between us as if we were very thick, and not the sexy kind. "You cannae tell me you didn't think of it. Two people"—he waggled his hands in a half-suggestive, half-magical gesture—"and then boom, life."

I suddenly had a great need for a drink of something stronger than water.

"No," Eilidh said blandly, "we really did not think we were *having a baby*."

"Well, many happy returns anyhow."

"Iain," I said, but I didn't have anything else I could add to it, so his name just hung there in the air like confirmation. I looked at the tree, then at Brac-Meanmna behind me, which was still radiating smugness. "Oh, don't *you* even start."

"Now he's bletherin' tae sticks, another bouncing bundle of joy," Iain muttered.

I closed my eyes and enjoyed the moment of dark silence.

When I opened them, Eilidh was rubbing her temples as if she had a headache.

Iain was giving Sailean a pat. She purred happily, leaning into his calloused hand. Traitorous cat.

I couldn't be cross with her, though, not with her contented warmth a ball of fuzzy joy in my mind through our bond.

"The tree's a gift, not a child," I said finally to Iain. "We're hoping it will help the town. It'll also grow once it's planted, so who knows what it'll be capable of as time goes by."

"So it is a living tree with abilities that grow over time, like a—"

"If you say 'like a baby,' I will kick you into the bay," Eilidh said, her face so implacable that I couldn't be certain she was joking.

"—normal tree." Apparently, that was not a risk Iain was willing to take, but he grinned impudently at her.

I'd seen them spar; he could take her in hand to hand, no doubt, but with swords? Pfft. Eilidh could have him julienned within two minutes if they hadn't been using blunted weapons and magical protection. Even with those protections, he'd moaned about the bruises for far longer than they took to heal with his ascended constitution.

Eilidh finally cracked a smile, but she shot me a bewildered look I returned with a shrug. The ethics of the ascended world were a job for philosophers, not himbo hamsters such as myself. "Tree pretty" was about where I stood with the current creation.

If it started calling us Mam and Da, though, we'd revisit the discussion.

This was not something I'd planned to have to think about.

"Was there a reason you came looking for us?" Eilidh asked Iain after a momentary pause that left me eerily certain she'd been thinking the exact same thing I had.

Iain turned to her as if startled out of his own existential crisis. "Hm? Oh, Mam's back and wanted to know if yous would be back for tea."

It was such a . . . mundane statement that both Eilidh and I just stared at him until he went on.

"She and the lads"—I knew *lads* in that context also referred to the other women who worked the fishing boat—"hauled in a cod the size of a pre-ascension dolphin, and there's enough fillets tae feed the toon, so she's currently a storm of pure, battered fury in the kitchen. Already sent Meeksy raiding the mages' magical hydroponics for tatties to make chips."

Never mind. Not so mundane after all.

"Well," I said slowly, "I cannae say no to an ascended fish supper. Eilidh?"

"It would probably be blasphemous to refuse," she agreed blandly.

Iain managed to look offended. "Dinnae sound so excited. You'd think I invited you to a toenail-eating competition instead."

"Iain, mate," I said, leaning forwards to pluck the kitten from the workbench and depositing her into her carrier bum bag, "think back over the last five minutes of conversation and compare it to the type of conversation we might have had two months ago, just for a second."

My oldest friend cocked his head to the side, and then he gave me a sheepish grin, scrubbing his hand through his already-messy blond hair.

"Aye, maybe you've got a point. Weird is the new normal."

"That ought to be our new battle cry," Eilidh said under her breath, glancing up at the tree.

I felt the bulge in my pocket where I'd placed the clach-cànain, again hearing that young woman's triumphant declaration that she'd learnt Gaelic in a handful of seconds. Brac-Meanmna still exuded its preening aura as I let it grab hold of my armour between my shoulder blades.

As we headed away from the workstation, leaving the tree where it was for now, I chuckled to myself.

*Weird is the new normal, indeed.*

·ᴄ ⚜ ᴐ·

The mood in the town was jovial as we made our way to Iain's house. At the pier, we could see one of the fishing boats' haul strung out with *mooring lines*—the fish hanging from them were too huge for smaller ropes to support.

I gawped at that view for a few moments, but Eilidh blurted out the question my brain snapped to a split second before she spoke.

"Thighearna," she said. "How the fuck did they even catch fish that large? Wouldn't they just break the nets?"

"Mam said they've been magically reinforcing the nets," Iain replied with a shrug of his muscular shoulders. "But aye, I think they had to do that because the fish *did* bust out of them like they were paper."

Images of people bursting out of cakes filled my head unbidden.

"No wonder the eagle said she'd be fine out there," I said under my breath. "One of those herrings would feed her entire nest and then some."

"Eagle?" Iain asked blankly.

Eilidh explained as we walked, and I added in details where necessary, somewhat surprised Meeksy hadn't filled him in yet.

Word had spread of the tree Eilidh and I had . . . birthed . . . and not a few people called out suggestions for its placement. Some, like the Oban Promenade, were clearly serious. Others, like an unpopular landlord's house up on Rockfield Road—which was still standing and would need to be demolished first—probably weren't.

Probably.

I wasn't entirely sure how we'd go about making the ultimate decision, but I supposed that was a strait we could swim when we got to the shoreline.

Already I could smell fish frying, hear laughing voices exclaiming over the size of the fillets. We all needed more energy these days, so it helped that our food sources were compensating.

Visions of dog-sized tatties danced in my head. The tatties that launched a thousand chips.

My mouth watered at the thought as we reached Iain's house. Sure enough, the smell of fried cod reached my nose almost immediately upon entering, and the windows were steamed up with the fryer's efforts.

"Oi, a Mham," Iain called. "Eil e deiseil?"

Eilidh quietly guffawed at Iain's *Oi, Mam, food ready?* I couldn't really blame her—from what I'd heard of her parents, she'd have gotten battered worse than a cod fillet if she'd hollered an *Oi!* at her parents, who were both Marines, if I remembered correctly, and not exactly fans of casual parent-child relationships.

Iain kicked off his shoes and somehow still managed to half stomp his way down the hall to the kitchen, and as Eilidh and I removed our own boots, she turned to me with a sideways smile to confirm what I'd thought.

"My mother and father would have *murdered* me for that," she said, a ghost of conflicted emotion struggling against her smile for a brief moment.

I reached out and squeezed her shoulder. She'd been closest to her grandparents, and now both her seanair and her seanmhair were dead. Who knew if her parents still lived?

"My own mum wouldnae be pleased with it," I said, "though she'd probably just give me a swat with a dish rag."

Eilidh's smile slipped, and her expression grew sombre. "I wish I'd gotten to meet her."

Aw, bugger. I'd forgotten that bringing up dead people tended to put a damper on any lightheartedness.

But Eilidh wasn't looking at me with pity, just wistfulness.

"I do too," I said after a beat. "She would have loved you."

Then, before my hamster brain could take over the himbo brain, I reached forwards and cupped her cheek in my hand.

"May I?"

Her eyes widened, but she nodded, her lips parting.

I hadn't planned our first kiss to be in the entryway to my best mate's house, each of us with one shoe on and one shoe off, but when my lips touched hers amid the smells of frying fish and potatoes and her clean, heather scent, I knew there was no way—none—that any other venue would have been more perfect.

Even with Iain laughing boisterously at something his mum had said as the accompanying music.

Eilidh was in my arms in a heartbeat, her lips soft against mine, and though the kiss only lingered briefly before we both pulled away, the flash of heat between us was undeniable.

Her pupils dilated, and with the flush that rose in her cheeks amid the smattering of freckles across her pale skin, she looked as dazed as I felt.

Eilidh gave me a shy smile, one hand somehow half on my shoulder and half on my chest where tingles spread out from that light pressure even through my armour.

"Yous get lost or something?" Iain bellowed down the hall.

"Aye, fell through a portal into another dimension!" I yelled back. "Be right there!"

Eilidh's hand lingered on my shoulder for a fraction of a second longer, and when I met her eyes, we both chuckled. Gods, I felt like I was back in high school around her, gangly and utterly clueless—though I wasn't sure that had ever really gone away.

At the same time, though, there was peace I never could have managed in high school with my sweaty palms and unfortunately timed pubescent erections.

Aye, no, this was nothing like high school.

Thank god.

"What?" Eilidh said as we walked down the hall towards Iain's loud banter. "Your face did a thing."

"Did a thing?"

"A classic Calum yikes thing."

"There's a classic Calum yikes thing?" I wasn't sure whether to be horrified at my face's betrayal or amused and touched that Eilidh recognised when it did "a thing."

"Yes," she said. "Why'd it do the classic Calum yikes thing?"

Oh, god.

"Erm, it was an embarrassing thought about high school."

"You should *definitely* tell me, then," she replied with an absolutely evil smile.

So much for my palms *not* being sweaty.

But what the hell, she'd asked for it.

"I was thinking that I feel a bit like I am back in high school around you, but then I remembered that high school was a mess of sweat and"—*no way, Calum, you cannot say the word* erection *to the woman you just kissed for the first time where your best mate and his mum can hear you*—"and, erm, shall we say 'unpredictable and uncontrollable tent pitching' and leave it me being utterly grateful to be a whole entire adult?"

Eilidh's peal of laughter made the sweaty palms worth it.

# CHAPTER
## NINE

Dinner flew swiftly by us in a haze of delicious fish for all —including Sailean, who thought she'd gone to kitten heaven—and Meeksy and Rhona showed up in time to eat with us too.

Rhona chattered on about the wolves she'd been tracking, not even cross with me for having her day rerouted.

"Real wolves! Real-life, actual wolves!" She exclaimed this at least four times throughout dinner. "God, they're amazing! Oh my god, did you know there are, like, four words for wolf in Gaelic? Mac-tìre, madadh-allaidh, faol, sitheach—wait, is 'faol' like 'am Faoilleach'? Is January the *wolf month*?"

That got Eilidh talking, because it was indeed, and the rest of dinner swung wildly between Gaelic etymology and the "real-life, actual wolves" with the conversation meandering between English and Gaelic with ease since we now all had the language in common.

It was still strange to hear Rhona happily chatting to Catrìona in flawless Argyll Gaelic, but it was the kind of strange that came with watching a dream you didn't know you had come true. Like a surprise gift you'd always wanted and never voiced, a homecoming, a boon.

Several times, I caught Eilidh and Meeksy exchanging a glance with eyes a little too bright to not be holding back An Emotion.

Which made it all the more jarring when someone pounded on the door.

All six of us froze, Iain's mouth still open in the middle of a rabbit hole he'd gone down about how listening to Irish felt like squinting with his ears, and Catrìona got up from the bench at the long, wooden trestle table, perfunctorily folding her linen napkin and placing it on the edge.

We all watched in silence as she made her way down the hall. The pounding came again, this time accompanied by a voice.

"Catrìona! It's Donnie!"

I looked at Iain, trying to place the voice with the name—"Donnie" wasn't exactly an uncommon name in Scotland—and drawing a blank.

"Fisher," Iain said.

I wasn't sure if he meant the profession or a surname, but considering his mother's choice of career, I figured it had to be the former.

Catrìona reached the door and flung it open. "Fuck's sake, Donnie, you've got to give a person time to walk to the bloody door."

"The *Sheila* didn't come back in today. No one can reach them." The man paid no heed to her words, and even from where I sat, I could hear the pain in his.

"Bugger," Catrìona muttered. I heard the slide of a mac's vinyl as she grabbed it from the hook by the door, heard the fumbling sound of feet going into boots.

Iain was up and moving with no less grace than his mum,

sliding down the hardwood hallway on his socked feet. "The *Sheila*?"

I couldn't hear Donnie's answering nod, but from the tension in Iain's shoulders, it had happened.

The boat's name was familiar, of course, but I didn't know who worked on it. Iain did, it seemed.

Our plates were mostly clean by now, and I saw Rhona pushing a chip around in a small puddle of malt vinegar, her face drawn.

The silence that had descended was heavy, oppressive. It landed in sharp contrast to the lighthearted mood of our dinner, and it jolted all of us back to the reality that this world really had changed, and we still weren't entirely sure how much —or how dangerously.

The disappearance of the *Sheila* had sucked all of the cheer out of the atmosphere.

The six of us—seven, including Sailean—plus Donnie all made our way to the pier, where folk had gathered in a humming drone of speculation and worried murmurs.

"There's the *Cuilean Donn*," Donnie said, pointing to a small boat moored at the edge of the wharf where the Muilich had been berthed when they came after the battle. "They were the last to see the *Sheila*."

"Mary!" Catrìona called above the buzz of the crowd.

Folk moved to the side so we could pass through, and a short cap of straw-blond hair appeared coming up the ramp, the woman's weathered face appearing a moment later with two men behind her. One I vaguely recognised, but the other was unfamiliar to me.

Mary I knew—peripherally, but enough to say hi to her at

the supermarket. Right then, her normally cheerful face was set in a stony expression of grim resolve.

She glanced at Catrìona's entourage—Iain and Meeksy, me and Eilidh and Rhona, and Donnie—and gave us a tight-lipped smile that barely touched her lips, let alone reaching her eyes.

"I can't tell you bugger all," Mary said bluntly. "We didn't see what happened. They were just there one moment and gone the next."

"Where?" Iain asked.

Mary pointed. "Literally just the other side of Kerrera. We were heading back for the day a bit late, but they were later. Communication crystal didn't even make a peep."

"I want to see where they were," Catrìona said darkly. "It's a calm day out there, and no boat will vanish without leaving wreckage behind."

"That's the thing," Mary said, her eyes still on the slopes of Kerrera. The sun was still up, but it was already turning the sky to gold to the west. "Nothing floated back up. Just disturbed waves."

Rhona's look of confusion prompted Eilidh to give her a quick explanation. "When you're on the sea a lot, you get to know what the wave patterns look like on any given day. If something large is underwater, it creates a shift in those patterns. Whales'll do it, but they don't usually swim this far in from the Minch."

Mary nodded to confirm Eilidh's explanation, but Rhona still looked bewildered, her blue-grey eyes narrowed.

"A whale wouldn't sink a fishing boat," the teenage banshee insisted. "Even an ascended whale, right? Even if a minke whale or a porpoise grew to be the size of a humpback or blue whale, what reason would they have to sink a ship? They're all used to us by now—any whales that come close to land know what humans do on the water."

Rhona had a point.

"An orca might," Catrìona said dryly. "Those things are monsters—they might sink a ship for fun if they got big enough to do it."

I had a feeling my face had the same look of horror as the one that drained the blood from Rhona's.

"They call them killer whales for a reason," Mary said in confirmation, sounding as unfazed as if she were discussing plankton.

"We're wasting daylight." Donnie cut in, pointing at the setting sun. "Catrìona, if you want to get back out there, we better do it now. I'd rather not be on the water after dark."

With that, we were moving. I followed the fishers down onto the boat, where a few other crew were still there, hauling the day's catch off in a chain of ascension-assisted tosses.

"Anything still on board goes into inventory," Mary barked. "We'll unload when we get back. Anyone who wants to stay on land, stay. We don't know what we'll find out there."

That was reassuring.

I exchanged a glance with Eilidh. I wondered if she was thinking the same thing I was—it was one thing to fight ascended monsters on land, something else entirely to do it on the sea.

Seasickness wasn't usually something that affected me, but jeezo, the thought of fighting for my life from the deck of a boat? Nausea sloshed in my full belly.

"Might regret that second fillet," Iain groaned as we stepped onto the boat.

"Took the words right out of my mouth," I told him.

Meeksy clapped Iain on the back—hard. "You'll be grand."

"Aye, you can just heal me if I boak," Iain said jovially.

"That's the spirit." Eilidh hopped over the gap between the pier and the deck with suspicious ease. At my look, she gave me a sheepish smile. "I worked on tourist boats in the summers when I was at uni. Well, the first couple years, anyway."

I blinked at that.

Before I could ask her how I'd never heard that in our years of acquaintance, though, Mary started barking orders at the crew, all of whom were clearly planning to come along. Not a soul stayed on the pier, though I saw fishers from the crowd come forward, picking their way down the ramp.

"We'll take care of the catch, no worries!" One man gave Mary a wave that was almost a salute.

"Cheers!" Mary called back over her shoulder as she ducked into the small cabin that enclosed the helm.

My boat knowledge left a lot to be desired, so I just tried my damnedest to stay out of the way. Iain and Eilidh both clearly knew their ways around, but Meeksy and Rhona did not, so the three of us clustered on the fishy-smelling deck where we seemed least likely to be a hazard.

A small fishing boat wasn't like the massive ferry , *An t-Eilean Muileach,* docked at the big pier. It didn't require a heap of running about to get moving, and within a minute or two, we were pushing back from the small pier with the bay's blue-green water churning beneath us. There was no smell of exhaust, no fumes, just a gentle hum and the lapping of water. It was like driving an electric car after being used to diesel your whole life—the sensation was entirely bizarre.

Magic. Literally.

Despite the frenetic movements of the crew, the tension wound everyone tight like a stretched mooring line. I didn't want to think of an orca that could do that kind of damage. My mind helpfully reminded me of a documentary I'd seen about how they would torture humpback whale calves and mothers, to the point that the humpbacks learned to coordinate vengeful attacks against the orcas for their murdered calves.

I shuddered at the thought. *Free Willy* was great an' aw, but damn, reality was a lot messier.

Really did not want this ascension to make whaling a thing again.

Then again, we'd seen the fuath and the beithir—what if whatever had done this was something entirely *other*?

"You know," Meeksy said conversationally, "they say these days that all the old tales of sea monsters with tentacles were because people saw whale dicks flopping out of the water."

It was such an *Iain* thing to say that I let out a guffaw in surprise, but Rhona's eyes lit up. "I've heard that! And seen pictures. Terrifying. They're like the size of a *horse*. The entire horse, not a horse willy."

Iain himself appeared from wherever he'd been. "Is your working hypothesis that ascended whales are sinking boats because they're trying to fuck them?"

"Iain!" Catrìona barked. "Inappropriate!"

But amid all the tension, the grossly inappropriate—and inappropriately gross—comment eased the mood ever so slightly.

"What?" Iain said innocently, and as he'd done a million times since I'd known him, I could tell he was doing a bit purely in order to diffuse that tension. "It's not any weirder than half the hentai I've seen. Humans are down for *anything*, so why wouldn't whales?"

His mother's groan was louder than the hum of the boat's magically altered engine. "You see what I live with," she said to Mary, who snorted.

Meeksy wore an expression of mock horror. "Please tell me you did not just start a conversation about porn in hearing distance of your mother."

"Brave," Rhona said with an admiring, if silent clap.

Eilidh, however, was staring at my best mate. "Just how

much hen—you know what? I'm not going to ask a question I don't really want the answer to."

"Wisdom in action," Meeksy muttered with a grin at Iain, which Iain returned with a wink.

The rest of the crew doggedly went about their business, though I saw a few smirks here and there.

They lasted as long as it took for us to exit the natural harbour of Oban—once we started to pass through the gateway that was the islands of Kerrera and Lismore, tension crept back through the boat like a cold wind.

The air itself felt unnervingly still, the only wind in my face from the movement of the boat. The seas were calm, with minimal swell.

On the southern edge of Kerrera, the Oban Marina looked like a small forest of yachts in berth, most of them likely awaiting owners who would never return.

We sailed westward until we came round the western edge of Kerrera, where we turned south. Or to port, if I remembered my fuzzy boat knowledge correctly. My shoulders felt so tense that I had to exercise both mindfulness and sheer force of will to coax them back downwards where they weren't practically invading my ear canals.

Silence came over the boat, punctuated only by the waves that splashed against the hull.

The sun slowly sank over Mull in the distance, and I felt an irrational urge to leap from the boat and swim there. A strange, intrusive thought of the sort I'd not had in a long, long time.

Mary kicked the engine down a notch. Moving about as slowly as a fishing boat could, we crept along the shoreline of Kerrera.

Any other time, I would have appreciated the jewel-like green-gold of the setting sun against the island's slopes, but that day it may as well have been black and white.

Farther and farther to the south. I alternated tracking the edge of Kerrera's land and the southern edge of the Ross of Mull, looking for familiar landmarks and finding none in my distraction.

I needed a distraction terribly—this stretch of water was a lot of things, but "full of hidden coves or anything an entire boat could simply duck behind" was not one of them.

"Eleven o'clock!" One of the fishers bellowed it from above me, and I jumped, craning my neck to see him atop the fishing boat's cabin with a pair of binoculars in his hands.

The boat swayed as everyone aboard tried to look where he was pointing.

In that moment, I regretted my ascension-enhanced vision.

Because the first thing I saw was a corpse, floating face down in the gentle waves amid the wreckage of the *Sheila*.

Until that moment, I think all of us had held onto hope.

"That's Auld Rootsy," one of the sailors said in a hushed voice.

"The boat," whispered Eilidh, her voice nearly throbbing with horror.

Because the boat was pulverised. It wasn't like it had simply taken damage and sunk. No, the *Sheila* remained only as practically matchsticks, bits of flotsam floating in the brine.

"We'll ask questions later. Right now, we use what's left of our daylight to retrieve the bodies. The rest we'll leave to the sea," Mary said from above, her voice harsh and emotionless.

No one said what I was pretty sure everyone was thinking: that the light was moot for all but our own comfort. The *Sheila* had been crushed in broad daylight, by something that had no reason to wait for nightfall for a second strike.

Regardless of the danger, we all sprang into action. Or rather everyone else did. I was set to the task of spiritual lookout. I stayed where I was as people moved around me in erratic orbits, and I pulsed Connection.

I felt Sailean's agitation in her carrier, but I wasn't about to let her out. As I let my spirit expand into the—relatively—shallow waters amid the chunks of wood and fibreglass that remained of the fishing boat, I tried to soothe the kitten as best I could. At the same time, I took her nervousness as a possible omen. Animals could often sense what humans had forgotten to acknowledge.

My webs of spirit swirled outwards from where we were. With my ability now ingrained into my muscle memory, using Connection felt like second nature. It catalogued the herring, the mussels, the lobsters, the oysters, the occasional larger fish and the kelp and seaweed that was starting to unfurl with the returning of the lighter months.

The water didn't get that deep here, wedged between islands as we were. Certainly not as deep as the Minch or farther to the west towards Iceland, past the bounds of the Outer Hebrides.

Connection caught sight of a small pod of porpoises, as yet untouched by the ascension's more radical changes, and a momentary, flighty thought flitted through my head, wondering how they were finding hunting when so many of the fish were now the same size they were.

I caught the errant thought and let it pass, breathing in time with my spirit and my use of Connection. My awareness grew with the meditative state where the sailors' shouts and the slosh of water and the sounds of choked-back grief simply floated around me, acknowledged without taking hold of my heart and my mind. Nothing could pull me from my current task.

Pulse. Salty water, fish, crustaceans.

Pulse. A minke whale in the Sound of Mull, headed west-ward towards the Minch.

Pulse. Dolphin, by itself, returning to its pod.

Pulse. Seals on the other side of Kerrera, basking in the last rays of the day's sun.

Pulse. Seagulls, a cormorant, a gannet.

Pulse. Quiet waters.

Pulse. More dolphins.

Pulse. A school of herring, clumped in the face of the dolphins' interest.

Pulse. Octopus swimming lazily—or not so lazily.

The octopus got my attention, because for the first time since I'd begun, something seemed to respond to my pulse of spirit with curiosity.

But the octopus wasn't a threat, just an intelligent being even before the ascension, and now, it was simply exploring its new senses. I sent it a gentle tendril of thought to say hello, and then on impulse, I followed that up with a query spun from Tàthadh, like I'd done with the eagle.

*Danger-boat-death.*

The octopus, observed through my webs of spirit, gave a start at being addressed directly, a swirl of water and its tentacles showing it retreating, then pausing behind a small outcropping of rock to the south.

Just as I was about to give up on hearing anything in return, I felt a nudge of the animal's mind.

*Danger-death-danger-boat-death.*

It came like confirmation.

It came with images.

It came upon a wave of disturbed water, bubbles and breaking, an underwater hurricane, with little else to explain it.

I pulled back from the octopus with a gasp, renewing my pulses as if I could see such a thing coming.

My heartbeat rattled in my chest like a maraca shaken by a giant hopped up on speed.

It took me what felt like an hour to calm my breathing

again. The octopus was long gone, off on its way and unbothered—whatever it was that had destroyed the boat, my eight-legged friend did not see it as a personal threat.

Whether it was an outsized, sadistic orca or something else, it didn't really matter.

The tingle in my mind began at the farthest edges of my awareness. I was stretching Connection to near breaking point, practically all the way to Corryvreckan to the south at the northern tip of the Isle of Jura and nearly to Tobermory on the northwestern edge of Mull. Up Loch Linnhe, searching out any hint of danger.

The thinnest threads of spirit caught hold of something halfway between Mull's Loch Buie on the southern edge of the island and the small Isle of Colonsay farther west.

And whatever they caught was at least as aware as the octopus, but instead of retreating, the thing spun into action.

"We need to go!" I barked out, my words pulled from my larynx almost without my own volition, and to my utter surprise, they overlapped with Eilidh's voice saying, "We can't stay here—it's not safe!"

I spun to find her and found her staring at me from the boat's stern where a trio of bodies lay with tarps over them. One had lost a welly, and for the briefest of moments, I fixated on the pink-and-blue-woven wool of the dead person's sock.

All eyes were on me and Eilidh, and I heard one or two muttered "What the fuck" from different positions on the boat.

Mary came round the starboard side. "You're sure?"

"Yes," I said at the same time Eilidh said, "Get us *out* of here."

The boat's skipper wasted no time, bawling out orders immediately.

My mind was already calculating our window of escape.

Danger, danger, danger, danger, danger.

It had taken us about twenty minutes to get where we were from the harbour. Twenty minutes in a boat that wasn't built for speed.

Whatever it was that was coming our way? It was on the move and coming *fast*.

The thing wasn't close; we had maybe five kilometres between us and the safety of land. Less if we jumped ship or made for Oban Marina on the other side of Kerrera. Whatever it was that had been alerted to our presence—that *I* had alerted to our presence—it had at least five times that distance to cover.

And it could, far faster than we could escape if we were any farther from home.

The engine hummed, a sound far too placid for the urgency of the situation.

Eilidh came to stand by my side, taking my hand at the same moment Sailean let out a plaintive mew, sensing our distress.

"I know, love," I said to the kitten. "We're going."

"This is what I was—this is what I felt," Eilidh murmured to me, referring to the day I'd caught her staring out to sea.

"How did you feel it?" I asked her carefully. "Is it your—is it your specialised affinity? The Seer one?"

Eilidh startled, her hand going still in mine for a moment before she squeezed both her fingers and her eyes closed.

"Aye," she said, her voice hardly above a breath. "An dara-shealladh."

It was my turn to startle. The second sight. Something our people had always known of, always respected. "Is it—is it new?"

Eilidh's eyes opened, and she turned her head to look at me, a sweet-but-uncertain smile on her face as if she were afraid to admit it. "No. It's not new. Seanmhair was helping me understand it."

Oh. *Oh.*

The boat beneath us sped up, cutting through the calm ripples of this sheltered bit of water, and for a moment, I couldn't even think about the thing that was gaining on us. I wasn't sure why I said it, only that I felt—to my core—that it was the right thing to say.

"Her spirit lives in you now," I murmured to Eilidh. "Chan eil càil a dhìth ort ach èisteachd rithe."

*All you need is to listen to her.*

At Eilidh's fierce nod, I knew my gut had been correct.

"Trust yourself," I said to her, squeezing her hand. "I trust you."

A piercing shriek cut through the air, making the sailors shout in surprise.

I looked up, my gaze tracking west towards the southern tip of Mull, maybe as far as Iona, where an enormous shape winged its way in our direction.

"It's okay!" I called out. "The eagle won't hurt us—I think she's trying to warn us."

When the huge bird circled, my heart stuttered in my chest.

"She's trying to warn us," I said again, awe touching my voice. "That's where it is."

The sailors relayed what I'd said across the boat, and a couple of them scrambled up atop the cabin with binoculars.

"Track the bird!" one of them yelled it out as we neared the northern shore of Kerrera where we could turn into the bay.

The boat seemed to inch in comparison. Even at the distance we stood from the eagle, she was closing on us. Pre-ascension, I'd have only made out a blip like a bizarre plane in the sky, but now I could see the flapping of her huge wings, and though I kept Connection closer in to not give away our position any more than I already had, I could feel the monster gaining on us.

It was a monster. That was clear. Whether it was an ascended animal from our world or something from folklore and imagination, all that mattered was that it was coming.

The eagle circled again.

"Fuckin' hell," one of the sailors said up top. "At least two clicks closer."

I glanced at Eilidh, unsure if I knew what the sailor meant.

"Two kilometres," she murmured.

"That thing's moving a hundred meters every couple seconds," I said, unable to keep the alarm from my voice.

In answer, Sailean gave another distressed mew.

"We ought to have left you at home," I murmured to her. "Duilich, a ghràidh."

The second meow was indignant, as if the kitten were saying, *Don't you dare.*

The eagle loomed in the sky, graceful despite her mahoosive size, and her cry sounded again. For a moment, I wondered how long the delay had been from the first one, considering her distance—and just how loudly she would have to scream to be heard over the intervening kilometres.

"Remind me to ask her not to yell like that too close to human habitations," I muttered. "She'll break all our eardrums."

A shaky laugh bounced about the boat, from the sailors and from Eilidh, and I finally caught sight of Meeksy and Iain and Rhona, who had all been near the helm when we'd stayed to stern.

Rhona buffed her fingernails on her armour. "If she screams at me, I'll just scream back."

"No banshee-eagle noise contests, please," called Catrìona from out of sight.

We finally reached the edge of Kerrera just as the eagle circled again. Now she was parallel with the arm of land that jutted out around Loch Buie, which meant the monster had closed almost two-thirds of the distance in the time it had taken us to go a bare two kilometres, if I was calculating my distances correctly.

"I hate this," Meeksy muttered. "Was never one for sea monsters."

"Mate, I don't think anyone's having a good time," one of the sailors said. "I love the sea, but there are times you've got tae remember—she's bigger and wilder and more unpredictable than you could ever guess, and the moment you stop respecting her is the moment she swallows you. Or something that lives in her does."

It was a relatively young man who'd spoken, rangy and weathered with ruddy cheeks and dark hair flattened beneath a wool cap.

At my look, he gave me a brief nod, his cheeks turning pinker.

"Ask any Gaelic song, and it'll say the same thing," I murmured.

"Aye, she gives us life, but she is hungry."

We rounded Kerrera, now wedged between the mainland and the island. Dunollie Castle rose up to the left on its hill, and I had the sudden wish that we use the castle the way it had once been meant to be used—a guardian at the gates of Oban.

The eagle was closer now, her shape moving with urgency even as she circled again. She was passing the inlet of Loch Spelve, more than halfway up the southern coast of Mull now. Soon, she'd be coasting along Kerrera.

I started counting familiar landmarks as if it would somehow get us home faster. Dunollie Point. Clach a' Choin, the Dog Stone. The parade of bed and breakfasts. St. Columba's Cathedral.

When the eagle rose up over Hutcheson's Monument on the northern tip of Kerrera, my stomach clenched.

"Bloody hell, that thing is fast," one of the sailors muttered, fear dripping from his words.

I knew without a doubt that he did not mean our eagle friend.

She banked away, turning back towards Mull, and circled once more.

The monster had already reached where we'd just been. If we'd delayed another few minutes, we'd have been pulped.

Eilidh's hand was damp in mine, and it was far from the sweaty-palmed nerves I'd had after kissing her.

I did the only thing I could think of. "Brace yourselves—I'm going to try to speed us along!"

The sailors relayed my words again, and I dropped Eilidh's hand to make for the stern, watching the boat's wake churn the waters without the accompanying roar of a motor.

Spèird came easily to me, my spirit dipping as I wove it together like an enormous paddle, imagining the tail fin of a huge whale that could propel us faster into the harbour. I couldn't push us too fast or we'd simply run aground without control; no, this required a certain amount of finesse, and with the pressure of a monster gaining on us every second, I wasn't sure finesse was in my wheelhouse.

But I had to try. The sun had dipped behind clouds and probably below the horizon by now, and the sky darkened with the oncoming twilight, turning everything to a desaturated state of blues and greys. Soon, we wouldn't be able to see what was coming. I had to act now.

Glancing over my shoulder, I looked at the distance remaining between us and the pier.

With a little—okay, a *lot* of—luck, I could both push us to safety and shove whatever was coming backwards on my resulting wave.

The eagle turned and circled the mouth of the bay.

*Now.*

I released Spèird like a humpback whale propelling itself forward with all its might.

The fishing boat surged forwards with startled yells despite everyone having been warned.

The resulting wave from my spell swelled the sea without cresting, an enormous ripple cascading westward.

And then, I saw it.

Subconsciously, I'd grown used to the patterns of the waves today, their calm and their serenity despite the gravitas of this expedition.

When my Spèird-enforced wave rushed into the west, it wasn't just on the surface of the water, but plunged metres deep into it—and it encountered resistance.

The eagle shrieked again as my wave shoved the whatever-it-was backwards from the mouth of the bay, and the wave crested over the sudden shallowness caused by something *huge*.

When the splash came, it arced like a bomb had gone off, drenching even the shoreline where the Oban War Memorial stood guard over the harbour's mouth.

I felt like everyone on the boat collectively held their breath, waiting for an attack.

"The eagle!" Rhona called out.

The massive raptor plunged into a dive.

# CHAPTER
# ELEVEN

Yelling exploded behind me—towards the boat's helm—
but all I could concentrate on was the eagle's sudden
plunge out of sight.

My wave must have pushed the monster back far enough
that Kerrera was in the way of seeing what was happening, and
in a moment of near desperation, I reached out with Tàthadh. I
wasn't trying to do anything but see what was going on, but all
that came back was a tumult of splashing.

Bare moments later, the shape of the eagle vaulted into the
skies again with a cry, and she came in to land on the outcropping of rock that housed Hutcheson's Memorial on Kerrera, her
gaze trained on the sea beyond the harbour.

This time, when my tendril of thought touched her, she
latched on to it.

A surge of satisfaction permeated her, though her feathers
were ruffled, both literally and metaphorically.

All that came through in terms of the creature was that it
was far bigger than she was and that it was on the move back
out to deeper water.

"It's retreating," I said aloud, sending a pulse of thanks to the eagle. "She's standing guard."

I turned to see that we were in the harbour proper now, and Mary had killed the engine to let us coast on the residual propulsion of my hasty Spèird.

Catrìona came on deck from where she had been at Mary's side at the helm, peering at the shape of the eagle, which was nearly the same size as the monument side by side.

"That," Catrìona said, "is a problem."

"It is a very big problem," I agreed. "And I think it coming after us was my fault."

I was still peripherally connected with the eagle, though we hadn't established a formal bond, but her immediate rejection of that thought caught me off guard. I hadn't realised she could hear me without my projecting thoughts at her.

Catrìona noticed my surprise and peered at me closely to ask what had happened. "Dè thachair?"

Motioning at the eagle and glancing around at the mostly English-speaking crew—all of whom were blatantly eavesdropping—I winced. "The eagle says it wasn't my fault, but I would like to know how she came to that conclusion."

I had the sudden image of the eagle preening her feathers, and not from seeing her do just that.

"Ask her," Iain called from behind me.

"I was planning on it," I replied, a small amount of waspishness creeping into my voice.

This time, when I reached out with Tàthadh, I *did* propose a bond, if only a temporary one. The eagle accepted with alacrity —she was at least as curious about my own memories of what had just happened as I was about hers.

A torrent of images and impressions roared through my mind, as incisive and piercing as her whistling call, and I was almost thrown off balance by the force of her personality. Everything else I'd bonded with had been meek as mice in comparison, and the silver-white gelding of Bawbag's who had helped us escape him the first time had been anything but meek.

But the eagle was in a class of her own. She showed me where she had been hunting off the coast of Staffa on the southwestern coast of Mull, where she had seen a disturbance in the waters circling Iona, the sacred islet that punctuated the end of the Ross of Mull.

What struck me about this was that she didn't mean *seen* with her eyes. Oh, her eyesight was appropriately sharp as the idioms we had about being eagle-eyed, but since the ascension, it had become something more, something other.

It seemed she'd developed something like Connection herself, but more innate than my active usage, where she could simply observe and track patterns in spirit much like she could sense a warm updraft or see the currents in the waters.

I'd thought that it had been my use of Connection that had alerted the creature, but when I'd first caught wind of it, it hadn't been off of Iona at all; it'd been farther south and east, closer to the Isle of Colonsay.

"Oh," I breathed. "Oh, that's not good."

The eagle, satisfied that I'd understood what she meant to convey, released the bond with a click of her beak that I could hear in my mind.

"What's not good?" Iain said, practically in my ear.

I jumped. He'd come much closer than he had been when I'd started talking to the bird.

"The monster had already been on its way to us." I felt sick, and it wasn't that the boat was rocking as we approached the pier. "Or maybe on its way back to the site of the wreck."

"It's defending its territory," Meeksy murmured, the big Persian Scot peering out over the waves.

"Well," Catrìona said after a beat. "So are we."

The loss of the *Sheila* had spread through the town by the time we'd secured the mooring lines, and we were all too aware at the three bodies we'd returned to shore with were only a third of the souls who'd been onboard.

Cries and sounds of grief filtered through the crowd at the news—though I was as certain as I possibly could be that we would not be finding the other six corpses, I knew there would be six webs of human connections, of families and friends and loved ones, who would always wonder.

At least the three we'd come back with, their families would have some closure.

The evening went by in a blur of questions I couldn't answer, to the point that I'd almost forgotten about the tree.

I was just about to head back to the house and was looking around for Eilidh—Iain and Meeksy had already taken Sailean with them to go sleep—when a familiar face wove through the crowd and approached me.

Angus, followed by his wife Eliza.

The two of them had been the first to welcome us into Oban, lending us their lounge when we'd arrived, exhausted, with the primary school pupils of Kilninver.

Gods, it felt like an age ago.

Angus's sea-blue eyes were darkened in the gloaming, but the slight stoop to his posture I'd noticed upon first meeting him was gone—more ascension miracles, it seemed. Eliza was similarly clear gazed, her silvering hair pulled back in a chignon as she came towards me and took my hands fondly, leaning in to kiss me on the cheek.

"Town's decided they want to put the tree up at the tower,"

Angus said without preamble, and I froze, my hands still in Eliza's as she pulled back from her greeting peck on the cheek.

I dropped her hands and clasped his in mine with a firm handshake. "You're sure? It's not exactly easily accessible if someone has mobility issues."

"Och, we've found ways around that," Eliza said, the *och* sounding strangely cute in her blended English-and-Argyll accent. "Some of the mages have been working on a funicular."

I blinked at that, deciding I'd leave them to it if they wanted a funicular in Oban. And the how-to that such a thing would necessitate. It made me think of the funicular in Barcelona where a hungover Iain had once boaked all over his own feet, much to my chagrin and a resulting torrent of Catalonian expletives.

"The tower it is," I said slowly. "So long as folk are sure that's where they want it."

"It makes the most sense," Angus said. "Especially if that thing's gonnae grow."

Fair play.

"Tomorrow, then," I told him. "I reckon everyone's had enough of today."

"I'll get people to move it into place for you." The older man clapped me on the shoulder in farewell, and then he and Eliza swept off into the milling crowd again.

It took me several minutes to find Eilidh, and when I did, she was talking to Alison and looking harried. I kind of couldn't blame her; Alison had been oddly infatuated with me when we first met her, and that had ended up making everyone uncomfortable—Alison included.

When I approached, Alison looked like she'd swallowed her tongue. "Calum—I, erm, thought you'd gone home."

I motioned at Eilidh. "We were about to, I think."

"Not quite," Eilidh told me dryly, one auburn eyebrow

twitching as if she were holding back a frown. "Alison's just said there's a pack of anomalous badgers out at Loch Nell that need dispatching. The mages on patrol have them corralled for now, but Alison says Ronald wants to keep one."

If her *not quite* had been dry, the *Ronald wants to keep one* practically sucked every drop of moisture from a hundred-mile radius.

I groaned. "Badgers?"

At least it wasn't pine martens. Small favours from this new universe.

"Are the mages who have them trapped unable to separate them or something?" I asked.

"They're a bunch of level fives," Alison said apologetically. "One of them has Ring of Fire, and the others are basically feeding her spirit to keep it going."

That pulled another groan from me. "Right. We'd better get moving, then."

Without waiting for confirmation, Eilidh and I broke into a jog, and I heard a stutter step as Alison hurried after us.

Sea monsters, land monsters, zombie badgers for pets.

I wouldn't have been totally surprised to find out I'd knocked my head back in my Glasgow flat and all of this had just been a strange, surreal dream.

And yet here we were, trotting through a magically powered Oban on our way to find a corrupted version of Tommy Brock, who'd not be half as cute as Beatrix Potter's grumpy badger of that name.

Darkness had well and truly fallen by the time we made it to Loch Nell, but the glow of Purifire lit up the surrounding land-scape like a beacon.

Visible from a mile away, we followed that glow to the makeshift "corral" the baby mages had created to contain the anomalous badgers.

"It's us—I brought Calum!" Alison called ahead of us when we approached.

Eilidh gave me a sideways glance as if to say *And me, chopped liver.*

"And Eilidh," I said blandly, and Alison visibly jumped.

"And Eilidh!" she chirped, almost a squeak.

The baby mages weren't exactly babies; most of them were middle aged, but the one who was maintaining Ring of Fire was a thirty-something-year-old woman who looked like she was on the verge of collapse.

Without waiting another minute, I surveyed the badgers where they clustered at the very centre of the ring, occasionally snapping at each other.

I drew on spirit and cast my own Ring of Fire, expanding it outwards from where the other mage had made hers, which was solid but small, and I wanted to lull the anomalies into spreading out enough that I could lasso one away from the others.

A quick count showed seven of them, which was unfortunate. An entire sett. Most likely, anyway. Badgers weren't all that common this far north, so I had to wonder if these had been pushed up from England on the orders of the entity I'd sensed through the creepy rabbit in Kilmelford.

"You can drop your ring," I told the woman who'd been holding hers for who knew how long.

Well inside my own, hers fell, and the mage collapsed with it.

"Shit," said Eilidh. "Is one of you a healer?"

"I am," Alison said, hitting her knees beside the fallen woman.

The other mages gaped at me, obviously not seeing a strain.

"I'm level twenty-one," I told them with a small, tight smile. "You'll get there. Work on your crafting if you want to get stronger faster."

How they were only level five after all this time was beyond me, though that was far from the point at the moment.

The badgers were not very quick on the uptake, which was lucky for me. With the collapsed mage in good hands, I turned back to the anomalies, tracking them as they slowly realised their prison had expanded. For a moment, I thought I'd not expanded it enough and they were just going to stay clustered at the extreme centre, but then one let out an ungodly squawk and peeled away from the others.

Through the haze of the Purifire wall, the thing still looked like an impressionist nightmare, and the moment it was far enough away from the other six anomalous badgers, I slammed down a smaller Ring of Fire around the intrepid pioneer.

My spirit took a large dip with the double cast, since I was pouring more into it to maintain both rings. It was just slightly higher than my regeneration, and I kept part of my mind trained on the awareness of how much spirit I had left.

I hadn't tried to create concentric Rings of Fire before, but it was good to know I could, in a pinch. Especially where it came to the anomalies.

My second cast had also had a more immediate effect on the other badgers—they did not like their sudden proximity to more Purifire, and now they all frantically scrambled with long claws tearing into the turf as they tried to get away from the newest addition.

The easiest thing to do would just be to flambé them all where they were inside the big ring, but I wasn't sure that was the best option. I also wasn't certain I could cast a third ring to further corral the clump of six, not without putting myself out of commission for the battle.

A groan behind me pulled my attention, and I turned to see the collapsed mage sitting up, eyes blearily searching the small clearing. She looked a bit green, but I thought that was just the effect of the Ring of Fire's lighting—not particularly a healthy look on anyone.

Loch Nell was a short distance away, its night-black waters reflecting the blue-green Purifire in ripples that cast strange shapes on its surface like a scrying pool.

Naturally, that was when the loch erupted.

# CHAPTER
# TWELVE

"The fuck is that!"

I couldn't tell who said it, because I was too busy throwing a wave of Spèird at whatever it was.

A golden glow told me Eilidh was flying into action, her two-handed claymore glinting in the cooler glow of my Ring of Fire even as she put herself between the loch's edge and the mages.

My instinctive defensive cast didn't take much spirit, and for a pair of heartbeats, I debated whether Keen Eye was worth the risk before deciding that *not* figuring out what we were up against was a far greater risk.

I cast it, homing in on the centre of the splash where it'd broken the surface of the water.

The answer was not a surprise, but it was unwelcome.

•‹ ⸎ ›•

*Fuath Mòr*

*This monstrous creature has taken over the neighbouring areas, terrorising most native fauna into migrating outward. While not immediately different to the lesser fuathan encountered more commonly, this one has a voracious appetite for flesh, though it is sluggish after a meal and generally rouses only when hungry again.*

That was all I needed to know. I pushed the information to every person in the clearing.

Eilidh slammed her claymore point down in the bank of the loch, blazing gold with the power of her will.

The fuath screamed, a wet, grating sound, and the light of Eilidh's magic lit it up as bright as day.

I practically flew to her side, pointedly ignoring the images assaulting my vision—slimy, slack flesh dripping with algae and loch flora, a mane of bristly hair like reeds I instinctively knew would stab like a porcupine's quills—and together, we formed a wall between the fuath and the unprepared mages behind us.

The fuath, momentarily blinded by Eilidh's magic, struck me with inspiration.

Dubh was a skill I'd unlocked after Blàr Ghaineamhain—it could be used with my ogham skills, or it could be used to blind an opponent.

Gritting my teeth against the further expenditure of spirit, I triggered Dubh. Power rushed out of me, and the fuath flailed.

Eilidh advanced to the water's edge.

"It's blinded, but be careful," I said to her sharply. "It might not need to see to hunt."

I forced myself to take a deep breath, moving in one of my forms to encourage my spirit to regenerate faster than I was spending it.

That woman—that brilliant woman—she simply glanced over her shoulder at me and winked. *Winked!*

And then she triggered a skill I'd never seen before.

Her sword flicked out like a whip, and indeed, a lash of pure will seemed to plait itself together from the hilt past the tip of the blade. The rope of energy caught the fuath around the neck —and Eilidh didn't stop there.

Bracing herself at the water's edge, she fell into a slight crouch, and then she yanked with all her might on the hilt of her sword.

The fuath flew free of the water with another ear-ripping screech and a squelch of mud.

Eilidh spun as it hit the ground, shaking her blade free and releasing the plait of golden will.

With my spirit flowing into me faster, I shifted forms to a more combat-oriented one, watching as Alison prudently motioned the baby mages back away from the fuath even as she herself advanced with care.

With a flash of inspiration, I pulled a tiny sliver of Purifire from my Ring of Fire and cast it into Eilidh's sword. For her part, Eilidh was so used to the feel of my spirit that she didn't even react, but Alison jumped, though she recovered quickly.

Eilidh's sword arced towards the fuath like a blue-green comet as the fuath itself scrambled in the now-muddy earth. I spun into a similar strike with my staff, using it as a blazing bludgeon without casting anything further. Brac-Meanmna, of course, also had a will of its own.

It lit up gold like Eilidh had, that will practically dripping from it like flaming honey as my strike connected with the back of the fuath's head.

A web of Purifire hurtled towards the creature. Alison. I leapt out of the way just as it collided, covering the length of the monster from head to webbed toe with a fine, delicate mesh of blue-green energy. With a start, I remembered that Alison had used that to attack a flock of anomalous starlings—Ronald had told me about it. It was an effective attack even against a non-corrupted monster. The fuath screamed again.

"Baby mages!" I yelled. "Hit the fuath with any ranged spell you have, and do it quick!"

I was tapped out of the arcane fight. Still maintaining my Ring of Fire around the anomalous badgers and at the same time landing physical blows on the fuath with Brac-Meanmna, I had to wrestle with my own focus to concentrate on the monster. My bloody staff was "helping" with its pervasive smugness as it smacked the thing with its will over and over again. I had the strangest impression of an old-timey film with a pair of overdressed gentlemen slapping each other with pairs of gloves.

Gleeful absurdity.

That was it.

Bolts of Purifire flew towards the fuath from the baby mages even as Eilidh brought her sword down on the creature's midsection.

If I expected that to be the end of the battle, I was sorely mistaken.

Like something out of a kung-fu movie, the goddamn fuath launched itself off the ground with a spinning motion that could not have happened without the help of spirit.

Eilidh's attack still landed, but instead of cleaving the monster in half, she caught it in the hip as the centrifugal force of its spin sent it flying away.

It landed a short distance from the Ring of Fire and recoiled from the flames, hissing and spitting loch slime at the fire. It sizzled and popped where it made contact with the arcane blaze.

"If anyone has Spèird, try to stomp it from the top!" I bellowed.

"Why don't you do it?" someone called snidely.

For fuck's sake.

"Aye, you take over badger babysitting and I'll get right on that, mate!"

The answering silence sent a very clear message.

A moment later, Spèird smashed down on the fuath's head.

The creature was still reeling from Eilidh's even glancing blow—a glancing blow with a blade as sharp as that claymore was like calling an amputation a mere flesh wound—and even though the baby mages were level fives, whoever had cast it had clearly given it a proper go.

It had the effect of a bowling ball falling on the monster's head, and the fuath stumbled.

I darted in to capitalise on the creature's dazed staggering, slamming my staff against the back of its neck and then whipping back to dip Brac-Meanmna in the Ring of Fire to light it up for my next strike.

The fuath's grotesque mane continued to blaze a good ways down its back, and my next hit caught it between the shoulder blades where the mane went up with a sizzling *whumph*. I hadn't expected something that dwelt underwater to be so immediately flammable.

I didn't have time to look that particular gift water-horse in the mouth, because Rhona threw another net of Purifire at the creature just as Eilidh let out a yell and leapt through the air, sword blazing gold.

She landed and struck at the same time, the force of her two-handed blow shoving the fuath sideways into the wall of Purifire at its left shoulder.

The creature screamed as the Purifire spread up its mane and also burned away at its left arm, but Eilidh was prepared. Her claymore had cut deep into the fuath's chest this time, and to my surprise, she dropped the heavy sword where it was lodged in goopy flesh, drawing a forearm-length dagger from her belt and plunging it upwards into the fuath's chest.

The blade emerged between the fuath's shoulders, and after a split second of consideration, I swept Brac-Meanmna through the Ring of Fire once more and touched it to the blade where it raced down the steel into the monster's chest.

My vision flashed gold.

*You have killed a fuath mòr.*

Thank all the gods.

"Badger, badger, badger, badger, badger, badger, badger—it just sounds wrong to stop at seven," I muttered under my breath, staring at my unfortunate charges.

Harvesting the fuath mòr had been significant for the baby mages, who I think I'd offended by calling babies, which was fair. They'd all been close to level six as it was, and since the fuath mòr had been far closer to my level than theirs, they'd all hit level seven even with their comparatively meagre contributions.

"Mushroom, mushroom," Eilidh said helpfully, pointing off to the side of the loch where a couple fungi indeed grew on the trunk of a tree.

"There better not be a snake. I've had enough snakes for one lifetime," I told her.

Alison, who had been crouched quietly nearby through this entire exchange, stood up, staring at us both sideways. "What on earth are yous on about?"

"Clearly preparing to drop dead from age," Eilidh said dryly.

The younger woman looked at her as if trying to decide whether she was being made into the butt of a joke or not, and Eilidh clearly saw that, so she went on in a hurry.

"It's a meme. An old meme, from, like, twenty years ago? Oh, god." Eilidh groaned. "It was literally over twenty years ago, wasn't it?"

"You're not *that* old, are you? Aren't you, like, twenty-eight?"

Eilidh let out a burst of a guffaw. "You're off by a decade, darlin'."

"You're *thirty*-eight?"

"Will be in July," Eilidh said.

"Wait, how old is Calum?"

"Calum is thirty-six," I said blandly.

I could almost see the vestiges of Alison's crush turn to dust, a sight I greeted with no small amount of relief.

Eilidh gave me a barely concealed smile.

"Your turn, lass," I said to Alison. "Only fair."

"Oh! Erm." Alison blushed, which painted her a strange, bruised colour in the light of my Ring of Fire. "I'm, erm, twenty-three."

Jeezo. I'd not thought she was *that* young. "Kilninver must have been your first teaching position, aye? Hell of a way to get chucked in the deep end."

Alison breathed a sigh of—what I perceived as—relief at the subject change.

"Whilst it's very enlightening to know that a pair of weans were calling us babies when we could be their parents," someone said from behind us, "perhaps we'd like to deal with the badgers?"

Both Eilidh and I winced. "For the record, we were referring to your levels, not your ages," I said, though I didn't think that helped. "How *did* a quintet of level fives end up on patrol alone, anyway? Angus wouldnae send folk out that unprepared, not this far into the ascension."

I motioned at the patch of earth where the fuath had dissolved into motes a few minutes before.

The man who had spoken looked like he'd choked on half a lemon.

A younger woman, who I recognised as the mage who'd been holding the Ring of Fire upon our arrival, rolled her eyes.

"Ignore Doug. He's just cheesed off that his attempt at heroism turned into us getting rescued," she said.

"Ex*cuse* me?" Doug looked about to go into apoplectic shock.

"Calm yer tits, mate," I said. "It was just a question, and you've managed to answer it anyhow."

"I didn't ans—"

"Doug," said a much larger man beside him, "you're answering it more and more with every word oot yer mouth."

Doug shut up.

I decided to move on. "Doug's right about the badgers. What's your name?" I asked this of the Ring of Fire woman, who gave me a beaming smile.

"Angie," she said.

"Fab. Angie, if I show you how to make a Purifire spear, do you reckon you could use it to skewer a few badgers?" When a couple other mouths opened, I waved one hand. "Anyone who has Purifire in their arsenal is welcome to try, but it is a bit more complex than the basic spell. Should help you level it up though, even if you can't manage to shish-kebab any anomalies."

"Anomalies?" This came from the bigger man who'd told off Doug.

"The badgers—we'll explain the rest after those are sorted." I squinted at the one in solitary confinement. "Though how we're going to transport that thing to Kilmelford is a trickier question."

I cursed under my breath. The damn purification cage blueprint I'd gotten when we'd finished the last stage of the quest.

Had Eilidh gotten it too?

Without my asking aloud, she answered. "We got that blueprint for a 'purification cage'," she said, making air quotes around the name, "but I didn't look closely enough at it. We got a bit distracted by the *Sheila*."

"The what?" Doug said.

Bugger. We had a lot to catch them up on.

Eilidh and I exchanged a glance, and after a moment, she suppressed a resigned sigh. "I'll head back into town and see if the crafters can make it—also we can figure out if it's something we can put on a cart or any other way of actually transporting it."

"Wait, why are you leaving?" Alison asked.

"We've got a way to transport the badger, but Calum needs to stay here to maintain the Ring of Fire until I can get back," Eilidh replied. She glanced at the five mages, who were all shifting their weight uncomfortably. "You lot can come with me, except Angie."

"Why don't we at least kill the other six first so—Calum, right?—so Calum doesn't have to hold the entire thing?" Angie frowned as she spoke.

"Too much margin for error. If we kill all six and then something happens with the seventh, we've lost the chance for the capture altogether," I told her.

I didn't like this. With my spirit tied up in the Ring of Fire to this degree, leaving me alone with a single level-seven mage did not seem prudent. Eilidh seemed to be thinking the same thing.

"Alison should stay too," she said after a beat. "You're what, level fifteen now, Alison?"

Alison started. "Aye, well, level sixteen after that fight."

Eilidh nodded perfunctorily, meeting my eyes. Though her

expression was serene, I couldn't help but notice the slight glint of amusement lurking in her blue gaze, the light of Purifire making her look like her irises had been touched by the will o' the wisps.

I returned her gaze just as serenely until she cracked a smile and beckoned at the other mages to follow her back towards town.

A sigh desperately wanted to escape as I looked at the badgers, seeing Alison blushing again in my peripheral vision and Angie looking back and forth between us as if trying to figure out why everyone was being weird.

It was going to be a very, very long night.

# THIRTEEN

I'd been exhausted before our excursion to Loch Nell, and by the time three in the morning rolled around, I was so bloody knackered that I was tempted to just kill all the badgers myself and go hunt new anomalies after stealing a few hours of sleep.

My stomach grumbled as I paced the clearing. Both Alison and Angie had fallen asleep with their backs against a large elm tree, leaving me awake and on watch. Since sitting down bore the distinct danger of me passing out, I was painstakingly putting one foot in front of the other as I walked circles around my Ring of Fire.

The badgers inside it followed me warily with their eyes, though they didn't move. I'd learnt my lesson about reaching out to them with Tàthadh, but that didn't stop me from using Connection every few steps just to make sure I wasn't missing their creator spying on me.

I had to admit, it was an immense relief knowing that I hadn't sicced the sea monster on our boat. I didn't think I'd have been able to live with myself if it *had* been my fault, but the corrupting entity that had spawned the anomalies? Aye, that was credit I had to take for myself.

In spite of the experience of the past couple months, we were *all* babies. None of us knew what the hell we were doing.

"Calum?" Eilidh's voice broke through my zombie shuffle, and I stopped short, pulling the communication crystal out of my bandolier.

"Are you on your way back?" I asked her, watching the small pulse of light at the heart of the crystal as if it might show me her face like some bizarre, arcane version of FaceTime.

"Not yet. I had to wake some folks up to find out who could craft this thing and then more folks to find who had the right materials. It's a bit . . . complex."

"Thighearna," I muttered. "I'm not sure how long I can keep this up without sleep."

"If all else fails, you could have Angie reinstate her own ring and separate out the lone one again later."

"There you go with reasonable suggestions again," I said, stifling a yawn that threatened to split my face in two.

Eilidh chuckled, the sound far too distant for my tastes. "I'll ask around and see who else we have with Ring of Fire—if we need to set up shifts so you can get some sleep, that's what we'll do."

Her voice grew sombre at the end of her sentence.

"What happened?" I asked.

"Nothing new, just that one of the people I needed to wake up for the cage lost her son on the *Sheila*."

"Fuck."

"Aye."

I blew out a breath.

After a moment's pause, Eilidh went on. "I think she welcomed the distraction, but waking her up made me feel like a monster. Her eyes were puffy and bloodshot, and I just wanted the ground to swallow me."

A sudden lump in my throat made me swallow. "And here we were all hoping things would get easier after Bawbag."

"Maybe someday." Eilidh paused, and I heard voices in the distance. "I think we've got everything we need for the cage. I'll either let you know we're coming back or send someone to give you a break as soon as I can. It'll depend on how long the cage will take to craft and how easy it is to transport."

"Taing mhòr an da-rìreadh," I said softly.

"'S e do bheatha."

With that exchange of thank you, the connection slipped away, leaving me again alone with my thoughts and a sett's worth of corrupted badgers watching my every move.

Dawn lightened the southeastern sky before Eilidh's voice returned in my ear, breathless and as exhausted sounding as I felt.

"We've got it, and we're on the way to you," she said. "We're also bringing a few mages with Ring of Fire so they can relieve you. We'll be there in twenty minutes—just hold tight."

"Taing do Dhia," I muttered.

"Greasamaid!" Eilidh said loudly, and I didn't think that was meant for me to be included in her *let's get a move on*. In confirmation, her voice softened. "Chì mi a dh'aithghearr thu."

Soon. She'd be here soon.

I nearly collapsed where I stood, but I forced myself to keep on my feet. While I'd been through some ordeals in the past couple months, the struggle of holding not one but *two* Rings of Fire in an active state for hours at a time on no sleep after a stressful and emotional day was eating away at what remained of my reserves.

Angie and Alison were still asleep, too, so I'd been at this alone. A small, petty part of me took some measure of solace from the raging cricks in their necks bound to make waking a bit miserable.

Actually, come to think of it, waking them up now would be a kindness, right? Give them time to get their feet under them before zombie badger stomping duty?

Maybe it was me being a brat, but I'd been awake all night, and my spirit was only holding steady at thirty percent because every so often, I'd stopped my circuits of the Ring of Fire to do moving meditations and cast Fuaran, which had allowed it to tick up a ways, but it slowly slipped downwards again after those breaks.

I waited until my current circuit took me as close to their elm tree as possible and paused, listening to their duet of light snores. "Oi, Angie and Alison. Dawn's breakin', get tae wakin'."

Taking a moment to be proud of my half-delirious rhyme—which I'd pulled out of my arse on the spot—I waited while the women stirred sleepily. Angie had a bit of tree bark stuck in her tousled waves, and Alison's dark hair had started to turn greasy. The latter sat up straight and wiped a bit of drool from her mouth, looking a bit wild eyed at coming face to face with me first thing in the morning, newfound revelation of my ancient advanced age notwithstanding.

I prudently removed myself, calling over my shoulder, "Eilidh's on her way with the brute squad and a badger cage."

With that, I resumed my pacing, hoping the fact that there were another two sentient people handy would wake *me* up a bit. It didn't seem to be true, but I reserved the right to be fool-ishly optimistic.

When I came round the circle again, they were both on their

feet and yawning. Alison was making a point of not looking at me, but Angie, for her part, stared.

"You look exhausted," she said.

"How long did you hold your Ring of Fire?" I asked her pointedly.

Her answering wince told me enough. "An hour. We got hold of Alison with the communication crystal not long after."

"Aye, well, it's been about ten for me."

"I can count." She didn't sound like it was meant to be sharp, so I shrugged and kept on, which prompted her to ask, "Why are you walking in circles?"

"Got tae get my steps in," I deadpanned.

When she was still staring at me on my next badgerial revolution, I gave her a tight-lipped smile.

"I'm bloody knackered. If I stop, I'll drop."

Angie frowned at that. "Isn't Alison a healer?"

That made me miss a step. "Apparently, aye."

Alison's head snapped towards us. "Oh! Oh, god, Calum, I'm sorry. I could have—"

She broke off mid-sentence and practically flung Slànaich at me.

I recognised the spell, since it was one of mine, too, and the relief of spirit rushing into me was enough to almost make me sway on my feet.

Taking what felt like the first real breath all night, I nodded at the young woman. "Cheers for that."

Her face was beet red in the glow of the rising sun, and to hopefully spare her further mortification, I continued around the ring again, wondering if I ought to turn and go the other way, just for spice.

Spell or no spell, I was reaching the loopy stage.

The minutes waiting for Eilidh and the others to arrive were worse than the hours that had piled up before. Every minute seemed to drag out longer than the last, my heartbeats even seeming to space themselves out in my chest to the point that I would have welcomed an attack if it kicked some adrenaline into my system. Probably prudently, both Angie and Alison kept their distance.

I could have wept with relief when I felt Eilidh's presence coming near, and when the group came into view, she broke off from the main group with a trio of mages, staves strapped to their backs as they all ran our way.

If the minutes before had dragged, now I blinked and everything seemed to happen in flashes.

One of the mages cordoned off the lone anomalous badger before I could so much as make a gesture of hello, another slamming a Ring of Fire in place right inside mine.

Eilidh caught me by the upper arms as I staggered with the relief of dropping the magic I'd held all night. Gold flashed in my vision, and I wasn't sure if it was the rising sun, Eilidh's beauty with the first rays of dawn, or notifications—or a woozy combination of all three.

"Shin thu, a ghràidh," Eilidh said, hearing herself a split second after I processed that she'd just called me *love*.

"Shin thu fhèin, a ghràidh," I replied reflexively, unwilling to let her overthink it.

The momentary panic in her eyes faded, and she threw her arms around me. After a moment, I sank to the ground in the dew-damp grass, more than content to let other people handle it. Not caring about what it looked like, I lay back, and after a beat, Eilidh joined me, her hand working its way into mine.

I didn't even realise I'd fallen asleep until a commotion made me sit bolt upright.

Eilidh scrambled to sitting herself, blinking in confusion as we looked around for the source of the noise.

Most of the people with her were folks I only vaguely recognised, but I did see someone I knew among them.

"Ealasaid, dè tha dol?" I called to the old woman, who was tinkering with a little red wagon—or, more precisely, with the cage that sat, glowing, *in* the little red wagon.

Christ, we were going to put a badger in a little red wagon.

I hoped she'd answer my question and tell me what was happening, but before she could, whatever was happening *happened*.

A surge of spirit made me scramble to my feet, and I absent-mindedly flung out a hand to pull Eilidh with me. The group she'd brought with her clearly had the badgers well in hand—as one, lances of pure Purifire flashed through the Ring of Fire and speared clean through three of the corralled anomalies, followed in an instant by three more that dispatched the rest.

Part of me wanted to protest, because if they bollocksed the seventh, I would have kept that bloody magic going all night for nowt.

I needn't have worried.

Alison, had the final badger in a stare-down, the monstrous creature snarling at her from within her net of Purifire even as the mage holding the Ring of Fire around the only remaining subject let it drop.

The badger didn't move, every inch of its disgusting, putrid pelt quivering as it flinched away from the net.

Ealasaid trundled over—never in my life had I had the opportunity to use the word *trundle* more appropriately—with the little red wagon and the purification cage.

She carefully removed the cage from the wagon, and with a ripple of spirit, the front of it opened, swinging upwards without her touching it, where it remained perfectly perpendicular to the roof of the cage.

What a time to be alive. Physics be damned.

The first rays of sun lit a sheen of perspiration on Alison's upper lip as she moved the net bit by bit, like she had a massive spider under a laundry basket and was trying to nudge it over the threshold into the garden without the basket coming into contact with the arachnid.

I could almost feel everyone in that clearing at the edge of Loch Nell collectively holding their breath.

Inch by painstaking inch, the disgruntled, zombie-esque badger crept towards the cage.

And then inch by painstaking inch, it went *into* the cage.

It wasn't until there was a solid hand's width between the badger's arse and the cage's opening that Ealasaid slammed it shut with an eerily silent and anticlimactic gesture, and Alison let go of her net, breath heaving her chest with the exertion.

"Uill, ma-tà," Ealasaid said brightly. "Why don't you lot let us get this to Ronald's laboratory, and you can all go get breakfast?"

The old woman then squinted at me and Eilidh.

"Or maybe skip breakfast and sleep for a day or two," she said after a moment's consideration.

"Aye, that sounds like a good—" I was cut off by the sound of a voice yelling from what seemed like five different directions in the clearing all at once.

"All hands, all hands—monster sighted in the bay! All fighters to arms!"

"Uill, ma-tà," Ealasaid said again, much less brightly, "fuck a duck."

# CHAPTER
# FOURTEEN

If I could go a few days without having to literally run from crisis to crisis, I'd be very happy.

A small, snide part of my mind helpfully reminded me that I'd had a few weeks of just that after Blàr Ghaineamhain, but I —in a fit of perfectly warranted pique—punted that snide part of my mind tae fuck.

I'd cast Fuaran on both myself and Eilidh the moment we started to hoof it back towards Oban, leaving the others to deal with the badger's locomotive conundrum, but it barely seemed to take the edge off my exhaustion—or hers.

Oban was in full alarm mode.

That was evident the moment we got even close to town, since every church bell rang out in frenzied, dissonant urgency.

People rushed from houses, still attempting to equip themselves as they moved.

If the monster was in the bay, I'd no idea how we were even supposed to fight it, let alone what the bloody thing *was*.

But by the time we made it into view of the harbour, we didn't have to wonder what the bloody thing was.

Because the first thing we saw was an enormous tentacle cracking the mast of a sailboat in half.

"Jesus fuck, it's a goddamn kraken," I said as I skidded to a halt, grabbing Brac-Meanmna from my back.

Already, magic assaults of Purifire and Spèird and a hundred others I couldn't name flew from the pier, creating concussive blasts that sprayed water in enormous gouts.

"How do we fight this thing?" Eilidh said, sounding as if it had stolen her breath.

"From the relative safety of land," I said without thinking, then winced, but Eilidh was nodding her head violently.

"Fight that thing in a boat? Nope." She looked horrified by the very thought.

"Let's go," I said, kicking myself into a run again despite the ongoing heaviness of my legs and the way my mind and spirit were screaming for rest.

Without another word, we ran for the pier and arrived just in time to see another tentacle swipe across the fighters, sweeping about twenty people straight off the quay and into the drink.

I heard a horrible crack as someone hit the exposed ramp where the *Cuilean Donn* had moored earlier, followed by a yell of pain that ended in a splash.

Angus was at the front line, having narrowly avoided the tentacle, and when he saw us coming, he yelled, "Stay back! That thing has too much reach!"

We still had to be able to hit the thing, but *how?*

Since the monstrous squid—Octopus? Kraken? Hard to tell from a pair of tentacles—clearly knew precisely where we were, I triggered Connection to the best of my strength, concentrating on the harbour to see what other fauna were possibly in the line of fire.

The answer was fuck all. Everything bigger than krill

seemed to have buggered off entirely—normally there were a few seals, maybe an otter, all sorts of sea birds large and small, and plenty of fish who enjoyed the natural foraging for scraps that were abundant in water near humans. Today, there was only the monster.

"There's nowt else in the harbour!" I yelled to Angus.

"Well, can you blame everything else for getting tae fuck?" He swore something unintelligible and threw himself to one side, landing in an impressive roll just as another tentacle came sailing by.

What could we do that would hurt this creature?

I wracked my brains, thinking through the possibilities. The only one I could dredge up that had a shot at doing anything beyond peripheral damage was probably the worst idea I'd ever had.

"How many people here have Purifire or another fire spell?"

I bellowed out the question at the top of my voice, purposely leaning on Òran na Cloiche, my skill that amplified the magnetism of whatever I was saying, and the nearest tentacle actually twitched. Interesting.

A disjointed chorus of *ayes* rippled through the crowd.

"Everyone on the Piazza side of the pier, circle around to the ferry terminal, and when you see us launch, aim as much fire-power as you can at the water." I saw confusion hover in faces around me.

"The water?" Someone piped up from the Piazza side, where the pizza restaurant was in danger of getting slapped with a tentacle as much as Ee-usk on my side.

"Aye, the water. If we can't find a safe-ish way to attack this thing where it'll hurt, we'll bloody well poach it in the bay," I said grimly.

"Fuckin' hell," the person muttered, but I saw them run a

hand through shaggy hair as they took off towards the ferry terminal.

I cast Fuaran on the widest range I could from where I stood, hoping the extra spirit regeneration would allow us to do some damage. This time of year, the water was a far cry from tepid, let alone the temperatures we'd need to actually poach a giant order of calamari, but if it worked, it gave us an edge.

Assuming the goddamn thing could feel pain.

Connection helped me keep tabs on the mages who were sprinting around the harbour, and I was relieved to see that they were strategically spreading out.

I couldn't tell if it was a blessing or a curse that it was almost low tide—I thought a blessing, because that was less water to heat, but it also meant that those who were in the inlet between the ferry terminal and the pier where the bulk of our fighters were had a disadvantage of distance. Some of them hopped down onto the exposed beach, making my stomach clench. We still didn't know the full reach of those tentacles or whether this creature, like an octopus, could survive a strategic self-beaching out of pure spite.

A painful-sounding *crunch* split the air along with a crack that sounded like a bridge snapping in half. I spun to see that that was more or less what had happened—the monster had cracked the floating wharf off the north pier with the flex of a tentacle.

"Greas oirbh," I muttered under my breath, urging the mages to hurry.

They were almost in place. Almost.

"Mages, conserve your spirit!" I called out, watching as some of the ranged fighters rained down futile arrows and bolts from the edge of the pier.

Then *I* had to hit the floor, because not one but *two* of the creature's many arms struck out in annoyance.

My armour shielded me from the burn of sliding on concrete, but adrenalin spiked with the impact as I felt not only the ripple of the tentacles' displaced air but also a pulse of spirit from the monster.

Fuck.

When I clambered to my feet, the pier was in barely contained chaos, and I heard a scream. Wheeling on my feet, I spotted the source of it just as it cut off with a crunch and a gurgle. The sea monster's tentacle had properly caught a fighter this time, someone I couldn't recognise, and with one squeeze, had crushed his spine.

Chills cascaded down my back even as the fighters flung out attacks on the still-raised tentacle. It must have felt like getting pelted with pebbles to the thing—the monster didn't even flinch.

Gods, I hoped my harebrained plan would work.

The creature had every advantage in this battle—short of fucking *cannons*, which we did not have, at best we could hope to blow off a tentacle at a time, and the thing could simply retreat underwater to avoid our attacks. Or flee the bay entirely, heal quickly with the ascension's spirit, and return to rain down hell.

A pulse of Connection told me the mages were finally in place.

"Get ready to target the water around the monster!" I yelled, my blood heating in my veins as my mind tracked the creature's movement.

I didn't think it could understand us, which was a small point to be grateful for amid our many disadvantages. Our ability to coordinate may have been our single best shot at doing any damage.

The sound of pounding footsteps behind me made me turn

to see a breathless Rhona, brown hair wild around her face as she hit the pier at a dead run.

"Jeezo, what the fuck is that, a bloody *kraken*?" Rhona blurted out.

"We're about to try to poach it in brine," I told her quickly. "When we fire—literally—hit anything above water with your lightning if you can."

The bloody teenage banshee's eyes actually lit up.

Trying to ignore her eagerness in the face of Oban's impending doom, I called out, "Ready?"

The answering chorus from everyone, including Eilidh, who had been standing by with her calculating gaze trained on the beast. If I'd thought she'd be gnashing her teeth in helpless anger, I was dead wrong. I was certain she had a plan when she turned to me and gave me a sharp nod.

I gathered my spirit to me in a torrent, Brac-Meanmna spinning in my hands with the type of glee that reminded me of Rhona's.

"You two are impossible," I muttered to it, receiving a glow of pride in response.

Spirit surged around me as the other mages followed my lead, a heady rush of magic that set my skin to tingling and made every hair follicle on my body prickle with anticipation.

"Now!" I loosed my Purifire, aiming it like a Ring of Fire around the body of the kraken with as much force as I could pour into it.

And in a wave that curled around the harbour in an enormous C shape, the other mages did the same with a blast of spirit, pathos, and will that charged the very air with our combined determination.

The bay exploded.

Steam filled the air instantly with the smell of seaweed and brine, blocking my view of everything beyond the pier, but a concussive wave of force slammed outward from the pier's very edge with a bloom of vibrant gold.

Eilidh.

Before I could reflect on that, my scalp prickled as the crack of a hundred lightning bolts struck in the centre of the billowing steam.

The sizzling hiss of water turning to vapour filled the air just as someone screamed, "Get down! The water!"

Hidden in the mist, I could hear the beast thrashing, and it was churning up seawater.

Seawater we had just flash boiled.

I threw up a hasty wave of Spèird like a brolly, but I was a moment too slow, and a massive drop of near-boiling water splashed against my neck with a flash of sensation almost too visceral to be called pain.

My spirit was still recovering from the first volley, but my heart exulted at the knowledge that we were hurting the thing. Maybe one more could—

A screech pierced the air at the same moment I felt another raging fork of lightning soar past me from Rhona's magic.

Through the column of steam rising from the water, the eagle went into a dive.

"No!" The word came out almost as a gasp, and I reflexively grasped for the eagle with Tàthadh to warn her.

I was too late.

Her second scream was a sound of pure agony, and an explosion of spasming wings and splashes warred with the cries of the people around me.

"It's fleeing!" I heard someone yell, but I couldn't even process the words even as someone else yelled, "Aye, awa' an boil yer heid!" which my tired brain managed to catalogue as one of the most literal uses of the Scots saying I'd ever heard in my life.

I felt more than saw the eagle lurch skyward, and only moments later, fighters dived out of the way as she plummeted to the pier.

The enormous raptor hit on her side, feet akimbo, her foot-long talons scrabbling in futile twitches as electricity coursed through her body.

Without hesitation, I spun Brac-Meanmna to bolster my flagging spirit and poured almost everything I had into Beannachd Slàinte.

More shouts rose as fighters tracked the kraken's retreat, but all I cared about was the bird. Knowing the fucking monster was on the run was enough. It would be back.

"Tha mi cho duilich!" Rhona cried, and I turned to see her stricken face as she apologised—to me or to the eagle, I wasn't sure.

"Na gabh idir dragh—chan fhaca thu i," I assured her, which was the honest truth.

Rhona had loosed her spell before the eagle made her presence known; there was no way she could have recalled her magic in time, and I'd been too slow to warn either of them.

Pinions the length of my leg scratched across the wet concrete of the pier, making a spasming, grating percussion to the counterpoint of frenzied footsteps of people regrouping and calling in healers for those who'd been injured.

Instinct told me my spell was working on the eagle, but with my spirit almost drained and my body on the verge of total shutdown, all I could manage was a handful of staggering steps in her direction before I fell to my knees in exhaustion.

The eagle herself took a shuddering breath and collapsed, unconscious.

# CHAPTER
# FIFTEEN

The first thing I saw when I opened my eyes was a cat butthole.

"Classic," I groaned, my voice a hoarse croak. "Sailean, I prefer your other end."

The kitten, perhaps mollified by my return to the land of the living, gave a half chirp, half mew and turned about to look at me head on.

"Taing." Reaching a fumbling hand out from under the duvet, where I was suddenly *roasting*, I gave her a pat before plucking her from my chest so I could remove the smothering pile of down.

I swallowed with relief—dry mouth introduced a gummy new problem—once I felt cool air on my bare chest, though I had a moment of minor regret when I replaced the kitten only for her tiny needle claws to poke me in the now-naked nipple.

Only the vaguest memory of getting home remained in my brain. Both Eilidh and I had been in a state after the bizarre battle, that much I knew, but after the eagle had passed out, the two of us had been bundled inside Ee-Usk and given a restorative dram—Angus's words, not mine—while Meeksy looked after the eagle with a pair of hedge healers and some of the braver sailors had taken a speedboat to follow the retreating kraken to make sure it buggered off.

Just the fact that I'd been allowed to sleep until I woke up naturally seemed to indicate it had, indeed, gotten tae fuck.

I wasn't nearly naïve enough to think we'd killed it, and though my notifications were pulsing at the edge of my vision, I instinctively knew it was for other reasons.

Sailean settled down on my sternum in a small loaf, which meant I was not getting up to pee no matter what my bladder said. Her eyes slow blinked once, then twice, and then closed altogether, her tiny purr rumbling against my skin.

That alone was almost enough to lull me back to sleep, but instead I took a couple deep breaths. Focusing my intake on filling my stomach, I tried a small experiment of seeing how little I could move the wildcat whilst still controlling both my breathing and my meditative cycling of spirit.

It was a morning ritual I'd taken to doing anyway, kitten or no kitten—sometimes she liked to sleep with Eilidh—and it was nice to have a small indicator of normalcy in this brave new world.

While other mages had worked out certain types of wards around Oban, something still bothered me, like a word on the tip of my tongue.

As I breathed, my focus on the duality of breath and spirit cycling through my physical body and energy body alike, I dredged up memories of what I'd learnt on our trek to rescue the captives Bawbag had corralled at his manor.

I listened.

Since that day, my reach with Connection had tripled; miles instead of metres. But there was some vital piece that I was missing, some sneaky wee nugget of knowledge eluding my every attempt to track it down.

Awareness permeated Oban, and like the thoughts that simply floated by in my mind, I was able to sense others without getting dragged into the minutiae of the thousands of other people in the range of my spirit.

My spirit was simply one eddy within those flows, but try as I might, I couldn't figure out where I was blocked.

Blocked.

Maybe that *was* the right word.

Even as I thought it, I drew the deepest breath I'd taken since waking, feeling the air reach down into my belly, aware of the oxygen waking my red blood cells and travelling throughout my body with every subsequent beat of my heart.

Blocked.

Something was blocking me.

A flash of triumph came and went in the stillness of my meditation. That was the right way to think of it, like cutting off access to one lung and thinking you knew what a full breath was when you'd only ever gotten halfway.

"Oi, look who's awake!"

I startled, as did the Scottish wildcat kitten with her needle peets in dangerous proximity to the all-too-tender skin of my nipples. A dozen tiny claws buried themselves in my skin, and I yelped.

"Iain," I said through gritted teeth, "there are easier ways to give me a nipple piercing if you're that dead set on it."

Because Iain was Iain and utterly incapable of shame, he didn't give a toss about my close brush with an unnecessary mastectomy. Sailean, being a kitten, also failed to see the problem, giving a drop of blood a dainty lick where it beaded on a rogue nipple hair and leaping from the bed with far more excitement than Iain deserved, the prat. She also let Iain scoop her up as if they'd coordinated this ignominious attack.

Rude.

Iain simply told me there was food and abandoned me, kittenless, to heal my punctures and wounded pride. Thankfully, neither took long.

Whatever I'd been on the verge of in my meditation had escaped on the wind, and my stomach gave enough of a rumble that I couldn't ignore the promise of scran.

I didn't bother with armour, simply clothing myself in pre-ascension trackie bottoms and a T-shirt that must have been twenty years old, since it fit me like a second skin. My muscles hadn't grown *that* much, and Iain was still broader in the shoulders than I was likely to ever be.

The kitchen was the height of our new normalcy—kettle boiling on its magical hot plate, sausages sizzling on a griddle powered by the same, and Rhona sprawled in the far corner on the bench seat at the trestle table, one foot on the bench and the other on the floor as she absently shocked herself with her own lightning.

"Morning!" she chirped when she saw me. "Or, you know, afternoon."

"What time is it?" I asked before I remembered I could consult the system clock, which I did at the same time Rhona said, "Half three."

Jeezo.

"Is Eilidh still asleep?" I asked, glancing over my shoulder in the direction of her room.

"Aye," said Iain from his position by the kettle with Sailean perched bravely on his shoulder. "Mam's fishing—"

"She's *what*?" I blurted out. "With that thing still out there?"

"—off Lismore," Iain finished as if I'd not spoken, "and Meeksy's with the eagle."

"Still?" I'd been out a while. Definitely over fifteen hours, which told me I'd been in bad shape from running myself to the brink of collapse.

"Not still. Again," said Rhona. "He made sure she was okay last night, and there's another mage who was able to convince her to stay where she was instead of trying to fly off."

Despite the teenage wraith's lackadaisical sitting position, her voice was tight and stiff.

"Hey, a ghràidh," I said to her. "It wasn't your fault. If anything, blame physics. Even if she'd seen the lightning in time, a bird that size in a full-on dive would be tough inertia to arrest that fast."

"Maybe she'll listen now that you've said the same damn thing Meeksy and I told her," Iain muttered over the sound of hot water splashing into a teapot.

Rhona's pale cheeks turned a bit pink.

"It really wasn't your fault." I went and sat on the other side of the table from her, and she gave me a wobbly smile.

"Fine. It wasn't my fault."

"Keep repeating it until you believe it," I said. "If it'll make you feel better, I'll ask the eagle myself if she blames you."

All budding flushes of colour drained right back out of Rhona's face. "Oh, god, no. I couldn't bear it if she said yes."

I rolled my eyes. "I promise you she doesn't blame you. She seems a very sensible sort."

"Another normal day in normal Scotland," said Iain.

He came over with two metal teapots piping steam from the spouts and set them on the table, where they were instantly joined by a certain Scottish wildcat passenger who decided that the tabletop was her stop on the Iain Express.

"I'm not sure the table is the place for tiny kittens," I said to Sailean mildly, though from the twitch of her whiskers, she truly did not care.

"Och, she's fine." Iain waved a hand, turning round to grab the sugar bowl and another ascension oddity: fresh milk.

I didn't quite understand how Oban's local dairies were keeping up with demand or adapting to using magic instead of electricity, but seeing milk in old-style milk jugs etched with a glyph that shimmered slightly in the light was not something I was quite used to.

Honestly, it was the little things that threw me these days.

"Did they get the badger to Ronald?" I asked suddenly, the thought plunging into my mind like the memory of a particularly surreal dream.

Iain squinted at me as he set down the milk jug and the sugar with a clatter that made Sailean jump and puff out her tail.

He gave her an apologetic pat.

"Did they?" I prompted.

"I don't know about a badger."

"Lemme ask," Rhona said, dropping her leg from the bench to dig in a pocket for a communication crystal. "Oi, Alison, got a badger?"

I looked at Iain, who snorted.

"Erm, yes, we got the anomalous badger to Kilmelford. Ronald's running experiments as we speak with a couple people who came to help after the battle. You all holding up?"

Alison's voice had a strained quality to it that I didn't dare speculate about, but perhaps that had to do with the nature of Rhona's very polite greeting.

"Aye, we're fine here. Thanks. Toodles!" With that, Rhona shoved the crystal back in her pocket and replaced the foot on the bench, leaning back into the corner. "They've got the badger."

"We heard," I said dryly, holding back a chuckle.

"Oh."

Iain did not hold back his own chuckle and continued his domestic undertaking after a moment, finally settling down next to me with a plate of sausages and tattie scones, along with what looked like fish cakes.

When I asked, he nodded. "They are fish cakes. We've got heaps of fish. Heaps."

I had a feeling the people of Oban were about to be proper sick of fish.

Then again, with that monster out there, we were lucky to have that problem.

A scuff of a foot made me turn to see Eilidh in the doorway in an oversized T-shirt and—presumably, since they were invisible beneath the T-shirt—short shorts, rubbing her eyes like a cranky toddler. Her loose auburn curls were frizzy and sleep-sweat dampened, squished to her head where she'd been lying on that side but wisping away from her forehead on the other in perfect ringlets.

Eilidh looked at the three of us with half-closed eyes. "Tea?" she said plaintively, shuffling towards the bench Rhona occupied and slumping onto it with a face-splitting yawn.

Sailean, who had been sniffing at the sausages and fish cakes with whiskers puffed forwards and pupils all the way dilated, was unceremoniously plucked from the table into Eilidh's arms, where she squirmed for a moment and then grudgingly started to purr.

Iain prudently pushed one of the teapots towards Eilidh and got up to put the kettle back on just in case.

I, however, had no such presence of mind, because I'd seen Eilidh MacIntosh in a hundred different forms, but *adorable* was, heretofore, not one of them. Hastily averting my gaze and stabbing a sausage seemed like the best option so I didn't get caught staring, but when I looked up again, Rhona was smirking at me where she leaned in the corner, and she made heart hands, mouthing *You loooooove her.*

Sailean, thankfully, chose that moment to lose control over her ability to refrain from sausage theft.

It seemed she'd been biding her time purring in Eilidh's embrace, because she launched herself at the plate of sausages, sank her teeth into one, and leapt from the table with all four feet splayed out like a skydiver jumping out of a plane.

# CHAPTER
# SIXTEEN

I f you've never seen a bunch of fully adult elves chase a sausage-stealing, growling Scottish wildcat kitten around a house, you might be forgiven for expecting it to be nimble, full of beauty and grace and the ephemeral mysticism of Tolkien's Rivendell.

Aye, well, that'd be a load of pish, and the reality was more like Monty Python had an unfortunate lovechild with the Three Stooges.

For something barely bigger than the banger she'd nicked, Sailean was *fast*, and she was hugely advantaged by the pure fact that while easily ten of her could have flown through a doorway all at once, the four of *us* absolutely could not.

Iain and Eilidh collided first, with Eilidh pointing to the left down the corridor and half squeaking, half grunting, "That way!"

They went barrelling off down the hall, and when Rhona and I reached the doorway behind them, we were just in time to see Sailean—growling like the world's tiniest outboard motor and almost tripping over the sausage—come gallivanting back down the hall towards us. The kitten skidded to a halt, tumbling arse over tit—arse over banger, really—and then bolted for the stairs.

"Oh, for fuck's sake," I said as I closed the distance between kitchen and staircase in three long strides.

Rhona, however, was faster, and like with the door, the stairs were not wide enough for two grown adults to vault up at once, so just as I hit the first step, I tripped over her foot as she bolted past me, causing both of us to fall *up* the damn stairs as Sailean miraculously seemed to grow a jetpack from her furry wee arse for the ease with which she vanished from view.

"Mate," said Iain from behind us, "maybe we should just let her have it."

"I'm not sure 'let' is the operative word here." I could almost hear Eilidh's eye roll. "She is clearly winning this game of Hide the Sausage."

Eilidh seemed to realise what she'd said the moment she said it, and I decided that being in a pile halfway up a flight of stairs with a teenage banshee's knee in my ribs was safest so the woman I fancied couldn't see the Herculean effort it was taking not to burst out laughing.

Iain, bless him, had no such compunctions.

His laughter roared through the house like Purifire through the late Lord Bawbag's barn, and from the accompanying thud, I could only guess that Eilidh had decided to bang her head against the wall.

Rhona flailed enough to get her knee out of my ribs— narrowly avoiding kicking me in the baws in the process—and scrambled up a few more steps.

"What's funny about 'Hide the Sausage'?" she asked, *far* too innocently.

Freed from the indignity of the staircase entanglement, I turned around to another thud to see I'd guessed correctly.

"Iain can explain," I said hurriedly and vaulted over Rhona up the stairs to find the ... erm ... literal sausage.

With my bond with the kitten, it wasn't difficult to track her down, but by the time I found her, she was all the way under the twin bed in my room. She'd already eaten half of the sausage and was gnawing at the rest of it with extreme determination. Her ongoing growl exuding from the darkened corner of the dust bunny kingdom lessened in its ability to strike terror into my heart by the fact that it was punctuated by her kitteny wee *nyam-nyam-nyam-nyam* noises.

"Yer gonnae boak," I told her sternly, both aloud and with an image through our bond. "Bangers are not ideal foods for eight-week-old kittens."

Her growl grew louder in disagreement.

After a long moment of listening to that tiny sound, I came to a conclusion I found both prudent and prophylactic.

I cast my healing spell on the kitten. Sailean gave a startled squawk that sounded like a mew mated with the *nyam-nyam-grr*, but then she quickly resumed eating.

If nothing else, my surrender could at least ensure the dratted cat didn't die of stolen banger.

It felt like an age had passed since we had created the tree.

Craobh an Òbain, a living entity.

And the town had obliged with what seemed like the perfect venue: McCaig's Tower on Battery Hill. The tower was already home to a garden, a peaceful and park-like atmosphere that allowed visitors to take in the whole of Oban and on a clear day see all the way to Mull and beyond.

The tree, once situated there, would be a beacon to all.

Angus had seen to moving the tree, but even so, as Eilidh

and I made our way up the hill to the tower, I don't think either of us were prepared for the sight that would greet us.

While the ascension had worked miracles on people's bodies, healing everything from old wounds to genetic diseases to any number of other ailments, the mages had not rested on their laurels.

How they'd done it was beyond me, but it seemed they had convinced some of the homeowners of Ardconnel Road to literally *move their houses*. A wide footpath now sloped gently up the hill from the bay side of the tower, where usually if anyone wanted to get there on wheels of any kind, they had to take the road around it.

When we stepped on the path, though, both Eilidh and I got a minor start as *something* shifted in the ambient spirit.

"Dè fon ghrèin—" Eilidh cut herself off abruptly after her exclamation, her eyes widening.

I, for one, was speechless. With a pulse of Connection, I took a step up the hill. A bizarre sensation rippled through me, and when I looked straight ahead, it appeared as if the path spread out in front of me perfectly level.

"Accessibility blueprint," someone called from behind us, and I turned to see Angus striding towards us. "Ascension healed all the genetic and pathogenic ailments that made getting around hard, but so far I don't think limbs have regrown. There are a few people in town who still need wheelchairs, and someone got a quest for a community improvement that included this blueprint. It basically creates an optical illusion that you're walking on a flat surface whilst spirit helps you move in whichever direction you're going. If you're going up, it pushes you up. If you're going down, it keeps you from, well, turning the hill into a luge into the bay."

"Thighearna," Eilidh muttered, and I almost echoed it.

"You said 'so far' limbs haven't regrown—do you think

that'll change?" I asked suddenly, my brain belatedly processing the man's explanation.

Angus gave a gruff nod in the direction of the tower, and we started to walk together. The sensation was vaguely disconcerting for just how *normal* it felt . . . as long as I didn't, you know, try to walk whilst looking anywhere off the path. I tried once and almost fell on my face.

"We've a few healers who are getting pretty advanced in their skill trees, and there *are* spells for it. They're just very complex." Angus grunted. "Makes sense."

Then he scowled, turning to glance over his shoulder at the bay, which the man seemed to regret an instant later when he stubbed his toe on the path and almost pitched sideways. Eilidh caught him by the arm, steadying him.

"Unnatural," he said with a scowl, shaking himself and training his gaze firmly on the path ahead. "I was just thinking the kraken can almost certain regrow *its* limbs naturally, without any spells. Next time we get the chance, we need to make sure it's dead."

I fought the urge to look out to sea myself, and the three of us continued up the magical path to the tower, silent in grim agreement.

A sense of peace spread over me when we reached McCaig's Tower. The tree Eilidh and I had created awaited us in the middle of the open space at the centre, and it was clear landscapers had not only prepared a place for it but had also rehomed any existing flora.

The tower itself had been built in 1897 as a means of employing local stonemasons—and to memorialise the McCaigs, of course—and rather than being an enclosed building, it was a wide circle of arched stone windows with battlements atop the entrance. Open to the sky, the tower's size meant that even if the tree grew to epic proportions, the arboreal giant would get sunlight.

For now, though, that was hardly a problem. The tree looked much smaller in the large ring of stone than it had in the workshop, but it still looked resplendent.

And to think it had been moulded from a pair of doors looted from a walking personification of duck butter.

On second thought, maybe I didn't want to think about where the wood had come from.

People already gathered around our creation, which sat innocuously in its central location. I think even if the ascension hadn't imbued everyone with magic, I would have noticed something ethereal, something *other* about the tree. It exuded calm and, for a bare, surreal moment, I had the strangest sensation of having just walked into the kitchen of my mother's house, the smell of her brewing mint infusion with herbs from the back garden. It was a home feeling, a belonging feeling.

My lungs sucked in a breath more deeply than I had all day to that point, and I heard Eilidh do the same beside me, though her face held an odd expression.

When I cocked my head at her in questioning, she gave me a wry, crooked smile. "Iain got in my head."

What? At my confusion, she nodded towards the tree. "Our . . . sapling."

Oh. *Oh*. Oh, god.

My cheeks warmed, and the blasted staff on my back seemed to nestle between my shoulder blades both snugly *and* smugly. Eilidh's pale skin had a decided pinkish cast to it as well.

The tree, however, seemed far more mature than the staff—

or Iain, for that matter—despite its relative infancy, because the sense of calm spread out even more eagerly.

For a moment, I stood silently, tingles climbing up my spine at the sheer potential of the moment. This tree would be a living library, a place of learning not just theory but practice. A repository of memory, of priceless generational knowledge.

The air hummed with it.

People filtered into the tower around us, but I kept my attention focused on the tree itself. I felt more than saw Eilidh do the same.

Despite the gradually filling park, a hush came over the tower. The day, imbued with the golden hour sun, still held the briskness of a Scottish spring, but it seemed as if the tree lent us some of its warmth.

Not long later, I saw Angus waving at me to get my attention, and I met his gaze.

"Get on with it," he mouthed at me.

I snorted, looking at Eilidh. "You want to make a speech?"

She gave me a look that said she'd rather strip naked and do cartwheels out of the tower and down the hill.

Most likely best to keep it simple, if that was the case. I certainly wasn't trying to win the title of Oban's premier orator.

"'S ann dhuibhse a tha seo." I tugged lightly on my sense of Òran na Cloiche as I said it, then repeated it in English. "This is for you all."

I couldn't explain how I knew what to do, but spirit flowed even before I took a step towards the tree in tandem with Eilidh. Her own magic swirled about mine, mingling with it like intricate threads plaiting together to create something stronger, more.

Awareness spread through me, as if I were using Connection even though all I was doing was allowing my spirit to circulate. Every individual spiritual signature around me sharpened with exquisite clarity; I may not have known every name of every person present, but I knew that I would recognise each of them for the rest of my days.

It happened so effortlessly that the startled gasp from the gathering crowd surprised me, and I almost lost concentration.

The tree was already alive; at the first brush of our combined magic, it reached out with its own.

On my back, Brac-Meanmna practically preened.

The entirety of McCaig's Tower lit up like the setting sun had relocated to directly above our heads.

# CHAPTER
# SEVENTEEN

Voices hushed as the light grew to illuminate the tree. Cracks appeared in the smooth trunk, running in glowing flickers like bolts of golden lightning from root to crown.

A sound of strange popping filled the air, like stretching out your spine after holding a single position for binge-watching an entire Netflix series. The pops travelled down the tree and into the prepared earth below as the roots flexed of their own accord. Where Eilidh and I had created a mere suggestion of roots—something like you might see on top of the ground that wouldn't show the full, breathtaking reach of their network under the soil—now they elongated. They pulled from the ambient spirit and from both myself and Eilidh, delving into the dirt.

I felt as they eagerly dived downwards; with access to the earth as well as the spirit around us, they drew upon the ecosystem with every bit as much alacrity.

Something shifted in the air as the tree took root, and the entire thing began to buzz. Like the roots, the branches were present but far less intricate than a tree that grew naturally—or they had been.

Even as the roots had found their home beneath our feet, spreading out palpably under the garden of McCaig's Tower, the branches had expanded, reaching up and outward where they could catch the sun and spirit alike.

The branches elongated, drooping downwards in flexible cascades like the waving whisper of a willow.

Slowly, ever so slowly, the glow receded, leaving only a tree that looked as though it had been planted there as a seed, but a seed of some alien arboreal species none of us had ever seen before.

The silvery sheen of its bark was much like Earth's birches, but the buds that suddenly dotted its draping crown of branches were so deep a green, they'd be more at home in the heart of a pine forest. Even that didn't do it justice; the colour was such that it called to mind an oil painter's most saturated hues.

Each trailing branch swayed in the breeze, and at the tip of every one was a splay of tendrils.

As if in a trance, I pulled the Clach Cànain from my pocket and reached out to the closest waving frond.

The branch reached back, and the tendrils took hold of the stone almost reverently.

A chime rang out through the tower grounds like someone had struck a singing bowl.

Gasps rippled amid the crowd in a quiet susurrus that blended with the sound of the tree's whispering movement.

As I watched, people stepped forwards from the encircling community. I wasn't the only one with such a stone. Branches took the other offerings just as gently, and a warm glow took hold where each stone then dangled. My mother had loved jewellery made with stone and wires where the artists would wind thin, delicate strands of silver or copper into intricate designs to cradle semiprecious gems. The image of stones of knowledge surrounded by careful swirls of living wood brought a lump to my throat.

I cleared it, glancing over at Eilidh, whose blue eyes were wide with awe as she craned her neck to look upwards.

I followed her gaze, and my own eyes threatened to mist as I lost my breath.

The canopy of the tree above us was already unfurling its leaves. They shone like emeralds, lit from within with the glow of magic. And among them danced flecks of gold, drifting like motes of dust in the afternoon sun but brighter than fireflies.

"Craobh an Òbain," I said in a hushed voice that nevertheless reached the farthest stretches of the tower, borne on flows of effortless spirit. "Stòras ar daoine, sòlas ar saoghail."

*Repository of our people, solace of our world.*

I thought I'd be exhausted after the emotions of settling the tree in place, but I found that being in its presence filled me with peace. The tree exuded calm and serenity, and everyone seemed to feel it. People soon exclaimed softly at the deep green grass that spread out from its base, plush and dense. It didn't take long for folk to find places to recline amid the roots or with their back to the trunk. Children wandered amid the dancing branches in wonder.

And the tree seemed to mirror their awe.

Eilidh found me when I had wandered a short distance away and sat reclining on my elbows in the grass, looking up at the tree. The sun had set, but the tower was still filled with gentle light like it was lit by a thousand tiny candles.

"Is math seo," she said to me as she sat down beside me.

I nodded my agreement; it absolutely *was* good.

"Imagine what it'll be like when the branches are full," I said after a beat. "Languages. Music. Science. Magic. Anything this new world has to offer, this tree will guard from harm and share with all those who seek to use it for good."

Eilidh exhaled a shaky breath. "It's almost too big for my brain."

I glanced over at her and gave her a wry smile. "I know the feeling."

She stared up into the glowing canopy for a moment. "I feel awful even saying this out loud."

"That it's too big for your brain?" I squinted at her swift shift in thought process.

That earned me a rueful head shake. "Not that. This: sometimes I'm actually thankful for the apocalypse."

Oh.

It was my turn for a shaky breath, this time on my inhale, which stuttered into my lungs. "I know the feeling. There must be so many people dying around the world, but—"

"But people were already dying around the world for asinine reasons. Some country wants more land; another has a shiny thing someone else wants. It's always the ordinary people who pay in blood—both those fighting and those just trying to survive being caught in the middle."

"Exactly." I looked over at Eilidh, her hair haloed in muted light that deepened the auburn into a mahogany brown touched with gold. "But now everything's different. Everything."

"I can't help but wonder how different our world would have been if we'd figured out ourselves that it didn't have to be that way." Her words were barely above a whisper, but they struck like a defibrillator to the chest. "A pandemic didn't get through to us; it took a literal apocalypse."

I gave a laugh that was more of a croak. "Guess we ought to carpe this diem, yeah?"

Her answering smile was off kilter but genuine. "Aye. And we've made a good start today."

Eilidh lay back on the grass, and after a heartbeat or two of hesitation, I joined her, reaching out and taking her hand in mine.

"Imagine a world where scarcity isn't even a question because we know there's *enough*," came her voice beside me, but sounding very far away. Then, stronger and underpinned with ferocity, she went on. "The old world is gone. The new one *will* be better."

I could think of nothing to say to that. My hand squeezed hers tighter, and I gazed up at the branches of the tree as I seemed to feel its fronds weaving together to form an unbreakable silver cord between us.

But it didn't stop at us.

All at once, it was as if that cord stretched from the centre of the earth and through the tree, so large it encompassed the tower as a whole. A direct line from our planet to the source of our newfound power—to the Ascended Alliance.

We would show them we could rise above our mistakes. We would show them we could rise above *their* mistakes and the apocalypse they'd unleashed upon our world.

We would. We could.

We would settle for nothing less.

The next few days were a flurry of activity, underpinned by the buzz of excitement about the tree. Mages entered a fervour of arcane experimentation and brainstorming, creating a priority list of things to add to the tree to enshrine everything they'd learned so far into the collective archive.

Branch by branch, Craobh an Òbain gained knowledge—and person by person, that knowledge spread like a candle flame passed in a vigil.

Humans were wont to take things for granted, as a species. Hell, people had happily forgotten the horrors of polio, measles, mumps, all the diseases that used to ravage communities before a poke in the arm made us safer. But I was certain those first few days of the tree's blossoming power would remain in the minds of everyone who lived them. We weren't even really human anymore—if we were anything like the elves of Earth's fantasy worlds, we'd have long, long memories.

The funny thing about knowledge is that it grows almost exponentially when shared. New viewpoints, new experiences, new perspectives—sometimes it takes a fisher to explain why placing a tidal power plant in a particular place is detrimental. Just like that, it took a child saying something breathtakingly simple for the rest of us adults to shift our own thinking about the kraken.

We were in the crafting workshop, and the child in question, a wee lass called Cara with hair so red that the sun hitting it made it look like she'd caught fire, had a long leather strip in one hand. On the other end of the strip was a very determined Scottish wildcat kitten who, despite the borderline argument drawing taut tension through the air around her, pounced the toy in a dedicated display of ignoring the exasperated huffs.

"If we don't hunt the damn thing down, it'll just come back bigger and stronger," said a man I didn't know and whose name eluded me like trying to grasp a fart in the wind, if anyone would ever wish to do such a thing.

The bloke had broad shoulders that made a near isosceles triangle of his torso, and he gave off the general impression of an old Clint Eastwood film, his face tanned and his mouth looking like it was missing a cigar or a piece of grass wedged between his teeth.

"No one is disagreeing that we need to fight the thing," Eilidh said, her tone far more level than I would expect—probably due to Sailean executing a particularly cute pounce-and-roll combo on the leather strip. "We just have to do it wisely. This can't turn into a long, drawn-out series of battles. We're the ones who will lose a war of attrition. That damn overgrown squid can literally regrow its own limbs. We can't resurrect our fallen fighters."

"No shit"—the man choked on the epithet with a guilty glance at wee Cara, who didn't seem to notice—"If it sees the harbour as its territory or humans as a food source, it'll come back sooner rather than later. Which is why we should go to it. Calum can track it even if it dives into the depths."

"I'm not suggesting we simply twiddle our thumbs and wait for it to slap us with its tentacles again," Eilidh said, irritation creeping into her voice. "Just that the harbour is our territory, but the open sea is the kraken's, and no matter how big the boat, we're going to be at a horrible disadvantage out there. We can't breathe underwater, for one."

"The mages are working on that," Angus muttered, but when What's-His-Name lit up as if he'd been handed his gotcha moment, Angus shook himself. "Even if—when—they succeed, it's a far cry from going for a leisurely swim in the North Atlantic and fighting a literal kraken in its natural environment whilst cosplaying the Little Mermaid."

What's-His-Name visibly deflated.

"What do we think it *wants*?" I asked, choosing to sidestep the entirety of their back-and-forth battering of the point. "It's a big ocean, and even if we're fishing it, it's not like it's trying to colonise Oban."

"The fish are so big now," Cara said out of nowhere. "It wouldn't need that many to live anymore."

Every eye turned to the wee ginger lass, who continued to dangle the leather for the kitten. Sailean, for her part, looked as if she were literally drunk on the endorphins of playtime. Her pupils took up her entire irises, and her fledgling whiskers puffed out as her tail twitched and her hindquarters did the telltale wiggle—if wobbly.

"I said *want*, but I think Cara might have hit the proverbial nail on the head," I murmured. "If it doesn't need fish, what *does* it need? What would be driving it to shallow waters?"

"Maybe it's scared."

Again, every eye landed on the child. This time, she felt it and looked up from Sailean at the realisation that four adults were staring down at her.

"You think it could be scared?" I asked her slowly.

That was an unpleasant thought; the kraken was fucking terrifying. If *it* was frightened, what could it be frightened of?

The other adults didn't seem to like that idea any more than I did.

Cara, thank goodness, just shrugged, more uncomfortable with the attention of the grown-ups than with the implications of what she'd said. Maybe she didn't quite realise what she was implying—or so I hoped, up until she proved me wrong with a worried glance to the west as the leather strip fell from her trailing fingers.

"Sea monsters."

# CHAPTER
# EIGHTEEN

Cara had been absolutely right—there was little way the squid was so desperate for food. But there were even more basic needs than that, like not being eaten yourself.

The thought of what kind of sea monster could threaten a kraken—itself a literal sea monster—made me feel like I was on the *Titanic* serenaded by the dulcet tones of the infamous iceberg tearing through the hull. Something else was niggling at me, though. We'd seen strange animal behaviour before, and my gut was screaming at me that there were few coincidences.

When Eilidh and I returned to the house, she gave me a troubled glance as I put the kettle on to boil and settled Sailean on the bench, where she curled up in post-play bliss and was out in moments.

"There might be another explanation," Eilidh said slowly after smiling fondly at the snoozing kitten, "but it's not any more appealing than the simplicity of an alarming post-apocalyptic food chain."

"Never in my life have I been so disappointed to *not* trust Occam's razor," I said. "If you're thinking what I'm thinking, you're absolutely right, and I hate it."

"On three?" Eilidh's tone hit a remarkably dry note as she nudged me to the side to access the cupboard of mugs above the kettle's home on the bunker. "One, two . . ."

"The anomalies," I said at the same time as she said, "The corruption."

"Damn it," we both said in eerie unison.

"George is wrong about hunting the kraken in the sea, but we may have to hunt down the source of the corruption sooner rather than later," she said.

"Thanks, I hate it."

George must have been the name of the bloke I didn't recognise. I filed that away in hopes it would survive in the recesses of my mind. So many names, and I *could* use Keen Eye every time I saw someone, but that just seemed like a waste of spirit and vaguely like cheating.

The kettle began to steam, and I sighed, disturbing the plume with my exhale. "I've been thinking the same thing. I've just been hoping naively for Ronald to have some sort of genius breakthrough that will give us an edge."

Eilidh's brow furrowed at that, but she nodded. "Honestly? Me too."

We both let that steep along with the tea for what couldn't quite pass for easy silence, if only because we were both stewing in the slow simmer of ever-increasing danger. Whatever gratitude we had for the ascension's gifts, it didn't erase the grief, the pain, and the growing pains of a world that had not been ready to play nice.

My communication crystal, for once, remained quiet. That was almost as unsettling as the thought of waterborne anomalies. The only thing worse than a kraken was probably an anomalous kraken that could poison our food supply as easily as it could ravage the harbour. Okay, so that wasn't the *only* thing worse than a kraken, but it was what I had to go on at the moment.

Eilidh and I were just draining our mugs when a knock came at the door, and we both flinched instinctually.

Served me right for thinking about the suspiciously quiet crystal.

At the door, however, was good news for once, in the form of Ealasaid.

"Halò, a ghràidh," she said to me, breezing past me as soon as the door opened wide enough to admit her. "Halò, a ghràidh eile."

Eilidh snorted at her "hello, love—hello, other love" and closed the distance to give the old woman a kiss on the cheek, which Ealasaid returned perfunctorily before eyeing me askance and pointing at her other cheek.

I obliged her with a peck, receiving one right back . . . and a swat on the arse, which would have earned my ire from literally anyone other than the inhabitants of the house or its current house guest.

"We've got company," Ealasaid said without further preamble. "From down your neck of the woods, a Chaluim."

I blinked at her in confusion for a moment before I realised what she meant. Argyll was my home, but I'd spent my whole adult life in Glasgow.

"Weegies?" I blurted out.

"Bless him," Ealasaid said to Eilidh. But after a moment, she snorted. "Or bless me for forgetting this is his neck of the woods."

"Bless you both," Eilidh said, her voice solemn.

"Weegies," I repeated. "Where are they?"

"Well, I didn't come to just tell you they existed." Ealasaid tapped her foot. "Faigh an cat is trobhadaibh."

I snorted at that, obeying without a second thought. *Get the cat and come on.*

I did just that.

The Weegies were a surprisingly robust group.

Not in the sense that they were hardened fighters or anything, just that there were a *lot* of them.

They'd gathered at the pier, and Oban had gathered around the newcomers in a murmuration of exclamations and movement.

I scanned the group with hungry eyes, looking for any glimpse of a familiar Iranian family that would lessen some of Meeksy's worries. No such luck. Glasgow was a city of half a million people, and no familiar faces stood out to me in the two score gaggle of new arrivals.

Ealasaid managed to part the sea of people with her very presence, and she led Eilidh and me through the throng to where our own community were already on the move, bringing out chairs and tables and using Purifire to free the weary travellers of grime.

". . . heard there was a proper community up here," a tired-looking white man was saying to Angus as he leaned forward on his elbows at the table someone had just placed in front of him. "There might be more headed this way with what's happening in Dundee."

That sent a nervous thrum through the crowd. Fan-fucking-tastic, more trouble.

Sitting next to him was a Black woman with her hair twisted atop her head in a coil of braids, and from the way she placed a splay-fingered hand between the man's shoulder blades with familiarity, I guessed he was her husband. "We can tell them about that later, love," she said in a thick Glaswegian accent. "It's no so urgent tae bother wi' the now."

The man leaned back into his wife's hand, closing his eyes. Poor bloke looked half dead.

His wife met my gaze, though her eyes also flickered to Eilidh at my side. "You're them."

Even in my peripheral vision, I saw one of Eilidh's auburn eyebrows hike almost up into her hairline. "Beg your pardon?"

"Sorry, pal," the woman said with a small smile. "That was rude. I'm Sammy, and this is my husband D.D."

"Calum," I answered, and then gestured to Eilidh. "And Eilidh, as I think you already guessed."

"You're both younger than I expected but also older than others guessed."

I didn't know what to say to that, so I just shrugged awkwardly.

Eilidh seemed to decide that if Sammy was going for blunt, she would too. "You didn't come all the way here just to see us, did you?"

Sammy chuckled at that, which made D.D. next to her start out of his light doze, and a nervous laugh spread through the newcomers. "Hardly. More that we wanted to see what you're building here in Oban and to ask if we could be a part of it."

I glanced at Angus, who shifted his weight from one foot to the other, scratching at his cheek and then giving a small start as if his hand or face had somehow betrayed him.

"Everyone's welcome so long as they mean no harm," I said carefully. "Let's get you all something to eat and drink, and then you can tell us about your trek—and about whatever's happening in Dundee. Or pass out and do that tomorrow. We've still got heaps of homes, along with hot showers and working plumbing."

"Oh, thank *fuck*," someone exclaimed, which sent another burst of laughter through the group.

They must have all hit the punch-drunk stage of tired, because the laughing turned into giggling, the exhausted level of emotional release that came from finally being able to relax.

I went with Ealasaid to see about food for them after a nod to Sammy, and once we'd supplied them with mahoosive fish suppers—a few people outright burst into tears at the sight, another hint that emotions were all over the shop—I sat back whilst they stuffed their gobs.

The group was large and diverse, but the ages were all between maybe thirty and sixty. I didn't see a single child among them, which had me feeling alarmed.

Sammy came up to me just as I was about to go back to her, and I figured I might as well just ask straight away.

"Why all adults and no kids? Lots of parent-age folks here," I said to her after enquiring after the fish and watching the tall woman almost swoon.

Her skin was quite dark, but an unmistakable tinge of pink bloomed on her smooth cheeks, and she cleared her throat.

Uh-oh.

I don't know what I expected to hear, but whatever it was, it wasn't what I got.

After a moment where Sammy glanced nervously around—which did nothing to settle my own anxiety—she gave me a bashful smile.

"Erm. We're a community of child-free swingers."

I wasn't sure whether my memory would be more scarred by the running loop in my brain of "community of child-free swingers"—no judgement, only a wildly unexpected combination of words—or my awkward finger guns as I moonwalked away from Sammy.

The moonwalking may have been an exaggeration, and I didn't *really* flee on the spot, but my mind was trying to convince me that that was exactly what had happened.

Sammy, who was presumably used to every reaction any person had ever had to that wildly unexpected combination of words, had given me an amused smirk and gone back to D.D., whose head had fallen backwards where he'd dropped off to sleep and whose Adam's apple bobbed with every resonant snore.

A raucous laugh, followed by a whoop and an admiring "Mon the Weegies!" from the other side of the pier suggested the rest of Oban was also about to learn of our new compatriots' bedroom habits, and I decided that was my cue to leave before I had to witness a child innocently asking about swinging.

I'd leave that to parents and guardians to explain. I was infinitely grateful in that moment that the closest thing I had to a wean was a sausage-swiping wildcat and a literal tree.

The arcane lights that lit the streets of Oban had turned on, bathing the harbour in a soft glow under the deepening blue of twilight above my head. I was ready to head home, see if Iain and Meeksy and Catrìona were back, and try to find something to occupy my brain.

The evening had other plans.

A familiar ripple in the ambient spirit at least gave me an immediate glimmer of hope of a distraction.

Rhona materialised just as I was crossing the street away from the pier, popping out of seeming nowhere, which I took to be bad news.

Bracing myself, I fixated on the wrinkle between her eyebrows and the decided lack of a smart-arse quip.

"What's wrong?" I asked her.

"Anomalies," she said. "Didn't see them myself, but one of the patrols squawked in my ear while I was in the loo."

Not the distraction I was hoping for.

"Too much info, Rhona," I said absently, and it was a mark of her mood that she didn't have any cutting remark primed and ready to launch. "Fuck, that bad?"

"Dinnae ken, d' ye reckon 'giant corrupted cat' is a problem or no?"

I swore. "We're not bringing Sailean, then."

"*That's* your first thought? I mean, fair, but—"

"All I know is I have developed a soft spot for the average moggy, and I don't relish the idea of killing any cat, even a corrupted one." Ugh. Understatement of the evening. "Just the one?"

"Aye, just the one."

"How big is giant?" I figured that was a relevant question. "On a scale of beithir to kraken."

"What a scale," Rhona muttered. "I'll ask."

"Do that. I'm going to gear up and grab Iain and Meeksy if they're home. Can you go find Eilidh?" I wasn't sure where she'd vanished to, but I'd not seen her since the Weegies had finished eating.

Rhona gave me a mock salute—but with two fingers in a decidedly *not* honourable formation.

"Meet me at the station," she called over her shoulder as she vanished into the gloaming.

Creepy-ass kid.

The new arrivals had been good news. Why did I have the uneasy feeling that was the last good news we'd get for a while?

Fuck. They hadn't even told us what was happening in Dundee yet.

It could wait.

We'd an anomalous cat to hunt down.

# CHAPTER
# NINETEEN

"About half a beithir," Rhona said when I met her in the square abutting the now-unused train station.

"That's . . . a giant fucking cat." I couldn't be more eloquent.

Guess we would *not* be bringing this kitty home to Ronald for his experiments.

Sailean still sulked in a corner of my awareness, her hissy kitten tantrum about being left behind still prickling me with guilt. I'd promised I didn't want to leave her behind anymore, but I had to draw the line here. She was still tiny, and half a beithir was the opposite of that. I'd explained to her as best I could; how much she understood was anyone's guess. I truly didn't want her to watch me murder another feline. Also, maybe it was irrational, but come on. Some things you couldn't unsee.

Eilidh wasn't with Rhona, but before I could ask, Rhona piped up.

"She's going to meet us on the way. She was halfway to Ganavan to help Meeksy with something. He and Iain are both coming too." Rhona glanced northwards, her expression far too troubled for my liking. "Do you get the feeling something bad is about to happen?"

I wanted to come back with a snarky reply to that, but considering I'd been all over the shop myself, all I could do was nod. "Too many variables. Like trying to play chess on a snakes and ladders board but with random blokes also kicking footballs at your head."

"That's a weirdly spot-on analogy." The teenage banshee raised her eyebrow at me and huffed a sigh. "Come on. Let's get this over with."

"Where is the damn thing?"

"Northwest, which is also bothering me since most of the anomalies have made a bee line for us from the south. George's team's tracking it for us. They didn't want to engage before we showed up."

George again. I gave Rhona a terse nod, and we broke into a trot.

If the beithir was the snake and Bawbag's doors a ladder, were we players, pawns, or about to take a football to the face?

Eilidh, Meeksy, and Iain fell in with us when we reached Pennyfuir just inland of Ganavan, and while they all looked clean enough, Iain kept shuddering like a dog with wet fur as if he could shake off the a lingering unwanted substance.

We were in too much of a hurry for me to ask questions about what they'd been up to, and instead my mind turned to what Rhona had said.

*Most of the anomalies have made a bee line for us from the south.*

She was correct. The only thing I could think of that had changed to explain it was my unfortunate and accidental connection to the whatever-it-was that was the source of the anomalies.

If they were gaining intelligence or sapience and beginning to act tactically when so far they'd been anything but strategic, that was going to put a bee in our bonnets right quick. Not a singular bee. More like an entire nest of hornets.

I punted that imagery right back out of my mind. The last thing I needed to fret about was anomalous hornets. I fought the urge to shudder like Iain had, my own hackles suddenly raised and twitching.

Rhona, as usual, scouted ahead, occasionally materialising amid the four of us to update us or adjust our course via an approaching junction. Her own demeanour grew more and more tense with each mile we covered. The crease between her eyebrows seemed permanent, deepening each time she flashed into visibility.

Some people grew fidgety when faced with the unexpected, but not Rhona. The closer we drew to danger, the more her slight teenage frame grew taut and still, though anyone to look at her would know it was the type of contained energy that begged to be unleashed on a foe.

Iain was the fidgety sort, and even as we ran with Meeksy still huffing and puffing alongside us to keep pace, my oldest friend clenched and flexed his fists, adjusted his shoulders. His energy also demanded release, but he himself was a pressure cooker's steam valve, letting it out in controlled movements rather than allow himself to explode.

Eilidh I'd expect to be like Rhona, but instead, she seemed to mirror me. I felt her pull on spirit as we moved, both of us pulsing Connection to check our surroundings, though she interspersed it with something else, too. As it was, both of us rooted ourselves in the ambient spirit, listening and trusting it to warn us of something unseen.

And Meeksy, well.

The Persian bear of a Weegie was cool as the proverbial cucumber in most situations, but running? All his energy and focus went to making sure he didn't fall over. I'd be amused, but it wasn't really funny.

The miles melted under our steady pace, the sky above dark with clouds that obscured the stars except in a few patchy holes that promised clearer weather when they reached us from the west. My own trepidation grew when Rhona told us we were almost there.

George's team had been told not to face the thing alone, and I was thankful they'd listened. One of the things we'd tried to impress on everyone was not to attempt heroics if there was no immediate danger to others. We'd had a few smaller instances of people blithely biting off more than their levels could chew and swallow, but shockingly *only* a few.

We picked our way overland from there, turning southward about halfway between Connel and Taynuilt where the ground was boggy and where there'd soon be summer swarms of midges plaguing anyone nearby on a still day.

"George says it's just sitting there," Rhona said softly right beside me. "He and his team are on its other flank, but we should be able to see it any minute now."

"Gasta," I muttered. "Just peachy."

For an ambush predator like the average feline, "just sitting there" wasn't necessarily a sign of inaction. Whatever trigonometry cats calculated with their strategic butt wiggles pre-pounce could be unleashed with devastating—and rapid—fury.

"Tell them not to get comfortable and not to take their eyes off of it, under any circumstances. It's behaving unpredictably for an anomaly, and even if it wasn't a cat big enough to snap our spines like a moggy toying with a mouse, it would be far, far more dangerous than anything we've faced besides the beithir and the kraken." Saying that out loud really did not help my apprehension. "I'd say Bawbag too, but . . ."

"We killed him the first time we saw him," Rhona finished for me.

Beside her, Eilidh nodded, her own gaze distant as she combed the darkened landscape ahead of us. "Let's aim to do the same with this one. I might be able to wreck its night vision if we're careful."

"If we're careful?" Meeksy asked between gulping breaths.

"If I'm reckless, I'll also wreck ours," Eilidh murmured.

"Oh. Let's not do that." Meeksy straightened; now that we weren't moving at a run, the ascension-boosted recovery worked to his advantage.

"Yes, that's my plan," Eilidh said dryly, though I now knew her well enough to catch the undertone of amusement.

Connection told me that, as usual, other forms of wildlife had fled the presence of the anomaly. What my spell didn't have to explain was that we were at an extreme disadvantage. George's group of five scouts and fighters was in range on the other side of the feline, which itself sat in the cleft between two hillocks, partway up the side of the one closest to us. Its presence oozed through the otherwise natural surroundings in my mind like a glob of crude oil in an otherwise pristine bay.

I wished Ronald's experiments had yielded any answers— or rather that the answers they'd yielded had held anything actionable.

The anomaly here, though, was unlike anything I'd encountered so far. The badgers had been feral and ready to fight like wolverines. So had the enormous rabbits. I couldn't use Keen Eye outwith the creature's line of sight, but something told me this was not an ascension-twisted stray moggy that had had the misfortune of encountering the corruption. Dread crept into my stomach lining, eking out to permeate the whole of my gut.

"Tell George to get its attention," I said under my breath to Rhona. "They're closest to its range of vision. Eilidh, pass on a signal when you're going to use your flash-bang so we don't incapacitate George's crew too."

Even in the darkness, I could see Eilidh's small frown when she nodded her assent.

Rhona muttered into her communication crystal, and my next pulse of Connection told me that the anomalous feline hadn't budged but that George's gaggle were on the move.

"I don't like this," Eilidh said just as Iain muttered, "This feels wrong."

"Nothing about these anomalies is *right*," said Meeksy, his tone uncharacteristically curt.

I didn't have time to wonder what had shifted, because a shower of sparks fizzled on the far side of the wrinkle in the hillside, and all five of us sprang into action.

The ground was boggy under our feet, but with Eilidh's expert crafting, other than pitching ourselves into an unseen deep pool, that was barely an inconvenience. Connection helped me avoid that, at least.

A glow of magic and a yowling screech told us that the battle had well and truly joined just out of sight, and when we crested the hill, the strobing effect of George's group's magic provided a surreal silhouette of the cat.

"Half a beithir" might have been factually correct, but that was only if we were talking length alone. The beithir, despite the distance from nose to tail, was still a snake. A cat half the length of the average adder would be a *very* large cat.

A cat half the length of the beithir?

This thing was a monster of epic proportions.

"Turn!" Eilidh barked at us, and Rhona echoed that into her

crystal just as Eilidh fired off an arcane bolt that accomplished its goal just as I spun away.

The beast had turned towards the new aggravator just in time for whatever Eilidh did to light up the gully bright as day.

Even with my eyes shut and my back to the flash—there was no accompanying bang—I winced against the possible loss of my night vision. My eyes had adjusted to the night, and with the ascension-improved vision, I could probably see as well as a pre-ascension house cat.

It still didn't prepare me for what Keen Eye showed me when I turned around to cast it while the feline was blind.

*Anomalous Eurasian Lynx*

*Long extinct in the British Isles, the ascension has reintroduced indigenous fauna, and this lynx was among the first to emerge. Unfortunately, the lynx encountered the corrupting influence of the anomaly, fundamentally altering it both in size and intelligence.*

*This lynx's behaviour has already proven different to other anomalies you have engaged with in combat.*

*You would be wise to tread lightly.*

"Fuck," I said. "Melee fighters, attack while it's unable to see, but the second its eyesight recovers, pull the fuck back."

The others were already moving, and Connection told me George's squad were doing the same. He'd three melee and two mages with him, and I could only hope that between six close-combat fighters, they could do some damage to this creature.

My hope was short lived.

Eilidh and Rhona were by far the fastest of the fighters who ran into the fray, and they were the only ones who managed to land a blow before the lynx let out a yowl and spun on one of George's mages with perfect precision.

"Get back!" I bellowed, snatching my staff from my back. The moment there was a meter between the lynx and the fighters, I cast Ring of Fire.

Purifire had been the single most reliable weapon we had against the anomalies, the ace in the hole, the holy hand grenade of weapons.

Before, it had stopped them in their tracks—even the beithir.

The lynx?

The enormous feline simply snarled and leapt right through the curtain of blue-green flame.

# CHAPTER
# TWENTY

The only sign of the lynx's reaction to the Purifire was a growl of irritation.

Purifire was the reason we hadn't hashed out a more tactical plan; if these anomalies were able to now pull a Taylor Swift and shake it off?

We were buggered.

"Calum!" Eilidh called, brandishing her claymore.

She didn't have to explain. I'd interrogate *why* she didn't have to explain later; for now, I just pulled on my spirit and poured more Purifire in her direction, spooling it around her blade. Meeksy had hung back with me, but now he closed the distance to Iain and Rhona and did the same.

If external Purifire wouldn't slow the thing down, maybe slicing into it with flaming blades would. It was worth a shot.

I mentally rummaged through my own arcane arsenal. Brac-Meanmna seemed personally offended that we hadn't managed to damage the thing yet, and that gave me an idea.

Whether it was a *good* idea remained to be seen.

I didn't wait to find out if the blade-wielding fighters would land a successful blow on the snarling anomalous lynx. Instead,

I took a breath, expanding my awareness through the root-level passives in my Nature skill tree. Gu h-Àrd, h-Ìosal, Taobh a-Muigh, Taobh a-Staigh. Underlying those—or perhaps surrounding them—was Tuairmse. A series of impressions flowed through me with the air I drew into my lungs, and while time seemed to slow in the darkened battle, I poured my spirit into two things at once.

I'd never tried to funnel one spell through another before, only combined things by instinct alone. This time, though, it was less trying to direct the flow of wild magic and more dumping petrol on a bonfire.

Or rather dumping Purifire into the unpredictable wildcard that was Tairm.

Fighting a feline at night in the Scottish Highlands would have been laughable pre-ascension, but even with heightened eyesight and the glow of magic, the battle was a chaotic blur of barely lit shapes and the occasional glint of razor-sharp teeth.

With half my spirit gone in one cast, I almost lost my breath, but the effects were instantaneous.

At first, it looked as if the ground began to glow.

A blue-green light illuminated the underbelly of the enormous lynx, which was spiky with moisture from crouching in the boggy hillocks. In an odd moment of beauty, the glow caught droplets of water like sparkling jewels.

And then the ground erupted.

Fledgling thistles burst forth from the earth amid the heather and gorse, and while normally they didn't climb, now they snaked towards the lynx like vines.

Several things happened in near-immediate succession.

One of the vines caught hold of the lynx's hind leg on its left side, and through the cat's dense fur, it didn't seem to notice. Or maybe that was a side effect of the rotting, suppurating sores permeating its hide. Either way, it tried to spin to face Eilidh's charge and found itself slowed—then stuck.

George let out a bellow as he charged side by side with Iain, and as the lynx lashed back and forth, its stubby tail's jerky movement accompanied by a snarl like someone tearing a spinal cord in half, Eilidh's Purifire-coated blade landed in a devastating overhand strike aimed directly at the joint of the lynx's front right leg.

The only flaw of her attack was that this joint was nearly at shoulder level for her, so the cut didn't have as much momentum as it could, but even so, the lynx let out a grating yowl as Eilidh danced backwards.

The cat stumbled.

With one leg snared in a noose of Purifired thistles and another effectively hamstrung, the feline teetered.

Iain was fighting with a bastardised version of a bo staff; George struck with a pair of dual daggers not dissimilar to the ones Rhona was busy plunging into the cat's free hind leg.

The thistle vines Tairm had unleashed were still moving, some of them grasping for the lynx's other legs, others whipping the feline's underbelly. I couldn't see Meeksy from where I stood anymore, but I felt a pulse of spirit that had to have come from him.

A roiling wave of unease hit me even as I realised what Meeksy was doing—he'd cast Sgiath, a shield spell, on Eilidh. Her claymore still glowed with Purifire, and I heard a squelch of boggy ground as she charged once more, this time at the lynx's midsection.

If the feline wasn't *quite* tall enough for an average adult person to walk under, it only missed the mark by maybe a few inches, and a few inches was more than the length of Eilidh's sword.

Its hilt grasped in both hands, Eilidh executed a strange

move that would have left her wide open if her opponent were another person. As it was, the feline was focused on evading Rhona's attacks and trying to snipe at George's mages, one of whom had a bow and was loosing Purifire arrows at the creature. Three had already hit home and burned like obscene candles sticking out of the lynx's chest.

Eilidh's charge took on the appearance of an Olympic discus-thrower's routine, but instead of a heavy glorified frisbee, she had a deadly sharp claymore. The centrifugal force of her run thrown into a spin gave this bizarre strike the extra oomph her original cut had lacked, and when the blade struck the cat's soft primordial pouch, it didn't stop there.

I had a vague memory of my mother explaining that all cats had that extra layer of saggy skin to perform a variety of different functions, but this lynx's primordial pouch failed to prevent Eilidh's Purifire-blazing blade from slicing straight through fur and membrane until it collided with bone.

At first, I thought the accompanying squelch was the weight of the panicking lynx's body on boggy ground, but then a further flash of Purifire from one of the other mages lit up the cat's underbelly—and the steaming pile of intestines that had spilled out of the gash.

Eilidh's cut had hit on the upswing, and any other time, I'd have been impressed at her ability to spin her way out of there despite her sword striking the cat's ribs, but as it was, the lynx's sudden thrashing put all of us in the danger zone.

I quickly used some of my remaining spirit to cast Fuaran on everyone in range, in hopes it would help me regenerate enough to adapt to whatever was coming next. It washed over me with a skin-tingling cascade of relief that lasted precisely two heartbeats.

Then the lynx did something that threw us all into chaos.

The fucking thing cast Spèird.

One second, I was holding my ground and thinking we may have this thing. The next, I was landing on my back with the wind knocked clean out of me.

Brac-Meanmna surged with indignant annoyance at the ignominy of being thrown through the air by the ascension's version of a zombie cat. I reacted as quickly as I could, clambering ungracefully to my feet and orienting myself instinctively with a cast of Connection.

All ten of us fighters had been scattered with the burst of force from the lynx, and while my brain screamed at me that it shouldn't have been possible, it had happened. Which meant we had to adapt.

The lynx, once more, had not done what I would have expected either an actual cat or an anomaly to do. It hadn't fled, hadn't tried to circle around to ambush us, hadn't gone after the closest foe. Instead, it still stood above the pile of its own innards, the horrid stench of offal and rot blending with Purifire-singed fur and cauterised flesh.

Almost worse than the creature attacking was not understanding why it wasn't.

"It is studying you."

The voice nearly made me jump out of my skin, and I spun to see a familiar figure not five feet away. A cry went up as someone in George's group noticed the glaistig, and I held up a hand to stay them. We'd made her existence known. That said, knowing a mythological half-woman, half-hind creature existed was one thing. Seeing her in the middle of a battle when she's managed to sneak up on you despite the near-constant use of Connection was something else entirely.

"You think?" I asked her, unwilling to waste time.

"Le cinnt," she said.

She was certain.

"We must end this thing. I would prefer not to let it see me."

With that, the glaistig vanished more thoroughly than even Rhona could manage, and I cast Ring of Fire again. We had weakened the beast—maybe it would hold it this time. Not that it was going anywhere anyway.

When Rhona appeared beside me, I took a gamble on the anomaly not being able to understand Gaelic. Hell, I wasn't sure if the thing could understand *English*, but it seemed more likely than it having taken an interest in a small indigenous language with a handful above fifty thousand speakers pre-ascension.

"Seachnaich do chleachdaidhean," I said to her. "Innis dha na h-eile."

*Avoid your habitual actions. Tell the others.*

Just like that, Rhona was off and I was stumped.

Only for a moment.

Eilidh's blinding attack on the creature had been fruitful, even if short lived. And I had a spell that could add to that.

### Dubh

*The Draoidh knows there is nowt to fear in darkness.*

*To the contrary, darkness is the source of all things, including light. It is from darkness the universe was born, and in that darkness is the potential of all creation.*

*Dubh allows you to tap into the creative power. Coupled with Bas-Ogham, it can be used to write ogham into your skin. In the heat of battle, the Draoidh can use Dubh to obscure an enemy's sight. While it will only work upon a foe who lacks the Draoidh's understanding of the true nature of darkness, on a fearful opponent who relies fully upon sight and light, it is a powerful weapon.*

*The skill taps into our most ancient connections to a time before time itself, before light, when all was one in the womb of the endless void. Dubh does not ascribe fear to this void; for the Draoidh, it is a source of comfort and solace. In returning to Dubh, the Draoidh finds the will to write reality into existence.*

*Affinity: Draoidh, Wild*

*Skill Tree: Draoidh*

Without further hesitation, I cast Dubh in battle for the first time. My spirit was already depleted from the additional Ring of Fire, and it almost drained me. Only ten percent of my spirit remained, but I could feel through the web of spirit that connected me to my spell's target that the anomalous lynx was engulfed in a void of inky black.

"Move! Now!" I bellowed at my compatriots, who were already obeying.

I sucked in a breath and began to move through a staff form, simultaneously cycling spirit through me to regenerate it faster and drawing spirit from the world around me to funnel through Brac-Meanmna. My staff took to this with alacrity, a surge of hatred boiling through it as it loosed bolts of pure spirit at the gaping wound in the lynx's belly.

Golden light exploded, lighting the lynx in silhouette as Eilidh released a stun, and George charged the lynx head on. I didn't know his class, but I had to guess he was similar to Rhona's usual strike-from-the-shadows strategy. With the lynx blinded, though, George went for the eyes.

Daggers flashed with Purifire, and the cat screamed as first one eye and then the next fell to unseen stabbing.

Iain may have looked like a walking, kicking stack of bricks, but he punched like a wrecking ball, tossing his bo staff to the side to concentrate the brunt of his attacks on the front leg Eilidh had nearly hamstrung in her first strike.

Still, the lynx stood unmoving. It didn't retaliate. It just hovered there, teetering and quivering.

Meeksy had abjured his usual support mode and was firing off what looked like darts of Purifire that soared, not in a straight line but in an implausible arc up into the belly wound along with my own attacks.

And then the ground began to rumble.

It was as if someone had unleashed Tairm like I had, but from every direction at once.

The wet moorland beneath the anomalous lynx seemed to disappear—except nothing was unmade. It was simply as if the hummocks of heather collapsed into a sinkhole. A few startled yelps reached my ears as fighters scrambled backwards, then more as thistle spines the size of spears plunged inward, impaling the freakish feline like weaponised spokes of a giant wheel.

It had to be the glaistig.

My spirit had climbed to about thirty percent, and I wasted no further time, forming Fist of Flame with Purifire with as much spirit as I dared.

I aimed it straight for the nearest eye George had obliterated.

My Purifire slammed into the vulnerable eye socket.

Almost immediately, my vision flashed gold.

It should have made me feel better to know the lynx was dead.

So why did I feel sick?

# CHAPTER
# TWENTY-ONE

Y ou have killed an anomalous Eurasian lynx.

*Long extinct in the British Isles, the ascension has reintroduced indigenous fauna, and this lynx was among the first to emerge. Unfortunately, the lynx encountered the corrupting influence of the anomaly, fundamentally altering it both in size and intelligence.*

*This lynx's behaviour has already proven different to other anomalies you have engaged with in combat. Your allied glaistig suggests the creature was studying you.*

*Such creatures frequently contain common crafting materials such as: lynx pelt, lynx claws, lynx teeth, lynx bones, lynx meat. These anomalous creatures, however, contain only a petrified heart. This is of unknown value.*

*Do you wish to harvest this anomalous Eurasian lynx?*

I hit yes with no small feeling of trepidation.

The moment it was done, I shook myself out of screen time.

The glaistig stood before me. She gave off a soft glow, which took her already golden hair to a paler and more ethereal tinge. Her skin was still that inhuman colour closer to silvery birch bark than what we'd consider a natural skin tone, and her emerald-green robes still draped over legs that hinged backwards like a hind's rather than our own knees. It made her silhouette feel *other* in a way someone might not be able to fully classify if they didn't know. Uncanny valley, like AI art where there's one too many teeth and a wisp of a finger wedged between two others.

She, however, was entirely real.

"It's good you came along when you did," I told her. "It used magic—Spèird."

"I saw," the glaistig said softly. Her gaze lingered on the patch of earth where the anomalous lynx had dissipated into motes. "You must be very careful. It knows of you, and it is watching you."

I winced at that. "It's my fault. I attempted to make a connection with one of the anomalies—"

The glaistig waved her delicate hand dismissively. For a moment, I got the surreal impression of not bones but branches beneath her silver-smooth skin.

"It is of no consequence. You would not have been able to make such a connection at all had the entity not wished it. It is always seeking footholds."

"Why are you here?" Eilidh asked her, her tone far less combative than the words were blunt. "I'm grateful, of course, but you've not shown yourself since, well. Before Bawbag."

The glaistig's lip quirked with distaste at the mention of Bawbag, but she nodded in the direction of the spike-lined crater that remained where the beast had died.

"We are neighbours, are we not? And you two, I trust with the land. We are all stewards of this place, and you are good ones. The little one is learning."

Rhona was in an easy crouch nearby, but her back straightened with indignant instinct at those words. The glaistig didn't miss the teenager's reaction and gave her a small smile.

"You are young."

"Older than you, technically," Rhona muttered.

The laugh that emerged from the glaistig's pale throat was like the rustle of autumn leaves and every ounce as satisfying as stepping on one such leaf with a gleeful crunch.

"You will learn, little one," the glaistig told her. She glanced at Iain and Meeksy with surprising fondness. "As will you."

The others, George's group, still hung back warily, which the glaistig greeted with a small, amused smile.

In my mind, I heard, *Those ones must wish to learn before they will be able to learn.*

I startled at the thought, which wasn't mine. Eilidh's gaze snapped to meet my own, and without having to ask, I knew she'd heard it too.

A question lingered in her blue eyes, dark as sapphires in the dim glow given off by the glaistig.

The strange woman's own eyes looked almost black. Already darker than walnut even in broad daylight, they may as well have been onyx.

"You came to warn us," I said, keeping my voice low enough only for those of us in within arm's reach to hear.

"Not only about this . . . thing." The glaistig nodded distastefully at the pit she'd created. "I have heard whispers that you are keeping these anomalies captive. This is dangerous."

"We're hoping to learn to reverse the corruption, if we can." I spoke the words carefully. "Are you saying it's futile?"

"Anything but. I am simply telling you that you must be very, very careful. It is not something that can be undertaken from a place of ego. The arrogant will be humbled if they do not proceed with extreme caution."

Eilidh's expression darkened, as did Iain's and Meeksy's. Rhona, being Rhona, just snorted.

"Ronald's a goner, then," she said under her breath.

"We'll tell him to be more careful," Eilidh told the glaistig.

George and his group, having realised they were being excluded from the conversation, inched closer. I held up a hand to them with a slight shake of my head. While I wasn't a mahoosive fan of excluding people on principle, the last thing we needed was any more rumours flying about Oban than already would after tonight.

The glaistig turned back to me, her dark eyes fathomless.

"The only way to cure the disease is to fight the disease itself. Easing the symptoms may increase your patient's comfort, but it does little if the source of the infection goes unchecked." Those eyes bored into mine. "You cannot heal in the conditions that are making you ill."

Then she was gone, leaving her words hanging in the air.

Our journey back to Oban was a grumpy one. George peppered me with questions for most of the way, trying to figure out what the glaistig had said that he hadn't heard until finally, I grew irritated.

"Look," I said, "the most important thing you need to know is that these anomalies are now apparently watching *us*. Not just attacking, not just seeking out me and Eilidh, not simply mindless and ravening beasts. That lynx was somehow relaying information back to whatever entity created it. That should be enough to put you on your guard. I'm putting you in charge of spreading that knowledge. Tell people to get creative when they fight them from here on out. Don't put yourselves in undue danger, and for Christ's sake, if you get in the shit, end it fast, but any way we can muddy the waters to make sure this entity doesn't have a clear view of our capabilities—"

"Or make sure it thinks we're a bunch of bumbling buffoons," Rhona said helpfully.

"—will maybe help us in the long run." I gave Rhona an acknowledging nod, because she was right.

George frowned at that, pulling his head back slightly, which made his already nonexistent chin almost vanish.

"An enemy that underestimates you is an enemy you have a better chance of surprising and beating," I said shortly.

I could almost see the gears click in his head, and after a moment, George's chin reappeared and dipped with his agreement.

"I'm in charge of spreading that to the other squads?" He brightened as he said that, and I almost wanted to groan.

Rhona actually did, but she was a teenager and could get away with it, whereas I needed to be more circumspect, even if I kind of wanted to roll my eyes.

"Yes," I said, keeping my voice clipped. "But don't get cocky, and I need you to emphasise that people are *not* to get flamboyant. Work together and strategise and make sure absolutely everyone has a fallback plan if you get in the shit."

"Of course," George said, sounding mortally offended.

That, thankfully, ended the conversation.

The sky was already lightening with the coming dawn. May in Scotland meant very little darkness, and with the coming solstice, the sky would remain twilit through the peak of midnight. Even so, I wanted to get at least an attempt at sleep.

Eilidh and I needed to pay Ronald a visit.

The closer we got to Oban, the more a sulky, furry awareness became unignorable in my mind.

A visit to Ronald, absolutely.

And I had some major, major sucking up to do to a certain wildcat kitten.

Maybe I could bribe her back into my good graces with a gift of sausage.

Never in my life had I thought a kitten could put on an act until I reached the Whyte house at four in the morning only to be pelted with a fur-based missile.

Sailean vaulted up my leg, much to Brac-Meanmna's amusement where the staff had firm hold of my armour between my shoulder blades, and soon there was a little rumbling purr in my ear as the kitten head butted the side of my jaw.

"You cheeky wee liar," I murmured to her fondly, plucking her from my shoulder to hold her in front of my face.

I swear the tiny creature actually looked pleased with herself.

Cuddling her to my chest, I bade everyone goodnight— Eilidh far more reluctantly than Iain and Meeksy—and made my way up to my room. Sailean's curiosity about the fight meant I spent the next fifteen minutes attempting to explain the lynx. She hissed in all the appropriate places, and while she demonstrated her very dangerous swiping paws for me—and almost tipped off my bare chest in the process—I could sense through our bond that Sailean was secretly relieved *not* to have been brought along.

As a crepuscular creature most active at dawn and dusk, she didn't cuddle with me for long, instead heading off to make mischief with Catrìona, who was still getting up at the arse-crack of dawn to fish, kraken or no kraken.

I passed out to the now-familiar sounds of Iain's mum making her full Scottish breakfast to fuel her for the day.

When I awoke, it was only about nine in the morning. I

made my way downstairs to find Eilidh already sitting at the table with a steaming metal pot of tea and two mugs.

Touched by the thoughtfulness, I sat down across from her.

"Hey," she said with a small smile.

"You knew I was getting up?"

For a moment, I thought maybe she hadn't. Her blue-eyed gaze fell on the second mug as if she'd only just realised it was there, but then she gave a rueful laugh.

"I guess I did. This seer business is taking some getting used to."

*That* was something I'd have to ask more about later.

"Ronald day," I said, sounding about as enthused by it as I felt.

"Ronald day." Eilidh echoed both my words and their tone, her lips pressing together in a firm line. "I really want to believe he'll listen, but . . ."

"Blokes like him tend to go hackles up first, listening ears second if at all, aye."

"Exactly. We'll have to frame it in a way that won't puncture his pride."

"You mean 'the glaistig said you're a danger to yourself and others, so you better be careful or else' isn't likely to go over well?" I dropped a couple lumps of sugar into my teacup and poured tea over it. "I am shocked and dismayed."

"If you're up for suggestions, I'm happy to help," Eilidh muttered. "I've got plenty of practice managing a prickly man's ego, though you might have to be the one to do it."

"Your dad?" I asked the question carefully. We hadn't spoken much about her parents, and while I wasn't sure they were even still alive, I *was* sure their relationship had been complex at best.

"Aye. He had exactly one idea of strength, and diplomacy sure wasn't it when it came to him dealing with literally anyone else, but if you needed to approach *him* with feedback or, hell, a suggestion on what to have for tea?" Eilidh's mouth twisted in remembered annoyance. "You needed to tread lightly."

"Sounds like the type to make everyone else walk barefoot on eggshells while he stomps around in steel-toed combat boots." I didn't even know if combat boots came in steel toes, but from the quirk of Eilidh's smile, my metaphor was spot on.

"Precisely," she said. "Ronald's not quite *that* bad, but I still get the sense that he will take advice better if it's coming from, well. Someone he respects."

The unspoken undertone was that she thought he wouldn't listen to *her*. Maybe any her. Gods, it was the twenty-first century, were we really still doing this? Despite the annoyance, I'd been raised by a single mother. I actually knew damn well what it was like and how maddening it had been for Mum when I—as a literal *child*—got treated like the "man" of the house right in front of her, a grown adult who was keeping us both alive.

So I simply nodded.

"Give me all the notes you've got, and I'll deploy them at our cantankerous ally," I told Eilidh.

# CHAPTER
# TWENTY-TWO

R onald had been *busy* while we'd been away.

I shouldn't have been surprised, considering the face of Oban was changing daily with our arcane advancements and understanding that rapidly shifted what was possible, but what had been a glorified bothy on the edge of Loch a' Phearsain was now a walled compound with a separate living area that was akin to barracks.

Alison was coming out just as we arrived, and her expression was pensive, though she brightened when she saw us. She also blushed, but that was perhaps to be expected. After all, she *had* discovered that Eilidh and I were, in fact, ancient.

Practically senile, really. More than a decade on her.

My mental jokes were likely a coping mechanism. It was strange when someone had developed a crush on you without actually knowing you—like you're just an image on a pedestal rather than a person. Thankfully, the pedestal had crumbled, and I was now firmly situated on the ground.

*That* was a relief.

"Hiya," I said to her. "You leaving?"

Alison nodded, glancing at Eilidh. "Ronald needs a few

things from town. It's safer that he's doing this out here, but it does mean some inconvenience."

"Need anything we can get?" The place looked a bit Spartan. "Duvets, pillows, a cast-iron pan to hit Ronald with if he gets too annoying?"

"Oh, god, all of the above. He's sent me with a list that'll take up my entire inventory, but if you can bring some of that stuff out here soon, that would make everyone's lives easier. Or at least less insufferable." Alison cracked a genuine smile at my salute.

"Any news?" Eilidh asked.

The younger woman gave an uncomfortable shrug. "I honestly don't know. He doesn't tell me much."

"That's encouraging," I said dryly.

Alison scuffed her foot on the path, which was newly paved. "He's always been very particular."

"Well, he really should be communicating with the people helping him," I said. "If anything happens to him, his research won't do anyone any good if he's kept it locked up in his skull."

"But didn't you hear?" Alison said, her lips now curling in a smile that didn't reach her eyes. "He's *invincible*."

"God," Eilidh muttered, but she chuckled, gazing thoughtfully at Alison, who I thought had just risen in her regard with her use of sarcasm.

Mine too, to be honest. She'd always been so on edge around me—due to the whole pedestal thing—that seeing her relax enough to gripe about a colleague was a relief.

"Even if he is, the rest of us aren't," I said, my long-suffering sigh only a little put on. "We'll talk to him."

"Good luck with that," Alison said, shaking her head. "Since that'll probably take several days, I guess I'll see you when I get back."

Two zingers in as many minutes? I stared after Alison as she made her way back to the A816 and turned to Eilidh after a moment to see her doing the same.

"I like her better without the rose-coloured glasses," Eilidh murmured.

"I think we can chalk her previous behaviour up to ascension anxiety," I said. "Something-something any port in a storm."

"You do make a very nice port," Eilidh said with a wink, then seemed to hear herself. "That sounded kinkier than it was supposed to."

Without another word, she strode into the compound, leaving me to follow, bemused.

Whilst the outside of the research compound had changed remarkably, the inside of the bothy had not, other than the fact that the cages were now of arcane construction and there were a hell of a lot of them.

The badgers we'd helped corral were each in individual cages now, and there was an entire wall of smaller critters, including a very unfortunate dormouse and a pair of squirrels. A starling squawked at our entrance, its voice a croak that would make a crow sound like it was singing an aria.

Ronald crouched in front of one of the badgers, his rail-thin ultra-runner figure folding like laundry drying rack, all sharp angles.

"Hello, Ronald," I said. "What news of the enemy?"

I hadn't really expected him to turn at that, but he did, eyeing me sideways. "Why'd you say that like you're LARPing *Game of Thrones?*"

"Excuse you, if I were to LARP anything, it would be *Lord of the Rings.*" At Eilidh's startled glance, I hastily changed the subject. Hell, we'd ears to match Tolkien's elves now, so none of us were that far away from the concept as it stood. "Look, it's been a long couple of days, and neither of us slept much. Oban grew a contingent of Glaswegian swingers, and apparently lynxes are back in the British Isles, because we killed one last night that was akin to these monstrosities."

"You killed it? Why didn't you bring it to me?" Ronald unfolded his wiry frame to standing, looking as if I'd just squatted and dropped a jobby in the middle of the floor.

"Mate, it wouldn't have fit in this bothy," I said. "The thing was massive."

For a moment, I thought he was going to protest, but then he sighed. "It would have been good to study."

"Not that one," Eilidh said softly. "That one was studying us."

It wasn't exactly what she and I had planned as a segue, but it slotted so perfectly into the conversation that I rolled with it.

Ronald's ears had pricked up at her words, and he latched onto it. "What does she mean?"

I fought my eyebrows' impulse to hike upwards at him choosing to address me about it rather than ask the person who was standing right there, but she took a couple steps away, twitching one finger on her hand to tell me to go for it.

"Something's changed. The entity that created these things seems to have figured out how to use them to relay information back to it."

"Because of what you did?" Ronald asked shrewdly.

"Not entirely, but partly," I admitted. "The glaistig paid us another visit. She's the reason we were able to kill it as fast as we did, and she said the connection I made with the last anomaly you had here was only possible because it was actively seeking it. But they are beginning to behave differently—unpredictably."

"Define that."

Not a man to beat around the bush, this one. He pulled a small notepad out of his pocket and looked at me expectantly.

I walked him through the differences, how the anomalous lynx had circled around to the north, how it had used an actual identifiable spell, everything I could think of. His brow furrowed more and more with every sentence.

Beyond that, I reported what the glaistig had said without editorialising. Neither Eilidh and I were going to deny that he was an intelligent person—just more the type to dig in his heels if he thought he was being told what to think or what to do. I was just hoping if we led this horse to water, he'd actually drink it.

The whole time I was talking, I was acutely aware of the anomalies around us. None of them gave off the sense of the lynx, the ineffable *off*ness that had characterised our interaction with it, but that didn't mean they weren't observing us every bit as much as we were observing them. Part of me wanted to keep Connection going as almost a constant trickle rather than my usual pulse, but I didn't quite dare. I instead went with what was characteristic of me for that, at least. Nothing seemed out of the ordinary, other than the ongoing fact that these anomalies shouldn't fucking exist.

Eilidh occasionally chimed in with supporting bits of information—how the lynx had responded to being blinded, how it hadn't responded to being gutted—which Ronald jotted down with almost feverish fervour.

He didn't surprise me even a little when he said, at the end, "I should like to study one of those creatures, whether in the field or here."

"Do you think it would be wise to bring one here if we think it's also watching us?" I asked, doing my best to keep my tone as neutral as possible.

Ronald pondered that for a moment. "Perhaps not."

Then his eyes lit up, and I braced myself.

"Perhaps a different facility for such a creature—just the one."

Over his shoulder, I saw Eilidh's worried look and did my best not to react to it visibly.

Instead, I pretended to think about what Ronald had said. All I could think of was the line from *Watchmen* that Eilidh had referenced when we were captured by Bawbag's men. Except if we had a sapient—or spyware-infested, for lack of a better term—anomaly in captivity, I couldn't believe for a second that it would work to *our* advantage.

I said the only thing I could think of that would be both noncommittal and hopefully a deterrent. "Well, at this point, we don't know how anomalous the lynx was compared to its fellow anomalies. It was unique on many levels. Hell, I hardly expected that the first time I saw a Eurasian lynx it would be half the size of the bloody beithir and a bizarrely zombified feral monster. We can't guarantee we'll even see such a thing again. And I'll reiterate that there's very little chance of us trans-porting something that large or containing it on short notice. Purifire didn't seem to do the trick."

There was no real way for me to know if my second Ring of Fire had had any effect on the creature, seeing as how the glaistig had stepped in with her on-the-fly spike trap, but Ronald didn't need to know that right now. Better for everyone to assume Purifire *couldn't* contain this shiny new version of anomalies.

Ronald remained silent except for his frantic scribbling and the sound of turning pages for a long moment, but then he nodded. "I suppose we can address that if and when more show up."

"Aye, that sounds prudent," I agreed. "Focus our efforts on

what we have. Care to walk me through what you have learned?"

This was another step to Eilidh's and my strategy—get him talking.

I didn't have to ask him twice.

By the time Ronald was done, my eyes felt ready to glaze over, but at least I was more confident that he was taking precautions.

"Do you have any of this written down somewhere accessible?" Eilidh asked him curiously.

Whether her curiosity was feigned or not was beyond me to figure out in the moment—the smell of the anomalies was making my exhausted eyes water even with the windows open —but Ronald was frowning in response.

"Some of the mages have taken some notes, but—"

When he paused for a moment, I jumped in. "You know, we've got Craobh an Òbain now, the living tree?"

"All trees are alive," Ronald said, his frown deepening.

"You didn't hear about the tree? Eilidh and I created it from the doors we stole from Bawbag's manor. It's functionally a library—we're using the memory stones to create a repository of community knowledge, and your contributions would be very welcome." Eilidh and I hadn't really talked about this part, but from the grin she flashed me, I'd nailed the tone. I'd figured framing it as a contribution rather than homework might be more effective, and it seemed I was right.

"Hm, yes, it would be good to ensure there's a coherent record of my—our—work here for posterity." Ronald's eyes lit up. "Yes, that could also be of service to us so I don't have to repeat myself when new mages show up."

"Brilliant," Eilidh said, winking at me over his shoulder.

The warm glow in my chest seemed to have decided her praise was for me—I'd take it. I'd seen how bullheaded Ronald could be, so getting him to do what we needed him to do in a way that he would jump onboard with rather than being dragged by a team of oxen? Aye, this had been a much better plan than barging in and telling him what to do.

"There is one other thing the glaistig said that felt relevant to share," I said finally after another ten or so minutes of hashing out details. "Though honestly, it felt a bit common sense."

That last had been my own idea. Make it seem like I was placating the glaistig rather than bringing direction. Eilidh had wholeheartedly agreed. This whole thing felt manipulative tae fuck, but I'd worked with shite managers and excellent ones in my pre-ascension days, and the worst ones were the ones who came in all bossy and "my way or the highway." It may have been a rationalisation to say that we were manipulating him for the greater good, but his job was dangerous, and I wasn't about to risk the people he was working with if he was getting high on the smell of his own farts.

Ronald waited expectantly.

I hesitated. "She warned us that however much we have learned about these anomalies, the entity creating them is far beyond our own capabilities." Here was where I was going to fudge the truth a little, stealing a line from, ironically, one of my more pompous professors at uni. "'Only a fool thinks they know the full extent of what they don't know.' I think she meant that we can learn a million things and think we understand some-thing, but if we don't recognise that we might not even have access to all the *questions* we need to ask, we're basically looking at the tip of a T-rex's tail and calling it a snake."

"Simplistic and yes, common sense, but it is a good

reminder," Ronald said after a beat. "The bulk of the iceberg does lie beneath the surface of the water."

I nodded. "And sometimes, the surface of the water is frozen and covered in a layer of snow, so we don't even know it's there."

"Indeed." Ronald gave me a sharp glance at that, and I had the immediate impression that I had earned another point or two of his respect. "I will bear in mind that these anomalies may be, as you said, the tail of a T-rex." The skinny man snorted. "Best not to pull that tail, eh, Calum?"

I nodded vigorously, refraining from the immense sigh of relief that wanted to gust out of my lungs.

"*Definitely* not a tail I want to pull." I held out a hand to Ronald, who shook it. Final phase of the plan, and it was fully genuine. "Thank you for your work here, mate. We can't beat these things if we don't understand them."

While none of the anomalies had shifted their behaviour in the time we'd been talking, I suddenly couldn't wait to be out of their presence.

# CHAPTER
# TWENTY-THREE

"Have I mentioned that I hate this?" Eilidh said as we made our way back to Oban.

"At least five times and me as many as that, but you can say it again."

"I hate this."

"Me too."

The afternoon was bright but mostly cloudy and warm enough that I was sweating in my armour. We were taking it at a leisurely pace—which was to say we were walking—but that was more due to needing processing time than anything.

Ronald had told us that the corruption behaved, on a basic level, like a virus. Except it wasn't a live pathogen or anything that could be fought with a vaccine or a course of antibiotics or, god forbid, drinking disinfectant like a few unfortunate souls had tried in the peak days of the pandemic.

That was good information to have, but it also didn't tell us much else. Like how to fight it. How it infected someone. How it had taken hold of these creatures. How it made them rot. On top of that, why it existed in the first place when even the

Ascended Alliance seemed to have no experience with it or any explanation.

Earth was a fucking Petri dish, and after years of a global pandemic, let's just say I was over it *before* the ascension.

I guess the plus side of the current reality was that it had done away with Earth-borne pathogens, though the implications of that for our gut flora and general ecosystem balance remained to be seen.

That was a question for the science of tomorrow, not for himbo hamsters just trying to survive.

"At least he behaved like you expected," I said to her. "Those safety measures he lined out before we left sounded sensible, and he was open to bringing in new perspectives to help him sketch out the T-rex, as it were."

"Aye, that's a plus for sure." Eilidh still looked pensive, and I couldn't blame her.

"Something bothering you?"

"Heaps." She gave me a wry smile. "The anomalies, the kraken, whatever news the swingers brought about Dundee."

That had been in the back of my mind too. "We can make that priority one when we get back."

"Good plan."

Something else seemed to be hovering in the air between us, but I didn't know what it was.

Without anything else to go on, I assumed it was just the litany of life-or-death problems we were trying to keep at bay.

"Shall we pick up the pace?" I asked her after a moment. "Burn off some steam?"

"Absolutely."

•ᴄ ⸎⸎ ᴐ•

If I had known what I was going to hear when we got back to Oban, I would have suggested *slowing* our pace to a snail's slimy trudge.

"Say that again, please. Slower, just to make sure I'm hearing you correctly." I fought the urge to get up from the table on the pier, walk to the edge, and hop into the drink like that scene of Denholm Reynholm in *IT Crowd* casually hopping out the skyscraper window.

At least jumping in the harbour wouldn't kill me. This news might.

"There. Is. Another. Bawbag. In. Dundee." Iain gave each word its own sentence, and he looked as if he found the mere act of repeating himself offensive.

I didn't blame him.

"Fucking hell. Who is it? Another lordling who fancies himself the next Duke of Sutherland circa 1814?" Maybe I wouldn't just jump in the harbour. Maybe the Muilich would like some company. I could swim to Mull. Or across the Minch. Had anyone heard from Uist yet? Barra? Benbecula? St. Kilda?

The pier wasn't yet overwhelmed with people for teatime, but the buzz grew around us nonetheless as I suddenly lost my appetite for my bowl of steamed mussels, lit by a finger of sunlight that poked through the dotted clouds above.

"Other end of the class spectrum this time, from what the swingers said." Iain shrugged, squinting into the sun since it was aimed directly into his eyeballs. I got the feeling he was almost more annoyed by what he'd just said than the reason he'd had to say it. "Someone fancies himself more the next Godfather than the next Sutherland, though if you ask me, they're basically the same turd with slightly different gilding."

"You've got that right," Eilidh murmured. "Regardless of the gilding on the jobby, this isn't good. He's not reached Bawbag levels yet, or the system would have hit us with a bounty like it did with him, but Bawbag managed to do plenty of damage before we got the headhunting quest."

"Fuck," I said.

I didn't want to say it. I knew *Eilidh* didn't want to say it. Which was, inevitably, why Iain said it. If there was anything I could count on my best mate for, it was saying the quiet part out loud.

"Reckon Susanna's in Dundee?"

I closed my eyes, dreaming briefly of Tobermory's colourful harbour. Soon, we'd be able to teleport. Soon. Soon.

"I do not know," I said after a too-long beat. "Does it matter?"

"Oof, cold."

Eilidh raised an eyebrow. "No, that's fair. Wherever she is, she's on my list of concern somewhere around Maggie Thatcher's formaldehyde-ridden corpse."

"*Also* cold." Iain slow clapped.

"Also *fair*," I said.

"What do we do about Dundee, then?" I asked.

"You campaigning to be the next Police Scotland, mate?"

"You kidding?"

"Fire brigade, then."

"None of the above!"

"We are making a bit of a habit of cleaning up messes," Eilidh said, popping a mussel in her mouth.

"I'm also not trying to be the national kicker of bawbags and burier of jobbies." I groaned.

"I would *happily* be the national bawbag kicker," Iain said vehemently. He spread his hands out like he was in a musical and not an apocalypse. "Can you imagine? Just go fae appointment tae appointment, kicking Scotland's worst cunts all day?"

"If I see a job posting, you'll be the first I let know," I told him. "Until then, we really do need to decide what we're going to do. I'd rather not wait until he's graduated to the next level of bawbaggery to figure it out."

"A stitch in time, et cetera," Eilidh agreed.

Iain just stared at her blankly.

"Saves nine," I supplied.

Now he blinked at me.

"A stitch in time saves nine," Eilidh said, rolling her eyes. "It's an expression that means if you act prudently, you do less work later. Patch the hole before it's a gash."

"Kick the bawbag before he enslaves half of Argyll, got it." Iain glanced towards the southeast. "Or Angus, I guess, in this case. Or is it Fife?"

"Angus," I answered absently, still contemplating long-distance swimming away from my problems, but then I eyed my friend askance. "Did you really just ask if Dundee was in Fife?"

"What?" Iain crossed his arms in front of his chest with a defensive scowl. "Geography was never my strong point."

"He has plenty of other strong points," Meeksy's low voice rumbled from behind me, and I turned to see him making his way across the few remaining intervening metres between us.

Iain winked and actually blushed. Still besotted after all these years. It was enough to bring a tear to my eye.

"Mussels?" Meeksy asked, peering down at the table after giving Iain a peck on the forehead.

"You can have mine. I lost my appetite talking about Dundee's Bawbag 2.0." I pushed back from the table and motioned at Meeksy to take my place next to Iain. "I think I'm going to go practice my superpowers."

"I'll come with you," Eilidh said, then hastily added, "if that's all right?"

In answer, I just held my hand out to her. Iain's blushing

must have been contagious, because there was a decidedly pink cast to her cheeks when she took my offered hand.

I've never been threatened by strong women. To the contrary, I'd happily let Xena open my jars for the rest of my life—or step on me if she really wanted to.

That said, getting the wind knocked out of me for the fourth time sparring with Eilidh was enough to dent the auld ego just a tad.

"It's what I get for putting all my points in magic shite," I managed to say between wheezes as she helped me to my feet.

Eilidh, for her part, was having an absolutely glorious day. She gave me a roguish grin that suddenly made my knees want to give out all over again, but then she attempted a curtsey so badly that my wheeze turned into a guffaw.

"It's honestly great fun," she said, then cocked her head to the side. "How far could I throw you, d' you reckon?"

"Erm, I'd rather leave some mystery in this relationship," I said with extreme haste.

Her answering peal of laughter made a few of the other folks nearby turn their heads.

"I think we're safe on that score." Eilidh's voice turned husky, and her eyes held mine for a moment longer than usual, just long enough to make me contemplate the bedroom ramifications of her Strength stat.

"Hm," I said to disguise my suddenly rerouted blood flow, "you're right. Too much mystery. We need . . . less mystery."

If she'd caught me off guard, it was clear my words returned the favour when her pupils dilated visibly and her breath hitched through her parted lips.

"Eilidh!" The voice that broke the sudden magnetism

between us earned an immediate spot on my shit list—or it would have if it hadn't been Ealasaid, whom I adored.

The old woman waved from the far side of the sparring field, and I waved back.

"Later?" Eilidh murmured to me, regret easy to read in her voice *and* the light press of her hand against my deltoid.

"Later." I took her by the waist and pulled her close, my hand flush against her lower back as our lips touched. "Most definitely later."

For the first time in our two hours of sparring, Eilidh actually wobbled on her feet.

Fascinating. I had a secret weapon: seduction.

One point for the pathetic hamster.

Eilidh's smile was every bit as wobbly as her balance, and I kept my hand on her back as she steadied herself.

"You're going to pay for that," she murmured.

"Promise?"

Her answering look threatened to turn me to dust on the spot, and when she swivelled on her heel and strode away, I half expected to hear an actual sizzle from her feet on the grass.

I gave myself exactly seven seconds to stare at her retreating figure—sensible armour or not, Eilidh MacIntosh made it look *good*.

We had been taking things at a pace so glacial, one might mistake it for the beginning of a new Ice Age rather than two people falling head over heels for each other. For my part, Susanna had burned me bad. Hell, for Eilidh's part, Susanna had burned her bad. We were both grown adults, sure, but we were also rowing the same shitty boat of trying to get over deep betrayal by someone we loved. I couldn't blame either of us for wanting to go slow.

But the tension? Woof. There'd been sparks for a while, but I think they'd just caught the tinder.

Suddenly, I had the overwhelming desire to do some push-ups. I may not have wanted to be the Rock, but my own personal hills were alive with the sound of sweet, sweet music that sounded suspiciously like Barry White, and my Strength stat could use a boost.

# CHAPTER
# TWENTY-FOUR

Naturally, it was when I was dripping a cascade of sweat down the waterfall of my spine and stretching out my now-aching lats that a cry of alarm wiped my satisfaction off my face. I'd been feeling smug about a successful plus two to Strength—after a gruelling two hours of everything from burpees to pull-ups—but from the commotion bubbling over at the pier, our run of quiet had ended.

"It's the kraken attackin'!" Someone bellowed this, followed by a return volley of uneasy chuckles and epithets.

I gave myself a quick once over with Purifire and started gearing back up. It wasn't nearly as satisfying as a shower.

By the time I'd made my way over to the pier, I'd already gathered that the attack wasn't ongoing. To the contrary, the kraken had struck Ulva Ferry, of all places. Ulva Ferry was the aptly named tiny village in Mull where a signal-based ferry operated between the large island of Mull and Ulva a bare hundred metres across a strait.

No one had been killed, but the ferry had been demolished.

Rhona and Iain were deep in conversation with Catrìona, who had apparently brought the news herself.

Iain's mother looked up at me, scrubbing a hand through her salt-and-pepper hair where it had been flattened against her skull from being under a fishing cap all day.

"He wants to meet you," she said to me without preamble.

"He who?" I said, perplexed.

"Am Bàrd Muileach."

The Mull Bàrd.

It was he who'd first rallied the islanders, and my wee friend the wren had met him—as I understood it, he could actually speak to all the wrens of the island—but beyond that and the fact that he was a keeper of island lore even pre-ascension, I knew nothing of the man. Not even his name.

"Deagh bheachd a th' ann an sin," I murmured.

It *was* a good idea, one that we'd already left too long. Glancing around the pier, I made a quick inventory of who was present.

"Someone find Ealasaid and Eilidh, will you? Meeksy too. Also Angus and Eliza, and if Alison's around, she'd be good to bring along as well. Oh, and Diana from Kilchurn if she's about." After another moment's thought, I rattled off a few other names of mages and people who'd landed in some semblance of community leadership around Oban."

Iain and Rhona had immediately dispersed, but Catrìona was watching me with a gaze far too like our enormous eagle friend's.

"What are you up to, Calum?" Catrìona asked. "Assembling an entourage?"

"What? No!" My face grew hot at the very thought. Ugh, really? "Look, the Ascended Alliance says our strength is in community, yeah? Well, I figured it might be good to show the Muilich ours. We're doing almost frighteningly well here, kraken and anomalies notwithstanding—or maybe especially with them in the mix, all things considered—and once upon a time, the islands weren't isolated. They were interconnected. We can be that again, but we need to actually demonstrate that we *are* a community. We have Craobh an Òbain here now, but we can share knowledge with the Muilich, and if we bring the people who have spearheaded our progress, we can do that faster. Maybe help whilst we're there."

I hadn't meant to make a speech, but halfway through, Catrìona's face grew pensive, then softened altogether. When my mouth snapped shut with an audible click of my teeth at the end, she took my face in her calloused, fishing-boat-hardened hands, pulled my head down to hers, and kissed me on the forehead.

"Abair gum biodh do mhàthair pròiseil," she said softly, patting me on the cheek.

*Your mother would be so proud.*

I didn't have time to formulate a response before she strode away, barking an order at one of the crew from her boat.

I'd always loved the crossing to Mull. It's not particularly far, and on the ferries pre-ascension, it was forty minutes from Oban to Craignure or, if you wanted to avoid the tourist-clogged passage, a much quicker few minutes from Lochaline to Fishnish from the Ardnamurchan Peninsula.

This time, though, with a dodgy giant squid monster ravaging the shores of Argyll, it was a very tense hour until we landed at the familiar pier in Craignure.

Craignure, Creag an Iubhair. Literally the Crag of the Yew. Or possibly a reference to dwarf juniper—I'd no idea.

I didn't see any yews nearby, but I'd never seen Craignure so busy even in the peak of the season. We hadn't taken the fishing boat but a repurposed yacht someone had commandeered and retrofitted a week earlier from the marina in Kerrera, which was surreal. Eilidh and Rhona stood on the port-side rail, talking in low voices as Rhona scratched wee Sailean's head. The kitten, it should be said, had taken remarkably well to her first maritime outing.

Everyone else I'd asked for—except Alison, who had already been back with Ronald—milled about. Angus sprawled on a deck chair, looking for all the world like he'd discovered his calling as an affluent hobbyist sailor—or he would if he weren't dressed in scuffed armour and lazily playing with a lightning spell like magic was a simple fidget toy.

I shook my head, looking at the rapidly approaching Craignure.

What had been a sleepy port village with a tourist office, a couple wee cafes, and a campground of caravan hookups and pods alike now bustled with movement. The tourist centre seemed to have been turned into an all-new type of hub, and the local Spar—the only shop many island villages had if they were too small for a Co-Op—had a stream of people flowing in and out.

Our docking did draw attention, but not much of it.

"Are they expecting us?" I asked Catrìona as I tossed her a mooring line where she'd hopped onto the pier.

"Aye, they'd said it was safest to keep the crossing short and go overland to Ulva Ferry and that someone would meet us." The second half of her sentence got muddled when she turned her back to me. Catrìona straightened after a moment, squinting into the diffuse light that brightened as a patch of thinner clouds teased us with the promise of elusive sunshine. "There's Rabbie now."

I didn't know who Rabbie was, but I presumed that was the portly bloke in a jumpsuit and neon yellow wellies stumping towards us on the pier.

Melding with the tang of the sea, a familiar-yet-bizarre aroma reached my nose.

"The chocolate shop is functioning?" I said, perplexed.

Catrìona now squinted at me as if *I* were the sun and had just said something confusing, but after a sniff or two, she shrugged. "Reckon so."

I wasn't sure why that of all things had awoken my cognitive dissonance. Scotland was not known for its growing of cacao pre-ascension. Though I supposed if we'd managed sugar cane and beetroot and all sorts of agricultural feats in Oban, why couldn't the Muilich figure out how to keep making truffles? I wondered if they'd also kept up with those lemon melt cookies I loved so much. Those things were crack.

Rabbie reached us just after we disembarked, clearing his throat as he gave Catrìona a gruff hug that was closer to using her back as a bongo drum. Most of the others made their way up towards the main road—and the enticing aroma of chocolate—but I hung back with Eilidh and Catrìona.

Rabbie's greeting escaped my ears when I heard an all-too-familiar trill and tweet and a tiny wren dive-bombed my face.

"Oi, it's you!" I exclaimed to the wee bird as his feathers brushed my cheek.

I held up a hand for him to land on, which he did, puffing up his feathers until he was even more spherical than usual.

Rabbie squinted at me, leaning around Catrìona to do it. But when he spoke, it was to her. "Another one, eh?"

It took me a moment to realise he was referring to the bàrd's ability to speak to the wrens.

"Erm, not entirely. I just know this particular bird," I said. "I'm Calum."

I held out my unoccupied hand, which happened to be my left, and Rabbie grasped it without hesitation.

"Rabbie," he said. "Finn's in Ulva Ferry, and I'm meant to lead the way there."

"Finn's the bàrd?" I asked slowly to his answering nod, which came with a delighted chirp of a soundtrack from the wren.

"Good lad. His dad worked the ferry with me for years before, well, you know." At my blank look, Rabbie waved his hands in the air before shoving them deep into his pockets uncomfortably. "The ascension. We didn't lose too many folk straight away, but there was a nasty pack of stoats in Gruline, and they got him. Size of horses—they don't look like much when they're normal sized, but I'll be damned if they don't give ye the fear when their teeth are as long as your thumb."

"Eilidh and I fought a warren's worth of enormous rabbits, so believe me, you don't have to explain." I cleared my throat. "I'm sorry, though, for your loss."

Rabbie cleared his throat again, his eyes shifting away from making contact with mine. "Aye, well. We adapt."

"We do," Eilidh said softly from beside me.

The wren lifted off from my arm and, inexplicably, fluttered over to Eilidh, where he perched on her shoulder to her bemusement.

Eilidh introduced herself to Rabbie, and he gestured with his chin up at the village.

"We'll get yous all sorted with some lunch, and then we'll get on the road. Shouldn't take too long, but we do have to be careful—been a muckle eagle making noise in the skies, and I reckon none of us feature getting carried out to Staffa to *become* lunch." Rabbie glanced upwards nervously, scanning the skies.

"Eagle?" My feet were all too happy to move in the direction of chocolate. "Just the one? There's one we know, and she's a friend. If it's the same one, you're probably safe."

Instead of relaxing at that, Rabbie scowled at Catrìona. "Yous didn't mention that."

Catrìona snorted, patting the man's shoulder briefly. "I think other news took precedence." After a few steps up the pier, though, she chuckled a rueful laugh. "Never thought in my life that an eagle to make Tolkien swoon would end up as a low-priority news item."

That got a laugh from Rabbie, though even his laugh sounded like brittle paper crumpling. The man was a sun-dried, windswept man of the sea, and I suddenly looked a bit closer, going against my own usual "don't spy on friendly strangers" rule to cast Keen Eye.

*Robert "Rabbie" Watson*

*Level 14 Windsinger*

*Affinities: Nature, Storm, Arcane, Seafaring*

*The Windsinger class is a rare class offered only to those with the Seafaring affinity at Level 9. A highly specialised tree of skills and spells allows them to not only read the currents in wind and water but to manipulate them. At higher levels, a Windsinger can navigate a rowboat through a hurricane unscathed. A boon to any maritime expedition or battle, this Windsinger earned his affinity through decades of hands-on experience in his home waterways.*

The bloom of pride I felt at those words caught me by surprise.

I followed along after him and Catrìona, listening to them banter back and forth as the wren on Eilidh's shoulder trilled his accompaniment. Sailean poked her head out of her carrier to mew at him, and the kitten and wren struck up an unlikely conversation—at least it seemed so to my ears. They certainly chattered at each other back and forth enough to look like it.

Maybe they were playing people. *Look at me, I make some noise and then you make some noise! Mew, mew, mew, mew. Chirp-chirp-chirrup! Nailed it.*

It took me most of the way up the pier and across the road for me to put my finger on exactly what it was that had sparked the sudden rush of emotion at Rabbie's class.

Before the ascension, folk who worked the ferries, the fishing boats, the docks—they were often written off with the rest of the working class. But now? We'd an entirely new class system, and their hard-won skills were treated with the honour they deserved.

The ability to know when it was safe to sail had been a vital one for most of human history. I had to admit that seeing that acknowledged made the world feel just a wee bit more just than it had.

We'd adapted, and we'd continue to adapt.

Bells jingled as Rabbie pulled open the door to the Craignure chocolatier, engulfing us in a wave of warmth and delicious aromas.

Wind magic and chocolate.

Suddenly, I couldn't wait to see what else the Muilich had to show us.

My stomach grumbled its fervent agreement.

# CHAPTER
# TWENTY-FIVE

"**O**h, god, I might actually pass out."

Iain's rapturous moan made me feel like I should tell him to get a room with his chocolate.

A laugh rippled through the room, followed by slightly more tempered words of agreement, some of which were spoken through a mouthful.

Of course, I'd not bitten into my own yet. I almost didn't want to—almost.

The little chocolate was pure art even to look at. I'd always been impressed by the shop here in Craignure, but they'd truly ascended—ahem—to new heights with the addition of magic.

My own wee chocolate was moulded into the shape of a breaking wave, studded with jewel-like crystals of sugar. Even better? It came with a small piece of paper that saved me a use of Keen Eye.

*Spirit-Infused Bon Bon (The Wave)*
*This meticulously hand-crafted bon bon is a delicacy of sea salt, dark chocolate, and divinity. Luscious and decadent, it doesn't stop at epicurean delights.*

*Spirit Regeneration: +10% for 24 hours*

*All sea-related activities have a +5% chance of unlocking affinities for 24 hours.*

It may not have seemed like much, but affinities could be powerful. As I'd seen with my snooping on Rabbie, the right affinity could open you up to rare classes that could provide enormous benefit. I'd take it.

The chocolates weren't the only treats we found in the chocolatier.

Their local chefs had clearly been levelling up their food-craft, because everything from the sandwiches to the garnishes offered bonuses. Calorie dense and mouthwatering, the rich, nutty bread energised me palpably, and any muscle fatigue I felt from my earlier intense workout washed away.

Intellectually, I'd always known that food was fuel, but the ascension had made it empirically unignorable. Meeksy looked like he might actually weep when he took a bite of his sandwich.

Not a whisper of my lemon cookies, though. More's the pity.

By the time we got on the road, everyone had a spring in their step, and the wren—who had been spoilt tae fuck with crumbs and seeds to the point I worried he might not be able to achieve liftoff—flitted into the air to chirp above our heads.

A few people prudently kept an eye on his alignment with their strides, and I just as prudently sent him a wee tendril of thought to aim his feathered bum away from our procession.

Sailean, for her part, was over the novelty of the wren and decided it was time for a wee snooze.

I hadn't been to Mull in a while, but the first major difference that hit me as we walked up the silent road towards Fishnish was that the once-dense, non-native sitka forest had been felled. People moved amid the exposed underbrush, occasionally giving us a wave, but there was also the glow of magic that permeated the clear-cut area.

"What's going on there?" I called ahead to Rabbie.

"Finn wants the sitkas gone," he called back. "We're replacing them with indigenous trees. That was already the plan before the ascension, but we can do it faster now!"

For several minutes, his reply left me—pardon the pun—stumped. Not in the sense that I didn't understand what they were doing, because I did. Scotland had once been richly forested, but humans had stripped the Highlands bare of trees. Mull was one of the few islands in the Hebrides that *had* trees; one of its many poetic names was Muile nan Geug, Mull of the Branches.

But when the Clearances came, it wasn't just the sheep that supplanted people. It was also the introduction of the invasive sitka. They'd taken over the island with no balance, only the oppressive, dark growth of forest so thick that almost no light could permeate. A blot on the landscape and an all-too-on-the-nose symbol of the death of the Gaelic way of life.

Eilidh's face beside me had also turned pensive, and we glanced at each other, the work of the Muilich beyond a strange backdrop to her sombre gaze.

"Silver linings" was all she said.

I reached out and took her hand.

Had it really taken the end of the world as we knew it to give the land back to the people?

I knew the answer to that question, of course.

Suddenly, I couldn't wait to meet this bàrd.

The bàrd was . . . not what I expected.

We reached Ulva Ferry just as the sun escaped the east-ward-moving cloud cover. To the west, the sky was clear and promised a night of sparkling stars, but my unease didn't let me feel excitement.

The wreckage of the ferry itself had been dragged into the shallows—and it *was* wrecked.

If the hull hadn't still been intact, it would have been hard to even recognise as a boat at all.

The kraken had smashed it to so much tinder.

Amid the boards, sleeves rolled up and dark green shirt showing darker, almost-black damp patches from sweat, was the bàrd. Finn.

Even from a hundred metres away, I could *feel* his spirit's signature. His presence was beyond the physical; raw power poured off of him as he laboured beside an older woman with her hair piled atop her head in a messy bun. Together, they lifted an enormous plank of jagged wood, their feet sunk deep into sand at the shoreline of the receding tide.

Finn couldn't have been more than thirty-five. I would have even thought he was younger. He'd a boyish face framed by golden curls that would have made Narcissus weep. His face even from side profile was flushed with his efforts, and he might have looked cherubic had his skin not borne laugh lines at the corner of his eyes and mouth. The visible side of his jaw was marked by a scar that was still healing, which meant it must have been very recent indeed—or magical in nature. Either way, whatever had caused it had dug deep. A couple inches away and it would have sliced his carotid artery.

Even as I thought it, he glanced over his shoulder, still heaving the plank, and met my gaze.

Electric blue eyes pierced mine even from that distance. For a bare moment, there was nothing but recognition, as if I'd known this man my entire life.

I'd never laid eyes on him before, but his brow furrowed as I snapped myself out of the bizarre sensation, giving me an acknowledging nod.

"Did you—" My jaw snapped shut almost involuntarily as I looked at Eilidh, because at the same moment, she simply said, "Jesus, did you *feel* that?"

Iain and Meeksy were close enough to hear us, and they gave us the same perplexed look, but Rhona was staring at Finn with an intensity that said *she* knew what we meant.

For that matter, so was Ealasaid. The cailleach's own blue eyes bored into Finn's back as he and the woman he was working with heaved the plank into a more orderly pile farther back on the beach where the next high tide wouldn't wash it back into the strait.

Scanning over the rest of the people gathered with us, no one else seemed to be reacting to Finn the way we had. Why just the four of us? I couldn't have explained it, had anyone asked, but out of the corner of my eye, I saw Rhona shake herself like someone had dumped ice water down her back.

She spun to look at me, a question in her eyes. I didn't know what else to do, so I just nodded at her with a shrug to say I had no more answers than she did.

Finn strode back our way, wiping sweat from his forehead with a bare arm as golden as his hair.

He closed the distance to us in silence, and even if the others with our party hadn't been as struck by his sheer presence as we had, he didn't have to give off an aura to be striking.

Iain and Meeksy, in my periphery, both wore almost comical looks of appreciation. They weren't gawping, but I knew them well enough to know that Meeksy's slight hike of his left eyebrow was like a cartoon character's heart beating out of his chest, and Iain scratched the back of his head almost bashfully. Iain was a brash brick of a bloke, but when he thought a boy was cute? Ha. He ceased to function. Bless his wee gay heart.

Ealasaid, however, was far less subtle.

"Well, aren't you handsome?" she exclaimed, followed by a low whistle. "Thighearna."

A ripple of nervous laughter filtered through the Oban folk and the locals alike, but Finn gave a good-natured chuckle and went straight to the old woman, leaning down—*far* down, because the man was as tall as me—to give her a kiss on the cheek.

Ealasaid turned as red as a boiled lobster, patting Finn on his own cheek as he straightened up. "Well," she said, sounding flustered. "Well."

"It's good of you to come," Finn said after a moment, making eye contact with me. "Our meeting is overdue."

His gaze moved to Eilidh, then to Rhona, then back to Ealasaid.

Yes, he most definitely had felt whatever we had. The question was what, exactly, that meant.

Finn gestured to a building that overlooked the strait. "Follow me."

I wasn't sure what I expected when we entered the building, but whatever that was, it wasn't what I got.

Before the ascension, I thought the building had probably been a terminal or office or something, but it had been remade at least twice—once into a crafting workshop and the second time a field hospital.

Most of the makeshift pallets were unoccupied now, thanks to ascension healing, but there were still four or five people lying flat and unmoving. Their chests moved with shallow breaths, and I turned a questioning look to Finn, who sighed.

He pointed to the healing scar on his cheek. "The kraken. Most cephalopods only have a beak in their mouths, but the ascension changed the game. It's got some sort of stinger or spine on its tentacles. I almost lost my head, and this lot wasn't as lucky as me. The spine's got some sort of venom—healers are struggling with it."

"You're up and about," Meeksy said, immediately going into healer mode himself.

"I barely got nicked." Finn's smile, a mirthless baring of teeth, didn't add to the crinkles at the corners of his eyes. He gestured to the nearest pallet. "Sue didn't realise there was venom in the stings and seemed fine until after the battle. Her cut healed over and sealed the venom inside her, and she collapsed an hour later, convulsing and literally frothing at the mouth."

"Jeezo," Iain said at the same time Rhona said, "Thighearna."

Finn pointed to the other beds. "Ailean's why we figured out it was venom—a tentacle had him wrapped up like a mummy, and a few of the mages managed to sever the end. The spines aren't just at the tips but embedded along the length of the tentacle."

A low whistle came from behind me, and I turned to see Angus shaking his head distastefully.

"Ailean had punctures all over him, but we couldn't figure out how he was so injured when his only broken bone was the arm." Finn's lips thinned as he pressed them together. "The others got infected when they were trying to get him free from the tentacle after it was severed."

This time, Angus did speak up. "We didn't see anything like that when it attacked us in Oban."

"Our only deaths were from drowning or being crushed," Catrìona added. "No punctures of this sort."

Silence settled over the room, broken only by someone's uneasy cough.

"It's changing," Eilidh said finally. "Just like we are—It's gaining strengths and abilities."

The sense of dread intensified. For a long moment, there was only the light sound of shallow breathing from those of us standing around and a high-pitched wheeze from Sue where she lay comatose.

"This meeting was most definitely overdue," I murmured. "We need to kill this thing, especially if the reason it's coming so close to our shores is that it's fleeing something worse."

Finn's attention snapped towards me so tangibly, I could almost feel a taut cord resonate like a plucked harp string. "You think that's what's driving it?"

"It's a theory," I said slowly. "That or the anom—"

I didn't have a chance to finish my sentence because the door we'd entered threw flew open so fast that it almost broke off its hinges.

The older woman I'd seen on the beach with Finn caught the door before it flew back to hit her in the face. "Iona," she said. "It's back."

Fuck a duck.

# CHAPTER
# TWENTY-SIX

As the ascended eagle flew, the sacred islet of Iona was a bare few miles away from Ulva Ferry. As the ascended elven humanoids could paddle or run? That distance might as well have been to the moon and back.

The ferry had been destroyed, but there were other boats in the strait that had been ascension retrofitted with arcane means of propulsion. Not many, but there were a few.

Even as we poured back out of the field hospital, the Muilich were on the move.

Finn sprang into action, and those of us from Oban, well, without knowing more, we stayed back so as to keep out of the way. The only thing worse than an urgent scramble was an urgent scramble tripping over ignorant wannabe "helpers."

Catrìona stood with Angus and Ealasaid, discussing distances, from what I could hear of their conversation over the sudden yelling from the Muilich. My own tension grew as I looked around. The other Oban folk who had come with us, Angus's wife Eliza and a handful of mages and crafters, all stood in a clump as if itching to do something as much as I was. Their eyes followed Finn and the older woman, who had herself an air of command that complemented the bàrd's rather than detracting from it. His own presence, though—Finn gave the impression of what I imagined of the ancient Irish hero Cú Chulainn.

"I hate just standing here." Eilidh's voice broke through my staring.

I could almost feel her heartbeat rat-a-tat-tatting out a skittering beat beside me. I'd say it was just my own, but *that* I had access to inside my chest, and the rhythms were just different enough to make me feel even more jangled.

The one thing I could think of doing to contribute—using Beannachd Slàinte to heal one of the people lying in troubled sleep—might be needed for someone who was far closer to death.

Falling into my customary pulses of Connection out of habit more than anything, I felt a jolt as my spirit caught a familiar presence at the farthest edge of my awareness.

The eagle.

She was somewhere just beyond Staffa, the islet formed of columnar basalt that lay on the far side of Ulva, obscured from my view.

I wasn't sure it would work, if I could even get her attention when Connection was usually like radar and not a beacon. But I had to try. I had to do something.

Here went nothing.

I concentrated on my spirit, teasing out pathos and will to weave together what I hoped was a delicate but pointed plait of magic. It didn't quite resemble Tàthadh, which would establish a bond with the eagle if she agreed, but it wasn't too far off, either. I wasn't trying to build such a bond with her; all I wanted was to get her attention and maybe her help.

Whether or not my attempt would work remained to be seen. I released my spirit with my next physical exhale, and in my peripheral vision, I thought I saw a head of golden curls twitch.

Finn didn't look behind him. He and the others were chattering into communication crystals, and on the other side of the strait in Ulva—clearly visible since it was less than a hundred metres from the Mull shore—someone gestured widely as a medium-sized boat pulled away from the Ulva pier.

Meeksy and Iain had their heads together as they spoke in low voices, but one glance at them told me they were just as focused on the commotion.

"What are we even going to do?" Rhona burst out. "Can we get to Iona in time to help?"

"We can always help, a ghràidh," Ealasaid said, moving away from where she'd been standing with Catrìona. "Though sooner would indeed be better than later."

Before the ascension, it was easy to watch the news and feel helpless. War in Ukraine, Syria, you name it. But that had always come with a certain level of dissociation when there wasn't much I could feasibly do to help aside from sending money to relief organisations. Here, knowing the kraken had struck Iona but being powerless to close the relatively small distance—that hit different.

Even as I thought it, Finn did turn this time.

"Anyone coming with us, get on the boat!" His voice boomed out through the tiny village with a timbre that jolted me.

Was that how I sounded with Òran na Cloiche? I didn't think it was the same ability as mine, but that was moot.

We all broke into a trot to get on the boat.

Finn clasped my shoulder as I stepped across. "Others will follow as soon as the next boat can get here."

He didn't have to explain that we *all* might be too late to do anything but tend wounded or search for the dead.

· ᴄ ᴄᴋᴊᴅ ᴐ ·

If standing around in Ulva Ferry had been bad, standing on the deck of this schooner was brutal.

I wasn't used to sailboats, and again, I didn't know enough to help, so my attention stayed fixed on simply remaining out of the way of the few people who worked on the rigging.

Sailean had remained in Ulva Ferry, which for once had been her own choice. Maybe she hadn't been as sanguine about the sea after all.

The one thing I knew was that it was *not* the wind propelling us out of the strait. There wasn't much wind at all, for one, but beyond that, the schooner cut through the water like a hot knife through butter.

Coastline slipped by us and then opened up into the wide bay that was Loch na Keal. Inch Kenneth appeared off to port, the flat island pointing the way out towards the sea.

There wasn't much to do but watch the southwestern ripples of Mull's ragged shoreline. My Mull geography wasn't great, but I knew Iona lay off Fionnphort on the Mull mainland, another short ferry that took people from the Ross of Mull to see the monastery and cloisters of the place Columba had brought Christianity to Scotland. The island had been considered sacred long before that, though. That the kraken had attacked there felt . . . significant.

It could have been coincidence, but with the ascension, anything was possible.

Mull was not a small island, but every minute that passed made it seem bigger and bigger. Iona was so protected that it wasn't even legal to bring your own car over without a permit. The thought of anything happening to any of our villages was bad enough; Iona felt blasphemous.

Religion and I'd never gotten on well, but regardless of what

I believed or didn't believe, I didn't have to be a believer to care. That was the thing about having empathy for others and the things that matter to them. Sometimes it's not about you; if something attacks a place any human holds as holy, it feels like an extra pointed affront. Mosque, synagogue, temple—it didn't matter which, when it came right down to it.

Iona was sacrosanct to many for a multitude of reasons that all counted, whether they were founded in religion or simply the island's special place in history. Or, hell, just because the beaches were pristine.

Despite knowing that my mind was trying to distract me from what we might see, it didn't prepare me for when we rounded the headland at Kintra and spotted a rising plume of inky black smoke.

"Is that the abbey?" Eilidh asked, her blue eyes narrowed as she tried to see what was still over a mile away.

"No idea." But even as I answered, I felt a tug on my spirit that rippled through me like wind in . . . feathers.

The eagle.

"Taing do dhìa," I breathed. "The eagle's almost here."

Not almost, as it happened—she appeared even as I turned towards Staffa, her silhouette breathtaking even at this distance.

A cry of alarm went up as one of the sailors spotted her.

"It's okay! I called her! She's safe—she's going to scout for us." From the uneasy chuckles and nervous looks that greeted my words, people weren't convinced.

Rhona's face crumpled for a split second in mortification; though the eagle had forgiven her for the unfortunate near-electrocution, I thought Rhona still lingered under the weight of guilt and shame. I gave the young lass what I thought was a reassuring smile, which she returned, albeit reluctantly.

She'd have to get over it. We needed the eagle's help.

Now that the enormous raptor was closer, I could reach out to her, which I did.

Her mind was focused on the task at hand. Despite Rhona's discomfort, the eagle showed no trace of anger or resentment through our delicate bond. It wasn't quite Tàthadh—I couldn't actually see through the eagle's eyes—but the eagle's mind fed me both impressions and images. Considering the deadly hunter she was, I was more than happy to defer to her assessment of the situation. Especially because while she did not hold any hard feelings against Rhona for the friendly fire incident, the eagle hated the kraken with a repulsion so visceral that when she called out above our heads, it was all I could do not to let out a piercing shriek of my own. Real eagles didn't sound like the films—my mum had always rolled her eyes and told me Hollywood used red-tailed hawks most often because eagles sounded less scream and more seagull.

An eagle this large, though—her yell was almost a roar.

The wind from her powerful wing beats rippled the sails and my hair, accompanied by more than one sharp gasp at her proximity. Then the eagle was past us, winging her way towards Iona's "Baile Mòr"—the big village that was anything but big.

My own breath caught as I saw the source of the smoke.

The mechanics and physics of combustion had shifted with the ascension. Someone had explained it to me, but all I really cared about was "car no go, gun no shoot." That didn't mean flammable substances ceased to burn.

From the deep, billowing black pouring into the air, something had sparked a fire and had caught petrol or oil or, hell, a pile of tyres.

And I could see the kraken.

The goddamn thing was almost completely out of the water.

It had crawled *up the pier*.

"Fuck," I said under my breath.

It was one thing fighting it from the water if its reach were limited by its need to be submerged. If the giant, Cthulhu-looking cunt had *gone for a fucking walk?*

"Calum, what?"

I realised Eilidh had had to repeat herself, because I was staring blankly past the now-visible white sand of Iona's most famous beach.

"The kraken's on land," I said, then raised my voice. "The kraken's on land attacking the village!"

"Right, then we'll smash it into unagi," Iain said. "It can't stay there long, can it?"

"I don't know, mate," I said at the same time Angus burst out irritably, "We don't know what it can do. It seems to grow new skills every time we bloody turn round."

Finn, who until now had been locked in conversation with the woman who'd summoned us, finally spoke up. "We can't assume it would purposely weaken itself that much. It would be foolish to believe it's so desperate that it will beach itself. That's far too much of a risk without cause."

The unspoken question—*what could cause it to take such a risk?*—hung in the air.

"What's the eagle seeing?" Eilidh asked me, and every eye turned to stare at my face.

With a pulse of spirit, I asked.

I regretted the glimpse immediately.

My stomach churned, and I held tighter to the rail. "It's grim" was all I managed to force out of my mouth.

If I hadn't stopped there, I might have boaked.

It had been bad in Oban, but it hadn't been carnage.

There was a difference—a stark difference—in a body that

died of a broken spine and a body that had been torn violently in half.

The image intruded in my mind of that poor, poor couple I'd stumbled upon when I was fleeing Glasgow. The beithir's work.

When I'd collected myself enough to speak again, I took a shaky breath, thankful that the wind hadn't yet brought us the stench of burning petroleum or whatever it was. All that met my nostrils was the scent of the sea and the tinny undertone of my own anxious perspiration.

"Prepare yourselves," I said at last. "It seems to have learned to strike for pain."

# CHAPTER
# TWENTY-SEVEN

We'd been expecting a sea battle.

There was no other harbour besides the one that was currently occupied by the kraken, which meant we had to get creative—fast.

The options? Option, singular.

There was no other harbour on the tiny island, nowhere we could easily disembark the schooner, no easily deployed rafts.

Which meant we had one real choice: jump overboard close to a beach, swim, and run a few hundred metres to join the fighters at the pier.

As far as plans went, it was by far the safest option for those of us who could swim, which was most.

The water was not warm when I hit it—not that I expected it to be. A shock of cold and salt to the face, and I was paddling for the small strip of white sand ahead.

The others followed, none of us concerned for the indignity of our manoeuvre. It was this or risk the schooner, and all it would take was a rogue kraken tentacle to render the boat useless.

At least we didn't have far to swim.

The narrow strait between Mull and Iona wasn't particularly deep, but I swam until the water was barely waist height to avoid a clumsy scramble through sand and waves, as much as anyone could.

A quick tug of Purifire dried me off. I waited just long enough to see that everyone was doing the same, and I took off at a run for the tiny track that cut across the field.

Eilidh was beside me, and a blur there and gone in an instant told me Rhona was already ranging ahead.

Connection gave me precise knowledge of where everyone else ran, from Ealasaid ten metres behind me to Finn bringing up the rear and swiftly gaining on my heels.

Above the Baile Mòr, the eagle screamed.

Purifire lit the air in the village as I vaulted the chained gate between me and the single-track road. Barely more than a track itself, it connected the smattering of crofts and houses along the eastern shore of Iona.

I didn't wait, only heard as metal clanged and the baas of startled sheep punctuated the sounds of feet thumping down on the road side of the fence.

After standing on the schooner and feeling helpless, relief pulsed through me at every pounding footstep. My body was ready to fight. Ready to defend this island as best we could.

Flashes of familiarity lit up my memory, times I'd come here with Mum as a wean. Sunrise over the abbey filled my mind even as my present-day eyes saw the ancient edifice of stone framed by sickly smoke.

Only a few hundred metres.

Rhona wasn't the only person who was faster than us; Finn ran like Cú Chulainn himself, and a few of the other Muilich blurred past as we ran.

It didn't matter that all of us could have crushed a pre-ascension Olympic sprinter; every step might as well have been through rib-deep mud for the way it felt achingly slow.

Then the smoke hit.

The wind had picked up, blowing in from the west off the North Atlantic, but even though the smoke tilted midair to buffet Fionnphort across the strait in Mull, the moment we entered the village proper, my nostrils flared with the acrid assault of burning fossil fuels.

That was nothing compared to the screaming.

When we finally turned down the final wee road past the Iona Craft Shop and their wee Spar, we saw the source of it.

I'd heard of canny octopuses in aquariums around the world getting bored and letting themselves out of their tanks to treat fish displays like an all-you-can-eat buffet. The creatures would mosey on out for a snack on dry land—or floor—and then head back home after they'd eaten their fill, leaving the aquarium keepers scratching their heads at the missing fish, at least until they checked the CCTV. So I knew that certain cephalopods could survive out of water for a time.

But I would have expected one this size to struggle more with the increase in gravity. It was one thing to be the size of the fucking Iona nunnery ruins when you were under the sea— it was something else entirely to manoeuvre that kind of bulk on land.

But it was doing it.

By every creature great and small under the Ascended Alliance, the kraken seemed to have shucked off all earthly constraints and assumptions of physics.

It looked like half octopus, half Lovecraftian nightmare. Its enormous body had already swallowed the carpark at the mouth of the pier, and its skin rippled both with movement and colour as it continually shifted itself to look like the tarmac or the beach grass or the rock-dotted sand. One mahoosive tentacle wrapped around a metal shipping container, the corrugated steel crumpling and bending where the kraken flexed its strength.

The smoke rose from a flaming drum, and a few people who weren't directly engaged with the fight were trying to smother it by using Spèird or something like it to dump great gouts of sand on the fire.

It didn't seem to be working.

I tried not to look at the bodies. Some were practically pulped; others looked whole until you realised they were missing their entire bottom half or that that rope of seaweed draped over their neck wasn't seaweed at all but their own intestines.

More than one person stumbled to a halt and vomited on their own shoes. It only took me a heartbeat or two to take all of that in, but that was a heartbeat longer than we had.

"Do anything you can to disable it!" I roared. "Go for the eyes, the tentacles, anything—even if it can grow them back, make it work for it!"

Even as I said it, I had Brac-Meanmna in my hands, and I threw myself into the fray.

The kraken's eyes—those, I hadn't even seen, but the monster had heard my voice, and I saw a ripple of shiny, still-wet flesh as the beast moved.

Along with the ripple of its enormous girth shifting across the concrete beneath, I felt a tingle of something else.

Recognition.

Even without seeing me, even without further contact, I suddenly felt down to my marrow that this creature knew beyond any doubt who I was—and that we'd met before.

Before I could react, Rhona began to shriek.

It had been a while since I'd heard what that slight, teenage voice box was capable of, but nothing I'd experienced before then could have prepared me for the noise she unleashed.

Rhona's scream struck like a physical blow, if the very air could attack from every possible angle at once. Cries of alarm rose around me, barely audible over her siren that blossomed into an ultrasonic vibration that I thought could cleave the atoms of my body apart like a nuclear bomb.

My impression wasn't accurate, but that was only because I'd gotten hyperbolic. The reality was almost as terrifying.

I'd seen the damage wrought by the kraken's inlaid spines; even now, they quivered up and down every single one of the creature's monstrous appendages. Far more than the usual eight, this thing may have begun as an octopus, but it had long since left such simple geometry behind.

Counting could come later. For now, staying upright against the onslaught of Rhona's preternatural voice was all I could handle.

The kraken's spines? Those were not up to the task.

At first, I thought they were merely quivering with discomfort. The spines, thousands upon thousands of them, slowly lifted from the monster's twitching flesh like a dog raising its hackles.

Maybe it was the pulse of Connection that I now did reflexively, but all at once, my mind recognised a pattern in the vibration.

The spines moved not only *with* the resonance of Rhona's shriek but *because of it*.

The image of a million champagne flutes humming intruded into my mind, and not a moment too soon.

"Get back!" I bellowed as loudly as I could. "The spines are—"

The spines began to explode.

At first, it was like tiny hisses of escaping steam, barely

audible over the banshee wail, but as Rhona's shriek continued, it quickly became louder until it sounded like someone had punctured a house-sized pressure cooker thousands of times.

I had no shield like Meeksy did, but I improvised.

Finn and a handful of other fighters were in my range, and I threw out a net of Spèird and Purifire with as good a combination of haste and care as I could manage at such short notice.

Venom from the spines sizzled as it hit my net. All around me, I heard shouts of alarm even as I felt swirls of spirit where others threw up barriers, shields, or whatever they could to protect themselves from the sprays of vicious venom.

Not everyone was successful.

A scream erupted on the other side of the kraken. Then another, just a few metres from me where someone had taken an arc of venom to the face. It burned her skin like sulphuric acid, and those fortunate souls who had narrowly avoided the same stared in horror.

I cast Slànaich as fast as I could, but the woman was already going into convulsions. Finn reached her in a lightning-fast leap, pulling her to the side and as far out of range as he could.

A scrabbling sound, muffled, vibrated the concrete beneath my feet.

It filled me with dread. I couldn't pinpoint it, but I also didn't have time to try. Rhona's shriek was dying off, and sprays of the kraken's venom as well as needle-sharp spine fragments littered the ground. The creature shuffled its enormous bulk, and it twitched as Purifire raced up and down its tentacles.

I joined the onslaught as acrid smoke poured into the air, this time not a result of the barrel of fuel but because of the venom.

Which was flammable.

*Very* flammable.

"Try not to breathe the fumes!" I yelled the words without

thinking, only flashing back in my mind to my short-lived chemistry studies when someone had once forgot to turn on the extraction hood and nearly asphyxiated the entire lab.

Mages summoned the wind to blow it away from us in the only direction that wouldn't immediately damage the village or wildlife—up.

I searched the sky for the eagle and saw her circling near the abbey, her presence grim in my mind.

"We've hurt it!" Eilidh's voice cut through the air. "We need to finish this—now!"

I locked eyes with her. Lightning hadn't been hugely effective before, but on land, maybe fire was our best weapon. Weaken it. Dry it out.

On the far side of the kraken, I could see Rhona and Ealasaid. Next to me and Eilidh was Finn, a polearm in his hand and looking every inch the golden warrior of old. And someone else —an old man with brown skin and sharp dark eyes, his aged body dressed only in the simple robes of a . . . monk?

I wasn't about to ask questions, not with time slipping away.

"Purifire, as much of it as you can!"

We'd gotten lucky, or as lucky as we possibly could, in that the kraken had to have overextended itself very literally by dragging its sorry arse onto dry land.

And Rhona's sonic attack had obliterated its spines and hurt it; the kraken's flesh twitched with pain.

So when I felt an unfamiliar tendril of spirit extend towards me like an offering, I flung my own to meet it, taking a full step backwards as I realised Eilidh, Rhona, Ealasaid, and Finn were doing the same.

The old monk—it was he who had reached out, and now those six tendrils of spirit wove together like rope high above the huge hump of the kraken's body. It formed a wheel-like net, filling my head with the surreal memory of playing parachute as a wean where each panel of the parachute was a different colour to form the spokes of a fabric wheel that billowed in the wind as we flapped it.

This didn't billow.

It burned.

Spirit rushed through me and out of me, swirling through the channel I'd created to combine in a seething maelstrom of flame that rained down upon the seaborne creature's vulnerable flesh.

The scrabbling sound returned, along with the squelching of sticky flesh, and I recoiled as I realised what it was that was hitting the concrete, buried under tonnes of kraken.

Its beak.

Cephalopods had a beak, razor sharp and deadly. The beak of a normal-sized octopus could cleave a clamshell with ease; on the kraken? It would have been able to snap steel cable like dental floss.

It grated against the hard tarmac of the street, then shifted —the kraken was fleeing!

"Keep the fire on it!" Eilidh's voice strained with the effort.

My own spirit drained quickly, too quickly, and heat buffeted me where I stood.

The monk was the first to move; he stood between the kraken and the water, and he grimly pulled back to one side, Finn's side.

This left a gap, and I couldn't blame him. With every passing heartbeat, the kraken moved metres. We weren't going to kill it before it hit the water. Not by a long shot.

More Purifire poured onto the kraken around us, and I smelled cooking flesh, briny and sharp and touched with the bitter tang of the monster's vaporised venom.

Then, all at once—or so it seemed, anyway—the kraken hit

the sea and with a splash and a wave of fighters diving away from one last lash of tentacles, the kraken was gone.

Again.

My ears rang with the remnants of Rhona's shriek, and the release of tension nearly turned me into a puddle where I stood.

Someone was squawking loudly—maybe someone who'd been hit with the venom.

But no, the sound was closer. Like right on top of me.

Not someone here.

Half flinging Brac-Meanmna onto my back and ignoring its swirling mix of triumph and indignation at the kraken's retreat, I snatched my communication crystal from the pocket on my chest.

"—lum, can you hear me?"

I didn't recognise the voice. "I hear you! We just got out of battle with the kraken. Who is this?"

"Moira," said the voice, which explained why I didn't recognise it. "I—we need you to come home as fast as possible."

Any relief I'd felt vanished. "What happened?"

The kraken was here, which meant it had to be something else.

"It's Ronald. He—he did something with the anomalies. Alison's been corrupted."

# CHAPTER
# TWENTY-EIGHT

"We'll come to you," Finn said to me as the the Oban folk piled back onto the schooner, which had moored at the pier in Iona after the eagle's confirmation that the kraken had gone out to sea. "Bheir mi an cat ann."

Sailean, of course, was still in Ulva Ferry. I hated leaving her in Mull to return to Oban, but this couldn't wait. Knowing she'd be with Finn at least assuaged some of my fears.

"Ceud mìle taing," I said to Finn. I'd forgotten he had Gaelic, but I ought to have remembered.

"We're going," Angus called out from the deck of the schooner.

"We'll get to Craignure before first light and sail with the sun," Finn told me in English, loudly enough for everyone to hear. "And now we've got the . . . rockie-talkie network, so we'll be in communication."

My soul left my body at the word *rockie-talkie* and from the small explosion of adrenalin-fuelled laughter that bubbled over both the schooner deck and the pier, that new name was going to stick.

"Aye," I managed to say. "We'll beat this thing yet."

I don't think I sounded half as confident as I'd wanted to, but my mind was understandably occupied.

"Beir buaidh," Finn said, slapping me on the shoulder.

The phrase meant, very literally, birth victory.

Everyone else was already aboard the schooner, so as soon as I crossed the gangplank, the sailors sprang into action casting off lines.

I didn't know how long it would take us to make the crossing, and with the sky darkening above us, it would be slower. One look at Eilidh told me she was in full screen-time mode, and I had to admit, that sounded like the best possible distraction.

When was the last time I'd gone through all my notifications? I suddenly felt like that *Titanic* meme. It's been eighty-four years.

Unsurprisingly, there was a veritable mountain of them. Between my training and sweating that felt like it had happened a decade ago, the various battles, craftings, and the instalment of Craobh an Òbain in McCaig's Tower, going through everything might indeed take the entirety of our voyage.

For expediency, I dismissed all of the minor increases and quickly allocated all of my attribute points. I'd gone up three levels somehow, and I figured the bigger notifications—the anomalous lynx among them—would cover that, but it still came as a bit of a shock to see the leaps when I'd finished.

Name: Calum Green

    Age: 36

    Level: 24

    Class: Draoidh (Further class specialisation at: Level 27)

Affinities: Nature (Level 19), Healing (Level 7), Synthesis (Level 11), Staves (Level 17)

Specialised Affinities: Wild (Level 11), Coimhearsnachd (Level 5)

Marks of Esteem: Life, Connection, Justice

Alteration:
Strength: 39
Dexterity: 54
Agility: 57
Mind: 113

Regeneration:
Constitution: 39
Stamina: 71

Manipulation:
Spirit: 111
Pathos: 45
Will: 51

Boons:
Blessings
Làmh na Glaistige
Glòir a' Ghiuthais

Blàr Ghaineamhain

I'd almost forgotten about the active quests, and now I couldn't avoid it anymore. Dread seeped through my bones as I read.

*Quest updated: Blood From a Stone*
*The destruction of the anomalous lynx provided you with further information about how the anomalies are changing alongside the ascended world.*

I had to stop there and reread that first sentence. The word choice seemed significant—"alongside" the ascended world, not "within" or "in"—and I didn't like the strange accompanying sensation of the anomalies existing somehow parallel to our world without being truly part of it. If that were the case, the implications were far above my pay grade.

The thought almost spiked my heart rate even higher, but then I took the deepest breath I had in what felt like days. It wasn't my job to fix everything. That was the entire point of the ascension, right? If something was outwith my own capabilities, maybe it would be within someone else's. Community over solipsism.

Remembering that gave me a small amount of comfort, and I read on.

*The destruction of the anomalous lynx provided you with further information about how the anomalies are changing alongside the ascended world. Some seem to have developed the ability to utilise spirit-driven spells and skills, as have the usual shifts in indigenous flora and fauna.*

*With the arrival of the glaistig, she has confirmed also that the originating entity of the corruption is aware of you and your community—and has warned you about the danger.*

*That danger has now been realised. In Ronald's examination of anomalies, a young woman (Alison) has been infected with the anomalous corruption. You must seek out further information by any means necessary if there is to be any hope of saving her life or her mind.*

*Will Grayson and Ezekiel Bosworth III discovered that the corruption is not immediate, nor is it total.*

I stopped there again to reread.

The use of "infected" also felt significant to me, and the last sentence heavily implied that Ezekiel, the poor sod, had not been lost on the spot. What was the word for diseases that slowly took over and progressed? Degenerative. Like Parkinson's or multiple sclerosis or Alzheimer's. All of them began with small symptoms and crept up on the patient until they became debilitating or fatal.

If—and this was a big *if* I'd have to trot by others with less of a himbo hamster brain—that analogy was truly a hint, it also implied that the corruption didn't completely erase the person.

Alzheimer's might seem like it did, but that disease worked by developing masses and breaking down the pathways, not eliminating information stored in the neurons themselves, if I was remembering correctly. It was closer to taking a puzzle, throwing it in a box with some children's blocks, and giving it a shake every now and then until everything was well and truly muddled together. The whole puzzle was still in there, but now bits of it would be stuck into a DUPLO and the corner pieces would lounge on top of something in the centre.

All of those degenerative diseases were nightmarish, cruel in their banality.

It should have been a gut punch, and it wasn't *not* a gut punch—but it had the opposite effect on me than I'd expect.

It gave me hope.

In an ascended world, we'd seen people *healed* of MS, of Alzheimer's, of cancer. The same cancer that killed my mum, gone in a day.

If something of Ezekiel remained even now, maybe—just maybe—we could dump out that box, sort out all the DUPLO from the puzzle pieces, and start putting him back together.

And Alison? Alison. What if we could make sure the box didn't get shaken?

Resolve snuck up on me, overtaking the dread.

I wasn't certain of anything; I was still a fairly himbo-esque hamster, as it were. But I was also a stubborn cunt, and Alison deserved our best. I didn't know what Ronald had done, but a nagging feeling lodged itself into my gut like a burr, hooked spines nestling in deep. Whatever he'd done, I wasn't gonnae like it.

Snapping myself back to the quest, I read on.

*This has become an evolving quest.*

*Objectives:*

*-Create Purification Cages to house any captured anomalies (Complete)*

*-Capture three different species of anomalous animals (Complete)*

*-Explore further uses for Purifire*

*-Examine the remains of the conduit anomaly (Ronald) (Complete)*

*-Contain the corrupted person (Complete)*

Oh, fuck that.

The thought of Alison in a cage made me want to vomit. If it was already done, it was already done, but I didn't have to like it. She may have been a bit naïve, and yeah, maybe she'd made me a wee bit uncomfortable with her doe eyes, but she was a good teacher, a good person, and I had to hand it to her—when her crush hadn't worked out, she'd simply straightened her back and got to work. That alone was more than most folk could handle.

We owed it to her to do whatever we could.

*-Assess the effects of corruption on Alison*
    *-Seek out other examples of corruption in sapients*
    *Rewards:*
    *-Experience (commensurate with current level progression)*
    *-1 skill point*
    *-1 item (ascension dependent)*
    *-Blood From a Stone: Part II*

Swearing under my breath, I shuttled that notification off to the side.

Most of the rest of the notifications were mid-level stuff that were useful to know—Brac-Meanmna could now store small amounts of spirit that I could tap into in an emergency—but not immediately applicable.

In the back of my mind was the increasing knowledge that I was going to have to leave Oban. That, paired with the presence of the kraken and knowing that Ronald had done a cock-up big enough to result in an innocent person's corruption did not make me eager to plan any outings. Even if we managed to get the Ionad-Siubhail up and running to allow us to teleport, even if we used our—groan—rockie-talkies to perfect effect, even if we killed the kraken tomorrow, there would still be enough threat to make me uneasy.

We were getting stronger. That was without any doubt. As a community, as a people, as individuals.

It didn't mean we'd survive.

Just like an individual couldn't go it alone in this new world —even Bawbag had been fully, ironically dependent upon other people until he gasped his last breath—I was starting to think that the same went for communities.

It was obvious, really. Even just looking at it from a reductive, simulation-game level, if you needed lumber and only had rocks but the people over yonder had quarries and no trees, you had to figure out a way to trade.

I also didn't think going about it the Earth way would work, with each group just trying to look out for their own and pull one over on the others. No, not against the anomalies and whatever had spawned them.

What I needed right now was to organise my brain.

Our biggest threats in order of immediacy were the kraken, the corruption, and the source of the anomalies. Somewhere beyond that was whatever that gobshite in Dundee was up to, and at an unknown immediacy level, the possibility of bigger monsters in the depths of the North Atlantic.

Out of all of them, the kraken was almost a relief in that we could see it, measure it, and fight it, even if killing it felt nearly impossible. The beithir had once felt that way too. The kraken had evolved venomous spines, and Rhona had exploded them. If it could adapt, we could too.

But the kraken was still unpredictable. Two attacks in a day, and who knew how quickly it could recover?

No, as far as priorities went, haring off to fight something we both couldn't find and didn't know how to guard against felt like a numpty move.

We'd stay in Oban for now, using what time we had to strategise on the kraken and learning about the corruption. By the time we did go off to find the source of the anomalies, we'd hopefully have enough information that we'd have some sort of weapon against it.

In theory.

I hoped.

Was it a good thing that the kraken hadn't pinged a quest? Digging through the rest of my few notifications, I found the lack of a kraken quest somewhat disconcerting. Did the system not consider it that much of a threat? Thighearna, that would be unsettling.

I didn't want to know what could make the kraken quest-level worthy of alarm.

My mind spun through other possibilities. If we prioritised the rockie-talkie network and getting travel points up and running, that would make any number of things easier. Cast a net for intelligence gathering, connect with other communities, you name it.

That thought solidified as I read through the ascension equivalent of headline news—global notifications.

• ( ◟☙◞ ) •

*World first!*

*In Fukuoka, Japan, there has been a community ascension that has combined with a legendary feat. The historical site of 17<sup>th</sup> century Fukuoka Castle has been designated as a sanctuary of Kyushu Island culture, language, contemplation, and knowledge. As such, the castle shall be a haven from all violence and a beacon of learning for its people.*

*For demonstrating reverence and non-violence towards their community to honour their history in the face of unexpected ascension, those involved have been awarded the following:*

*-Blueprint: The Resplendent Throne*

*-Blueprint: Spirit Well*

*-Blueprint: Communication Beacon*

*These blueprints can be shared with other communities for the betterment of your ascended world.*

My breath caught in my throat. At first, I couldn't tell if it was indignation that they'd gotten the same rewards we had after killing Bawbag or annoyance that rewards were repeated, but after a moment, I shook my head ruefully.

This was *good* news. I still didn't know what the throne was, but the spirit well? The communication beacon?

Those things meant something vital: *we could reach out to Fukuoka, on the other side of the planet.*

I scanned through the rest, feeling hope burgeon in my chest. Fukuoka wasn't alone. Maasai people in Tanzania had somehow purified bloody *Lake Victoria* in the African Great Lakes. Nyanza, as it was called in the local Kinyarwanda language, had long been a water source for the highlands of Eastern Africa between Kenya, Tanzania, Uganda, and the Democratic Republic of the Congo, but the ascension had given the people what they needed to enshrine it into legend. The second largest lake on Earth, apparently, by surface area—now it would do far more than hydrate.

The list kept going; no continent would be unreachable. Not even fucking *Antarctica*, whose international community of isolated scientists had, of all things, built their own communication beacon without a bloody blueprint. A legendary feat in itself.

By the time I snapped out of my screens, feeling almost drunk with what had to be the euphoric antithesis of the pre-ascension doom scroll, the schooner had just rounded the northern tip of Kerrera and skimmed into Oban's harbour.

I'd almost—but not quite—forgotten what we were returning to.

For all the hope my notifications had beamed into my brain, it didn't change the immediate danger as reality crashed back into the forefront of my mind.

# CHAPTER
# TWENTY-NINE

O f all the things I thought a corrupted person would say from the confines of their cage, Alison's "It was my idea to be in here" was not on the list.

She still seemed lucid. Or *was* lucid, rather.

Alison had preempted my question the moment I walked through the door into the newly constructed room where her cage sat, as if she knew I'd be outraged at the thought of a person in a cage. Everyone should have been outraged, but I'd learned long ago that human beings were far too good at justifying such things for me to assume.

"You're sure?" was all I said in response, even as Eilidh opened and closed her mouth beside me, her eyes fluttering shut at the same time.

When Eilidh opened her eyes again a second later, she echoed my question. "We might be able to think of another alternative."

Alison just shook her head. "This is the safest way."

From the way she said it, she had reason to *know*, not just to suspect that was true.

Eilidh glanced at me, which was all the confirmation I needed to know my guess was likely right on the mark.

The room wasn't crowded, but it also wasn't empty. A few lower-level mages lurked in a corner, ostensibly tidying up crafting materials they'd used to build the cage—we hadn't had anything person sized, that was for sure—but mostly eavesdropping. Beyond them, it was me, Eilidh, Ealasaid, and Meeksy. The biggest and most notable absence was Ronald.

"Would you excuse us?" I said pointedly to the gaggle of unfamiliar mages.

They ranged from Rhona's age to probably Catrìona's, but they all jumped like guilty schoolchildren at the edge to my voice.

"Aye, we were—we were just leaving!" The speaker was a lad with maybe a year or two on Rhona, but his voice sounded like it might crack every now and again.

I waited until they'd bustled all of their supplies into their inventories—which took some shuffling around and increasingly urgent whispers from the older members of the group—and once they were gone, I let out a breath.

"Are you all right?" I asked Alison. "Before you tell us what happened—are you all right?"

"No?" The young woman cracked a small smile as if she'd made a joke. "From a scientific perspective, it's kind of fascinating to observe first hand, but I'd really rather not."

This time it was Eilidh who let out a long breath through her nose, and her auburn head nodded at the young science teacher. Ealasaid said nothing, but Meeksy started to walk towards Alison, only to stop when she put up a hand.

"Don't get any closer. The mages were going to put down a line on the floor"—Alison gave a self-deprecating smile—"but they didn't get a chance before you arrived."

"It's that contagious?" Meeksy asked, frowning. "Proximity is—"

"No, no, no," Alison cut him off hurriedly. Her smile turned tighter to the point that her lips grew pale around their edges. "It doesn't seem to spread with droplets or anything, and it's not airborne like COVID was. It's more like a venom, for lack of a better explanation? Transfers with skin punctures. Like a bite or a scrape. We don't know why. So just being in the same room with me shouldn't make it spread. It just that the cage isn't great at containing my extremities. I can get a hand out, and, well."

"What did happen, a ghràidh?" Ealasaid asked gently. "Ronald's lack of presence here is conspicuous, to say the least."

For the first time since we'd entered the room, I saw a flash of anger light Alison's brown eyes.

"Ronald devised a—a lead, of sorts," she said. Alison licked her lips once, twice. It looked reflexive but strange, out of character and nowt to do with anxiety.

Hunger. The movement looked like hunger.

My skin began to crawl.

Alison was going on, seemingly oblivious to what her face was doing. "He thought he could restrain the anomalies outwith the cages, that if he got them out, they'd be easier to study." She paused, this time with her lip curling with distaste. "Like a dog at the groomer."

"That," Ealasaid said, "does not sound smart."

"Did anyone tell him not to do this?" Eilidh asked, with what I recognised as a valiant attempt to keep her tone mild.

"Everyone," Alison said, licking her lips again. "He didn't listen, and I stayed with him to at least make sure it didn't go too horribly wrong."

You could have bounced a haggis off of the taut, tense

threads of irony that stretched out between the five of us in the room.

"I'm going to kill him," Meeksy said, surprising all of us, if the way the rest of the group all turned to stare at him. "It's the equivalent of handling blood you *know* is contaminated with bare hands and open wounds and just being like, 'Oh, I'll wash them when I'm done.' We went through years of a literal pandemic. This is not something that requires a degree in medicine, for fuck's sake."

Meeksy was, often enough, fairly meek. Or maybe not meek, but quiet. A sleepy bear of a man, with his thick black beard and his rich brown skin and rumble of a laugh. But he was also the child of refugees, had put up with way too much bullshit because of his combination of Iranian looks and Glaswegian accent—not to mention his fluent Gaelic—and he'd inherited both tenacity and zero tolerance for fuckery from nature *and* nurture levels of life. Plus, he was a nurse. That took all the rest and turned it up to eleven. You didn't fuck with a nurse.

This, with Ronald?

Aye, that was some class-A fuckery that would tick all of Meeksy's boxes. Ignoring safety measures? Tick. Putting an innocent in harm's way? Tick. Escaping unscathed whilst said innocent got harmed? Tick.

"I think studying me will be punishment enough," Alison said after a long pause. She hesitated for a moment, then stepped back as far as she could in her cage and pulled up the bottom of her shirt to expose her midriff. "This isn't pretty."

I felt the blood drain from my face.

It was one thing to see the anomalous animals with their suppurating sores and living rot. It was something else entirely to see it on a person—worse when it was a person you knew.

Just a puncture, she'd said, and it seemed that truly was all it was.

"What happened?" Eilidh asked, her eyes glued to the spiderweb of sickly dark lines snaking out from a point on Alison's left side about halfway between her hip and lower ribs.

Alison let her shirt fall again. "Bird pecked me."

"What?"

Ealasaid had inched closer to the cage but prudently remained more than arm's length away, and she gestured at Alison to lift her shirt again, which the lass did.

"That's it. As stupid as that," Alison confirmed, holding her shirt in place against her ribs with her elbow so Ealasaid—and now Meeksy, who'd ventured closer—could examine the strange wound. "He had one of the starlings hooded and teth-ered by the foot, and he asked me to get something from the shelf above his head. It was in the main room at the bothy; we'd put up shelves to store crafting materials since they wouldn't be affected by the anomalies. I reached up, and he must have let his grip slip on the tether or something, because the bloody bird shrieked and pecked at me. At first, I thought it had just gotten my shirt. I was wrong."

It was so—so *stupid* and human. I might not murder Ronald, but we were going to have words. Never mind his guilt; there was being a bit of a numpty and there was treating a corrupted and dangerous flying creature like some medieval laird's trained fucking falcon.

On second thought, I really might murder him.

Meeksy seemed to be heading along the same railway line as me, thought train going chug-a-chug-a-choo-choose-violence.

I knew him too well to be surprised by how level he managed to keep his tone when he opened his mouth again, but even so, his words were unexpected.

"Ronald's not getting anywhere near you again, love," Meeksy said to Alison. "I don't care that he's been the main person to study these things for the past few weeks. He's going in fucking time out. *I'm* taking over. And you better believe me when I say that we will find a way to fix this."

Ealasaid nodded with an alarming amount of savagery. "We will, m' eudail."

For all that, it was to me that Alison looked, licking her lips as if she hadn't heard a word they'd said.

I could only stare back, sickness spreading in my core as if her very gaze could pierce my skin and infect me from across the room.

Even though I knew beyond any shadow of a doubt that Alison herself would not wish me harm, as she licked her lips one last time, it wasn't Alison at all behind those brown eyes.

It was the thing trying to devour her.

I had to fight the urge to shake myself like a dog when we finally left the room. Ealasaid and Meeksy stayed behind, and Eilidh and I started walking back to Oban. Her hand worked its way into mine as we picked our way through the darkness, her fingers cold and tight interlaced with my own.

It was as if I could feel her thoughts pressing against my mind, darting back and forth between *What are we going to do?* and pure, unbridled rage.

Before we'd left, in the brief few minutes I'd managed to remain in Alison's presence after she tore her gaze away from my face, we'd at least established that she would—to the best of her ability—chart the progression of the corruption. It would be very useful data to have, of course, but there was a major problem.

We'd have no way of knowing whether the data itself was

corrupted. I hadn't wanted to say that in front of her myself, not with the way she'd been staring at me like her jaw was about to unhinge and swallow me hole, but she had been the one to say it herself. She was sapient, and so was whatever had infected her. That meant intelligence, and that meant it could try to manipulate us. It could already be trying to manipulate us. I would have been shocked if it wasn't, to be honest.

Either way, up until the point a recognisable Alison ceased to exist—or at least retreated from our reach—she would give Meeksy reports, and he would also generate his own, as would a select group of other healthcare workers and scientists. He'd already identified people he wanted us to commandeer in Oban.

"I thought it would be awful, but I also thought having a plan might, I don't know, help me feel less helpless," I muttered to Eilidh as we approached Oban from the south. "Instead I just want to scream."

"I know what you mean," Eilidh said softly. Her hand squeezed mine a little tighter. "Did you read all those notifications? The global ones?"

I had a feeling I knew where her mind was headed. "You think they might be able to help if we can contact them? *They* being . . . literally anyone, I guess."

"To be honest, I was mostly thinking they deserve a warning."

Oh.

The thought made me queasy, because she was absolutely right. "They really fucking do."

"What happened with Ronald can't happen again," Eilidh said then. "Just—no way."

"Not just his asinine attempt to treat the anomalies like his very own pet freaks on a leash, and not in a wholesome Kornfan way," I said under my breath. "He's kept way too much to himself all this time. Everything we find needs to be subjected to scrutiny and confirmed as best we can—"

"Peer-reviewed anomaly study," Eilidh said mirthlessly.

"—and disseminated as widely as possible. They might not be in the line of fire yet, but we also might be too close to see an obvious answer." I shut my mouth with a click of my teeth. "Gods, I hope there's an obvious answer we're just too close to see."

"Forty-two."

"If the answer is forty-two—has anyone *tried* forty-two?" I snorted. "How would we even go about trying forty-two?"

Eilidh's chuckle felt far too brittle to be making light of the situation. "No bloody clue."

She was silent for a moment, but then she shook her head, her silhouette bobbing in the darkness.

"One thing my dad used to say that, you know, wasn't actively harmful, was that the bigger the problem, the bigger net you had to cast to find the solution. Not sure where he got that idea, but considering he was the king of 'my way or the highway,' it had to be something he learned the hard way." Eilidh squeezed my hand once more as the lights of occupied houses ahead up Soroba Road made her more than a silhouette. "If the first thing we do with the reinstatement of global communications is this?"

I gripped her hand back just as hard. "It's worth it."

Dawn was beginning to light the sky, which meant Finn— and Sailean—and the other Muilich would soon be sailing our way.

We needed three places at least three kilometres apart, if I remembered correctly, to begin the Ionadan-Siubhail.

Connecting us with our friends in Mull so they wouldn't

have to sail kraken-infested waters until we could kill that thing?

Aye, that was a good bloody start.

First the islands. Then we'd spread the net as far as it could go until we caught our answers.

# CHAPTER
# THIRTY

I onad-Siubhail

*Your human concept of borders died with the ascension.*

*Ascension Champions are able to collaborate in order to designate a specific location as an Ionad-Siubhail. Once at least three Ionadan-Siubhail have been established at points at least three kilometres apart, the network may be activated.*

*An activated network allows instantaneous travel to any connected Ionad-Siubhail.*

· ⟪ ⟫ ·

Staring at the thing didn't make it less intimidating.

Eilidh had left me to go take a shower, and while I was sorely tempted to join her, I didn't trust myself to do that *and* still be functional when Finn arrived with the dawn. Which meant I was standing in the crafting area, the former vehicle queue for the ferries, thinking about teleportation.

As much as I had expected people to be all over this skill, only about ten percent of Oban's Ganavan veterans seemed to have spent the three skill points to unlock it. Anyone who'd fought at Ganavan feasibly could access it; it was part of the Ascension Champion skill tree, a reward we'd received with our victory. Ten percent wasn't *nothing*. It meant we did have a decent number of people who could establish an ionad-siubhail, but since it was the middle of the night—or, more accurately, the wee hours of the morning—no one was about to whom I could fling that question.

From the first glance at the ability, it seemed like ascension crafting, but after unlock, it had gained an additional paragraph of text to complicate matters.

Considerably.

Most germane to our current predicament was one weaselly little line, and while of course I understood the reasoning behind it, it made my life more of a pain in the arse, and therefore I didn't like it.

The deflating paragraph, in its entirety, was this:

*The locale for an Ionad-Siubhail must meet a number of criteria established by the Ascended Alliance to promote peace. 1. Location must be undisputed and in sapient control. 2. Location must be accessible to land-dwelling and amphibious sapient beings—including their young—and safe to access. For example, an Ionad-Siubhail cannot be established on a rock that would be covered at high tide or require climbing to reach. 3. Location access may not be restricted. In the event of violation of these criteria, the Ionad-Siubhail will be disabled until criteria are met once more.*

The bit that was giving me trouble was the "must be undisputed" bit, because I wasn't sure what that meant. Did that mean if another Bawbag came trundling out of the woodwork to attack, our entire travel network would shut down? Or did it just mean an invading force couldn't access them and if someone from within our network tried to use them in a coup, *then* it would shut down? And how would it know? How did the system know anything?

I was in full agreement on the rest; even though many physical disabilities and restrictions had healed with the ascension, not all had, and I'd be damned if I let folk miss out on the magic of bloody *teleportation* because they used a wheelchair. Like, come on.

The message was clear: travel was public, free, and open to all. If it was built on community networks with community power, it was for the community. If someone learned to make their own farts into a methane-powered jetpack, they could toot their way to Tibet alone for all I cared, but what we needed was efficient and safe transportation for everyone.

*Could we even do it?* That was the question.

I read the whole thing again, then again.

Finally, something seemed to click. *Your human concept of borders died with the ascension.*

It wouldn't say that if "undisputed" meant there could be no squabbles at all. At least I didn't think it would. I could almost feel the light bulb illuminate above my head, cartoon style. It had to just mean you couldn't throw an ionad-siubhail into the middle of a battlefield. For whatever reason, to escape (which could endanger people on the other end if you were followed) or to teleport in reinforcements (rude).

Satisfied that we could, at least theoretically, do the thing, I dug into the itemised list of requirements.

Beyond the basic criteria, there was a quest-like enumeration of necessary items to gather for each and every ionad-siubhail we wanted to craft. Most were the same items—spirit-infused stone, spirit-infused wood, a crafter who could engrave a signpost—but others were location based. Specific to the location rather than specific items already listed. Stone or wood from within a three-metre radius of the ionad-siubhail's location, or in cases where there was neither, sand or clay. It boiled down to *something natural from the location itself*. That aspect made me think of spell craft, symbolic but given a purpose.

In an ascended world, maybe all the things we'd whispered over the centuries really would come to life. If our mythological creatures—and extinct ones, for that matter—could turn up on our doorstep, why couldn't folk magic also work?

That was a question for another time.

For now, I needed to snap out of it and find locations for the ionadan-siubhail.

The first thought that lodged itself in my head? The Tesco carpark.

Our crafting area and sparring area had taken up much of the harbour's immediate surroundings, and with the kraken still a threat, anything that needed the designation of "safe" had to be out of tentacle's reach from the sea. Granted, as we'd seen in Iona, the damn thing could and would heave itself up onto dry land, but that was easier to do in Iona than in Oban.

With cars' materials repurposed and the few that remained intact virtually extinct, the carpark had been used mostly as a thoroughfare. A market had sprung up within Tesco itself, the superstore's aisles and shelves long since raided and requisitioned by the community, but the carpark lay empty.

The sky was brighter now with the approach of the sun, and Finn would likely be on his way from Craignure even now. Even knowing that, I decided to scurry over to the carpark just to check it out.

It was just a couple streets inland from the harbour, and as I'd thought, it was almost entirely empty. And huge. The carpark now carried the faint whiff of obscenity with it; its purpose rendered moot, it just looked dead, and Joni Mitchell's voice in my head helpfully sang a few bars of "Big Yellow Taxi" to emphasise the point.

That was a bit too on the nose.

For all the surreality of the chunk of pavéd paradise, I found myself nodding.

Wide, accessible, flat, open. Sea level, unlike McCaig's Tower, despite the unsettling illusions that made that place easier to reach.

The only problem was that I didn't really think tarmac would count towards the location-specific requirements. A smile tugged at the corner of my mouth as my gaze fell on a darkened hummock in the pre-dawn dim.

No tarmac, but there was a hedge planted in the median at the end of a row of parking spaces.

Hawthorn. Indigenous wood.

We had somewhere to start this thing.

True to his word, Finn arrived with the dawn.

Let's just say the sun breaking over the hills to the east to bathe the man in gold did little to dispel my previous day's first impression that he looked like a god come to life. It seemed to light up his hair from the inside, the honey-coloured curls practically glowing.

It was probably good Iain was asleep, because if *I* was staring, jeezo.

I wasn't the only one, either—of *any* gender. This damn man had managed to drop jaws across the entirety of the early-morning Oban populace. Maybe the godawful hour lowered inhibitions, because folk outright stared.

Honestly, it was kind of a relief it wasn't just me.

And Sailean, the cheeky wee thing, was perched atop his shoulder like she belonged at sea. I'd half a mind to ask her if she'd decided to ask to become a parrot.

I knew the exact instant the kitten saw me, because the

little ball of emotions and spirit in the back of my mind lit up like, well, the morning sun hitting Finn's inhumanly beautiful golden hair.

She ignited pure commotion in her adolescent kitten mewling as the yacht—the very one we'd made the journey on yesterday—coasted breezily into its berth. No sooner had the mooring lines hit the wharf than Sailean had launched herself from the bàrd's shoulder and tight-roped across, hit the ground running, and parted the waiting gawkers like Moses in the Red Sea as she barrelled straight at me.

I caught the wildcat midair when she leaped at me, pulling her against my chest with pure, unfeigned relief.

"Och, mo chreach, a ghaoil. Bha sinn gad ionndrainn!" Yes, I had become an unabashed cat dad. Get tae fuck if ye don't like it.

I *had* missed the wee fur ball, and having her back made me feel like I could breathe a little deeper.

"Off on her ane adventure, eh?" The voice was familiar, and I turned to see Sammy, the dark-skinned woman who'd arrived with the Weegies.

Oh. Right. I'd forgotten about the swingers.

"She's one for that, aye," I said to Sammy hastily.

My hamster brain couldn't keep up with everything that was happening, but thankfully, Finn was making his way ashore, and that was a distraction on every possible level.

The appreciative murmurs lapped through the crowd like the morning waves against the wharf, but I immediately sobered as Finn drew closer.

"Thanks for looking after her," I told him earnestly, giving Sailean a hearty scratch behind the ears to the music of her rattly purr.

"She's a special wee thing," he said with a small frown. "There have been rumours of a wildcat or two in Mull that swam across from Ardnamurchan, but I've never seen them myself. Never thought I'd see one up close."

"How's Iona?" I asked, aware of the press of people crowding around us.

Finn glanced at the onlookers, looking unsettled.

"The kraken attacked this very harbour not long ago," I said. "You can tell them."

The Mull Bàrd swallowed, for a moment looking less like a Grecian Adonis and more like the floundering thirty-something I was myself. I gave him a tight-lipped smile that I hoped was reassuring, and he took a measured deep breath.

"Fourteen dead, three unaccounted for and presumed dead, another four stabilised. We've got healers and mages working on antivenin. Thanks to Rhona and Eilidh, we've got samples enough of the venom to study." At my questioning look, he gave me a lopsided smile that didn't reach his eyes. "Eilidh lopped off part of a tentacle with that monster sword of hers, and Samuel—the monk—had the presence of mind to chuck it into his inventory immediately to study."

Samuel. "Pass on my thanks to him, please."

"You can tell him yourself. I expect he'll be on the next boat over from the island. He needed to stay to look after his people, but he said he would follow once he was assured the kraken was gone." Finn paused, glancing around at the faces surrounding us. "Your eagle friend paid me a visit—she's the one who sounded the all clear."

Looks of awe had turned to horror with his recounting of the casualties, and any star-quality lustre seemed to have faded with the brine and blood. But the eagle brightened eyes again.

"Have you rested at all?" I asked Finn, fully expecting his answering head shake that confirmed he had not. "If Samuel is going to make his way here today, I think we should all get some rest and regroup. I've a couple ideas I'd like to address with you, and having Samuel around means Iona is also represented."

I hadn't seen Rabbie coming up from behind us, but he waved a weathered hand in the air, drawing my attention through the crowd. "We've got Ulva folk here too."

"And Coll!" called a voice from further down. "Tiree's here too!"

My eyes met Finn's with a flash of understanding. "Perfect—this—this is good. Someone who slept last night, can folk take charge of getting someone in from Kerrera and Lismore? Hell, Lochaline too, if it's possible."

"We've got rockie-talkies in Salen and Lochaline both," Finn supplied. "We'll send it down the relay."

"Scarba, Colonsay, Luing, Jura?" I asked. "Islay and Gigha might be too far to reach in a few hours, but—"

"Leave it with us, Calum." Catrìona had snuck up on us from the town side of the pier; she must have just woken up. The crowd moved aside to let her through. "If we can reach Jura, we can reach Islay and Gigha. Eigg and Rum might be a stretch, but this is a start no matter what."

I had to stifle the sudden tightness in my throat.

"It's a start," I managed to choke out. "Once we can reach them, we can reach Skye and maybe even over the Minch. Faster than going overland, maybe."

The Uists. Barra. Harris. Lewis. Gods, the folk out there must have felt marooned. Or, hell, maybe they were doing just fine, enjoying a springtime without tourists, romping through the white-sand beaches without the buzz of a handful of drones broadcasting to Instagram.

No. They might appreciate the landscape, but no one would have paid the steep price for the peace and quiet—not when it cost the planet blood.

We'd get there again. Our world would come back together. If it started with our islands . . .

For a moment, I couldn't breathe, and it wasn't the lack of sleep. Sailean purred louder in my ear where she'd nestled in the crook of my neck.

"Aye." Catrìona reached my side and gave my shoulder a squeeze. "Take Finn and the Muilich to get some rest. Come back down at noon, and we'll start bridging the waters to our islands."

# CHAPTER
# THIRTY-ONE

My mind raced so much that I barely managed a couple hours of sleep before I had to get up again. Eilidh was nowhere to be found—her bedroom was empty—and I had the house to myself.

The Muilich had all been given rooms in the Perle, which was somewhat amusing since it was a literal hotel, but for the people who'd been caught out in Oban without a way home and didn't feel comfortable requisitioning a vacant house for themselves, the hotel had remained a staple.

I couldn't shake the feeling that something was eluding me. Something important. Something we needed.

Tea first. I could think better caffeinated, right? Aye.

I put the kettle on to boil, absentmindedly dropping a teabag into the biggest clean mug I could find—as if I couldn't just Purifire any dish in the kitchen clean. Gods, the ascension had saved all future generations of children washing-up duty.

The one thing I hadn't taken care of on the journey back from Mull and Iona had been my skill points. I had nine skill points to use. Whether exhaustion or a gut feeling that I should hold onto them, I wasn't sure. Now, though, I thought it might be a good idea to look into the Coimhearsnachd skill tree.

It was the community skill tree both in name *and* function. Maybe more trees like it would open up down the line, but for now, it was the only shared skill tree I knew of. Each unlockable skill, blueprint, or bonus required multiple points to open. That was how we'd made Oban into a sanctuary—the keystone skill had been the first major advance for us after Blàr Ghaineamhain. Once we'd crafted and placed that, we were protected. Kids could play in Oban's streets without fearing incursion from beasties.

I frowned as that thought turned over in my head.

Our keystone hadn't stopped the kraken from attacking from the water. Why?

We'd placed the keystone at Argyll Square, at the centre of the roundabout where the A816 met the A85. It had seemed prudent at the time—central, accessible. There was a monument in the middle of a ring of small palm trees, and . . .

I pulled up the information about the clach-cheangail, the keystone.

*Clach-Cheangail allows for the creation of a keystone which, when placed in an existing community, will provide said community with a limited area invulnerable to attack. This can be used to protect the most vulnerable among you as well as serving the purpose of a repository of communal knowledge.*

"Limited area" was the salient point there, but how limited was it, exactly? The kraken had attacked at Ee-usk, a couple hundred metres away. That, apparently, was answer enough to my question. I wasn't entirely sure how we would test it, other than catching some sort of beastie and turning it loose in the centre of town to see what would happen. Or I could use Keen Eye on it.

While the kraken had attacked at Ee-usk last time, that

didn't mean it would do the same a second time. Argyll Square was less than a hundred meters from the bay at high tide. I'd put this on the list of things to find out as soon as possible. The kraken could only go so far inland, presumably, but a wide open area—invulnerable or not—would put our highest-risk people in full view of the damn thing. "Alive but deeply traumatised by front-row seats to vicious sea monster battle" was less than ideal for weans.

Unsettled by our collective oversight, I took a deep breath as my kettle boiled, breathing in the steam and pouring the hot water over my teabag.

Once my tea was sorted, I grabbed a stack of oat cakes and some cheese and sat down at the table, pulling up the Coimhearsnachd tree.

I almost spit out a mouthful of oat crumbs and cheddar when I saw the next skill, which required a whopping eighty-one points to unlock—and it was immediately evident why.

*Cumantas*

*With combined effort expended for the common weal, Cumantas adds to the benefit of working together.*

*The radius of protection from Clach-Cheangail increases by one hundred metres from the base fifty.*

I winced at that. Fifty metres. Ouch. That left at least twenty or thirty meters of no man's land between the protective space and the sea, but it also meant that our "invulnerable" area was literally wide open and indefensible. The thought of children huddled in the centre with an army of anomalies slavering at the boundaries? Nope. Nope, nope, nope. This needed attention.

Recriminations could come later, I guessed. Ugh. I read on.

*Those designated as Tosgaire na Coimhearsnachd gain the ability to direct others' spirit.*

I had to stop there again, my mind whirling. Samuel, the monk in Iona.

He had done this. He'd directed our flows of spirit into Puri-fire to make that net, and he'd done it without a thought. This had to be what he'd used to do it. I'd ask him when I met him officially, but I was already sure.

The bloody monk in Iona, a tiny island with barely a hundred fifty residents, had not only managed to get his community to unlock this shared skill tree, but they had also poured *how many* points into this? The root-level passives were three points a piece, but Clach-Cheangail was twenty-seven, and this was a further eighty-one. Clearly, this was exponential, but a hundred seventeen skill points from barely that number of people?

Fewer people now, even. The thought stopped my breath in my throat. Fuck.

I took a drink of my too-hot tea, ignoring my scalded tongue. We'd avenge Iona, whatever it took. They'd lost ten percent of their population in one day.

If I let myself think about that now, I'd never get through the rest of my necessities. Taking a deep breath, I forced my brain to do less personal maths. Points and people.

Points and people.

Okay, it was really only about one skill point per person in the end, but it made Oban's folk look positively miserly in comparison. The Scrooges of the ascension. I half expected the Ghost of Christmas Past to start pounding on the door to the back garden.

We were at about sixty points into Cumantas as it was for the Oban community, and I couldn't help the flush of embar-rassment that heated my cheeks. One of the things we'd need to talk about this afternoon was perhaps gently encouraging people to give this tree a wee look. There were several thousand people in Oban, for fuck's sake. We could do this with twenty of them levelling up. Especially once folk hit level ten and started getting three skill points per level.

Part of me was glad my own points couldn't make the difference alone this time.

It wasn't that I wasn't willing—hell, I'd chuck all nine of them into it without a thought—it was really just that this was a community. I'd already used a proportionately huge chunk of my points to unlock the last one. With six thousand people or so? Aye, they could chip in.

I still needed to finish reading the damn description.

*All communication crystals created within the radius of the Clach-Cheangail will function at a distance of an additional ten kilometres.*

Fuck me, we needed this.

My own skill points could wait. If I needed to bribe people by sacrificing my points on the altar of Cumantas, I'd do it—if we were going to rally the islands, I'd lead by example.

Maybe just the willingness would be enough to convince folk, if they needed convincing at all.

I closed out of my screens again and tugged on my bond with Sailean, hearing a sleepy "Prrow?" from the lounge, where at this time of day, a small beam of sunlight would cut across the floor.

Sure enough, when I made my way into the room, there she was, sprawled on her back with the sun warming her exposed belly.

I resisted the urge to put my face in it. I liked my face attached.

"Come on, you wee gremlin," I said to her fondly. "We've got a Hebridean council to form."

·ᐧ ⟨⟨ ﴾⟩ ⟩ᐧ·

Those had been perhaps the worst possible words I could have chosen.

You know what council meetings are like? Ever sit through the annual general meetings of a community organisation? Have you ever decided you'd rather die a death by a thousand paper cuts on your loins instead?

Aye, I asked myself that last question about fifteen times over the course of the afternoon.

There are some people who *live* for admin work. I applaud those people. We do actually need those people.

I am not those people.

A pair of middle-aged men and a very eager woman a bit older than them had positioned themselves at a table in the corner of Ee-usk, and they dutifully scribbled down everything anyone said. We hoped the choice of venue proved prudent. If the kraken showed up, the enormous windows weren't exactly tentacle proof. On the other hand, we should have warning enough to get out before we got impaled on venomous spines or shards of glass as long as my leg.

The view, at least, was serene. Blue sky, blue bay, some wisps of clouds. Moored at the wharf, I could see Birlinn an t-Seann Ghiuthais, which filled me with a slightly irrational annoyance that it wasn't being used. No one really wanted to risk it with a kraken on the loose, this mythic item, but I reckoned we'd have to eventually.

The room was crowded and warm. My core group plus everyone we'd taken to Mull with us, the entire Mull contingent of ten or so people, a handful from Lismore, Kerrera, and Luing, somehow a pair of representatives from Jura, Scarba, Coll, Colonsay, *and* Tiree—the restaurant was as packed as I'd ever seen it, and the default setting of Ee-usk during the dinner rush was *sardine-tin full*. The windows steamed up every now and then before someone would go nudge open a door to let the breeze through, which was always a welcome refresher.

I clung to wakefulness with desperation. One cuppa had stood zero chance against drowsiness, and the rousing emotion of Finn's arrival and talk of bridging the islands with magic had dithered into doldrums of recounting the ascension's day to day.

Don't get me wrong—it was good to know everything. We needed an accurate, current picture of what we were working with. But dear gods, I was not cut out for this. My brain wires fizzed and panicked in the face of processing auditory-only information. Podcasts had been my arch-nemesis pre-ascension. Sound passed through my eardrums and became noise. I was lucky to finish an episode of something with so much as vibes. No brains.

My ears finally pricked up when someone said my name.

Low bar, but in my current state, it was frankly a miracle I even heard that.

"Aye," I said, hoping I'd not only caught my name at the tail end of a question that'd flown through my skull unnoticed.

Small mercies.

"You think we can craft the ionadan-siubhail?" This came from Eliza, Angus's wife, whose English accent shifted to painstakingly rehearsed Gaelic for the ionadan-siubhail, bless her.

"We can, absolutely," I said. I turned to Finn, glancing at Samuel as well. "Is that a skill you all have as well?"

I didn't expect they did, because it was one of the ones we'd only accessed due to—I had to rummage in my screens to double check—the Mark of Justice we'd received for dispensing with Bawbag. It was impossible to say for sure, and I hoped maybe they had pulled off some legendary feat of their own, but their blank looks quickly removed that optimism.

Giving them a quick rundown left a room full of wide eyes.

"Why haven't you mentioned this before?" Finn burst out, and for the first time, I saw the man start to splutter.

Samuel's face remained as placid as the morning waters, but one eyebrow hiked a millimetre or so in what I assumed was displeasure.

Eilidh, thankfully, saved me. "They take resources, and a fair amount of them. One person is all it takes to activate the skill, technically, but unless they can fit a tonne—literal—of building materials into their inventory and haul it to the site themselves, they need help."

"The ascension does like teamwork," Finn said dryly.

I nodded. "It also requires crafters to help. From what I can understand, each is not only keyed to the locale with a signature of indigenous substance but also the hands of those who make it. There's a good number of folk in Oban who fought at Blàr Ghaineamhain and spent the three points to unlock the skill, but even then, they can't do it alone."

Angus surreptitiously unfolded his lanky body and got up to open the door again. I sucked in a cooling breath of sea air with disproportionate gratitude.

That gave me the strength to talk them through the special requirements, which caused no little amount of consternation, but after a few exasperating attempts to get everyone to quiet down, I sighed.

"You can probably understand why we haven't managed to get our ascended ducks in a row on this one, yeah? Between the kraken and the anomalies"—a collective shudder passed through the room, and I paused; Alison had been one of the major topics of discussion—"we've been in survival mode."

"We could stay in survival mode just reacting to threats as they come at us," Eilidh said then, "or we could get organised. The ascension keeps rewarding us for working together. If we're just scattered communities, no matter how tight knit, we're still vulnerable."

Samuel nodded, touching one calloused brown hand to his heart. He still wore the rough-spun robes belted with a length of rope. "It pains me to say it, but yes. We ought to have reached out sooner, before we lost . . ."

Silence filled the air where he trailed off.

He looked at me, dark brown eyes boring into mine, and once more, I felt the strange sensation of falling, of recognition. I didn't think this was a skill—by the way he twitched, he hadn't done anything any more than I had—and it had to be significant.

On the far side of the room where she'd stood leaning silently against one window, Rhona had an off-kilter expression on her face, like she was feeling it too. A brief pulse of Connection illuminated . . . something.

Wisps, as fine as a spider's silk. They trailed between us—between me and Rhona, Eilidh, Samuel, Finn, stretching back to Ealasaid who sat somewhere behind me.

Six of us, connected. It wasn't Samuel who'd done it, either.

"And?" Eliza prompted us, breaking whatever spell we'd all been under.

All over the room, the six of us jumped collectively—noticeably.

A chuckle, uneasy, followed.

"Where do we start?" Finn brusquely pushed past the awkwardness.

"Where hungry souls dare not venture unless they're seagulls," I said, my voice dryer than a month-old oatcake. "The Tesco carpark."

# CHAPTER
# THIRTY-TWO

There was no hope of corralling everyone we needed so quickly, but the decision had lit a fire under everyone's arses. We needed that fire.

Gods, we needed that fire.

I seized the moment before everyone dispersed to bring up Cumantas.

"If we can spread the word that we need to unlock Cumantas on the Coimhearsnachd tree as soon as hu—elvenly possible, that'd be grand." I gestured to Samuel, whose head had turned away from a murmured conversation with Eliza to look at me when he heard the word. That alone was confirmation enough. "Iona has a population a fraction of a fraction of Oban's, and they've managed to unlock it already."

"We're seventy points into the next one, too," he said with a wink. "Just, you know, to give you lot a push in the right direction."

My mouth opened and closed like a fish before I could stop it. "Right, aye, he's just put us tae *shame*. Rally the troops—this is just proper embarrassing."

Finn, however, grinned. "See if you can catch up with us.

Tobermory's onto the, what, fourth skill? Salen's at the third, so's Craignure, and Ulva Ferry's—"

"We get it, we suck," Rhona said, rolling her eyes dramatically. "We've been fighting disgusting rot monsters over here."

That seemed as good a time as any for me to yeet myself out of the stuffy restaurant. Even with the door open constantly, the afternoon sun pouring in from the west made it a sauna with what felt like a hundred people breathing their sticky, steamy breath everywhere.

"Fancy a date to the Tesco carpark before everyone else gets there?" I murmured in Eilidh's ear as I passed her.

"Ooh, baby, you know what I like," she answered, then as we snaked through the throng and escaped into the much-more-breathable pier, she gave me a worried look. "You know that was a joke, right? Tesco carparks aren't, like, my real turn-on. Not to kink shame or anything, but—"

The laugh that escaped me was more like a gasp. I was just thankful it wasn't a snort. Her nose was crinkled up like a bunny's and actually twitched with distaste.

"I promise you, Eilidh," I told her, "if I had to guess your kinks, supermarket carparks of *any* variety would not be in the top thousand."

"Good." She recovered with a dazzling grin, her teeth flashing almost gold in the sun. "Besides, if you want to know my kinks, you can just ask like an adult."

With that, she took my hand and pulled me towards the least private place in Oban.

Damn it.

Any lascivious thoughts evaporated when we got to the carpark. If the sight of tarmac and oil stains wasn't enough, it was also filling with heaps of people, and on my own *personal* list of kinks, exhibitionism lay somewhere below "doing it in a pit of cockroaches."

I was pretty sure I'd had some very nice dreams turn into nightmares that way—and I'm not talking about the roaches. There's being caught naked in class without having done your homework and there's getting caught in flagrante delicto with your crush at uni where grading your performance *is* the homework everyone's doing.

No, thank you. Nope.

Thinking stupid thoughts was pretty much my deepest ingrained distraction technique. A pathetic himbo hamster special, as it were. Manual labour was another one, so when Eilidh and I spotted people coming over from the crafting centre with the materials we needed, we both hurried to help.

Before too long, we were ready, except for the indigenous wood.

For that, I needed to do my draoidh thing and make friends with the tiny tree.

The hawthorn was only about waist height. It hadn't been pruned in the weeks since the ascension, and without getting spewed with car exhaust and churned-up antifreeze when it rained, the little shrub was the happiest it had ever been. It was practically giddy.

There was no way I was going to ask it to sacrifice its life for us—not when things were just getting good.

Instead, I sat down on the kerb next to it and simply listened. I'd not yet met a tree that could be called a chatterbox, but this wee hawthorn about fit that bill.

As the crowd gathered and Eilidh directed the crafters, I let the shrubbery talk itself out, sensing that it would eventually get curious about what everyone was doing there breathing on it. Not that it wasn't grateful, mind.

I showed it what we were wanted to do. All I had in my mind was a vague picture, since I couldn't be certain what the end result would look like exactly, but what I tried to convey was a sense of movement, joy, connection. Like a root system, but for us flighty folk who ran about on two legs without roots.

At first, I thought the hawthorn was showing exuberance out of pure excitement on our behalf, but then I caught the gist of its eager thoughts and had to laugh when it posed a tentative question: would there be other trees like itself in the new places we wanted to connect?

This hawthorn was young; that's what I was picking up on. It wanted to know about the world, and though it was part of the ecosystem here in Oban, it was marooned on a small island of earth in a sea of tarmac. Its root system connected to to the trees across the carpark only barely, with the help of mycelium.

Trying to reassure the plant as best I could, I showed it images of Mull and Iona. It greeted these offerings with amazement and curiosity—and on a wave of earthy insistence, the hawthorn returned an offering of its own.

Awareness crept into my mind as people around me took notice of what I was doing. The crafters readying to make the ionad-siubhail busied themselves with far more active and obvious work, but people had more senses than the previous five—or six, depending on who you asked. Now, the base number of senses *was* six, and in their awareness of spirit, the onlookers could tell I was every bit as busy as the crafters.

Tapping into my own well of spirit, I slowly fed it into the hawthorn to help it along. Its channels sucked it in like the roots would pull water from the earth, and just like the water would strengthen it, bolster it, the influx of spirit rushed in to seek out weak spots. Places damaged by the fumes of human pollution, bits where spatterings of oil had then overheated in the sun, torn branches at the hands of bored children—spirit poured in like a soothing salve.

A crack broke through my concentration.

The hawthorn's roots had flexed beneath the concrete kerb that surrounded its enclosure, and the tarmac had given way. I ignored the startled looks from the folk gathered round me and instead concentrated on coaxing the shrub to finish what it had started.

I knew it had something important to offer us. Eagerness filled me.

Gasps tickled at my awareness, but I ignored those too. The hawthorn was almost done. I had the silly mental image of a four-year-old concentrating very hard on an intricate piece of macaroni art, tongue stuck out between their lips as they painstakingly glued elbow-shaped pasta to colourful paper.

When it was done, it was a far cry from paste and dried carbohydrates but every inch as heartfelt.

I reached out to take the offering with gentle reverence, thanking the hawthorn with a tendril of spirit it returned with a visible wiggle of its branches.

Chuckling, I examined what I held.

The shrub had had enough nearly dead branches that it had been able to rework the wood into a gift. In my communion with it, I must have shown it how we needed to start with three possible ionadan-siubhail, because it had given me a threefold present.

Sort of.

I held in my hands a spiral triskele, a pattern well known to anyone who's ever set foot inside a Scottish tourist shop. The reason it was so ubiquitous, though, was that the design— three spirals turned in the same direction like a windmill's cloth-covered blades, a three-pronged wave always moving and never breaking—had been carved into stone across the breadth of Scotland and beyond for literal millennia.

This one was even more special, because each individual wave fitted at the centre into the other two like a woodworker's puzzle. Instinctively, I knew they were meant to detach; one would stay here, and the other two would go to Mull and Iona.

"Mìle taing," I murmured to the hawthorn.

If a bush could preen, this one would have.

I was impatient to get underway with the creation of the ionad-siubhail. Eilidh and Rhona seemed similarly antsy—Rhona fiddled with a very sharp dagger, oblivious to the wide-eyed gaggle of weans staring up at her—but neither of them said or did anything to hurry us along.

Because my spirit had been depleted by my funnelling it into the hawthorn, I sat on the kerb with the triskele in my hands and focused on my breathing, cycling spirit through my channels. It came more naturally now, but part of me wanted to hop up and get within the small radius of our keystone where it would recover faster.

The faces around me had grown familiar even if I didn't recognise everyone here. It left me with a sense of kinship, of home. In Glasgow I'd been so mired in my own bullshit with Susanna—gods, she felt a lifetime away now—and the capitalist grind that I'd kept to myself. Most city folk did. I'd forgotten that isolation wasn't natural to humans. No wonder social media had been so popular; humans were desperate for connection.

Something tickled at my mind again, but just as I thought I was finally going to grasp it and understand, Angus called my name.

"Calum, we're ready."

Getting to my feet, I straightened my shoulders. I felt Sailean a short distance away—with Iain. She sure loved him. Probably because he enabled her chaotic kitten urges.

The crafters had indeed been busy. I'd been so wrapped up in what I was doing that I'd missed them literally peeling through the tarmac, for fuck's sake. They'd cleared about a ten-metre circle that bystanders had blocked from my view, and a quick worried glance told me that at least it was within the required three-metre radius of the hawthorn's wee enclosure. Otherwise, my work would have been for naught.

The circle they'd created dug a crater into the carpark, and into that, they'd piled what had to be a full tonne of stones. Electric anticipation zipped through the air, and though most people stood silently waiting, I heard more than a few excited murmurs.

"This is just one step," I reminded everyone wryly. "Like a bridge to nowhere until we get the others in place."

Laughter filtered through the crowd.

The crafters came up to me when I beckoned them, five in total. I tried to make a mental note of their names—Amer, Ceitidh, Vic, Charlotte, and a man who looked like an anvil and called himself Nug—but I wasn't sure they'd stick.

To my surprise, Samuel made his way through the crowd with Finn at his side.

"We'd like to help, if you'll let us," Samuel said, gesturing at the rock-filled crater. "It takes spirit-infused materials, yes?"

At my nod, he made a small noise of assent.

"I also have access to that skill, but Samuel is more deft with it," Finn told me. "He's been using it to restore the abbey in Iona."

I blinked at that. "We're happy for the help—and the demonstration. We'll all benefit from this, if we pull it off."

Eilidh came up beside me, and she didn't have to say anything for me to hear the implied *We need to get on with it*.

There was no way I was going to make a speech, so instead I gestured to the crafters and to Finn and Samuel to join us.

"What do you need from us?" I asked Samuel.

He nodded at the crafters. "Ask them."

Nug and Amer exchanged a glance, but it was Ceitidh who spoke up. She reminded me a bit of Iain's mum, but a decade younger. Short blond hair that stuck up all over her head like straw, green eyes.

"Can you feed the spirit to us directly? It's easier for us to have it to work with rather than explaining to you how to do what we've learned. No offence." She added the last two words with some haste, scrubbing a hand across the back of her head.

"Of course," Samuel told her with a warm smile. "We don't want to fill your kitchen with too many cooks."

Ceitidh breathed out an audible sigh of relief at that.

"I will act as a funnel," Samuel said to me and Eilidh and Finn. "For you all, it will be like it was in Iona."

That had felt as natural and instinctive as breathing.

Right. We could do this.

"Let's build ourselves a bridge."

CHAPTER

# THIRTY-THREE

No matter how long I lived—and by ascension's best guess, that would likely be a bloody long time—I didn't think I'd ever really get used to magic happening right in front of my face. Crafting that turned a pile of stones into mouldable, pliable material. Engraving that happened in reverent silence rather than the buzz of machines. I didn't think I'd ever really get used to how it felt when spirit connected me to not only the earth beneath my feet but everything alive within and above it.

Once upon a time, I'd gotten very high and gone to the planetarium at the Glasgow Science Centre. Such things could be trippy experiences *sober*, and I'd thought the cheerful Weegie astronomer leading the show had been kidding when she said all exhibitions came with a wee existential crisis, but she had been one hundred percent chock-a-block full of earnest intent.

It was a catchy spiritualist tool to say that we are made of star stuff. It's also literally perhaps one of the most basic truths of existence.

Every atom in our bodies, every particle, every bit of energy within us was forged itself in the heart of a star.

Spirit connected me to that truth more clearly than

anything ever had—not only were we made of star stuff, but, even more simply, we *were the universe*. The universe alive, the universe breathing, the universe capable of looking around in wonder and thinking about itself. The universe falling in love over and over again.

As my spirit flowed through me with every breath lighting up channels I'd never thought really existed, Samuel took it into himself, a living vessel. The old monk moved in a meditative trance opposite the circle from me, reminiscent of qigong masters in his fluidity, and through him, the crafters got to work.

Stone may as well have been clay in their capable hands. They shaped it, first into an enormous lump at the centre of the circle, then smoothing it out, letting gravity pull it flat and level to spread itself across the prepared space.

Someone, at some point, had drawn a perfect circle within that crater, and the stone stopped there as if hitting a wall. Three of the crafters, equidistant from one another, crouched as one and gathered pliant stone between their palms.

It was strange to see Nug, the humanoid anvil man, move with such gentle grace. His counterparts were Ceitidh and Charlotte, and all three of them manipulated the clay-like rock with control.

Watching them in awe, it hit me that while they made it look easy, they were still bearing the weight of stone. They pulled it from the mass at their feet. Each time they crouched it was more like a squat. They lifted with their legs, backs straight and protected, and after several minutes of this, sweat beaded on their brows and upper lips.

I wasn't sure who started it; maybe it was one of the mages behind us or someone who simply thought this was a super intense leg day for the trio of stoneworkers building us a miracle.

A breeze began, a gentle swirl filled with the tang of salt from the bay. It whispered through the crowd and washed over my face.

I'd begun to sweat as well, which I'd not even noticed. The wind cooled me immediately. A collective sigh stirred the air in our little circle.

Charlotte and Ceitidh and Nug continued to draw the stone upwards bit by bit.

I lost track of time while we worked. Shadows changed and lengthened as the sun began to dip towards the horizon; at this time of year, that meant it was getting on towards eight or nine at night. Even though we were sharing spirit and using passives to both increase regeneration and pull from the environment along with our own wells, it was starting to take a toll.

My muscles felt like I'd just run an Iron Man, and even though I could see physical progress happening—the triune arms of stone now met over two metres above an intricate plat-form of quartz-dotted grey stone—I was a hairsbreadth away from whinging, "Are we there yet?"

And then we were.

There.

The crafters released an enormous, heaving breath, and the tug of my spirit ceased. Samuel took a half step, almost stumbling. Ealasaid caught him by the elbow before he toppled into the circle, which still lay a slight dip beneath the tarmac.

I was up.

Pulling the triskele from my inventory, I stepped into the circle.

When we learned spells by unlocking spaces on our skill trees, it was strange how the information and knowledge downloaded into us, like instinct.

The crafters had done their part; now it was my turn.

My foot touched the moulded stone, half expecting it to give beneath my weight like clay. It didn't. Instead, it was as solid as it should be. I stepped into the centre of the platform, under the three branches of arcing rock that met above my head. Connection helped me find the exact middle point, and it was there I laid the triskele.

Triggering Ionad-Siubhail, the ability, felt just like any other spell I might use, but unlike other spells, that was only the beginning.

The triskele began to spin like a child's top, perfectly balanced. The stone around it glowed gold, flickers of quartz refracting back the light like glitter. For one absurd moment, I thought that if the stone arches had been covered with a roof, the inside would have lit up like a disco ball.

When the triskele slowed and finally stopped, it lay in its own delicate circle, studded with mica and quartz. One wave-like spiral had embedded itself within the stone. The other two sat loose, and when I picked them up, I saw impressions in the rock.

A smile sneaked onto my face.

The hawthorn—wee scamp.

Three ionadan-siubhail, one triskele. Clearly, it wanted us to complete the puzzle.

As if thinking of it had alerted the shrubby tree, the hawthorn tugged at my mind, and my smile grew to a grin.

I got to my feet, exhausted and a little dizzy from watching the spinning triskele. I tucked the two other pieces back into my inventory and glanced at the awestruck crowd.

"It's done. Can someone fetch me two wee pots filled with good soil? The hawthorn wants to send a cutting of itself to Mull and Iona where it can see the other platforms."

I thought it was a mark of how the ascension had changed us that, aside from a few snorts and giggles, the only reaction was a flurry of movement as folk scurried off to get me containers for us to transport our wee foreign exchange hawthorn.

The eagle was waiting for us when we were done with the ionad-siubhail.

I barely had a chance to appreciate the enormity of our handiwork before her ear-piercing shriek made everyone jump and duck at the same time—an unusual and absurd combination.

Even though we were all aware of her existence, our lizard brains hadn't gotten the memo. Or maybe they were just smarter than the conscious bit in the driver's seat. There could very well be an entire population of enormous eagles who had every intention of eating us.

This was our friend. We really needed to give her a name.

She landed a moderate distance away from the crowd, as if as wary of us as we were of her, and I tore myself away from the ionad-siubhail to pay my respects.

If the eagle had come back here, I imagined that was because she had news, and it was probably news I wasn't going to love.

We didn't share a permanent bond. She surprised me by reaching out to me to initiate, her now-familiar spirit pecking at my own with a sensation not unlike spiritual preening of feathers. Kind of tickled.

My own spirit was still recovering, but I had enough for this. I opened myself up to her thoughts and braced myself for whatever it was she had deemed vital enough to come in to town to share.

What I got was unexpected, to say the least.

It took me a moment to orient myself in the images she

projected into my mind. My breath caught at the literal eagle-eye view over the Irish Sea, and finally, the sight I was seeing processed.

A large shape in the teal-blue water, swimming westward along the northern coastline of *Ireland*.

The kraken was headed out to sea.

*The kraken was headed out to sea!*

I could have kissed the eagle. As it was, her feathers puffed up in a ruff around her enormous neck at the onslaught of my gratitude through the threads of plaited spirit between us. Could an eagle look embarrassed? She had a downright bashful cast to her, like Toothless the Dragon attempting a smile.

"Thank you," I said to her aloud.

She surprised me yet again by leaning down—which put that terrifyingly sharp flesh-shredder of a beak in alarming proximity to my throat—and nuzzling at the side of my head.

Then she launched herself into the air with a self-satisfied scream.

The blast of wind from her mahoosive wings threw my hair into my face, and by the time I'd batted it back out of my eyes again, she was barely a smear on the horizon.

"I'll be damned," I said under my breath. She was surprising me at every turn.

"What did she want?"

I jumped at Finn's silent appearance beside me. He gazed after the eagle, a hungry look in his eyes that faded to wistfulness as soon as he turned to meet my own.

"I thought she'd come to tell us the kraken was coming back to attack somewhere," I said, shaking my head in bemusement. "She actually came to give us a reprieve."

Finn's blue eyes narrowed thoughtfully. "A reprieve?"

"The kraken's turned out to sea. She's going back to make sure it doesn't double back, but an hour ago, it was passing"—I wracked my brains for Irish geography, since I'd actually been to that particular corner once—"Malin Head."

At Finn's questioning look, I expanded on that just as Eilidh made her way over to us. From the curious expression on her face, she'd been eavesdropping anyway.

"Northwestern tip of the Republic of Ireland," I said. "Why it went that far south is beyond me, but if it did and it is injured, it implies—"

"That the kraken has a safe place to recover and retreat to," Finn finished for me.

"More than that, it suggests the kraken was injured enough to need such a place but not so debilitated that it had to stop sooner. It's been almost a day now, so it's moving slowly." Eilidh's interjection drew nods from both me and Finn. "You said our eagle friend came to tell us that?"

"Aye," I replied.

"That demonstrates some advanced cognitive processes," Eilidh murmured. "It's common animal behaviour to warn the group if a threat is coming, but it's a few steps beyond to go out of one's way to tell your group the coast is clear."

"I was thinking the same thing," Finn said.

Harrumph. I'd have gotten there if I'd not been immediately interrupted.

I glanced up at the setting sun. "I originally was going to suggest we all spend the night here and go back to Mull in the morning for the other ionadan-siubhail, but if the kraken's out of commission..."

"Carpe the fuckin' diem," came Iain's voice, punctuated by a confident "Mewp!" from the wildcat kitten perched on his shoulder.

Finn gave the kitten a solemn bow, and she sat back on her haunches and started licking her own chest.

Eilidh snorted and started walking back towards the group,

already calling out running orders. Finn followed, making a bee line for Samuel. That left me standing with Iain and Sailean.

"Not sure whether I tell you to take a nap on the boat or that you can sleep when yer deid," Iain said to me in a conspiratorial tone.

I feigned clutching my nonexistent pearls. "You've crushed all my expectations. I'd have thought you, of all people, would know when to deploy a good 'no rest for the wicked.'"

My best mate's face actually crumpled. "I've failed you."

"Aye, you'll have to fall on your sword."

"I haven't got a sword."

*That* made my eyebrow hike up almost into my hair. Unrelatedly, Sailean sneezed. Iain turned to the kitten with reproach in his eyes as he wiped kitten snot from the side of his neck.

"You tell yer da I have regrets about my last sentence's implications," he said seriously.

Just to get one more surprise in, the kitten—who took Uncle Iain's advice to heart, it seemed—pounced on our bond and filled my mind with a Sailean-POV image of an enormous Iain face repeating his words verbatim.

"Sailean," I said to the cat, "you do realise I am standing right here and heard him just fine when he told you?"

Her only reply was to sneeze again, this time right into Iain's laughing mouth.

# CHAPTER
# THIRTY-FOUR

By the time we were back on the schooner headed for Mull, I felt like I was in a fugue state. We'd taken a risk—one we'd all agreed upon—in only travelling aboard the one ship.

If we were successful, we'd finish the ionad-siubhail at Iona and be able to activate the network from there. Our first three would be connected, and we could travel directly home to Oban.

The thought was, admittedly, bloody tantalising.

It would have been even more attractive if I hadn't been nearly dead on my feet.

Finn and Samuel's conversations on their rockie-talkies formed a low background buzz at the back of my mind. While I was necessary for the act of building the ionadan-siubhail, I deferred to the Muilich and Ìthich when it came to where they thought was best.

I found myself dozing as the sun dipped behind Beinn Mhòr, Mull's highest peak and only munro. A few wisps of cloud touched the mountain with gold, and normally, I'd have stared at that view until the sky darkened. Today? Could have put the kraken in a tutu dancing the multi-tentacled can-can on the peak to a barrage of pyrotechnics and I'd have still nodded off.

By the time Eilidh gently shook me awake, it was almost full dark, and the sky shimmered with stars on the eastern horizon.

I got to my feet, accepting her hand up as I tried to shake off my exhaustion.

The pier where we berthed was unfamiliar to me, which meant we weren't in Fishnish, and we weren't in Craignure, and we weren't in Tobermory. Even at night, Tobermory's harbour would be impossible to miss—the shopfronts and houses are painted in a rainbow of colours.

"Salen?" I asked groggily.

"Finn's got her," Eilidh told me.

"Not Sailean, *an t-Sàilean*," I said, emphasising the Gaelic name of the village and it's much longer A sound.

"Oh! Aye, 's e a th' ann."

Salen—an t-Sàilean, in reference to the salt of the sea and not the kitten's namesake willow tree—was a small village that sat at Mull's narrowest point of land about halfway up the Sound of Mull between Craignure and Tobermory. One of my best mates at school had grown up there before her dad broke his back and the family moved to Oban. I'd been to the village with her in my adolescence, but I'd never been down to the pier that I remembered. Or maybe I had, but it was bloody dark now.

We'd taken the bare minimum of people. From Oban, it was just me and Eilidh. Sailean had almost stayed with Iain— whether he'd forgiven her for sneezing into his mouth or not was anyone's guess, but Finn had taken her now. Rhona had gone to Kilmelford to check in on Alison and Meeksy. That was a job I was more than happy to leave to her.

As it was, I was about to fall asleep standing up on the deck of the boat.

The Muilich were already securing a gangplank for us to disembark the schooner.

As far as locations went, Salen was smart, in my opinion. It really was about as central as you could get in the island, since you could both travel up and down the bigger road along the Sound of Mull and cut overland to Gruline at the head of Loch na Keal. That provided access to the more jagged southwestern—ish—coast of the island. Otherwise, folk would have to cut through the glens, up Glen Forsa and beyond through Loch Ba or go all the way down the Ross to Pennyghael to skirt Loch Scridain. From Salen, all that could be avoided.

These were only our first three, too—only a beginning.

I half stumbled onto the pier to find Finn waiting for me. "They're still working out exactly where to put the ionad-siub-hail," he said. "That and getting all the materials together. If you want to head up to the hotel, Deirdre's got rooms ready. We can sleep for a couple hours."

"Oh, thank god." I squinted at the well-lit pier; I couldn't see much beyond the pools of arcane light, but presumably, he meant *the* Salen Hotel.

Finn rummaged in the cowl of his cloak, retrieving a very drowsy Sailean. He handed her to me, and I tucked her into the crook of my arm, where she made one disgruntled squeak and went back to sleep.

"At least one of us will be well rested," I said, staring down at the kitten.

"I don't know—I think she needs about twenty hours of sleep a day and has probably only gotten sixteen or so." Finn's smile vanished into a jaw-cracking yawn.

Poor man. He'd gotten about as much sleep as I had over the past couple days.

He seemed to read my mind as he finished yawning, and

just before the contagion took over my own face, he said, "The price of being popular, I guess."

Laughing and yawning at the same time, as it turned out, was a recipe for choking on one's own spit.

Our relative popularity aside, we trekked our way past Salen Primary School and into the village proper, indeed heading to the building I recognised.

I'd never been so glad to see a whitewashed island edifice in my life.

I barely heard Deirdre's welcome; somehow I ended up with a key pressed into my palm and a gentle nudge in the right direction. Careful not to drop my weight onto the kitten, I landed in the middle of the bed and kicked off my boots, pulling the duvet up and over me from both sides like wrapping myself into a burrito.

I passed out almost before the door worked its way shut.

Someone, some blessed person, decided that we'd be better served by a full night of sleep than we would by getting dragged sobbing out of our duvets to do magic tricks.

Okay, maybe "magic tricks" didn't do justice to the work, but "sobbing" was not an understatement. I, for one, would have been in full crocodile tears.

As it was, when I woke up bleary eyed and disoriented at ten in the morning, having slept an estimated eleven hours or so, I had the unwelcome sensation of a day when an alarm fails to wake you up for work.

The bed was a tangled nest of duvet and sheets, and my neck had a crick in it from staying in one position too long. Sailean was nowhere to be seen, and after a brief spike of anxiety, I reached out for her through our bond and found her in the hotel dining room, where the blasted wee beastie was eating sausage again.

Sausage some traitor had *cut up into pieces* for her.

Whoever had done it was going to be on Sailean duty all day. They could deal with the biological weapon they'd created. One poot could burn the sitkas out of the nearest glen if they held up a match to her furry wee arse at the right moment. Wildcat napalm.

I shuddered at the thought, which was dangerous for my appetite. When was the last time I'd eaten?

The dining room was a-buzz with activity, most of which revolving around the kitten. Sailean perched on a two-top table like a dais, a linen napkin spread out beneath her. Said napkin was littered with sausage carnage.

Eilidh caught my eye from the other side of the room, where she sat beside a window that overlooked the Sound of Mull and Morvern on the other side of the water, Ardnamurchan beyond.

"I tried to stop them," she mouthed with an exaggerated shrug.

Sailean squeaked as I preemptively cast a healing spell on her again.

"Yous have created a time bomb," I told the gathered Muilich as I passed. "I hereby grant you kitten duty for today, and may the gods have mercy on your sense of smell."

I had time to see a few horror-stricken looks before I made my way over to Eilidh and sat across from her.

"How long have you been awake?" I asked her.

She gestured at the metal teapot that steamed in front of her. "Long enough to get this, not long enough to pour any."

Touché.

"Enough to share?" I eyeballed the extra mug on the table, and Eilidh rolled her eyes.

"Of course."

As much as they were culinarily abusing my kitten, the Muilich—well, Deirdre, who owned the hotel—wasted no time getting us a remarkably full Scottish breakfast.

I didn't ask questions about the eggs. Egg, singular, was more appropriate, since it took up half the plate and looked like it came from a chicken the size of a working dog. The toast was heavily seeded and perfectly browned. The black pudding was unlikely to be Stornaway, but it was rich and hearty anyway, and the tattie scones and tomatoes were proper lush.

A quick look at my stat sheet provided a peek into the special sauce of ascension food, just below my boons.

*Buffs:*

*+15% spirit regeneration for 3 hours*

*+5% likelihood to unlock agricultural affinities for 24 hours*

I'd take it, especially with the work ahead. As much as I hoped the second ionad-siubhail would go faster than the first had, I couldn't count on it. Three hours was a solid help, but it would still run out before we were done.

Eilidh and I usually had plenty to talk about. Today, we were so busy stuffing our faces—after she finished poking her enormous egg yolk with her fingertip to watch it jiggle, which almost made me inhale a bite of black pudding—that we barely made a peep that wasn't connected to swallowing or slicing something on our plates.

No sooner had we finished than we pushed our chairs back from the table.

I gave her a wry smile, then a careful peck on the cheek, aware that my breath was probably nothing I wanted share too magnanimously after all that black pudding and bacon.

"Two to go," she said, snaking her arm around my waist and nestling under my armpit.

The small gesture warmed me more than the breakfast had.

"Two to go," I told her. "Then maybe Deirdre will let us tele-port back for a mini-break at the hotel."

"I love the way you think."

It seemed the people of Salen had decided the best place for their ionad-siubhail was the village campsite, which over-looked the pier where we'd come in. While we had slept, the villagers had been busy hauling rock and preparing the area.

Our run of good weather had faded to a grey day scudded with clouds. The mountains on the mainland hid behind a shroud of mist, and to the west was a bank of puffy cumu-lonimbus heading towards us. It hadn't yet begun to rain, but it was only a matter of time.

"It's a little out of the way, isn't it?" I said to Finn dubiously when we arrived, thinking of the requirement of accessibility. "If someone has to walk all the way down here—"

"One of the crafters built a rickshaw." Amusement tinged his voice, and his words stopped me mid-sentence.

"A rickshaw." Eilidh's eyebrow looked like she was fighting a losing battle in keeping it from inching its way off her fore-head entirely.

"I think it started as a joke. A couple of the rugby lads have Strength stats that have had them throwing each other back and forth for run. That or someone lost a bet—really could go either way. No matter what, there's a system in place to get people here, and we're hoping other modes of transport make themselves known." Finn gestured at the campsite. "Besides, this is a wide-open space otherwise, and there's easy access to indigenous plants. You need that, right?"

"Aye." Glancing around, I saw a few useful candidates.

Unlike our Tesco carpark, there was no tarmac to clear

away, and the Muilich had piled all their materials in the precise location they thought best. Within a few metres of the heap of rock stood a scrubby blackthorn, some thistles, and wee maple sapling.

I disentangled myself from Eilidh, giving her hand a squeeze, and made for the blackthorn. Eilidh's murmured words to Finn got lost on the breeze blowing up the Sound of Mull. Out of the corner of my eye, I spotted the two little pots of hawthorn cuttings, which made me smile.

People trickled down the hill from the village proper, but I paid them no heed.

Even at a distance, blackthorn felt entirely different to the plucky wee hawthorn in its sea of carpark. Blackthorn was known for its protective properties—but also for being used in aggressive magics even before the ascension. Long, long before the ascension. The reason why couldn't be less surprising; the thorns that gave it its name could be measured in inches. Brutally sharp, they also provided a natural vehicle to cause injury in those pruning the bushes, and punctures could easily grow infected. The bush had a reputation as the "Devil's shrub" for that reason—it made sense to me that something known to cause injury would double as a symbol of protection.

For all that, blackthorn had plenty of medicinal uses—and alcoholic ones. Its berries made sloe gin.

This bush was in the tail end of flowering, with no berries yet developing.

It felt somewhat warier when I reached out to it with spirit, though my presence clearly woke its curiosity as well. For whatever reason, it put in my mind the image of an auld highland bodach sitting on a stump with a sprig of barley in his teeth and watching the world go by.

The explanation of our purpose went over a treat. If my approach had sparked curiosity, the idea of connecting to far-flung locations set it ablaze. I half expected to hear it hooting and hollering or feel a hearty slap on my back. With a small snort, I showed it the two-thirds of the triskele from Oban, and the blackthorn seized the idea eagerly.

It wasn't long before I had a second triskele in my hands.

My thanks to the shrub stopped short when all hell broke loose in the campsite.

# CHAPTER
# THIRTY-FIVE

Eilidh and I had fought off a veritable battalion of anomalous rabbits a few short weeks before, but neither of us could have been prepared for a rapidly moving furrow in the grass to erupt in a hare the size of a horse.

It tore a crater in the once-pristine green adjacent what had been a caravan hookup, exploding from the earth in a shower of pebbles and dirt.

I didn't have time to think.

Pulling Brac-Meanmna from my back, I threw up a Ring of Fire around the hare.

Which the enormous hare *launched* itself out of in one powerful thrust of its fucking hydraulic hind legs.

"Look out!" I yelled.

The bizarre Bugs-Bunny-esque entrance aside, there would be nothing cartoonish about a mammal that size landing on yer heid. I'd seen humans get splatted. It wasn't cute or funny, and they couldn't be reinflated with an air pump.

Gathering Muilich scattered, adults who had been bringing children down to watch the ionad-siubhail instalment throwing shields between the hare and the weans even as they high-tailed it back towards the road.

I felt the hare's landing in my knees. Its body slammed into the earth like a tonne of bricks, and the impact shuddered outward in seismic rings.

With non-fighters far too close for comfort, I didn't dare use Tairm. Thankfully, the familiar golden glow around Eilidh gave me a moment's warning before her stun provided the answering volley to the hare's leap.

Instead of Tairm, I cast Dubh.

Eilidh's ability had hit the hare, rendering it momentarily dazed, and Dubh stole its eyesight.

Finn, armed with a deceptively simple spear, leaped into the fight.

Other fighters were coming; I was certain of that. But Finn seized the moment of the hare's weakness to let his spear fly— directly at the hare's exposed throat.

His form rivalled the grace of an Olympian. The spear sailed through the air, targeted as precisely as a sniper. I wouldn't have been surprised if it split individual strands of the hare's fur.

It was almost a successful strike.

The hare, despite being blinded and stunned, must have retained a hair-trigger instinct for survival. Whether it was vibrations in the earth or those ears the size of kayaks, a split second before the spear would have lanced into the hare's carotid artery, it threw up an enormous foot and kicked.

Finn's own instincts were all that saved him—that and my frantic cast of Spèird.

My hasty spell knocked that powerful paddle off course just enough that Finn's dive got him out of the way. Almost.

The foot connected with the bàrd's shoulder instead of dead on his chest. I wasn't sure even ascension healing would have kept him alive with that kind of blow. As it was, Finn bellowed in pain as bones shattered.

One glance behind me told me the weans were clear enough. Eilidh took advantage of the hare's exposed flank to slash her claymore through the back of its knee, leaping out of the way as soon as she pulled the blade free.

My spirit was down to about forty percent, but I poured three quarters of what remained into Tairm.

At first, I thought nothing happened.

There was little in a grassy campsite for nature to really take hold of.

But in a moment of utter silence between breaths, Brac-Meanmna buzzing gleefully as I braced myself against the living staff in dread, my other senses kicked in.

I'd been thinking of what lay below—Gu h-Ìosal. I ought to have looked up—Gu h-Àrd.

All at once, when I triggered a small pulse of Connection, my spirit connected to everything.

Time slowed as microscopic filaments of spirit blazed to life. For one shining moment that seemed to stretch on into infinity, those filaments lit up the pathways in the air and in my brain alike.

I stood at the nexus of billions of them. They poured into my spirit channels, rushed through the length of my energetic body and physical body alike, and as if I were suspended in an intricately woven multidimensional spider's web, when I moved, those delicate filaments responded.

They delved into the earth; they soared into the sky.

It wasn't just me, either. Eilidh was her own nexus, brighter than the sun in her brilliance. Behind me, I couldn't see Finn, but despite his injury, I could sense the burning power of his own spirit.

In one shining, glittering moment, I felt Tairm take shape

high above my head, in the scudding bank of cumulonimbus clouds that had been rolling in from the west as I worked with the blackthorn.

In one shining, transcendent moment, I understood something fundamental.

Above, below, around—they were just prepositions to help us conceptualise our world. The truth was in those filaments.

They were *everything*.

They were energy.

And so were we.

For the first time, as Tairm rumbled into existence, I expanded into the conscious knowledge that I'd been grasping at for days.

There was no separation between me and the earth, between me and the universe.

We were one and the same.

I reached into the sky, gathered a trillion eager filaments of spirit, and Tairm split the cloud bank in a fork of blue-white lightning.

It cooked the hare on the spot.

"Calum, what the *fuck*?"

Finn's words squeezed out between gritted teeth, and I didn't think he was talking about the impact of Beannachd-Shlàinte as it healed the shattered left side of his body. I didn't think I'd heard the man swear before, and considering his baby face and angelic looks, it gave the odd impression of hearing curses from a toddler someone had woken up from a much-needed nap.

"Better?" I asked, trying not to laugh at my own mental image.

His only answer was a grimace and an impatient wave of his left hand, which, considering every bone from his radius to his scapula had been almost paste a few moments before, was pretty much answer enough.

Finn pushed himself to a sitting position, taking the skin of water Eilidh offered and throwing back half of it. That was less graceful; he drank too fast and some spurted out his nose.

When he'd recovered, Finn scrubbed a hand through his golden curls, leaving one side of his head frizzy and the other in sweat-damp ringlets.

"*I'm* fine. What I want to know is how you got possessed by Zeus to smite that beast with a literal lightning bolt. And I want to know why the hell I saw string theory come to life in front of my face in the instant before you did it."

"I'd also like to know that," Eilidh murmured.

I frowned in consternation. String theory. I was hardly a rocket scientist, and the closest I came to resembling Stephen Hawking was the fact that we shared two Es and one A in our respective names.

Even though that moment had stretched out for me, Eilidh, and Finn, it seemed that experience hadn't been universal.

While it had felt like an age to me, the three of us facing off against the hare alone, other fighters had been running at ascension speed to reach us. They'd still been fifty metres away when I barbecued the enormous not-a-bunny, and I'd turned to see them all skidding to a halt with comical expressions of awe and confusion on their faces. Now, they were cleaning up the site for the ionad-siubhail, and already crafters busied themselves exchanging hare meat and items and stashing things in inventory to take into the village.

"I'm not sure how to explain it," I said to Finn and Eilidh. "Or if I can replicate it. Usually when I've used that spell, it's been pure wild magic with a mind of its own. I've never been able to direct it before."

"What spell is it?" Finn asked.

"Tairm," I said at the same time as Eilidh, who gave me a sheepish grin.

"Interesting word," Finn murmured. "'S ann sa Ghàidhlig a tha sin, nach ann?"

"'S ann," I said automatically in agreement.

For the next few minutes, I explained my perception of what had happened with spirit, and Eilidh and Finn relayed back what they'd seen on their end. I was just about to go get one of the other witnesses to ask if they'd seen anything when Rabbie came stumping across the grass just as the sky let loose the rain it had apparently been waiting to dump on our heads.

Rabbie waved one arm, squinting up at the clouds as if they'd interrupted him. "We're ready to start if you are! All right, Finn?"

Finn got to his feet, brushing himself off. "Aye, let's get it done."

Great. If the rain kept up, we'd be out here for hours in it.

Thank the gods for ascension waterproofing.

The only differences in the creation of the second ionad-siubhail were the design of the crafters—instead of three arching, rib-like curves that met in the middle, they created a lattice of intricate stone that was more like a tunnel, open on two sides and enclosed on the others—and the addition of the blackthorn spiral to complement the hawthorn at the centre in the stone floor.

Well, that and the colour. I wasn't sure why Sailean had pink granite lying around, since that came from the Ross of

Mull far closer to Iona than here, but it *was* pretty. Even in the rain, it glimmered in soft, peachy salmon hues.

The exhaustion, well. That hit me like an ascended hare's kayak foot when we finished.

I took one of the hawthorn sprigs to the northwestern lattice side of the ionad-siubhail, where I gently planted it, using the dregs of my spirit to encourage its roots to take. While connecting with the earth do this replenished a bit of my energy, my fingers still shook with a fine tremor when I was finished.

The sun hid behind the clouds, so I wasn't sure what time of day it was. My brain swam with lethargy to the point that I forgot I could check the clock in my head until Eilidh caught me squinting at the sky and said, "System says it's half three."

"How am I still this knackered? I spent eleven hours almost comatose." I scanned the area around the ionad-siubhail, where most people had scattered, but a few milled about, touching the pink granite as if it were sacred. "Where'd Finn go?"

I'd been hoping to suss out what we'd experienced a bit more.

"Up towards the village. Someone said something about cake." Eilidh gave me a small smile. "Fancy some cake?"

Normally, cake got my attention, but right now, all I wanted was to sit down. Especially since my arse wouldn't get wet sitting in the grass. I did just that, and after a moment of looking down at me in bemusement, Eilidh joined me.

We sat in silence for a short time, watching people explore the ionad-siubhail. I couldn't hear their conversations, only a light buzz of voices I didn't really try to parse. One pleasantly sturdy middle-aged woman stood in the archway of the open end closest to us, her grey hair in a short mop of loose curls, which she tossed out of her face as she ran a hand up the twisting arc of pink granite. She looked vaguely familiar—

maybe I'd seen her at the mòd growing up back when Mum would force me to learn a poem to recite or a song to sing.

After a few minutes, I did start to feel better, but the thought of going through another hours-long travel-plus-gruelling-spellwork extravaganza made me feel like the rumpled toddler I'd imagined Finn to be earlier.

"Calum!" Rhona's voice made me jump when it came from the rockie-talkie in my . . . pockie.

I really needed a nap.

"Erm, hi, Rhona. Something wrong?" I pulled the communication crystal out, even though I didn't really need to hold it to use it.

Eilidh's face had been relaxed, but now her resolved, wary mask returned.

"Well, I mean, *yeah*, but not emergency-level wrong. It's Ronald. He's gone missing. And he took three of the anomalies with him."

# CHAPTER
# THIRTY-SIX

If things could stop happening for, like, five minutes together, I would be tremendously grateful. The weariness that washed over me with Rhona's pronouncement through the communication crystal made red flash in front of my eyes. I'd always rather thought that was just a figure of speech, but the pure vermillion fury left washes across my vision. At that moment, I would have punched a god in the face without hesitation.

The fucking *coward*.

Eilidh was still talking to Rhona, having—I think—pried the communication crystal out of my hand before I could accidentally crush it by squeezing it into sand. They may as well have been the parents in *Peanuts* cartoons for all the sense the noises made over the rushing in my ears.

Ronald had been secretive about his research, put people at risk, gotten Alison corrupted, and now he had the gall to pull a big scaredy run-away?

Forget punching god.

I was going to track him down and punch that string bean

so hard he'd be permanently folded in half like a fucking boomerang. Salen's rugby lads could practice throwing him from Fishnish to Lochaline and he could live out his days whipping back and forth across the Sound of Mull.

Or we could just put him in the cage with Alison and let her deal with him.

None of that was really even possible. Not yet. Not with one ionad-siubhail left to create in Iona and a kraken on the loose, somewhere in the North Atlantic where we couldn't reach it until it healed enough to rain down hell on our coastlines again.

Ronald had to know that. He had to know I couldn't drop everything and come after him.

Somehow, I'd gotten to my feet, and I was pacing back and forth over the grass. It took every tiny, minuscule atom of my self-control not to take out my aggression on the unsuspecting foliage.

Naturally, we'd had to get this news *after* I'd gone full smite on a horse-sized hare.

The few people who had been still milling around at the ionad-siubhail en masse seemed to recognise moving *away* from the ragin' mage as the prudent choice, but one shape walked against the flow of traffic, headed in my direction without flinching.

Finn.

When he arrived, he was carrying a white box in his hands. The rain had stopped at some point, and Finn paused a short distance away from me. His presence reminded me that I should probably make an effort at humane communication. I sucked in a breath as deep as my lungs could take, filled them to bursting. Oddly, Finn did the same, and when he let out the breath slowly and audibly like yogis did, I followed him without thinking.

"What happened?" he asked after we'd repeated the process a few more times.

I told him, and his face darkened.

Finn didn't know Ronald personally, but he'd heard enough about the anomalies to recognise the source of my fury.

"Could he be corrupted somehow?" This came from Eilidh.

She handed my communication crystal back to me, and I tucked it into its pocket on my chest, mentally reminding myself I'd need to apologise to Rhona later.

"I don't think so," I said after a moment. I shook my head more confidently. "No. I use Connection so frequently that I don't think I could have missed that. There are too many other people who also worked around him. From what Alison told us, if her information can be trusted, there would have been signs. He must be acting under his own volition."

"Could he be going to find the source of the anomalies?" This question, posed with the usual thoughtfulness that pervaded Finn's demeanour, gave me pause.

"I'm not sure he's that . . ." Eilidh seemed to grasp for words. "Not *stupid*, but—not that willing to sacrifice himself pointlessly."

I gave a mirthless laugh at that. "Eilidh's right." Pausing, I scowled as a bitter taste pervaded my mouth. "Did Rhona mention how he transported the anomalies he took? Three of them is a lot if they were badgers. I missed it if she did in my . . . rage haze."

"He took birds." Eilidh's soft voice held no recrimination—for me, anyway. Ronald was another story. "Rhona said one of the other mages at Kilmelford saw him with a strange contraption that looked like a modified containment cage with compartments, but they didn't think anything of it at the time."

"Why would they?" I agreed. "Gods, of all the fucking ideas, buggering off with the beasties was not something I expected *anyone* to do."

"I take it someone's gone after him," Finn said to Eilidh, who nodded.

"They said he went east, which doesn't say much. With a little luck, they'll find him and the anomalies before something worse happens." Eilidh's mouth curved downward. *Worse* could be a lot of things, but the anomalies getting free and corrupting more people was at the top of my list of worries. "But we ought to finish what we came to Mull to do—the sooner we connect our communities, the sooner we can warn people."

I nodded my agreement, torn between maniacal exhausted laughter and using Spèird to punch through a boulder or two.

Finn gave a tight-lipped smile. "Silver lining?"

"*Please*," I said at the same time Eilidh said, "Oh, god, yes."

"Don't get too excited," Finn said with a self-deprecating chuckle. He hefted the white box in his hands. "I just brought you some cake."

Most of the time, I was grateful for the lengthening days of a Scottish summer. As we cut across the central belt of Mull to Gruline, all the interminable daylight just stretched out time into infinity.

Mull was not a small island—far from it. We made good time as far as things go, but through the mist and intermittent breaks in the clouds, it still took us all the way to twilight to reach Fionnphort.

Samuel had gone ahead of us. It was a mark of my weariness that I hadn't even noticed his absence in Salen.

Between his preparations and the Muilich communication via their impressive rockie-talkie network, there was a boat waiting for us at the pier in Fionnphort to take us across to Iona straight away.

As thankful as I was for it, I knew this time we would not have the luxury of a full night's sleep. We needed to get this done and get back to Oban.

Finn and Eilidh and I had bandied about theories on the trek from Salen, but despite Finn having a surprising pet interest in quantum mechanics, none of us could come up with an explanation for why our perception had shifted so dramatically. The only helpful bit of information came from Finn, who had used his cake acquisition time out to ask around, and none of the other people present for the hare's heavenly judgement had seen the filaments.

My brain wanted to fixate on that. Luckily, the ferry from Fionnphort was a majestic five entire minutes.

It felt bizarre to step back onto Iona so quickly, but at the same time, it felt as if it had been a century. Aside from the crumpled metal cargo container, there were no outward remnants of the battle in view, something that further added an element of surreality to our arrival.

Samuel waited to greet us in precisely the spot where he would have been buried under several tonnes of kraken two days before. The old monk seemed to take us in with one quick glance, judging that none of us had the energy for small talk. He passed us each a packet of nondescript paper that contained a warm mutton sandwich with horseradish, a roll of dehydrated fruit of some kind, and a buttery tattie scone. I could have kissed him.

We all scoffed down the food as we followed him up the hill.

The older man stopped just short of the nunnery ruins, where there was an open grassy area bordered by hedges of gorse and hawthorn.

I stared at the stone pile in the middle of the grass with

mouth hanging open. My stomach gave an embarrassing gurgle.

"You want us to use *stone from the bloody nunnery*?" I blurted out, then closed my eyes. Way to put yer foot in yer mouth up to your knee, Calum, ya gobshite. "Sorry. I just mean—why?"

The monk didn't seem offended by my borderline blasphemous outburst, but a couple of the waiting crafters looked like they weren't sure whether or not to be affronted. Eilidh and Finn, on the other hand, each stood far too still to be doing anything other than waging an internal war with their urge to laugh at me.

"This place has been here a very long time," Samuel said with careful enunciation. "What better way to honour the nuns who spent their lives in contemplation than to use part of these walls to connect Iona to the wider world once more?"

Well, when he put it like that, I sounded like even more of a pathetic himbo hamster.

"It's a very lovely thought," I said after a beat.

Eilidh's restrained mirth softened into a genuine warm smile. "It is, Samuel. Thank you."

"It is the community who decided, not I." Samuel let that sit for a moment before waving one hand suddenly. "I agreed, of course. Merely—och. It's been a long day."

"Long week," one of the crafters said.

"Long year," Finn muttered.

"Long *decade*." I let out a small chuckle, which the others all echoed mirthlessly. "Not sure this was the reboot of the Roarin' Twenties anyone wanted."

"Definitely not," Samuel agreed. He straightened his shoulders with a sigh, gesturing at the pile of stone. "Shall we?"

"You all prepare the stone. I'll . . . talk to a gorse bush." That earned another chuckle, this one with a touch of actual levity to it. I wasn't sure why I'd said gorse bush, exactly, but it felt right.

I walked up to the gorse at the edge of the hedge. In range. "Hello, there."

The alacrity with which the gorse responded surprised me. My mind lit up so brightly, I had to glance up to make sure the sun hadn't reversed course and decided to break over the horizon again even though it had just set.

Gorse was a staple of Latha Buidhe Bealltainn, the old fire festival called Beltane in English. Yellow like the Gaelic name—the Yellow Day of Beltane—gorse wood grew saturated with its natural oils and burned fiercely when set aflame. It was a symbol of the old god Lugh, a hardy plant that forever chased the sunlight. Voracious and tenacious, gorse provided sustenance with its edible flowers, splashed colour over the hills year round, and shared its sunny yellow in dyes.

The plant, though an arch nemesis of Winnie-the-Pooh's fluff-stuffed behind, brightly shared itself with my mind. Gorse was resilience, hope—a beacon that felt right for Iona after the devastating losses from the kraken.

The triskele from my inventory was almost complete—one part hawthorn, one part blackthorn, and soon one part gorse.

This gorse was ready to help, and help it did.

Paler than both the deep blackthorn and the honey-gold hawthorn, the triskele the gorse gave me almost glowed.

I detached the three pieces where they met with a smile. Iona was where we would truly begin our journey to connecting the people of Scotland again—Iona's ionad-siubhail would receive the first of the completed triskeles from the moment we finished. Finn would take one spiral back to Salen, and we would take the third blackthorn spiral and the remaining gorse spiral to Oban, but into that ancient stone tonight, we would place all three as one.

Hawthorn's compassion and acceptance, blackthorn's ferocity and protection, gorse's optimism and hope.

The nunnery had stood for almost a thousand years. Maybe what we built today would stand for thousands more.

Eilidh and Finn and Samuel all waited for me, the crafters already in their places.

As tired as I was, I tried my best to remain present as I took hold of my spirit and shared it with Samuel once more. His magic somehow felt more potent here, in his own community.

The crafters began their work.

Spirit swirled around us as they shaped the stone. In the glow of spirit, I could see it for what it was, and my heart soared at the sight. The nunnery had mostly been built of grey diorite and granite, but it also contained some of the pink stone from the quarry near Fionnphort. It bound this place to both Iona and Mull, and the crafters' labour reflected that sense of intertwined destiny.

Oban's ionad-siubhail had been practical, serviceable. Beautiful and graceful, yes, but its arches' artistry was subtle. Salen's provided some shelter from the winds, a gentle weaving.

Iona's stone plaited together in the endless knot.

It rose from the ground in intricate whorls, the crafters physically turning strands of pliable rock this way and that. Like Scottish Christianity had always carried with it our older traditions, our older remnants, so did these stones blend our histories and the geology of both islands. Perhaps it was just exhaustion, but I found my eyes wet with tears.

The stone seemed to sing.

Minutes turned to hours as spirit flowed through us into the crafters, and through the crafters into the stone. When it was done, the ionad-siubhail took my breath away.

Like Salen, the Iona crafters had created a lattice, but here, pale grey and pink wove together in intricate knot work dotted with flecks of mica and quartz. But where Salen's ionad-siubhail was like a tunnel, Iona's more closely resembled a gazebo with open walls. When the sun rose in the morning and touched the ionad-siubhail for the first time, it would filter through that knot-work lattice roof. I had a feeling rain would not penetrate the spaces between the complex patterns of plaited stone.

Like Oban, the weaving stone rose up in three pillars to meet in the centre above our heads, but where Oban's remained almost entirely open, the crafters here had somehow made lace from rock.

My one remaining task took the last of my strength, even though it was simple. Easy.

I walked on tired feet to the middle of the platform beneath that graceful dome, and I placed the triskele on the floor.

Spirit rushed through me to meet it, and the spirals of the triskele spun as they had in Oban and Salen, but now with all three woods—hawthorn, blackthorn, gorse—it felt all the more dizzying. A few gasps rose around me; I hadn't realised we had an audience, but now I saw the entire island had turned up as we worked.

After what felt like an age, the spinning spirals began to slow.

The bell-like tone that rang out the moment the triune-wood triskele stopped spinning in the centre of the ionad-siubhail's platform made all of us jump.

Gold script flowed across my vision.

*World first!*

*In the Inner Hebrides of Scotland, the combined communities of Oban, Mull, and Iona have activated the first three gateways on Earth. This legendary feat has united all participating communities as one. All community bonuses shall now be shared to all members.*

*By their extraordinary cooperation and diligent efforts to recon-*

*nect mainland and island alike, Argyll has succeeded in taking a major step in the process of Earth's ascension.*

*Instantaneous travel now available between Iona Nunnery in Iona, Salen Bay in Mull, and Tesco Carpark in Oban.*

I couldn't help it.

I sat back on my arse and cried.

# CHAPTER
# THIRTY-SEVEN

"Deiseil is deònach?" Eilidh asked me as the sun crested the eastern horizon.

"Deiseil is deònach," I said.

Ready and willing.

I hadn't realised the sun was so close to rising. Once more, we'd been up all night.

Now, finally, we could step across the sea in a heartbeat.

Part of me remained apprehensive that the ionadan-siubhail somehow wouldn't work, but I stepped onto the platform with Eilidh anyway.

Finn and Samuel stood by, their entire demeanour a complex mix of excitement, exhaustion, and trepidation.

"We'll meet back here tomorrow, then," I said to them. "Assuming we don't step over an event horizon and end up in another galaxy or having swapped heads or anything like that."

"If we swap heads, we can still make our meeting," Eilidh said breezily.

At Finn's incredulous expression, she giggled—actually giggled. Eilidh must have been tired to the level of punch drunk.

"I mean, stranger things have happened," she said, giggling again.

"I will pray that your heads remain situated where they are," Samuel told us gravely.

"Thank you. I like my head where it is." Aye, it was time for us to go. Maybe we could sleep until midday tomorrow.

"Siuthadaibh," Finn said, making a shooing motion with his hands.

Framed as he was by the golden rays of the rising sun, all I could think about was the brilliant yellow gorse and the old god Lugh.

Maybe Cú Chúlainn hadn't been the right analogy after all.

"You're stalling," Eilidh whispered in my ear. Her breath tickled.

"I don't want to end up in another galaxy," I whispered back.

We stepped into the middle of the platform.

"Do we have to d—"

Eilidh's question cut off when a map of Argyll appeared in front of us. Two points glowed gold—Salen and Oban.

"Here goes nothing," I said, giving Finn and Samuel a nervous salute. "See you tomorrow, hopefully from this head and body fully attached."

I focused my attention on the Oban dot.

The image of Finn waving dissolved.

Into the Tesco carpark, where an entire crowd burst out in exuberant cheers.

If we'd thought we were getting to sleep, we were immediately disabused of the notion.

By "disabused of the notion," I mean "hit in the face with three fountains of champagne at once from shaken bottles."

The thing about world firsts in the ascension was that they were the push notification from hell. No way to turn it off, so if you were awake and not currently fighting for your life, that gold script was going to light up your vision.

Which meant that when we'd triggered it, every early riser in Oban had gotten the memo—and they'd helpfully played alarm clock to every other soul in town.

At least that's what it felt like.

The Tesco carpark had never seen a party quite like this.

"How the hell did we think people would just go about their days?" Eilidh half yelled over the blare of arse-o'clock-in-the-morning bagpipes.

"I blame the chronic lack of sufficient rest!" I hollered back, still scrubbing champagne out of my eyes.

Someone pressed a mimosa into my hand in a tin camping cup, and while I didn't know if my stomach could handle it, I figured my ascension-bolstered constitution would fix it if push came to boak.

"Eyyyy!"

The roar of a cheer that went up almost made me drown on my champagne-and-orange-juice death wish, and I turned, coughing, to see the older woman from Salen I'd thought looked vaguely familiar, standing with her husband—I presumed—and a gaggle of other Muilich.

For one long moment, she and I stared at each other in shared terror, and then someone yelled, "Una!" and her face lit up with pure joy as she barrelled off the platform into the arms of an Oban woman, who immediately planted a kiss on her cheek and handed her a stein of mimosa.

"Oh, god, what is happening?" I was going to die, and it was *not* at the hands of an anomaly or at the tentacles of a bloody kraken, but with a wheeze of bagpipes and an uncontainable crowd of my rambunctious Argyllians.

Eilidh had her own mimosa halfway to her lips but was staring into space like she'd turned a corner and found herself face to beak with the kraken's enormous orifice.

"Why do you look like you just caught your parents in bed with Cthulhu?" I yelled over the din, vaguely aware that Una, the newly arrived Muileach, had just found a bottle of sambuca on a table someone had set up and was *pouring shots*. Her husband stood by with a beatific grin, squinting into the dawn. A solid fifty people looked ready to fall down on their knees and worship.

We were done for.

"Pub crawls" was all that made it past Eilidh's strangled voice box.

Even as she said it, more people appeared in the ionad-siubhail, and another roar of joy went up, this time answered by the new arrivals as they held up bottles of whisky, gin, and something that looked suspiciously and terrifyingly like Jägermeister.

Oh no.

*Oh no.*

What had we done?

Forget the kraken.

We'd created a real monster.

"Blàth nan cailin, Sìne Bhàn!"

"Thighearna, I swear, if they sing this one more time—" Eilidh broke off with a self-pitying moan as she vomited for the third time to the accompaniment of a massed choir of drunk

Gaels belting out their praise to the flower of womanhood that was Fair Sìne.

Thank all the gods and mages for the glory of a self-cleaning toilet. The public cubicle remained immaculate, even if Eilidh did not.

I held her hair back from her face, but considering that I was one more witnessed boak away from boakin' myself, my drunken grasp was not up to the task of catching *all* her hair. Purifire was a bit risky as a clean-up method, considering half of Oban at this point was probably ninety percent alcohol by volume, and I didn't feature my town exploding.

*World first!*

*Argyll blows itself up in celebration of their momentous triumph, the bloody lushes!*

It was all too easy to imagine. Not the push notification from hell I wanted to see. No Purifire to clean the puke out of my partner's hair. It would have to wait for water.

I'd apologise later, if we survived what was—by my best inebriated estimation—the eighteenth rendition of "Sìne Bhàn" in the past two hours.

For one long, inscrutable moment, I wondered what would happen if she stuck her whole head in the self-cleaning toilet. Would it wash her hair? Did I dare suggest she find out?

Blinking into the bright white tile of the public loo, I had a moment of lucidity as someone wailed, "Na caoin, a luaidh! Na sil na deòir!" on the pier outside, sounding as if they were not, in fact, following the song's urge not to cry.

No, I decided.

I would not suggest my vomiting partner stick her head in a toilet to see if it would get cleaner. I'd survived seventeen rounds of "Sìne Bhàn" and intended to make it through number eighteen.

Midday had come and gone, as had what felt like the entire

population of Mull, Iona, and everyone between Tarbert and Fort William.

That may have been an exaggeration, but I'd been low on brain cells before I was blootered. Three mimosas, two shots of Una's sambuca—the Mull woman was a proper menace, and also I would love her until the day I died—six pints of cider, half a bottle of wine, and an ungodly number of affirmative answers to a Gaelic "Och, dìreach tè bheag, dìreach tè bheag" and even my ascended constitution was crying *mayday*.

For another long moment, I lost myself in the existential crisis of how many tè bheag it took to make a tè mhòr. A question for the ages—at what point do many small drams make a big dram?

Eilidh had begun to quietly weep.

Alarmed, I dropped her hair, which fell into the toilet bowl over her trembling shoulder.

"Eil thu ceart gu leòr?" I asked her if she was all right, suppressing the triumph that rose in me as the lock of hair that had, a moment ago, been soiled now looked pristine.

I hadn't suggested she wash her hair in the self-cleaning toilet bowl aloud, had I? Had I made her cry?

"Tha an t-òran dìreach cho àlainn," Eilidh said into the crook of her shoulder.

Oh.

Eilidh had simply succumbed to the beauty of Sìne Bhàn.

I patted her back while she cried and sang along.

The public loo had unfairly nice acoustics.

"Mrph."

This whimper woke me from my state of being dead.

I peeled my eyelids slowly up the sandy orbs they shielded

from the light, expecting the invasion of whatever-the-fuck time it was to ignite bile or blood or some other bodily fluid heretofore untapped. Lymph?

My innards remained, miraculously, placid.

The auburn blur that materialised in front of my eyes was Eilidh shaped.

When it moved, I felt something dislodge from between my lips.

"Peh." I spit out . . . a chunk of her hair?

"Calum," came a muffled groan from under the still-solidifying cloud of fuzzy curls, "are we dead?"

"No," I said, my claw-like and half-asleep hand crawling its way out from the prison I'd apparently doomed it to sandwiched between Eilidh's knees. Pins and needles flared into being, and I pried more strands of hair from where they were stuck to my lips. "Not for lack of trying, I think."

"I think I'm still drunk," she said into the duvet.

A small mew came from somewhere.

Both of us sat bolt upright.

I braced myself for bodily retaliation, but aside from a light head rush, it didn't come.

Sailean emerged, blinking, from a cave of quilt and pillow looking as bedraggled as I felt.

Eilidh's hair was a glorious nest of red-brown frizz except where the shorter baby hairs framed her face with perfect little wisps of ringlets. We both looked at each other for a moment, and Eilidh reached out a pale hand towards me.

I waited to see what she would do, but all she did was lightly press against the side of my head.

Perplexed, I gave her a questioning look. "I don't think there's a button there."

Eilidh blinked at me. Beside her, the kitten padded onto the centre of a pillow neither of us had been anywhere near and sat down, immediately dozing off.

"Curl," Eilidh said vaguely, then made a gesture at the side of her own head, perpendicular to her skull and made a sound that was half duck quack, half "weh."

For some reason, that made perfect sense to me.

"Why don't I feel hungover?" I said, yawning.

"Still drunk?"

I thought about that for a moment, but aside from grogginess, I didn't feel drunk.

Both Eilidh and I came to the same conclusion at the same time, and I had a momentary, crystal-clear memory of our realisation from the night—morning?—before at the danger of teleportation-facilitated pub crawls.

"Forget the ascension. If we can get drunk but don't get hungover, that's going to cause the real apocalypse." Eilidh tipped over again and landed on the duvet with a *whumph*.

The impact sent Sailean springing into the air from the pillow like she'd been on a trampoline and someone had cannonballed onto it from a nearby rooftop.

The wildcat kitten landed on the pillow again with all her hair standing on end, bottle brush tail to hackles, claws lodged deep into the pillowcase.

Eilidh peeked out through her mess of hair. "Soz."

Sailean let out a plaintive mew, and I scooped her up, rolling onto my back to lie beside Eilidh.

Closing my eyes, I checked the clock.

"God, it's been—ugh." We hadn't missed our meeting with Finn, but that was only because Finn had been dragged to Oban, and then all of us had been dragged to Una's house in Salen, and *then* to Iona, where we'd gone swimming on the beach—skinny dipping, if my all-too-clear memory served—and by the time we'd made it back to Oban again, Finn had told us very seriously between whisky burps that we should reschedule.

"It's been what?" Eilidh asked.

"Like two days."

Her answering groan as she checked herself drew a chuckle from me.

"I think I found the downside of ascension drinking," I said, scratching Sailean behind the ears to her oblivious purring.

"Just the one?"

"We might have no hangovers, but I think we're going to find that we remember every—single—stupid—thing we did drunk."

# THIRTY-EIGHT

*You have been honoured with a Mark of Esteem.*

*For being the first ascension champion to create and activate a gateway network (ionadan-siubhail), you now bear the Mark of Passage.*

*This will be visible to all who have access to your information, whether by ability or your choice to share. A Mark of Esteem distinguishes you among your people as one who has taken vital steps on the path to ascension.*

*Should you survive, your name will be recorded in the Halls of the Ascended Alliance for all time.*

*The Mark of Passage also grants you the following bonuses, which you must accept to receive:*

*- An increase in an existing affinity of your choice*

*-Ability (Treeless): Waypoint. This ability allows you to establish preliminary gateway locations for activation where you do not possess the requisite materials or assistance to create the gateway at that moment. Doing this creates a waypoint findable to all those with access to the gateway network that slowly charges with ambient spirit to facilitate gateway creation by those who do not have access to the Ionad-Siubhail ability.*

*Do you accept this Mark of Passage and its requisite rewards along with the ramifications of renown that accompany such esteem?*

I immediately accepted. As far as bonuses went, it was the least flashy I'd seen in a while, but after the ordeal of the past week and the toll it had taken on all of us to connect Oban, Mull, and Iona, anything that could make future ionadan-siubhail easier to establish was a an absolute boon.

Before she'd left, Eilidh had told me she'd gotten the same notification, and that was a relief. Even though I had technically been the one to activate the skills, she also had the ability as an ascension champion, and she'd been present every step of the way. With two of us bearing the Mark of Passage, we would have a much, much easier road ahead.

Though to take advantage of it, we'd have to split up.

I punted that thought to the back of my mind. I wasn't ready to consider that. Not yet, not when we were still in the shit.

Oban had finally settled down in the past few days since we'd activated the ionadan-siubhail—the Gaelic came more naturally to me than the English *gateways* even if it had more syllables—but the threat remained. Our eagle friend flew through every so often to let us know the kraken still hid in its trench or wherever it lurked to lick its wounds, but each time I felt her approaching, I couldn't help the knot of unease that grew tighter in my belly.

Still no quest about the kraken.

No Bawbag-esque bounty on the anomaly's source, either. I wasn't sure if that was a good thing or a bad thing.

No news of Ronald. No real changes with Alison. Iain now spent most of his time going back and forth between Oban and

Kilmelford to see Meeksy. They'd both missed the party—Catrìona was threatening to drag them both to Iona for a day if they didn't let some of the mages relieve them. As soon as I finished digging through my piles of notifications, I planned to venture out there myself and add to the peer pressure.

Was it still peer pressure if the main person applying the pressure was your mum? Probably not.

*Through diligent use, you have increased the level of your skill: Connection (Level 12), Dubh (Level 2), Keen Eye (Level 5), Purifire (Level 11), Slànaich (Level 5), Spèird (Level 6), Tairm (Level 4), Tursa (Level 3).*

*Through physical exertion, you have gained a permanent +2 to Strength, +3 to Agility, +1 to Dexterity, +5 to Mind, +3 to Constitution, and +3 to Stamina. Please note that such increases have diminishing returns as your base statistics grow.*

*Through arcane exertion, you have gained a permanent +7 to Spirit, +2 to Pathos, and +3 to Will. Please note that such increases have diminishing returns as your base statistics grow.*

*You have increased your affinity: Nature (Level 20)*

*You have increased your affinity: Synthesis (Level 13)*

*You have increased your affinity: Staves (Level 20)*

*You have increased your specialised affinity: Wild (Level 15)*

*You have increased your specialised affinity: Coimhearsnachd (Level 7)*

*You have increased your specialised affinity: Justice (Level 2)*

Name: Calum Green

Age: 36

Level: 24

Class: Draoidh (Further class specialisation at: Level 27)

Affinities: Nature (Level 20), Healing (Level 7), Synthesis (Level 13), Staves (Level 20)

Specialised Affinities: Wild (Level 15), Coimhearsnachd (Level 7), Justice (Level 2)

Marks of Esteem: Life, Connection, Justice, Passage

Alteration:
    Strength: 41
    Dexterity: 55
    Agility: 60
    Mind: 118

Regeneration:
    Constitution: 42
    Stamina: 74

Manipulation:
    Spirit: 118
    Pathos: 47
    Will: 54

Boons:
    Blessings
    Làmh na Glaistige
    Glòir a' Ghiuthais
    Blàr Ghaineamhain

I'd nine skill points bumping around, and I had for a while. It was high time I did *something* with them, even if the thought of staring at more screens made my brain ache.

Might as well start with Coimhearsnachd to see how much our friendly little comrades-in-arms race had fared.

I was glad I was already lying down.

The damn community skill tree was lit up like, well, a bloody Christmas tree.

A full week of travel, battle, lightning, more travel, and copious amounts of alcohol had dimmed my brain's processing power even more than usual. I called up the notification we'd gotten upon activating the ionadan-siubhail.

*All community bonuses shall now be shared to all members.*

Holy galumphing shitebaws.

Is *that* what it meant?

My maths were not mathing, but no matter what, that tree had far and away more points than it should. We'd gained access to Cumantas.

We'd gained access to the next skill, Cala, and we were seven *hundred* points into the next skill on the tree, which was called Caithream.

I wasn't sure if I was reading it right, but unless we'd racked up over a thousand skill points from Obanites alone—possible, but how likely?—the system had merged all of the smaller local trees' points.

I lay on the bed for a moment, resisting the urge to kick my feet in elation. That would disturb the snoozing kitten curled up against my side, and that would be a sin.

Preening at my own restraint, I read over the unlocked skills.

*Cumantas*

*With combined effort expended for the common weal, Cumantas adds to the benefit of working together.*

*The radius of protection from Clach-Cheangail increases by 100 metres from the base 50.*

*Those designated as Tosgaire na Coimhearsnachd gain the ability to direct others' spirit.*

*All communication crystals created within the radius of the Clach-Cheangail will function at a distance of an additional 10 kilometres.*

That alone about made everything worth it.

But then there was Cala.

*Cala*

*Within the bounds of your community—defined as the area in which community members reside within one kilometre of one another—the aggression of all ascended animals will decrease. Only designated hostile beasts, noted within their description when studied with Keen Eye or equivalent skills, will actively attack sapient life within Cala's influence. This calming effect of your community's safe harbour may have additional benefits for local wildlife.*

*The radius of protection of Clach-Cheangail increases by 100 metres from the base of 150.*

This time, I did kick my legs on the bed, and while Sailean awoke with a startled burst of kitten annoyance in my mind, my excitement filtered through the bond enough that she chirped and puffed her whiskers forward.

"This is good, m' eudail," I said to her, my heart rate speeding to a march. "This is very, very good!"

I didn't bother hoping the kraken would be affected by Cala's influence, but the ambient stress of stoats, bloody brutal seagulls, badgers, any ascended fauna that could wreak havoc on the unwary? That evaporated with relief so palpable that I felt muscles actually release tension in my neck and shoulders they'd probably been carrying since I left Glasgow.

We were less than thirty points away from Caithream, and I did a double take as I looked again and saw it was down to less than twenty even in the time it had taken me to catch up on the others.

With a quiet whoop, I pulled up the description.

*Caithream*

*As the highest trunk-level skill in the Coimhearsnachd tree, Caithream marks the beginning of branching paths. While a community can, eventually, unlock all branches on the tree as a whole, most choose to concentrate on one or two branches that are best suited to their goals as a people.*

*Throughout an ascension process, communities frequently grow and merge through heroic, legendary, and mythic feats accomplished together over time.*

*Caithream can be unlocked only after two or more communities have merged. (Achieved) There are many paths to this goal; every community's ascension path leads them down a unique journey.*

*Unlocking Caithream creates a community quest. Depending on the branch(es) the community wishes to pursue, the quest or quests will align to the appropriate branch. It is for this reason the Ascended Alliance recommends a community reflect, discuss, and review their holistic strengths, weaknesses, and needs in order to choose the best options.*

Over seven hundred communally donated skill points to unlock whatever options these would be. The branches themselves remained shrouded, and as curious as I was, I also had too many memories of the absolute shitshow that was politics to feel anything beyond a tentative eagerness.

I decided, after a moment of letting my heartbeat slow down to a more normal zone, to leave that where it was for now. If anything, people would come banging on my door when it came time for decisions, and I was quite happy to make that Future Calum's problem.

For now, I would spend my nine skill points—some of them, at least—on myself. As a treat.

A memory tickled my brain with a feather, and I pulled up the Wild tree. I'd a vague inkling that whatever had been up next there was an active skill; maybe it would be of some use even if I was getting a bit overwhelmed with the skills I had as it was. Couldn't hurt to take a gander.

*Tuinn*

*As the name of this spell implies, Tuinn activates waves of wild magic through the ambient spirit. This can—and will—have unpredictable effects and will amplify other skills in the Wild tree when used.*

*At higher levels, Tuinn can animate non-sentient organic matter to first hinder and then harm an enemy, but its non-combat applications can include physical assistance with manual labour, entertainment, and more. Effects temporary.*

I squinted at the second paragraph. Entertainment, eh? That sounded dangerous. Humans had been making unsanitary sexual decisions since the dawn of time. Animating some mulch could have messy consequences.

That said, the last two words made me think of a time Susanna's rechargeable vibrator died when we were, erm, at a sensitive moment. That, combined with the word "unpredictable" in the first paragraph, might give all but the most intrepid adventurers a moment or three of pause.

One would hope.

I really wasn't sure about the skill, which was new. Usually, I was champing at the bit to snap up new skills as soon as I saw them. This one didn't quite spark joy.

Maybe it was that the internet had ruined me.

I'd go with that.

Leaving the Wild tree for now, I moved over to the Draoidh tree. The last skill I'd unlocked there had been Dubh, and that had been an incredibly useful skill so far.

When I looked through the tree, I skimmed through my existing skills. Bas-Ogham was a passive with active applications I hadn't even begun to explore since I'd barely had time to sit down, let alone think about tree writing. I would have been tempted to put a couple of my points into that to increase the skill, but it was an odd one for several reasons, not least that it improved based on attunements with different trees. Of those, I'd only unlocked oak, Darach.

But Dubh drew my eye. I reread its description to refresh my memory.

*Dubh*

*The Draoidh knows there is nowt to fear in darkness.*

*To the contrary, darkness is the source of all things, including light. It is from darkness the universe was born, and in that darkness is the potential of all creation.*

*Dubh allows you to tap into the creative power. Coupled with Bas-Ogham, it can be used to write ogham into your skin. In the heat of battle, the Draoidh can use Dubh to obscure an enemy's sight. While it will only work upon a foe who lacks the Draoidh's understanding of the true nature of darkness, on a fearful opponent who relies fully upon sight and light, it is a powerful weapon.*

*The skill taps into our most ancient connections to a time before time itself, before light, when all was one in the womb of the endless void. Dubh does not ascribe fear to this void; for the Draoidh, it is a source of comfort and solace. In returning to Dubh, the Draoidh finds the will to write reality into existence.*

*Affinity: Draoidh, Wild*

*Skill Tree: Draoidh*

While it wasn't directly related to Bas-Ogham, I felt a tug in my chest when I looked at it. I'd used it as an active skill in battle, but I hadn't delved into the applications of the skill on its primal, spiritual basis.

Before I could talk myself out of it, I added three points to it and confirmed my choice.

The notification popped immediately.

*Through use of a skill point, you have increased the level of your skill: Dubh (Level 5).*

That same pull faded once I'd settled the skill points. I still had six to use, but something told me to keep them in reserve.

Another skill in my Draoidh tree had caught my eye, and a spark of hope flashed deep within me.

A thought had lurked for some time in the recesses of my mind, with regard to the anomalies. I didn't know if the combination of my Faicte 's Neo-Fhaicte passive and Tursa could shine some light on the mystery.

All I knew was that it was the first inspiration I'd had on the subject.

It was time for me to pay Meeksy and Alison a visit.

# CHAPTER
# THIRTY-NINE

Because it was the decent thing to do, I called ahead on my rockie-talkie—gods, that name had well and truly stuck —to alert Meeksy to my plan to pester him.

He answered with the same beleaguered air of exhaustion I thought I must have been exuding in the days before, but he perked up when I told him I'd a glimmer of an idea.

"No promises," I told him. "I still don't know what the fuck I'm doing."

"Mate, we're all just throwing wet spaghetti at the wall to see if it sticks here. Literally about a hairsbreadth away from chucking actual pasta at Alison."

"*Hey!*" came Alison's voice, slightly muffled.

"She doing okay?"

"Creepy as fuck, but clinging on to her faculties so far, when she doesn't stare at me like a child of the sodding corn." I could almost hear Meeksy's eye roll, and when he went on, he wasn't talking to me. "What? You do. And it's not like that—you just look constipated. I can tell you're faking."

"Erm," I said, "I'm glad you two are getting on. I'll be there soon."

I withdrew my spirit from the communication crystal, unsure whether the jokes were a sign Alison was holding the corruption at bay . . . or a sign Meeksy'd been infected by an anomalous clown.

The mention of Alison fooling around made me remember the list she'd jokingly given me days ago. If nothing else, I could still bring that stuff out there. It was weird, but it might boost her spirits to know that I brought the duvets and pillows for folks—and the cast-iron pan, well, that could be mounted on the wall with a plaque.

We might never haul Ronald back here, and we might never cure Alison, but knowing there was the cartoonish promise of bonking him on the head with it lurking nearby could be a morale booster for everyone.

It didn't take me long to gather up all of what I needed. My inventory might as well have been full of dust bunnies for all the use it got these days, and it was almost nice to have it full of random bits and bobs.

Clouds obscured most of the sky when I left Oban, and thankfully, people didn't bar the way. More and more now, wherever I went, people wanted to talk to me. They wanted my opinions, my help, and in one uncomfortable case, my autograph. Iain had been with me for that one, and he'd laughed so hard the poor person had fled. I shook my head as I hurried down the road, a perfunctory wave to a man who opened his mouth to say something cutting him off.

Guilt needled at me when I had to give people the brush off. At least most folk understood that if I was on the move, I probably needed to, you know. Move it.

I hoped it wouldn't rain. Even if I would stay dry regardless, the low visibility wore on me, and any time I had to be around anomalies of any kind, it draped the entire situation in a cloak of claustrophobia. The cloud cover today wasn't total, thank the gods. High-altitude slabs of grey only intermittently allowed blue to show through, but at the extreme least, they moved at a fair clip across the sky and gave the weather a more comfortable air of transience.

Maybe it was my passives, maybe it was a fancy, or maybe I was just desperate to find some sort of pattern to latch onto, but the movement made me feel a smidge more hopeful. People grew sparser as I left Oban behind, and my pace picked up.

The route to Kilmelford was familiar on foot now, but one thing appeared to surprise me—something I hadn't seen on this route before.

Some*one*, rather.

Ealasaid appeared around a bend in the road, her own pace a decent clip. Every time I saw the woman, I swear she looked—not *younger*, not really, but it was as if the *effects* of age drained away. Her skin had less of the crepe-y look of collagen loss and more vibrance and brightness. She still wore her enormous Coke-bottle lens glasses on a cord around her neck despite the ascension providing planet-wide vision correction to all. I wondered if she was still afraid it would revert, that her vision would go one day and she'd wake up unable to see.

"Shin thu, a ghràidh," Ealasaid greeted me fondly when I got within speaking distance.

I stopped to kiss the cailleach's cheek, and she returned it, patting my other cheek with a soft hand.

"Have you been in Kilmelford?" I asked her. "I'm headed there now—had a wee idea I wanted to try."

Ealasaid nodded. "I brought Rhona some of her things."

That gave me pause. "Rhona's there? Wait, her *things*? Rhona's staying there?"

Ealasaid gave me a piercing look. "Nach robh fios agad?"

"Cha robh," I said, exasperated. I truly had had no idea

Rhona was spending time out in Kilmelford at all. "Carson a tha i—"

The old woman interrupted my asking why Rhona would be out there with a wave of her hand. "Ask her when you get there. Cuir ceist oirrese."

Harrumph.

"Aye, I'll do that." I paused, hesitating for a brief moment. Then, after a pulse of Connection to make sure we were alone—we were—I went on. "Ealasaid, you tend to notice things. When we met Finn, did you feel anything different?"

"I did." The cailleach's shrewd gaze grew pensive. "Six of us, to my count. You, Eilidh, Rhona, me—then that Samuel and Finn."

"Any idea what it means? Every time I'm around them, something strange seems to happen."

Ealasaid shrugged. "Something strange—m' eudail, that's the story of our lives the now."

"Stranger, then," I said. I took a deep breath, filling my lungs with cool highland air. "I suppose it's good to know I've not gone round the bend, at least."

"Whatever it is, it's meant to be," Ealasaid said, turning as if involuntarily to gaze westward.

Though the view of Mull lay obscured by the elbow of mainland that enclosed Loch Feochan in its armpit, I sensed instinctively that Mull was where Ealasaid's mind had gone.

"Meant to be?" My words drew the cailleach's attention back towards me, and she started.

"Did I say that? Hm."

I frowned. "You did, but—"

"Oh, never mind an old woman's fancies. You ought to get on towards Kilmelford. Alison will be happy to see you. Siuthad, a ghràidh."

With that, Ealasaid reached up, patted me on the cheek

once more, and set off at a power-walking pace that would have put pre-ascension suburban mummy groups to shame.

From Meeksy's banter with her, I half expected Alison to still look normal—or at least as normal as she had looked when I'd last seen her.

My first glimpse of her chased away that ill-placed optimism in an instant.

They'd moved her again. Ascension construction powers still left me gobsmacked, but the crafters and builders had outdone themselves. Far from the simple bothy that had begun the anomaly operation at the edge of Loch a' Phearsain, now there was indeed a full-on compound. And I'd been too late with my delivery of duvets and pillows and pots and pans, much to my chagrin—those remained in my inventory. Folks here had covered that whilst I was off flitting about the islands. Beyond furnishings, the crafters here had added an entire freestanding structure for Alison alone, and her new cage—the word still made me cringe—took up half of the room.

I wasn't sure that was a good thing. She'd more space to move around, sure, but if they'd expected her to pace like a caged tiger, they must have been surprised.

When I walked into the structure—house or containment module or prison, I wasn't sure what to call it—Alison stood stock still in the centre of her enclosure, equidistant between the two walls on either side of her, but instead of positioning herself in the very middle of her cage, she was as close to the weave of restraining spirit as she could safely stand.

The unnerving part of that was that she stood there as if she didn't even notice; her posture was tall but vacant, not slouchy or zombified, and at first glance, I had the unnerving impression of the young woman deigning to hold court.

In the back of her enclosure was a cubicle that I presumed contained a toilet; opposite that stood a trundle bed, made to military precision and disturbingly undisturbed.

The rest of the room held a corner desk opposite the entry, a few comfortable-looking chairs, and a very uncomfortable-looking Meeksy and Rhona, who both waited for me to process . . . Alison, I guessed.

Looking around the rest of the structure gave me a distraction and an excuse to not look directly at Alison herself.

She, by contrast, never took her eyes off me.

I instantly understood Meeksy's *Children of the Corn* reference. Surely, she had to blink sometimes, yeah? Her eyeballs didn't *look* like they had dehydrated into sultanas in their sockets.

Alison did not blink. Not once.

Her skin had an unnerving grey pallor to it, and even as I had noticed Ealasaid's losing the crepe-y texture that came with age and collagen loss, Alison's seemed to have gained that appearance. Except where in natural human ageing, the skin would also wrinkle and grow softer, looser. Alison's, by contrast, seemed stretched out over bone as if her muscles had calcified or as if there were some kind of mask beneath the epidermis. Her skin clung to it, a thousand times less natural looking than even a Botox addict's lack of expression.

"They won't show me what I look like, but from your face, it's bad."

I jumped when Alison spoke. My face immediately flushed. "Sorry for staring," I said hastily. "It's—"

"Bizarre?"

The one thing I couldn't bring myself to do was lie. "Aye, it's bizarre. Sorry."

Alison smiled, and it took every bit of control I had over my muscles not to recoil. Her skin didn't even wrinkle like normal skin; the corners of her mouth dimpled and *rippled*. It was the only way I could think to describe it. It was as if my impression had been truly correct, and only the thinnest layer of epidermis remained, flexible and pliant, but resting atop something that did not give way with it.

"You said you had an idea." Meeksy's chair squeaked as he stood, and oddly, it was that utterly normal, pre-ascension sound that made my own skin ripple into gooseflesh with its unexpected contrast to the uncanny-valley horror of our— Alison's—predicament.

Rhona remained shockingly quiet. I glanced at her, worried, and she gave me a tight smile. I'd ask her what was up later.

"Aye, I've got a thought. It's really more thought than idea, but I figured anything is worth a shot." I forced myself to meet Alison's eerie, unblinking gaze, hoping she wouldn't smile again herself. She didn't. "It shouldn't affect you directly."

"I am at your disposal." This time, when she spoke, Alison's words contained something *beyond*, and my skin prickled all over again.

Gods, this was creepy.

I didn't see much use in explaining myself if I tried what I was going to try and got a glorified fart noise in response, but I might as well get on with it.

My passives were meant to be just that, passive, but even so, I called up the ones I would lean on, just to reassure myself that there might, in fact, be some use to what I was doing.

**Faicte's Neo-Fhaicte** (*Passive*)
*The Gaels have long known that there are more worlds beyond*

*the physical, worlds into which people sometimes slipped, unseen or unheard or both. On occasion, they reemerged with tales of delight or horror or a mingling of the two.*

*Food so delicate and sweet all else would taste forever of ash. Beauty so rare and tantalising one could weep—but denying it would bring swift and brutal death.*

*The fuath, the glaistig, the beithir—all of these are creatures of your world and always have been. Now, though, they slink through the veil.*

*Faicte's Neo-Fhaicte alerts you to the presence of the otherworlds and may, for the canny, provide insight into its inner workings and motivations.*

*Affinity: Draoidh, Nature, Wild*

*Skill Tree: Draoidh*

· · ⟨⟩ · ·

**Liminality (Passive)**—*The Gaels and the Celts both venerated liminal spaces—the place where land meets water, dusk and dawn, and the traditional markings of the year for equinoxes as much as solstices. There is power to the between-places, where the world becomes veiled. Neither shore nor sea, yet both at once.*

*Liminality increases all Nature and Wild affinity abilities based on the following temporal-spatial locations: dawn, dusk, Imbolc, Samhain, Beltane, Lughnasadh, equinoxes, being within nine metres of a body of water, and being in places that house the dead.*

*Your magic shall respond with alacrity in these times and spaces, and you gain a 10% chance to bend others' magic to your own will to disarm it if it seeks to harm.*

*Any permanently bonded animal companions immediately unlock this passive skill.*

*As the bridge between the physical and the spiritual world, the Draoidh draws power from both.*

*This spell cannot be increased with skill points after unlocking, but mastery of its ways may trigger evolution.*

*Affinities: Synthesis, Wild*
*Skill Tree: Draoidh*

·ᴄ ⧼⧽ ɔ·

**Tuairmse** (Passive)—*Whilst most flounder with patterns in the wilds of nature, you thrive riding the waves of weather and landscape alike. Tuairmse is like a volcano; it may lie subtly dormant for a time, but when it wakes, the results can be course altering.*

*Tuairmse works best in tandem with the Nature tree's root-level passives: Gu h-Ìosal, Gu h-Àrd, Taobh a-Muigh, and Taobh a-Staigh. It is recommended to learn those skills prior to learning Tuairmse.*

*Once all of these are unlocked, however, your innate understanding of nature increases tenfold. You will not only be able to sense the turning of the seasons like the woodchuck who builds a thicker-walled den before an intense winter, but you will also judge the tides, the whip-quick shifts in weather, and most importantly, how to use those things to your advantage.*

*Affinity: Nature, Synthesis*
*Skill Tree: Draoidh*

·ᴄ ⧼⧽ ɔ·

The floor of the structure had the strange but increasingly familiar give of a professional running track. I wasn't sure how the crafters made it, but it made sitting on it ever so slightly more comfortable than gluing my arse bones to solid concrete.

I sat, not quite cross legged, on the floor well behind the line they had crafted into the surface itself in glimmering red. I'd not even noticed that until I got closer to it, and when I reached out a hand towards it, the line glowed brighter.

"A warning spell." Meeksy spoke in his bear-like soft rumble behind me. "It also makes a noise if you get too close and flashes."

"I'm very dangerous," Alison said conversationally.

She smiled again with a glint of too-white teeth.

"I'm going to ignore that," I muttered.

Here went nothing.

"You'll have to give me a bit of time," I said, shifting my weight. My legs were bent, one in front of the other like a sitting yoga pose. "I'm not sure how long it'll take me to know whether I'm onto something or not."

"Take all the time you need," Rhona said. "Not like she's got an appointment to meet the pope or anything."

Pushing my sudden wonder about whether the pope had even survived the ascension out of my head, I closed my eyes and started to breathe deeper.

CHAPTER
# FORTY

Like I had once upon a time at Bawbag's manor, I concentrated on the ebb and flow of breath and spirit, pulsing Connection as I went.

It came so much easier now, with an awareness I allowed to pervade my consciousness.

It was the difference between the reflexive and instinctive act of breathing and a yogi's ujjayi breath, the strange-sounding ocean breath where you consciously and audibly inhaled from the openness of your nasal cavity and exhaled the same way. The awareness of your diaphragm's contraction, the activation of your parasympathetic nervous system, the conscious level of an unconscious process that could be used to alter your reactive state.

In fact, I combined the ujjayi breath with my cycling spirit.

Like the heightened awareness of breath, the cycling of spirit rooted me in part of my body that I was gradually feeling out both consciously and subconsciously—the energetic body.

I had never understood what the woo-woo crowd meant when they said "energetic body" before the ascension, but now I did, and I had to admit—with no small amount of chagrin—

that they had grasped something the rest of us cave dwellers didn't. We'd pooh-poohed the woo-woo, even though plenty of traditions all over the planet asserted it, especially in cultures where they practiced yoga and reiki and qigong as spiritual practice beyond physical.

Turns out, they were right on the money all along.

We *were* energy; oddly, it was the matter that was the illusion. All atoms were mostly space. Everything in existence was energy.

*That* took it a wee bit too far for my himbo hamster brain, so I focused where I could make sense of things.

Like blood, spirit flowed through channels. Meridians, pathways, whatever we wanted to call them, our life force and our connection to magic worked like our other systems and then some. Blood was mostly limited to veins, arteries, capillaries. Spirit was and was not. It flowed more smoothly through those established avenues, but it also existed outwith the meridians. Transcended them, in a way.

By tapping into that network within me, I grew aware that my energetic body actually surrounded my "physical" body. It encompassed it and could overlap with others' energetic bodies, as it right now overlapped with Meeksy, Rhona, and Alison, as well as the much smaller signatures of creatures both creepy and crawly who went about their business obliviously beneath the floor and outside the walls.

As my breath and spirit cycling expanded, so did my energetic body. One of the ascension books I'd absorbed had described this as attunement, like what I'd done with the oak but instead with myself. It elevated the frequency of my energy, where my usual day-to-day goings on would contract and lower that resonance.

A glimmer filtered through my awareness.

When I had cast Tairm with the hare, I was used to the spell simply triggering and responding without any further direction from me. But something in that moment—something, I felt certain, that had to do with the proximity of Finn and Eilidh—had expanded my energetic body. *All* of our energetic bodies, along with our awareness, a collective ujjayi breath. From that space, I had been able to direct Tairm into that lightning.

Tairm was an active skill but had a passive element. It was like pressing an unlabelled button.

But something about the collective expansion of our energy had given me the instinct to reach into the machine and route the signal of the button to the desired result.

If that was possible, then maybe passives weren't really passive after all.

Maybe they could be accessed.

My diaphragm would move and respond to my breath whether I actively inhaled or not, but if there was anything I remembered from my mòd-related singing experiences—trust me, there wasn't much I hadn't repressed out of the terror of tween-aged public performance—it was that your control of the vital, powerful muscle had a direct effect on the quality of breath and sound that made a voice *go*.

I lost track of time as I sat on that floor. It warmed to the temperature of my body. I felt into the moment, into the flow of spirit.

While blood remained contained in my physical body except in an emergency, spirit, like breath, came and went in relationship to the outside world.

Unlike breath, spirit didn't only have a pair of entry points; spirit had multiple.

I was not even a little bit sure if Eastern philosophies had described those entry points. My mind retained a vague awareness of acupuncture and pressure points, but I had no way of knowing how what I observed matched up to pre-ascension human understanding.

What I did know was that we'd gotten the third eye right.

Within my energetic body, there were many points where spirit funnelled into my meridians, but the third eye felt like it had the strongest draw.

It was there I concentrated on the sensation, feeling spirit enter, circulate, and leave.

As I repeated the cycles over and over and over and over again, I did notice something curious.

Unlike with breath where we could inhale air through the nose and exhale it through the mouth and vice versa, spirit that entered the body through one point made a full circuit of my meridians before exiting the way it came in.

The experience rose to the forefront of my consciousness with the next cycle. Awareness lit up my third eye, entry points at my wrists, palms, shoulders. The crown of my head. At the base of my neck and the base of my spine. At the centre of my core. My heart. My hips. My pelvic floor. My feet.

And, suddenly, my third eye *opened*.

It was the only way I could think of to describe it, opening.

My awareness moved outside my "self" as pre-ascension me would have classified it, but that was only true in that my awareness raised itself beyond my physical eyes.

It was as if my body had become a three-dimensional model sat, straight-backed, on the floor. My energetic body surrounded me an egg-shaped space, and my mind immediately added more points to the ones I'd felt through my physical body. Spirit moved through my energetic body without a physical focal point, too.

And I saw them.

The filaments.

Just like I'd seen at Salen Bay, the world lit up with them.

Fine as gossamer, delicate and indestructible at once. They permeated . . . everything.

With every cycle of breath and spirit, the filaments swirled and shifted, moving through my energetic body in a dizzying dance.

Where my energetic body overlapped with others', those filaments twined around one another.

Something else caught my attention.

With Meeksy, the filaments felt familiar. They moved in and out of his the way old friends moved in one another's space; comfortable and safe. It brought with it a surge of affection that, in turn, hummed through the frequency of spirit and elevated it.

But that wasn't what had struck me.

What hit me was where my energetic body met Rhona's.

The younger woman's energy *illuminated* where it touched mine—and vice versa.

Where my filaments and Meeksy's danced, mine and Rhona's ignited.

Amplified.

I wanted to explore that, to see what was causing it, because the answer to what we'd experienced with Finn and Samuel and each other felt bound by that ecstatic interaction of energetic light.

That wasn't why I was here.

And the moment I directed my focus to my purpose at long last, all of that excitement fell away.

Because where my energetic body reached out towards Alison, where hers grasped out at me, it *hungered*.

Loch a' Phearsain had not stopped looking appealing.

All I wanted to do was dive into its murky waters as if I could wash the memory of Alison's energy out of my skin and psyche alike.

I'd left her still standing like a creepy-ass statue in her enclosure, her eyes glued to me and that terrible, tantalised smile wrinkling the corners of her mouth like the film of dried milk on hot cocoa.

No, *I* was the caged tiger, and I was not the one in a cage. I paced back and forth on the path between outbuildings, waiting for Meeksy and Rhona to join me.

Apparently, the mages had devised a warding system so they could keep Alison—and, by extension, the entity that had infected her—from hearing sensitive information. But they were careful with it. They hadn't even let her hear them discuss it, which meant to employ it, they had a system that they enacted from outside the structure entirely.

There was a small sign that I'd missed on my way in that, not unlike the Ulva Ferry's signal, had a slider from red to yellow to green. When it was green, we could speak freely as long as we remained two metres from the walls of the structure.

Right now it was yellow, which meant the wards were being activated. I had to wait until it was red, and already, the time stretched out to the point that I really was about to go dive in the gods damned loch.

I shuddered again, unable to help myself.

The sense of hunger, a ravenous and insatiable hunger, still ate at the edges of my mind.

What it was hungry for, I didn't know. Frankly, I didn't give a damn.

All I knew, and all that mattered, was that it would devour us all if we let it.

Compared to the vastness of that hunger, the kraken might

as well have been an adorable baby Pixar squid, big eyes and accidental inking. A cutesy whoopsie daisy.

We may have to deal with the kraken first, but if I'd had any doubt whatsoever that the anomalies were the real danger, what I'd seen in Alison had chased that doubt into the abyss.

The slider, moved with magic, flipped to red.

An exhausted-looking Meeksy opened the door to the structure.

He didn't say anything until he crossed the perimeter line, but the moment he did, his shoulders slumped even more. Meeksy squinted up at the sky, where the clouds had cleared to some degree, but the sun was still obscured, on its downward arc. I'd been sitting there on the floor for literal hours, but the ache in my butt was nothing compared to the pain in the arse that was coming for us.

"What did you see?" He asked the question as if bracing himself for the worst.

Couldn't blame him for that.

As best I could, I explained with a rundown of what I'd seen and how, and his face grew thoughtful.

"I'm going to need to come back and try again," I said. "I'm just floundering around with this, and while I *think* I should be able to at least consciously explore my passives' insight eventually, there's a steep learning curve."

I paused, mulling over my next words.

"I think there's a certain level of danger here, too, aside from the obvious. Whenever I've connected to the anomalies' spirit, however peripherally, there's been a risk of the controlling entity interacting." Blowing out a breath, I shuddered again. "It didn't see what I was doing this time, probably because I did the energetic equivalent of sitting there breathing at it, and that's it. But it *is* acting on the spirit around it, which opens a whole other, like, barge of worms. Forget cans."

Actually, worms were a strangely appropriate analogy. The anomaly's energetic body was crawling with grasping, squiggling filaments that felt alien compared to our own, like a parasite. A tapeworm, a botfly, anything.

My whole body twitched at the thought. I no longer wanted to jump in Loch a' Phearsain. I wanted to spiritually cleanse myself with preternatural bleach.

Meeksy watched me physically get myself back under control, his expression growing more and more bleak with every passing second.

"What?" I asked warily. Something had clearly occurred to him.

"You said the anomaly is 'acting on the spirit around it.'"

"Aye."

"Could that have an affect on behaviour?"

I frowned. Now that the image of parasites was in my head, I couldn't shake it, and my nature-documentary memory kicked in.

"Yes," I said, wishing I were less certain. "There are certain parasites and fungal infections that can affect host behaviour. I think we'd be pure numpties to think this would be somehow different or safer."

"Feasibly, could that explain Ronald?"

Oh, shit.

I'd been thinking of him as a cowardly wank stain, which might very well be true, but even if he weren't strictly corrupted by the anomalies to the point where he was as dangerous as they were, it didn't rule out the possibility of those hungry, grasping worms influencing him to do things he otherwise wouldn't.

There was, obviously, a difference between impulse and action. It was why I wanted to punch any man who blamed a woman's clothes for his shitty behaviour to her—it was infantilising to men who owned their own actions and choices, and it was grotesque. Human beings have impulses all the time; just because I might *want* to sic a pod of orcas on a billionaire's yacht doesn't mean I would act on the desire. Because I was a grown-arse adult who had the self-control of a grown-arse adult.

But certain things lowered inhibitions and made us more likely to act on impulse. Those things did *not* absolve the person of responsibility. They weren't going to make someone do something they didn't have the capacity and inclination to do already.

"Think out loud, mate," Meeksy said after a moment, and I realised I'd been silent for a long minute.

I ran through what I'd just thought of, and his beard moved as he chewed on the inside of his cheek. It was an anxious tic and one I'd not seen him do in a very, very long time.

"So you're essentially talking about two different things," he said.

"What do you mean?" I squinted at him, though I already thought I knew what he was going to say.

Meeksy paused as if needing to organise his thoughts. "A parasite that acts on the a host to change behaviour is something that can *force* the host to do something uncharacteristic. Whether the host is *aware* is another question, but they are helpless in the face of it and reduced to the level of observer. Yes?" At my nod, he went on. "The second example, of lowered inhibitions, like with drugs or alcohol, that's different. No matter how someone says they become the observer there, they don't. Their choice is inherent in their situation unless they're forcibly or coercively drugged. But someone who gets drunk and beats their spouse and then later says it wasn't them but the booze is full of shit or everyone who had a few pints would turn into an abusive shitbag. Lowered inhibitions just—

temporarily—remove the fear of reprisal for doing something we want to do anyway."

Silence stretched out between us. Meeksy was a nurse; he saw a lot of people come through the hospital where he worked, and I knew he got "regulars" in victims of intimate partner violence. It was his stories that had so heavily shifted my own understanding of such things, the patterns he saw play out over and over and over again. I fought the urge to shudder again.

"Right. The question is whether the anomalies function as a parasite or a drug, I guess." As soon as I said it, dread settled into my gut. "And I think it can't be a drug."

I remembered flashes, moments where anomalies I'd slain seemed to exude relief.

Like they'd been captive in their own bodies, a prisoner as they watched a nightmare play out with no escape, no waking up. For death to be a welcome reprieve, they had to be aware—and unable to stop what was happening.

Meeksy seemed to come to the same conclusion at the exact same time. "Alison is still in there. She's aware. She might make some jokes, but she's fighting for her life."

I looked over his shoulder at the innocuous-looking building.

"If the notifications we've gotten are any indication, she's also not the first." I thought of Ezekiel Bosworth, whose name I knew first because his family were notorious in pre-ascension politics and second because he seemed to have been the first to be corrupted by the anomalies.

"We need to find Ronald," Meeksy said. "If this thing is acting on him even without taking him over completely, we need to contain him. And we need more precautions for everyone here."

I reached out and clasped my friend's shoulder hard. "Aye, brother. We do."

His brown eyes met mine. I knew he was thinking of Iain, just as I was. And Rhona.

Meeksy returned my shoulder squeeze before turning back to the building. Just before he reached the line, I called him back.

"Meeksy—send Rhona out. I'm not sure why she's hanging out in here, but I think it's even more dangerous in there for her than it is for you."

His startled look faded after a moment, and he gave me a grave nod before crossing the threshold.

# CHAPTER
# FORTY-ONE

"You doing all right?" I asked Rhona as we made our way back to Oban.

She kept looking over her shoulder back towards Kilmelford —including right as I asked the question—and she jumped at the sound of my voice as if I'd caught her out.

Alarm started to gather inside my ribcage like wee bubbles at the bottom of a pot on the hob.

"You've been friends with Iain and Meeksy for a long time, right?" she blurted out.

I blinked at the non-sequitur. "Iain since we were kids, Meeksy since uni. Why?"

Rhona visibly relaxed for some reason. "I just . . ."

Her cheeks turned pink in the late-afternoon light. The clouds had finally given way to blue sky to the west, and the sunset was going to be a belter.

I stayed quiet, waiting for Rhona to go on. A small-yet-persistent suspicion had begun to dawn, and I didn't want to spook her if I was right.

"Okay, so you have to promise you're not going to take the piss out of me," she said at last.

"I promise."

Another time, I might have made a smart-arse remark, but my spidey senses were telling me she had something important she wanted to say, and I knew from my own personal experience with Susanna that being a smart-arse to someone trying to be earnest about something vulnerable was the fastest way to ruin their trust in you entirely. I'd eventually stopped trying to tell Susanna anything; I wanted Rhona to feel safe talking to me about everything. She was like a younger sister to me—part of the family.

"It's Alison," she said, all in a rush. "She and I—I mean, we —ugh. Before it happened, we were sort of . . . talking."

My spidey sense had been bang on. No wonder she'd been there all that time with Meeksy—between Alison's predicament and likely feeling safe confiding in our gentle papa bear friend, I couldn't blame her. That explained why she hadn't been around even before what happened to Alison, too. Hm. It was all coming together.

I stopped walking, put my hand on Rhona's shoulder to stop her own movement, and then I pulled her into my arms as tight as I could.

Rhona tensed up for a moment, but then she made a small wail and buried her face in my chest. I missed whatever she said next aside from the muffled vibration against my sternum.

"You're gonnae have tae say that again, a ghràidh," I told her.

The young woman pulled back, wiping tears from her eyes with the heels of her hands.

"I was afraid you'd think it was silly of me," she confessed. "I didn't think you liked her."

"Rhona, I like her just fine. I was just a bit uncomfortable with her putting me on a pedestal when we first met. Alison maybe started out a bit floundering, but who didn't? She's spent the last few weeks painstakingly learning from any mistakes, and that's a lot more than we can say about too many people." My tone darkened at the end, and Rhona's lip curled in disdain.

"I wanted to go after him myself," she said, venom in her words. She did not have to explain who she meant. "*She* convinced me not to. Said it wouldn't be worth it. I think she knew I'd kill him."

"That's something we can't take back." I reached out and gave her a gentle pat between the shoulder blades, beginning to walk again. "We've all killed people—or most of us have, anyway, at least in our wee group—but it's different when it's someone we know. Someone who has been part of our group and isn't actively trying to harm us."

Rhona wilted at that. "I know," she said in a small voice. "But he might have killed her."

Her voice cracked on the word *her*, and a pang went through my heart. "We're going to do everything we can to avoid that. I can't make any promises, but we're going to try."

She scrubbed her eyes with the heels of her hands again as if they were betraying her by crying. "Sorry I didn't tell you. I was scared—both because it's Alison and because, well. She's a girl."

"You don't ever have to be afraid of how I'll react to that, love," I told her as earnestly as I could. "I understand why you were, but you never, ever have to worry about that with me."

Rhona sniffled at that, shaking her head in annoyance. "Ugh, I knew I could trust you. There's just this—this bloody wee voice that wouldn't shut its gob in the back of my head, telling me I was wrong."

"I think I've got a one of those myself," I said wryly. "Does Eilidh know?"

Rhona shook her head. "You can tell her, if you want."

"If you don't feel safe telling her yourself, that's fine, and I can. But you can trust Eilidh as much as you can trust me." I snorted. "Honestly, probably more. She's less of a numpty about heaps of shite."

"Hm, true."

O-hò, it was like that? I chuckled. "Brat."

"Arse."

After a moment, Rhona looked over at me again.

"You can tell Eilidh. She can come—she can come talk to me if she wants to, but I just . . . ugh. I don't like the idea of coming out or whatever. I just want to be who I am and I don't know why it's still such a big deal."

"Because people are cunts?" I shrugged. "You got a word you want me to use or do you want me to just tell her our resident banshee's dating a possible future zombie?"

"The anomalies are *not* zombies!" Rhona actually stamped a foot. Then she grinned a sheepish grin. "But okay, touché. I don't love labels but other people seem to find them useful, so you can just tell her I'm pansexual."

"Pan heard." I brightened. "Our resident pan-shee, aw, yes. Ooh, I'm going to have so much fun with puns."

"Oh, no. Oh, *no*."

"Oh, yes."

"Oh-no-oh-no-oh-no."

In fact . . .

Yes, this was going to be excellent. The time for earnestness had passed. It was dad joke time.

Ignoring Rhona's sudden increasing horror, I rummaged in my inventory and produced the cast-iron skillet I'd brought out for Alison and held it out to Rhona with a bow.

"It you."

"Oh, for fuck's sake, Calum. You just had that *stashed*? Why?"

I briefly explained the joke with Alison—and my ingenious plan to boost morale by making it into a cartoonish Chekhov's gun in case Ronald ever returned—which made Rhona smile and say, "Like that scene in *Expendables 2* where Jet Li bangs his way through a kitchen hitting people with frying pans!" but her eyes still carried a shadow of wistfulness.

"I'm so proud that you know of that scene," I said, taking the pan in one hand and pretending to wipe my eyes with the other.

"Gimme that," she said, making grabby hands as I was about to stick the skillet back into my inventory.

I complied, and a moment later, the pan disappeared into Rhona's inventory.

"Do you really think taking it away is going to stop me from making pan puns every time I get the chance?" I asked, amused.

"Pfft, hardly. When I go back to Kilmelford, I'm going to use it to make a shrine. That was a good idea. *Not* the pun." She glared at me in mock rage, but after a moment, I could see when her mind moved to Ronald. Rhona bared her teeth in a savage smile. "And when we find Ronald again, you better *believe* I'm going to let Ali hit him with it."

"I'll hold him when you do. And with ascension healing, you can both bonk him with it a few times, and he'll heal just fine."

Rhona linked her arm in mine. "Yes, telling you was a good plan."

"An excellent pan. Of course it was."

"Shut up, or I'll bonk *you* with the pan."

"Och, all you need to do that is hit me yourself."

Rhona's groan startled a nearby tree full of birds into flight. Or maybe that was the fault of my answering laughter.

·( ᘓᘓᘓᘓ )·

A familiar chirp greeted me just as we reached the Tesco carpark, and I turned to see my wren friend . . . flying *out* of the ionad-siubhail.

"Please tell me the local wildlife is not, in fact, using our magical teleportation gateways," I said to Rhona, who blinked at me, then held her hand out to the wren, who landed on her finger and tweeted a wee song.

"I think he just used his wings," she said, holding the wren up in front of her face and making kissy noises at him.

The wren puffed up his feathers to make himself a perfect sphere, settling himself more firmly on Rhona's finger in a positive haze of self-satisfaction.

"Dè tha dol, a charaid?" I said to the wren.

His eyes had closed in bliss as Rhona stroked his chest with one finger, and he opened one of them again as if to ask me why I dared interrupting his massage.

As he had done a time or two before, though, his mind reached out to me.

He was getting much better at that. When I accepted the connection, the images that funnelled into my mind were clear, concise. And still occasionally cute—he'd seen some basking sharks, apparently, and he thought they were funny. The wee feathered friend had a point; they were odd creatures.

The salient point of his visit was far more important than the local shark population, glad as I was to hear they were neither mutated to monstrous size nor reduced to kraken chum.

Oor esteemed wren pal had been able to see said sharks because, in an ascension-level absurdist twist, he'd hitched a lift on a mutual friend, the eagle.

He explained to me—at least I thought this was the gist of his report—that Finn had asked him to go with the eagle, and since the wren could talk to both Finn and the eagle but Finn couldn't talk to the eagle, Finn had wanted his own eyes in the sky.

My brain hurt a little trying to keep up, but the wren's feathers had puffed up so far in pride at being chosen by Am Bàrd Muileach for such an important quest that I thought he might actually explode.

Just looking at him made me lightheaded.

That wasn't even all.

The eagle had made friends of her own.

"Breathe," Rhona said, peering more closely at the wren in concern.

I gave him a tiny poke with a tendril of spirit, and he squeaked. Clearly, he really had been about to pass out with the glory of his own self-importance.

"Why does he look like that?" Rhona asked me, reminding me that she could not, in fact, hear or see everything the rotund little ball of feathers was preening about.

"He's got friends in very high places," I said seriously and related the wren's excitement to her as fast as I could.

"*More* eagles?" she exclaimed when I was done.

"More eagles. It's getting Middle Earth up in here."

"Never say that again. The last thing we need is Mount Doom waking up in Ardnamurchan or Mull." At my blank look, Rhona rolled her eyes. "Haven't you read your Argyll geology? There used to be a super volcano or two there or something. You can still see the crater from the sky, but it was millions of years ago. Spread lava all the way into, like, the Borders."

I shook my head rapidly a few times. "I'll . . . ask the eagles to give me a lift up there one of these days, but till then, I'll take your word for it."

"Can I feed him?" This question made me turn, because it came from a child.

Not just any child—Cara, the terrifyingly insightful child who just casually suggested that the kraken was playing big, scary sea monster because it was scared by a bigger, scarier sea monster.

"Erm, sure," I said. "Just seeds, though, aye?"

"Mam!" Cara bellowed, making the wren squeak once more and flutter off Rhona's finger for a moment before settling back down. "I need bird seed!"

I watched, nonplussed, as a woman—presumably Cara's mother—bustled over and produced a bag of millet and sunflower seeds from her inventory.

Nope, this was never going to get less weird.

I listened to Rhona telling Cara about the volcanos while the wren ate his fill, and when he stopped, Cara pouted in disappointment.

"He's a very wee birdie," I told her. "And I think he just ate his weight in millet."

As if in agreement, the wren gave a tweet that sounded suspiciously like a burp.

An image of Ulva Ferry flitted into my mind at the same moment the wren darted away, straight back into the ionad-siubhail.

I watched carefully, but I did not see him emerge from the other side.

"Definitely not just feathers," I muttered.

"What?" Cara's mum asked.

"Nothing."

Cara, bored now that the bird had gone, started tugging at her mum's sleeve. Her mother glanced down with a bit of exasperation, but she gave me a small smile. "If you're not too busy, Calum, I think you'd be of some use over with the crafters."

"Oh?" I didn't want to be rude, so I kept my gaze trained on the woman's face, but over her shoulder, I could see Rhona slowly tiptoeing away. After a moment, she blurred into stealth. Our resident teenage banshee was allergic to crafting. And she was abandoning me. Bloody traitor. "What do they need?"

"They're working on the scrying pools."

My eyes widened. "I will head there straight away."

# CHAPTER
## FORTY-TWO

The scrying pool had been one of the blueprints we'd gotten as a reward for dispensing with Bawbag. Like the ionadan-siubhail, it had global implications.

Also like the ionadan-siubhail, it required more effort than the usual crafting items.

While plenty of average, everyday things used magic and spirit-infused materials, they were all meant to be used in one location without, for instance, traipsing across the entire planet. Just like we'd needed transatlantic telegraph and fibre optic cables and satellites in pre-ascension times for instantaneous communication, magic also needed infrastructure of a sort.

The scrying pools weren't difficult, per se, but the operative word was "pool," and the liquid that would fill said pool was tricky.

As much as my pathetic himbo hamster brain could understand it, it was essentially liquid quartz crystal that, like mercury, *remained* liquid at all temperatures we were likely to encounter on Earth.

To convert quartz into this liquid, it required an intense purification of spirit. To call it "spirit infused" was a bit like saying a diamond was just a hunk of carbon. Not *wrong*, but definitely not *right* or precise.

Anyway, I'd been a bit preoccupied with other things and hadn't had the time to sit down and spend days on end thinking really hard at sand.

Sand was usually the best source of silica in easy reach for people, and there was a sand mine in Lochaline. I knew that, because I think my mum's dad had worked there once upon a time.

While I'd been off doing other things, the crafters of Oban had found people to not only gather a whole heap of quartz sand but also, apparently, to think very hard at it for days on end.

That was a reductive way of putting it, but since I'd spent the afternoon essentially thinking really hard at my own electrons, I figured I was allowed to be cheeky.

I made my way over to the crafting station, only to stop short. I'd been absent for a couple days, and the place had expanded.

Significantly.

It had previously taken up the former vehicle queues at the pier where cars used to wait to get on the ferries. Now, it stretched down to the old Railway Pier carpark. A somewhat central hub had sprung up, and even from where I stood, I saw clear jars of herbs, stones, shelves with stacks upon stacks of different woods, a glasshouse of hydroponics, and an entire section dedicated to metals. The brilliant thing about ascension crafting was the quiet—no banging of hammer on anvil necessary, no saws, little waste because excess could simply be repurposed without losing its integrity.

It also made storage easier for things like junked metal from cars, since we didn't have to keep everything in ungainly heaps of salvaged doors and bonnets. Crafters could just as easily reduce the metal in a vehicle to purified and easy-to-carry chunks and stacks that slotted right into inventory and could be produced and shelved without dropping a sheet of steel on your foot.

No matter how handy all of this was, the sight of it struck me a bit speechless.

Every time I thought I was getting used to things, it hit me all over again. Maybe one day we'd really acclimate. Anyone younger than Cara would one day forget they'd ever known a time before magic was real. What a thought.

I wasn't sure where the scrying pool consortium had established themselves, but I figured someone would see me and lasso me.

Five steps—that was as far as I got towards the glasshouse.

"Calum!"

At least the person calling my name was a familiar face. Eliza, Angus's wife. She waved at me until I moved her direction, and when I got close enough to speak to her without yelling, she gestured excitedly back the way she'd come.

"We're working on the scrying pools, and the first three are almost ready." Eliza pointed towards the carpark along Railway Pier, the street that ran along the harbour side of the railroad tracks. "I've got to get something, but you should go see."

"That's exactly what I was planning to do," I told her with a grin. "A little bird told me yous were working on them, but I didn't realise they were that close to being done."

"The ionadan-siubhail"—again, her Argyll-touched English accent contorted to precise Gaelic with the words—"really fired folk up. Lismore and Kerrera will be the first to get one. Ours is going in Argyll Square with the clach-cheangail."

"Magic," I said without thinking.

"Literally." Eliza grinned and patted me on the shoulder, continuing on her errand.

I headed for where she'd pointed.

Even on the approach, I could see the glow of spirit. Not wanting to distract anyone, I didn't get too close at first, hanging back and trying to spy on them from ten or so metres away. Then someone closer shifted, turning an auburn head to look directly at me.

Eilidh.

It was like she'd known I was there—maybe part of her seer abilities was an eye in the back of her head.

On second thought, I wanted to scrub that entire idea from my brain with a scouring pad.

I made my way to her side, where she stood a short distance away from the crafters working on the pools.

"They're almost done," she murmured, standing on her tiptoes to give me a soft kiss on the lips.

Every time she did something like that, it gave me a wee shock all over again. The sweetness of it, her lips on mine—I couldn't have pinpointed why, exactly, but something inside of me relaxed at her proximity, her touch.

Like I was home.

I knew I ought to be watching them finish this important bit of Oban history, but instead I was just staring at the way the glow of spirit danced on Eilidh's auburn hair.

She caught me looking at her and replied with a quizzical cock of her head.

"Is tu tha brèagha," I said.

Her pale cheeks flushed, and she looked down with a small smile playing at the corners of her mouth for my having called her beautiful.

Eilidh's hand slipped into mine, and she gestured with her

chin towards the crafters.

There were three at each pool. Because the pools were only about the size of the average wok and situated at about waist level for an adult, I couldn't see much of them between the bodies of the people making them.

In a small gap, I caught a glimpse of what appeared to be pure gold and rippling, crystalline water. Light refracted off of that water and cast back rainbows like a prism. Except where the average prism's rainbows would be at least the size of a thumbprint, these were infinitesimal.

Had my vision not been more attuned to spirit and the arcane, it might have just looked like someone had filled a golden bowl with holographic glitter, but that made it sound cheap.

The bowls may not have been actual gold, but they looked it from where I stood, and they rested in intricate stands that cradled the pools in silver whorls of metal. The liquid quartz within them moved like water, but it had the same uncanny quality of mercury. One glance was enough to tell it was *not* our usual dihydrogen monoxide or any similar liquid like vinegar.

I watched, transfixed, as the crafters manipulated spirit in the bellies of the bowls.

Taking the moment to expand my senses the way I had earlier, I tried to work out what it was they were doing, exactly. It didn't quite make sense to me, but I hadn't given the blue-print more than a cursory glance when I'd absorbed it. Maybe digging deeper into it would shed some light on the process, but even from what I could see, it was complex.

Unlike what Samuel did with harnessing other people's spirit when granted permission, each trio seemed to be spinning spirit and passing it sunwise around their scrying pool. Threads of it flowed from each crafter, joining with a circle that ringed the lip of the golden bowl and twined together with the next thread. Around and around and around it went, growing many-plied and stronger with every circuit.

Just as rope grew stronger the more fibres you twisted into it, so this cord of spirit grew sturdier and more visible.

I couldn't be certain, but the longer I stared at the liquid quartz, the more I seemed to hear a vibrating resonance, a hum like a singing bowl.

That hum rose around us, first a distinct tone, then a branching harmony between the three bowls, swelling into a chord that built, each pool resonating the same note in first one octave, then two, then three, then more.

All at once, it ended, leaving behind the strange impression of its memory, like the afterimages you see after looking at a bright light, if such a thing could happen with sound.

A hush swept over the gathered crafters and the few onlookers the song of the scrying pools had pulled from their paths.

Something Eilidh had said clicked into place as a chuckle broke the silence and excited chatter picked up.

"You said two of them are going to Kerrera and Lismore," I said slowly, staring at the diamond-bright liquid quartz.

"Aye." Eilidh raised an eyebrow at me.

Boats weren't exactly notorious for travelling steadily without sharp movements, no matter how calm the sea.

"Well," I said, "I just have one question. How are we getting them there without spilling?"

One of the crafters overheard me and gave me a rakish grin. "Easy," he said.

And he promptly aimed a kick at the nearest scrying pool.

I felt my soul leave my body with the collective horrified gasp that cracked through the crowd like a rifle's bark.

A clang rang through the air—but that was it.

The pedestal with the golden scrying bowl on it didn't so much as budge.

Silence fell in the aftermath of the clang, followed by a titter, then a giggle, then a few good-natured swears.

The man who'd kicked the thing winced, giving his leg a shake. "I didn't think that through. Newton's third law."

"Serves you right," said one of the other crafters. "What if that hadn't worked?"

They started bickering about the blueprint's fine print, leaving the rest of us milling about now that the show was over.

"I'm going to go with them to Lismore and Kerrera," Eilidh told me. "They asked me to accompany them."

"Oh! Do you want me to come along as well?" I asked.

"I mean, yes. But while I'm doing that, if you could establish a couple waypoints for the next bunch of ionadan-siubhail, that would probably be best." Eilidh paused. "There's a list floating around here somewhere. Most people agreed that Kilmelford is top priority so we can get help there faster if anything goes wrong, but after that, some of the other islands. Tiree and Coll first, I think, since Jura and Islay and Colonsay might have to wait until the kraken is dealt with."

"It'll get easier," I said, trying to will myself to believe it.

Jura was close in theory, but sailing there meant circumventing the massive Corrievreckan whirlpool either by sailing south all the way around the island to reach the inhabited side or passing between Luing and Scarba, and I wasn't really sure if any of our sailors had experience with those routes. Or how deep the waters were or any of the other important bits of information that made seafaring less dangerous.

We'd gotten someone out there this week, but I wasn't actually sure how. Needless to say, the increased chance of unlocking sea-related affinities had not, in fact, unlocked any for this himbo hamster.

Eilidh's gaze had turned to the sky, and I followed her line of sight. "Calum," she said, her breath catching. "How many eagles would you say that is?"

Even as she said it, my eyes caught what she meant.

In the outer reaches of my awareness, I felt the presence of the eagle mind I was used to.

Apparently, she'd found some friends.

CHAPTER
# FORTY-THREE

If one enormous eagle had caused a commotion when she had perched atop Clach a' Choin what now felt like a lifetime ago, the sight of six more soaring above Oban harbour set the town to buzzing so frenetically, I briefly thought the vibration might shatter every window in town.

There were plenty of reasons eagles enjoyed reverential status around the globe—fierce hunters, striking silhouettes, sheer size even before the ascension—but watching birds big enough to see with perfect clarity with the naked eye showcased the pure enormity of their majesty.

My first avian friend was a golden eagle, and of the now seven who circled above Oban, another four were just like her. Their feathers were a deep bronze. Lit by the sun, the light touched those massive pinions with gold like a halo. I couldn't have guessed their wingspan, but it would have to be measured in metres.

For one long, stretched-out moment, I felt a flash of awesome terror. These raptors were so huge, they could easily pluck a person from the ground with the same facility a pre-ascension bird could have scooped up a stoat. The thought of talons longer than my hands and sharper than a sushi chef's knives—that was enough to curdle the blood of the stoutest heart.

I was very, very grateful these monarchs of the skies were on our side.

Among the five golden eagles were two white-tailed sea eagles, immediately identifiable as much for their larger size— if the goldies left me stunned, the white-tails made them look like adolescents—as for the eponymous tails. Fanned out in a blaze of white that caught the sun, their tails showed in stark contrast to the deep brown of their wings and backs. Their heads were paler. Not white like the North American bald eagles, but the white-tailed sea eagles' heads looked dappled. At least on these two, they wore a mantle of lighter brown that darkened as it flowed down their necks to blend with the rich feathers of their backs.

I wasn't alone where I stood gaping at them. Every face around me, upturned to the sky, gawped open-mouthed, at the spectacle.

Even before the ascension, if you'd stood behind a full-grown white-tailed sea eagle with your arms outstretched, one flap of its wings would dwarf your arms' reach. I'd a memory of Mum telling me about visiting one that a colleague rehabilitated—a monster bird of prey with an eight-foot wingspan, large even for them.

Staring up at these magnificent beasts, something in my heart gave way. I wished Mum could see them. The awe she felt with animals even before the ascension—she would have been thunderstruck.

For once, I let myself feel the old grief of losing her rather than punching it down to fester. People who'd never lost someone that close to them couldn't possibly understand the hole that opened up, how it would never really go away. All you could do was build your life around it—but every so often, you could still fall right in.

One of the eagles screamed, a fierce cry of joy.

Joy.

I didn't have to guess; I knew.

Their joy filtered through to me in the connection I shared with our golden friend. She circled with her brethren, proud of her contribution.

Because that's what it was. She viewed Oban as her community now; she didn't want to be alone, so she'd found friends.

This display, this exhibition of their glory, was meant to introduce us.

In that moment as I stood staring at the old Cal Mac pier and these tremendous birds, I couldn't help but think of how fiercely proud my mum would be. She might be gone, but if she knew I'd formed a bond like this with an animal like those? She'd be greetin' with the joy of it.

There weren't many places in Oban where birds that large could roost. We'd have to fix that.

I reached out to the familiar mind high above my head. She knew precisely where I was.

Now that there were more eagles, I *really* needed to know what to call her. She'd been out there working to show us that she belonged as part of our community, doing what we couldn't. Literal eagle eyes in the air. The name came to me out of nowhere, and even as it ricocheted through my mind, I exulted. It felt exactly right.

The eagle didn't understand words in either Gaelic or English, but when our minds met, I extended my thought to her, doing my best to encompass her fierce spirit and dedication to reporting back what we most desperately needed to know.

In English, I called her Scout.

Her delighted acceptance of her name resounded through the air.

I watched Eilidh's hair—an easy landmark with the sun shining on it—as the boat sailed towards Lismore.

She'd be back within a day, and she wasn't even going far, but I still felt nervous at the separation.

The eagles had returned to their task, Scout leading the way, and I was left with my own task.

People were right; having an ionad-siubhail in Kilmelford made sense considering the importance of the work there. Even so, restlessness took hold of me on the walk there. It wasn't that far of a distance, and with my Stamina what it was, I could run the whole way. The miles crept by despite my speed.

Everything around me felt charged, electric. Like a mahoosive thunderstorm lurked on the cloudless horizon.

When I finally arrived in Kilmelford and made my way up to the compound on the edge of Loch a' Phearsain, the first thing I heard was cries of alarm.

"Look out!"

The yelling seemed to be coming from behind the building where Alison's enclosure was, and I broke into a sprint, thankful for the work I'd been doing to up my Strength stat— I'd been an okay endurance runner for a while, but a strange benefit of increasing Strength meant the fast-twitch muscles necessary for sprinting responded in gratifying ways.

A crash reached my ears before I rounded the corner.

Between two outbuildings, a handful of people were hefting what looked like a slab of pure rock worthy of bloody Stonehenge. Well, a *small* Stonehenge—like *Spinal Tap* more than Salisbury Plain—but a small Stonehenge was still heavy.

Thanking my gains for the second time in a few heartbeats, I reached them in a hurry and lent my muscles to the equation. I was no Eilidh, but my added help righted the stone.

"That way—oof." One of the others grunted as he gave the rock a shove, and the rest of us followed.

It was still a bit odd to see such a mixed group in general, but especially in the context of moving something that weighed a literal tonne. The man who had spoken was in his early twenties, but the others around the stone ranged from a woman who had to be in her late seventies to a teenage—Andy.

It'd been ages since I'd seen the kid, and it felt like it had been a century since Eilidh and I had met him at Kilchurn when we were first trying to get to Oban.

We manoeuvred the stone into the prepared groove between the outbuildings, and everyone heaved a sigh of relief. My muscles had the familiar tightness of having approached a one-rep max.

*That* was something I'd never thought I'd say. Who'd have thought the ascension would have gotten me into lifting heavy things enough to have a reference for that? I blamed Eilidh, both for the incentive of keeping up with her strength and for the more . . . recreational applications of such things. Even if we could barely find the time to make out, let alone explore farther.

"Calum!"

Andy had just realised who had stepped in to help them, and he gave me a sheepish grin, thankfully derailing my poorly timed train of thought.

"Hiya," I said to him, returning the smile. "I didn't know you were helping out the operation here."

"My gran thought it would be good for me, but they don't let me work with the anomalies." Andy shot a look at the man who'd been guiding the stone slab, adding hastily, "Which is fine. They creep me out anyway."

"He's been a good help," said the man, whose name I didn't know as the others dispersed, heading off towards different outbuildings to get back to whatever tasks they'd put aside for rock duty.

That just left me, Andy, and the other younger bloke.

For a moment, I almost panicked, wondering if I'd met this man before and had just forgotten, but then he stuck out a hand.

"Brandon," he said. "I don't work much with the anomalies myself. I just do the grunt work."

"Nothing wrong with that," I said. "Is Meeksy with Alison?"

"I reckon so—also the wee lassie, your pal."

"Rhona?" Bugger. I really didn't love her taking this risk.

"Aye, that's her." Brandon shuffled his feet. "Well, I'd best get back to work."

With that, he turned and went into the nearest outbuilding. Andy, on the other hand, hesitated.

The past few weeks of relative stability seemed to have agreed with the lad, though he still carried a haunted look of grief around his eyes from the loss of his mum and grandfather. Not to mention the added trauma of then being captured by Bawbag and turned into a mindless, incontinent shambler before we rescued them. But Andy looked better for having a purpose, and the ascension's magic had given him a more solid form, a straighter back. Hell, even clearer skin.

"What are you here for?" Andy asked suddenly.

"I came to get a waypoint established so someone can come in and put in an ionad-siubhail. I should have asked Brandon before he left where they wanted it." I frowned.

"Oh! I can show you where it goes." Andy brightened at the idea of being useful.

"Lead on, mate."

Everything had been so up in the air that I'd forgotten they didn't want it up at the compound itself. Andy led me back down towards the village proper, but he stopped on the other side of the one house that shared the road up towards Loch a' Phearsain.

"Ah, no wonder I didn't see it," I said when the lad pointed.

At first glance, it looked as if the house's owners were just expanding their driveway to have more space to park, and despite my knowledge that cars were no longer a thing, a couple months of post-apocalyptic adjustment were really no match for over three decades of experience.

"Is anyone living there?" I asked dubiously, squinting at the house. "I reckon it might be a bit of a pain in the arse if folk are coming and going in their garden."

"No one's living there," Andy said in a hurry. "The people who own it moved to Oban where they felt safer, and they are letting us use the house when we need to take a nap or if anyone stays too late and doesn't want to go back to town in the dark."

"They just gave up their house?"

Andy shrugged his gangly shoulders. They weren't *that* gangly anymore, since he was filling out, but he still had the adolescent look of someone trying to reckon with sudden growth spurts.

When he didn't answer after another moment, I blew out a breath. "Okay, I guess I'll get started."

"Do you need any help?" Andy's voice had the hopeful quality that said he wanted to watch.

I wracked my brains to think of something he could do, but I couldn't come up with anything.

"I think this one's all on me, but you're welcome to hang out and observe."

The hopeful look faded. Just as I think he was about to turn and head back up to the compound, I got a spark of inspiration.

"Actually, if you could watch my back, that'd be great. I don't reckon anything will try to attack me, but you never know. I'll need to focus on what I'm doing—might not see a giant ant or something creeping up on me."

Mollified, Andy gave me a solemn nod, and I set myself up in the centre of the space where he directed me. They hadn't added any building materials for the ionad-siubhail yet, but they had carefully placed the site in easy distance of some native flora.

In fact, the presence of a stately rowan—a tree well known as a protector—gave me an idea that had nothing to do with my current project.

Andy took his job very seriously as I walked up to the rowan. He followed at a respectful distance, but I noticed he had a pair of daggers in his hands and out of the corner of my eye, I noticed that he took up an unobtrusive stance of wariness, his eyes scanning the surroundings.

He was a good kid; I hoped we'd keep nudging him onward where he could heal and come into his own.

For now, the rowan needed to occupy my focus.

Like any ascension skill, utilising the upgraded process for waypoint creation had been coded into me. Even so, I stretched out my awareness to the rowan. I wanted to feel out what I was doing, to articulate it to myself even if it wasn't necessary.

My part of the creation would be to integrate the indigenous tie to the point in space that was the ionad-siubhail. Like I had with the hawthorn, the blackthorn, and the gorse in Oban, Salen, and Iona, respectively, the rowan was a connection point between the physical and the metaphysical. The natural and preternatural.

When the crafters created the platform and the external structure, that was essentially window dressing. The vital piece of this mystical puzzle was mine. It didn't have to be a triskele like I had created for the others; it just had to make space for a link. I'd done that literally with the first three, but maybe it didn't have to be so with this one.

With my unrelated idea still fresh in my mind, I reached out to the rowan.

The tree's response felt almost silvery. Delicate but implacable. The rowan was ready to help without being eager. Where the hawthorn had felt young and excited, the rowan had a sense of grace and dignity.

Branches rustled above my head. They'd already shed their flowers for the year, but the telltale berries that made the tree so easy to identify hadn't yet shown themselves. The rowan's leaves were small and grew in saw-toothed clusters off of a central twig, usually at least ten or so in a group.

As I let the rowan guide me, I felt spirit lift the fallen branches around the tree's base. Loose twigs and broken sticks above joined them in front of where I stood, first a jagged ring of them end to end, then smoothing out and joining together. The circle did not end up perfectly even and uniform; the ends of twigs and branches kept small knots.

On impulse, I expanded my awareness into one of my abilities, Bas-Ogham.

To my surprise, the rowan leapt to attention with my concentration as if it recognised the ancient writing system.

A line sprouted and grew around the floating ring, expanding in both directions at once until it met on the opposite side.

More lines began to etch themselves across the length of it, and my mind made sense of the seemingly random scratch marks.

A diagonal slash for M, two vertical slashes for O.

When it was done, it read, *Mo bheannachd air an astaraiche.*

My blessing on the traveller.

I walked the hoop of silvery rowan to the site of the ionad-siubhail, but when I tried to place it on the floor, the wood seemed to resist.

With a seeking tendril of spirit, I concentrated my energies on the wood as I would have to activate an ionad-siubhail.

The air around the site grew somehow thick; that was the only way I could describe it. After a long moment of consternation, I let go of the hoop of rowan.

It wobbled ever so slightly—and then it hovered in the air of its own accord, a thrum of power surrounding it with a resonant hum.

"Calum," Andy said urgently. "Someone's coming."

I turned up towards the loch at first, expecting Meeksy or Rhona or Brandon, but Andy pointed the other way.

Even at that distance, I could see the broad shoulders and isosceles triangle torso. George.

And he wasn't alone. In a strange litter, he hauled a large containment cage—and in that cage was a snarling goblin.

A snarling *anomalous* goblin.

# CHAPTER
# FORTY-FOUR

Anomalous Ùruisg
Known throughout Scottish history as sometimes helpful,
sometimes mischievous humanoid creatures of folklore, this ùruisg
has been corrupted by the same entity that has affected native fauna
throughout the countryside.

*Already a sapient species, like the glaistig or the Homo sapiens sapiens of Earth, the ùruisg's natural abilities are inhibited by the anomaly.*

*The Ascended Alliance counsels against killing sapient creatures except in instances of self-defence.*

*Providing aid to this unfortunate creature as you would a fellow ascended person may be for the benefit of all.*

·· ⸪ ··

I stared at the information given by Keen Eye, reading it again and again.

I'd fought the fuath, the beithir. I'd met the glaistig more than once and engaged with her. Wolves roamed the Highlands, lynx were apparently back, and now here was an ùruisg, more commonly known as a brownie.

Dressed all in rags, the creature had brown skin that was covered in bristly hair. Of indeterminate sex, the ùruisg glared at me. I couldn't be sure whether the presence of the same bristly hair on the ùruisg's face meant male or whether that mattered at all whatsoever. Also, while brownies of lore were often described as very small, this ùruisg was easily the size of a small human with bulbous joints and limbs that seemed elongated for the creature's size.

My mind, having learnt to take most of these new developments in some sort of stride, needed a moment to catch up.

George was talking to Andy in a low voice, and I tuned in.

". . . the only one we saw, but that doesn't mean there weren't more. We were going to kill it, but Jack has a skill that gives information about creatures, and he stopped us." George did not look convinced that this was the wisest course of action. "Reckon bringing it here was the second best option."

"It was," I cut in, brain spinning through options.

*Think, hamster.*

"Is that really a brownie?" Andy asked me, his eyes glued to the creature, which sat sullenly in the containment cage, knobbly knees pulled up to a bony chest.

"Seems that way." I approached the cage, feeling a bit out of my depth. Did they speak English like the glaistig? Gaelic? Their own language? "Hello. Can you understand me?"

The brownie glowered but said nothing.

"A bheil sibh gam thuigsinn?" I asked, repeating my question in Gaelic.

I figured it couldn't hurt to use the polite form of address with a creature known for varying degrees of helpfulness or mischief.

"Tha," said the ùruisg.

So they could understand me.

That was, however, the only answer I could get out of them. After posing a number of other questions to no avail, I gave up, mind tumbling through different options.

"What do you want to do?" George interrupted my staring.

"I don't know," I muttered. "We can't let them go when corrupted. At least it's unlikely there were any others. Ùruis-gean are solitary as far as I remember. Andy, can you run up and get Brandon or Meeksy?"

The kid was off like a shot, eager to be of help, which left me and George.

"More of the anomalies," George said after a moment. At my grunt of assent, he went on. "We need to do something about them."

"Aye, we do, and we are to the best of our ability."

"Are you sure we shouldn't kill it?"

The ùruisg visibly stiffened, which I noted out of the corner of my eye because it indicated the creature also understood English.

"I'm not going to kill this creature. They're sapient—they understand us. It'd be no different to killing Alison." The brownie relaxed a little at that, which only confirmed my conviction. "I don't love killing even the non-sapient anomalies. They didn't ask for this any more than Alison did. They deserve our help as best we can provide it."

"Even if it puts people in danger?" George narrowed his eyes.

"For now, we have the ability to keep them quarantined," I said. "I'm not going to murder another sapient creature who isn't at fault for their predicament."

Thankfully, Andy was already returning with Meeksy *and* Brandon.

As they drew closer, I felt two additional pairs of eyes on

me, and unnervingly, it wasn't the anomalous ùruisg's gaze that felt the most threatening.

Brandon and the other folks at the compound had been busy in the previous days and weeks, and after Alison, they had prudently prepared a couple other larger enclosures just in case. When she'd been corrupted, they'd had to adapt on the fly, but they didn't want to be caught unawares again. Once the brownie was settled into a safe space—I stood back and let the others take care of it, since they had the experience and I didn't—I personally herded George out the door.

Grateful for the existence of a wealth of tasks for George that were far more pressing than standing about trying to change my mind, I stuck around at the compound long enough to make sure the man buggered off.

"We need to be careful with that one," I said to Meeksy and Brandon when George had gone. "He wanted to kill the brownie, and while that *might* become necessary down the line, right now it's not."

I watched Brandon closely to gauge his reaction, and the tension in my shoulders gave way when a look of reflexive horror crossed his face. Meeksy, of course, I didn't have to worry about.

"If he comes back up here, we'll keep him away from any of the anomalies, sapient or otherwise." Brandon stood up a bit straighter. "It's like suggesting we kill someone for getting sick. Why the hell would we do that just because they might spread their germs?"

It was a surprisingly good analogy, and I relaxed by further increments to hear it. "Exactly," I said. "It'd be a bloody point-less cruelty. We'll find another way."

I left it unspoken that we didn't know for certain it *wouldn't* eventually come to that—if we encountered more anomalous people, humans or otherwise, if we couldn't subdue them or contain them, it could become a matter of life and death. But I also wasn't going to entertain the idea of leading with violence.

There was too much we didn't know about the anomalies, and life was too precious.

Brandon and Meeksy went back to what they'd been doing, and after telling Meeksy I'd come in to see Alison shortly, I used my rockie-talkie to let the folks in Oban know I'd sorted the waypoint. The sooner we could get an ionad-siubhail finished here, the better.

The sky was clearing up to the west, and I wondered how Eilidh was getting on in Lismore. Maybe it was the arrival of the brownie or the hairline fracture in my trust of George—I didn't know the man well anyway—but the day suddenly felt like I'd drifted off on a picnic blanket and woken up to the sensation of a thousand tiny legs crawling across my skin.

"Everything good in Oban?" I asked Angus, watching as the sun broke through a small patch in the clouds, sending fingers of gold to touch the earth.

"Aye," the man said through the communication crystal. "We've got a few folks ready to come your way for the ionad-siubhail a bit later on today. Reckon you'll get out to Taynuilt before sundown or do you fancy waiting till tomorrow?"

I squinted at the sky. I *could* make it out to Taynuilt today if I hoofed it.

"Not sure yet," I told Angus. "I'm going to see Alison before I head back to town, and I'll figure it out from there."

Angus ran me through a couple other wee details before I disconnected, but I still felt jangled even though there was nothing of note that even implied immediate danger.

I put my finger on it as I made my way over to the building that housed Alison's enclosure.

One of my passives, Tuairmse, played off of my Nature affinity's root-level skills. I pulled it up briefly, more to confirm to myself that I wasn't crazy than anything, and while it didn't relax the antsy feeling, it did validate my unease.

*Tuairmse works best in tandem with the Nature tree's root-level passives: Gu h-Ìosal, Gu h-Àrd, Taobh a-Muigh, and Taobh a-Staigh. It is recommended to learn those skills prior to learning Tuairmse.*

*Once all of these are unlocked, however, your innate understanding of nature increases tenfold. You will not only be able to sense the turning of the seasons like the woodchuck who builds a thicker-walled den before an intense winter, but you will also judge the tides, the whip-quick shifts in weather, and most importantly, how to use those things to your advantage.*

I'd planned to go back in and work on expanding my awareness of my passives with Alison, but reading that made me veer towards listening to my instinct instead.

There was one other thing I wanted to do; Rhona had again come to visit Alison, and my instinct that this was especially dangerous for her won out over my sudden itch to return to Oban.

Sure enough, when I entered the outbuilding, she was cloistered with Meeksy, barely six inches behind the safety line.

Alison looked worse. Her skin had even more of an ashen tint, and her eyes tracked me the moment I stepped through the door. I had the immediate uncanny sense that she'd been following my movement even before I opened the door at all. It was like she was ready for me.

Rhona turned to see me, her eyes tired. Dark circles ringed them, making the nineteen-year-old look older than she was.

She gave me a small wave, turning back to Alison without a word.

I met Meeksy's gaze, and the concern on etched between his eyebrows said everything.

"I need to head back to Oban," I said to Meeksy, my mind digging fast for any kind of excuse I could give to Rhona to drag her with me. Lying just felt wrong. Then again, I did have an excuse to at least get her out of the room; I'd just been interrupted by the arrival of the ùruisg. "Rhona, I think it'd be good if you came with me. I've got something I want to make for you."

"Can't you give it to me next time you come up?" Rhona tore her gaze away from Alison to ask, and the fact that it seemed to take a visible effort just made me all the more certain.

"It's urgent," I told her truthfully. "Plus, I need to take care of a couple more waypoints, and I'd be grateful for your company."

Rhona's eyes narrowed as if she saw right through me and had latched onto the real reason, but I wasn't exactly trying to be stealthy. And it was the simple truth—I would be grateful for her company.

"Okay," she said.

Meeksy sank into his chair a bit more with relief.

Alison had been watching in silence all this time, and she didn't change now. Her brown eyes didn't blink, and when I met her gaze, it felt as if the sensation of ants crawling all over my skin moved internal, like they were swarming up my spine vertebra by vertebra. I fought the urge to shiver.

It didn't take long for Rhona to gather up her things into inventory, but she seemed subdued again as we made our way down the hill after a promise to tell Iain that Meeksy would be home later that night.

If there was anything I knew about being a teenager, it was

not to underestimate them. Sure enough, we were approaching the rowan when Rhona cleared her throat and said, "Okay, what's up? This is the second time you've dragged me out of there. Why?"

"Remember what the glaistig said about the danger?" I asked.

"Aye, I do. She said the creature was studying us."

We reached the rowan, and I paused for a moment, gaze focused on the ring of wood I'd left there; it still floated above the ground, looking strangely innocuous despite the obvious magic.

"I think—"

I didn't get a chance to tell Rhona what I thought, because I heard the eagle's screeching voice at the same moment Scout bombarded my mind with images.

Images of the kraken, attacking not a village like it had in Iona, but a harbour itself with a flat, level island splayed out beyond.

The kraken lay waste to the pier—and all the boats in berth.

# CHAPTER
# FORTY-FIVE

"Fuck-fuck-fuck-fuck-fuckity fuckles," I said, clenching my teeth so hard I thought I would crack a molar.

Forcibly relaxing my jaw—if such a thing wasn't a complete oxymoron—I quickly told Rhona what I'd just seen. I didn't even need to ask her; she immediately grabbed her rockie-talkie and started spreading the news. The eagle was already winging her way back out to sea, but I knew she would return.

I was glad she had help; this much flying for a raptor that large could kill her. As she reached the edge of my range for communicating with her clearly, she sent back a small wave of reassurance. Part of that help, apparently, included the other eagles hunting—and our communities providing their own supplementary snacks.

Somewhat comforted, I turned my attention back to Rhona's and my project.

Between the two of us, we could cover a lot of ground fast. My mind whirred through the various possibilities. It looked, from the glimpses I'd had, that the kraken was in Tiree. Tiree was one of the flattest islands in the Hebrides, so it was easily identifiable since Lismore was so close to the Ardnamurchan

Peninsula and the mountains of Argyll that seeing only open sea meant it couldn't be any of the islands within our immediate surroundings. That was somewhat of a comfort, if a selfish one. Eilidh was in the sheltered cradle of Lismore and Kerrera, not out at the edge of the Minch.

Tiree sat about an hour or so's sail from Mull and Iona, depending on where you left from. The Muilich would be able to respond faster than we could.

Did the kraken know about our ionadan-siubhail? Or was it a simple coincidence that it had attacked one of the islands we could only reach by boat?

The answer didn't change our course of action.

Rhona was still speaking urgently into her communication crystal when I disconnected from Finn with a terse "Bidh sinn a' bruidhinn" to promise I'd keep him updated, and the thing I'd meant to do for Rhona was at least still within my power.

"Don't go anywhere," I mouthed to her while she went back and forth with someone who seemed inclined to badger her with questions.

She gave me an exasperated wave of the hand, and I turned my attention to the ring of wood I'd left floating near the rowan, the site of our soon-to-be new ionad-siubhail.

Rowan rooted deep into our lore as a culture. A hardy tree, it was also a beautiful one. Silvery bark, yellow-white flowers in spring, bunches of deep red-orange berries in autumn, and fronds of splayed-out, serrated leaves that grew in opposing lines along their stem. Tradition had it that cutting a rowan was bad luck. They were meant to protect from harmful magics, and this one most certainly gave that impression.

I went to the tree, reaching out to it with spirit once more.

Spirit wasn't the only thing I reached for.

Bas-Ogham, one of my passive skills, lurked in the recesses of my mind.

It felt like muscle memory in my head, the way a practiced motion became second nature after cultivating it over years or decades. Iain's martial arts katas. An Olympic triple jumper's rhythm.

The tree responded with alacrity once more, its presence in my mind a swift, cool wind.

That made my job easier.

Carefully, I focused on the problem at hand. The rowan had seen the anomalous ùruisg, the brownie. This also facilitated what I wanted to do. Giving the tree a point of reference was important.

It surprised me still that "see" was indeed the correct word for the tree's awareness of the creature. We were so used to the word only pertaining to the sense we accessed through our eyes —or, if you believed in extrasensory perception, our invisible *third* eye—but plants were different.

They converted light to food; it was their first and most fundamental source of sustenance. Evolution would make absolutely certain they were capable of perceiving it. Anyone who'd ever taken the time to observe a plant over the course of a day could attest that they not only perceived sunlight but actively sought it. They might not move as quickly as we did, but they did still move. Flowers opened in the daytime and closed at sunset. Leaves reached for light.

And just like they could sense the source of their life, they could also perceive threats and danger.

The anomalies were, without a single doubt, a dangerous threat.

It didn't take much convincing; the rowan was eager to help. While it still bore its emotions with grace and dignity, the anomaly's presence and immediacy awoke a sense of urgency.

Through my bond with the tree, it fed back an analogy that was all too resonant: a parasitic fungus that entwined with the healthy root-and-mycelium network below ground, insinuating itself into the web until it overtook everything it touched.

*Yes*, I thought.

The image sickened me, left my stomach coated with a thin layer of bile that felt somehow slimy.

But the rowan had context I lacked. Trees lived longer than humans. That might not be true now in an ascended world, but it had been true on Earth long before the apocalypse.

Trees communicated with one another; they adapted to and learned their environments every bit as much as we did. And that meant the rowan had wisdom.

Unlike a human immune system, which depended on roving T cells to recognise and attack invaders—an oversimplification—plants did not have that kind of whole-body traffic. Instead, the rowan showed me that they fought invaders on a cell by cell level. Like a bunker designed to halt incursion and close off at every new gate, a plant's cells could armour themselves individually or, essentially, nuke themselves to contain whatever had come to hurt them.

Spirit swirled around me as I communed with the tree, providing an awareness of my surroundings that included Rhona. She stood not far away, glancing every so often over her shoulder up towards the compound as if gauging whether or not she could sneak away to see Alison one more time before I snapped out of my trance.

The rowan and I were almost done.

Tiny twigs rained down from its branches, drawing Rhona's attention like a magnet. Those twigs coalesced above my head, elongating and spinning themselves out like a weaver with a spindle and a fleece. Fibres of rowan, so thin and delicate they could have been gossamer, wove together.

Once upon a time, my mother had taken me to see a silversmith at work making a chain. Before that moment, I'd never given much thought to the process of such things. I'd thought machines made them, and I was sure that was true of some or most, but that day I got to see a master at work—jewellers had been hand making chains for millennia.

As the rowan drew from my experience as much as I was drawing from its own, I felt what went into each individual link. Every infinitesimal oval coded itself with the cellular defences of a plant's immune system. First one loop of links, then another, then another. Intrinsically, I felt not only that there were exactly three thousand, three hundred thirty-three but also that the rowan and I conspired to engrave every single one of them with ogham.

Tiny lines thinner than hairs encircled each and every link with powerful words written into the very fabric of what we had created.

When it was done, a thin sheen of sweat beaded on my forehead like I'd been sprayed with a mister.

The sense of the rowan retreated, and I got the sense of the leaves opening up to catch the day's diffuse light to replenish its energies.

"Mo cheud mìle taing," I thanked the tree.

Rhona was staring at me with an unreadable expression on her face.

Without explaining, I took the three steps to her, moving behind her with the necklace.

There was no clasp; fastening it required spirit.

Rhona let me encircle her neck with it, and as I closed it, the links far warmer than any metal would be, a shiver went through her. Her skin rippled with goosebumps visibly, the light dusting of peach fuzz across her neck more pronounced as every single hair stood on end.

When I stepped back, she shivered, shaking herself all over as if she were a dog emerging from chasing a ball into the sea.

"Fuck" was all she said.

It was as if putting on the necklace had flipped a switch.

Though Rhona was faster than I was, she kept close to me as we ran back to Oban, her fingertips occasionally drifting to her collarbone where the nearly invisible necklace's silvery fibres almost vanished against her skin.

At first, we only spoke about plans. Voices occasionally squawked through the rockie-talkies.

Just as I landed on the need to connect islands before the mainland, Rhona piped up, startling me enough that I broke my stride and almost tripped, ascension-level Agility and all.

"Tapadh leat," she said in Gaelic, then repeated it in English. "Really, thank you. I don't know what you did with that tree, but it feels like . . ."

The teen girl seemed to struggle with whatever she was trying to articulate. Our hurried gait punctuated the air with the beats of our running footsteps.

"It feels like waking up after a fever has broken," Rhona said finally. "Like when you've been so sick and out of it that you've forgotten how foggy your brain got, ye ken?"

Alarm, a fresh and unwelcome flavour of alarm, rose through me with a spike of adrenaline.

"You think you were almost corrupted?" I blurted out.

At Rhona's horrified look, I almost tripped again, but this time it was with relief.

"No, no." She veered towards me on the road to reach out and give me a pat on the shoulder. "Or maybe a little, but it just feels like sobering up or the sudden quiet after a neighbour stops blasting shitty dubstep when you're trying tae study."

I couldn't stifle the chuckle that spilled from my throat, but it wasn't really funny. "We're gonnae have tae unpack that later," I said, "but I'm glad the necklace is doing something."

"I still care about her, but"—again, Rhona seemed to have a slap fight with her internal monologue before going on—"there's a difference between care and getting obsessed. Something was tipping me towards obsession, and I don't think it came from me."

Ronald.

I did not like the implications of what Rhona was saying.

Her mind seemed to travel a similar road. "Calum, if Ronald—"

She broke off before finishing as her rockie-talkie blared to life with Angus's voice, clearly audible to me.

"You two almost back? Finn wants you in Mull as fast as you can. He says we need to get ionadan-siubhail in Tiree and Coll before anywhere on the mainland." The older man's voice crackled with urgency.

It was the same conclusion I'd come to myself.

I glanced at the Tuilich switching station approaching on our left.

"We'll meet you at the ionad-siubhail in ten," I said. Rhona repeated it, turning a worried expression on me. I went on before she could say anything. "If Ronald was under a similar influence, what's done is done. He's out of our reach now, but as soon as we can deal with this new crisis, I'll see about getting *everyone* up at the compound some new wooden jewellery."

The crease between Rhona's eyes smoothed out almost imperceptibly, but she nodded.

She didn't say Meeksy's name.

She didn't have to.

Iain was my oldest friend, but Meeksy was every bit as much a part of my life.

His soberness, the cloud hanging over him—I'd attributed it

to the gravity of the situation at the compound. I ought to have looked closer.

"We won't let what happened to Ronald happen to anyone else," I said, as much to myself as to Rhona.

From the way her lips pressed tightly together, I could tell she knew I wasn't making a promise both of us understood I might not be able to keep.

It didn't take long once we reached the Tesco carpark to get punted through our new portal into the not-so-sleepy village of Salen in Mull, kicked down the hill, and shuffled onto a boat heading up the narrow strait between Ardnamurchan and Mull itself towards the exact place we knew the kraken haunted.

Part of me wanted to connect every island with ionadan-siubhail just so I'd never have to experience the tension of being on a boat with an impending battle hanging heavier than a guillotine over our heads ever again.

I loved boats, loved being on the sea, but I did not love feeling water slip by like sand through an hourglass where every grain brought us closer to an inevitable confrontation.

I liked it even less when I didn't know what that confrontation might be—a sea battle? A repeat of Iona? An encounter with the kraken in the Minch? The eagles had lost sight of the kraken again, it seemed, and even mages with highly levelled Connection weren't able to track it. *That* was not a welcome sign. We didn't know if it was heading for Coll or planning to take a jaunt around Tiree to turn every boat it could find into driftwood.

Rhona had deserted me to go stare back towards the mainland, and I had half a mind to join her. The thought of Eilidh off behind me in Lismore while I was on an all-too-fragile floating contraption headed out to sea made me saltier than being surrounded by all that brine.

"You're sure you can't get out here?" I asked Eilidh through my communication crystal after she finished telling me about the scrying pool's successful instalment in a field just outside Lismore's post office.

The sea breeze picked up as the boat emerged from the Sound of Mull, and the swell of the North Atlantic lifted the boat beneath me with a reminder of just how much the Inner Hebrides protected the waters from the tumult of the open ocean.

"I'm sure," Eilidh told me after a beat. "The eagles say the kraken is going for boats now—Lismore and Kerrera know they're not on the immediate list for ionadan-siubhail with the danger to Coll and Tiree, so the least we can do is protect their only ways on and off the islands."

She was right, but that didn't mean I had to like it.

"Be safe," I said softly.

"You too."

The rockie-talkie went silent.

I could understand why the kraken went for the outer fringe of the Inner Hebrides. It was far from stupid or mindless; it had seen the eagles and knew we could track it that way. Deeper water meant it could stay, quite literally, below their notice.

The kraken was adapting to us.

I wished I knew what was possibly motivating it beyond simple anger or survival.

And, in that vein of thought, I had to wish on every possible lucky star that wee Cara, the lassie who'd scared the pants off us with the thought of bigger, badder maritime monstrosities goading the kraken into action, was wrong.

Just thinking about it summoned a cartoonish—if terrifying—image of a simplified food chain ranging from a cod the size of a bottlenose dolphin to a basking shark as big as Inch Kenneth to Cthulhu itself stirring up a maelstrom and swallowing the kraken whole.

Gods, please, no.

The northwestern coast of Mull skimmed past us. Already, the dark smudge on the horizon that was the Isle of Coll broke the flat blue. Again, I thought of the Outer Hebrides. Coll blocked any possible view of Barra or South Uist, and Kilchoan on the mainland obscured the Small Isles of Rum, Muck, Eigg, and Canna.

"Tricky game we're playing here," Finn murmured beside me, making me jump.

I'd not even seen the bàrd approach.

"Aye, it is," I agreed. "We're gambling, and I can't really tell if we're going all in. If we exhaust ourselves creating more ionadan-siubhail and the kraken attacks Oban or Salen or Tobermory..."

"Tha fhios am."

I *knew* Finn knew, but saying it out loud at least put it somewhere we could see it together. It felt a little less scary when it wasn't bouncing back and forth inside my skull.

A little.

We could connect all the islands to each other, but if we couldn't actually fight, how many people would we lose? We were far from the only capable fighters, but each of us had more experience than ten of the average villagers together. Trial by fire—or venom, in the kraken's case—wasn't exactly ideal for anyone to cut their teeth.

"We'll just have to hope we have enough time to take a nap after this," Finn said.

I followed his gaze, which hovered on the horizon, his narrowed eyes seeming to peer beyond the smudge of Coll.

"Has anyone from Coll or Tiree heard from Barra or the Uists?" I asked again. *Again* because I felt like I'd asked every day and no one had. "They can see each other, right? Even if they couldn't send a boat, you'd think someone would have, I don't know, signalled or something. Sent up a flare. Smoke. Anything."

"Nothing," Finn said. "And it's been weeks since the ascension, plenty of time for someone to get even a rowboat across the Minch if they really put their mind to it on a calm day."

He tore his eyes from the horizon and met mine. His were a frighteningly bright blue, and they bored into me. I had a feeling my own green ones did the same right back.

"One emergency at a time," I muttered after a moment. "All we can do."

Finn nodded. "All we can do."

Above us, eagles soared in circles, patrolling the waters to give us whatever warning they could. I only hoped they wouldn't see anything rising up from the deep.

Arinagour had not, thankfully, been hit by the kraken.

Yet.

The main ferry terminal in Coll was a small, whitewashed Hebridean building with a yellow placard on it that said COLL in big block letters. A small shop sold local pottery, and up the hill a short distance stood an enormous arch of a replica whale jawbone.

I had a vague memory of my first time in Coll with Mum.

There was a bench somewhere nearby that had a plaque, reading, "To those who pause and take a seat, spare a thought for 'Grumpy' Pete."

As much as I didn't love being on the boat knowing the kraken was wreaking havoc, it was almost worse to disembark at the small pier with the knowledge that we could return to find the boat smashed to smithereens.

Not that we were going far; our destination was the whale bones themselves. They formed an existing place of interest, and if Finn was correct—I suspected he was—the landmark had become enough a part of the place to already tie the natural gateway they created to the ionad-siubhail we sought to build. I just needed something organic to add.

The ionadan-siubhail needed to be built in sets of three. Even as we were moving to the whale bones, Oban folk had gone to activate what I had started in Kilmelford. After Coll, we'd move on to Tiree.

I was already tired.

"Should have slept on the boat," I said to Finn as we approached the massive ribs.

"I was just thinking the same thing," he replied under his breath.

A few Coll folk had already gathered around the bones, the lot of them dressed in practical island clothing. Layers, wellies —the only thing that didn't necessarily fall under the brolly of practicality was the dour expressions. I couldn't blame them for that any more than I could for the jumpers. Even though summer was fast approaching, the day was brisk and the clouds stubborn. Coupled with the wind that blew incessantly in from the Minch, it was no scorcher.

And none of us had any pressing reasons to be jolly.

"Hiya," I said when I drew near enough for my voice to triumph over the gale.

"You Calum?" This came from an older woman I took to be a fisher—though she looked nothing like Catrìona, she had the same weather-worn face and way of holding herself. At my nod, she scuffed one booted foot on the concrete base that held the replica jawbone. "Wish we were meeting under better circumstances."

I gave her a tense nod of agreement.

Rhona and a few others—Mull and Iona folk, including Samuel—were still making their way towards us, so we waited in awkward silence. I turned my attention and my spirit to the awe-inspiring remains that towered over us.

Replica or not, the jawbone looked like an enormous wishbone. Bleached by the sun and scoured by salt and wind alike, it reached easily the height of three pre-ascension humans stacked on top of one another.

"Finn," the fisher said when she saw me staring up at it. She gestured at the arch of the bones.

Both Finn and I turned to look at her.

"Beg your pardon?" Finn said.

She blinked, then glanced directly at Finn, her sun-browned face turning ruddy. "Oh, sorry. Fin *whale*. It was a fin whale that washed up here in Coll twenty years back."

"Oh!" Finn scratched his head with a small laugh that ricocheted through the gathered group just as Rhona and the others reached us.

"Jesus," Rhona said, squinting up at the spot where the arch crested. After a moment, she winced and shot a guilty look at Samuel.

The monk didn't react to her epithet; his only response was to give her a kind smile.

I wondered if he'd always been this chill.

"I'd say the sooner we start, the sooner we can get onward to Tiree, but honestly, it's more like the sooner we start, the sooner we take a nap," I said, which sent another small ripple of laughter through the group, though this second wave had a brittle edge.

"Either way." The fisher gestured at me.

While I didn't think she meant *get on with it*, it was hard to take it as anything but that. She was also right. Part of me wanted to ask for her name, but my brain was already bursting with names from across Argyll, and instead, I just got to work.

There was little beyond scrubby bracken and heather around the base of the monument, so for the first time, I turned to stone instead of flora.

Where Mull was a veritable cornucopia of rock even to my untrained eye, Keen Eye told me that Coll was not so much. This small island was almost entirely Lewisian gneiss.

I suppressed the urge to make a pun.

Even lacking geological diversity, the rock that poked up through the dirt beside the fin whale's replica jawbone showed beautiful striations from the lava that had formed it.

Pulsing Connection, I extended spirit into the stone.

It came as no surprise that rock moved more sluggishly than plants. This rock had been sitting here for about three *billion* years or something ridiculously impossible to conceptu- alise to someone whose lifespan, in comparison, couldn't even be equated to a sneeze.

The mere contact with the gneiss left me reeling.

My pathetic himbo hamster brain started to sing a song from a cartoon musical about everything having a soul, but even that couldn't joke away the sheer magnitude of encoun- tering . . . something so ancient.

Spirit whispered through me, threads connecting all my many layers of passives on a more conscious level now. Like the warp and the weave of a tapestry, spirit formed the framework for *everything*.

It was in everything, even before the ascension. Call it particles, call it strings, call it strong nuclear force, call it all of those things and none—spirit pervaded all of existence.

My puny brain struggled to comprehend yet another existential crisis. To work with this stone, to get it to work with me, I had to meet it on its own timeline.

As my own spirit meshed into the matrix of Coll's bedrock Lewisian gneiss, my mind felt as if every synapse and every neutron had suddenly expanded with the force of the Big Bang.

I fought back a wave of panic. This hadn't happened with other things I'd done with stone.

The entirety of my being seemed to hang suspended in the void between galaxies with this single stone on a round, wet little blue boulder hurtling through space at sixty-seven thousand miles per hour. And I needed to nudge this stone to move too—if not quite that fast.

Faster than it was used to, though. Faster than erosion, faster than the lava flows that had made it. Faster than the wind that had worn its exposed face away.

We didn't *have* several billion years. Not even a million or two. Not a few millennia, not a century, not even a decade.

Where I dwelt in that moment, I couldn't even see the face of Coll, of the people around me. Nothing but the vastness of time—and time seemed to laugh.

What did my linear thinking have to do with spirit?

Nothing, that's what.

Spirit was everything. Everywhere.

Like the film, spirit was all at once.

The void rushed up to meet me.

# CHAPTER
# FORTY-SEVEN

"Have a nice nap?" Rhona asked.

My nose stung.

And also itched.

I smelled salt and rock and heather and . . . whisky?

"Dè fon ghrèin?" I groaned and shoved a hand against something rough. Wool, not warm but slightly damp.

Without opening my eyes, I pushed myself up to sitting.

Coolness rushed over me, and I gasped. My eyes flew open as the healing spell hit me, and my first sight was an outwardly concerned Samuel, though the skin around his eyes twitched as if to hide a persistent smile.

"You passed out," came Finn's voice from a short distance away.

Rude that I didn't feel rested. To the contrary, I felt cheated.

It was still light out, but barely. This time of year, that meant it was approaching midnight.

I pulled my knees up to my chest and hugged them, more to give myself somewhere to put my chin than anything else. Woozy. That was the word.

Guess getting a crash course in the practical applications of Ascended Alliance astrophysics had side effects.

Oh, yeah.

And talking to a three-billion-year-old rock.

"An do rinn mi a' chùis?" I asked, swallowing.

Was this a migraine coming on? Why did it feel so bright inside my head?

I wanted someone to at least answer my question in the affirmative—had I done enough? Was our new whale jawbone gateway done?

"Rinn," Finn and Rhona said at the same time Samuel said, "What?"

Another wash of healing energy hit me like an ice bucket challenge down the back of my shirt.

I yelped, but in the aftermath of the rush of cold, relief bloomed.

"He asked if he'd managed to do the thing," Rhona explained breezily, ignoring my surprised noise and accompanying shudder. She eyed me askance. "Though *we* all managed, not just him."

"Am I the only one who passed out?" I asked her, irritation creeping into my voice. I wanted to pass out again.

"Yes," Samuel said. "You were out for about a half an hour."

He looked a bit like he wanted to ask something else, but my brain felt concussed. I had to do this again today? Ugh.

Maybe not technically today, but I'd have happily waited approximately forever.

My hand bunched in the wool I'd felt. Someone had laid me out on either a blanket or an unpleated traditional kilt. From the plaid, which I could barely make out, it was anybody's guess. I slumped backwards to stare at the sky. Every bone in my body felt as brittle as pumice. I'd have preferred something . . . gneiss-er.

If the kraken didn't kill me, these ionadan-siubhail might. Or my puns would.

The others continued a low conversation that eddied around me. Whatever healing spell they'd used had helped, but my body was still ticking through whatever ascension recovery meter existed. All I wanted was to go back to sleep.

Gods, I wished the kraken had taken a few more days off.

Maybe it was bored. Maybe the kraken just wanted to play with a toy boat. Or maybe we'd accidentally harpooned its mum before the ascension, and it had sat in its lair in impotent rage until the the apocalypse had given it a way to fight for vengeance.

The thought was an errant one, but it stuck in my brain like, well, a harpoon.

"I think he's broken," Rhona whispered, so loud it was clear she intended me to hear her.

I scrambled to a sitting position for the second time, no less woozy but with a frightening blend of hope and clarity. Could I be wrong? Obviously, yes. But Occam's razor and all that—what if it was just that simple?

"Boats," I said. My voice came out strangled.

"I think you might be right," Finn said, and I looked to him eagerly only to see that he was exchanging a perplexed look with Rhona.

"I'm not broken," I burst out. "Rhona, the first thing the kraken attacked was boats, right?"

"Yes," she said, sounding like she was addressing a toddler.

My brain shuffled through everything with the kraken. This time it was attacking marinas and any boat it could find, but even when it had attacked the harbour at Oban, it hadn't necessarily been trying to kill us specifically. Maybe we were just collateral damage.

Maybe it remembered boats as the threat and we were just incidental.

We were never going to beat the kraken just chasing it around the Hebrides. Ionadan-siubhail or no, even if we could teleport anywhere in Scotland at the drop of a hat, that didn't mean we'd be able to kill it if it could just dive and escape and heal and come back tougher.

I doubted we'd ever really know the thing's motivations, but we did have one—albeit tenuous—thing that it seemed to want.

"Boats," I said again. "If we want to beat this monstrosity, we need to give it what it wants."

"You want to . . . give a giant squid a boat," Rhona said. "Or plural boats. You're definitely broken."

"Not as a gift, you wee gremlin," I said to her, holding out an arm to Finn, who obliged by clasping my wrist and yanking me to my feet. "What's a staple of any typical fishing expedition when you're not using a giant net?"

To my surprise, Samuel was the one who looked utterly lost now. Finn gave me a sideways glance as he released my arm, and Rhona's concern-tinged teasing faded as understanding lit her eyes like the distant dawn.

"Oh," she said. "You mean *bait*."

I wanted to hash out the plan right then and there, but I couldn't. Extended range on our rockie-talkies or not, I could no longer reach Oban, and the Mull relay would take some time even if we wanted to spread our plan across the islands, which we didn't. Too much margin for error.

Instead, we tried to sleep. Our best and safest bet was to get to Tiree at first light and then go home via ionad-siubhail to hatch the plan. If we wanted it to work, we'd need a lot of boats, and if we wanted a lot of boats, we would need to move them carefully or the kraken would simply guerrilla torpedo them one by one before we could get everything into position.

Sleep was far less elusive than I expected. To my surprise, Finn began to sing softly, a Gaelic lullaby I thought I'd heard on a Gaelictronica album years before sung by, oddly enough or not oddly at all, another Mull singer I'd venture to call a bard, albeit one who hadn't had magic—yet.

Finn's voice turned it into a spell.

Within one or two repetitions, the world retreated, and I slept to the comforting counterpoint of Finn's baritone and Rhona's familiar soft snoring.

This time, much to my dismay, I did not receive the luxury of a lie in.

Rhona poked my shoulder until I woke up as the sun was just breaching the northeastern horizon.

"Tiree time," she said, not bothering to lower her voice.

I managed not to resort to violence.

Probably the only reason for my remarkable forbearance was that I felt cautiously rested, though I still avoided speaking to anyone until I was safely aboard the boat to head to Tiree.

Samuel approached me with enough caution that I felt a bit like a feral bear. I made a concerted effort to soften my surly morning expression as he handed me a rolled-up . . . burrito?

I squinted at the food in my hand, which did indeed seem to be a burrito. "Thank you."

"It should help perk you up," he said with a smile altogether too sunny for this godawful hour.

The sun may have been up, but in Scotland in early summer, that means four thirty in the morning.

Heinous.

I took one bite of the burrito and thought I might pass out

all over again. Where the man had gotten tortillas—I broke off mid-thought as I chewed the perfect, lightly floured wrap that tasted lightly of literal fire.

He'd made them. Bless him.

They were nowhere near the gummy monstrosities sold in UK groceries that turned to paste if they encountered moisture. No, this thing had some chew to it. It held a mixture of scrambled eggs, deliciously seasoned pinto beans, and a tangy cheese I'd definitely not experienced since the time I went to Mexico with Iain when we were at uni. Cotija cheese. The Iona monk had literal cotija cheese, probably stuffed in his inventory. Actually, I wouldn't have been surprised if he made that too.

By the third bite, I was ready to run up a mountain—not that I'd find such a thing on Tiree, which made a pancake look hilly.

I found myself eyeballing Mull off the port side of the boat. In a pinch, I reckoned I could skim myself across the water with Spèird and trot up Beinn Mhòr.

Samuel had finished passing out all of his burritos and caught me thoughtfully assessing my chances of expending the human—or elven—rocket fuel he'd handed me.

"Have you considered opening a restaurant in Iona?" I asked him, barely managing to swallow another enormous bite before talking. "Scotland's idea of Mexican food is Taco Bell. One time in Glasgow I ordered a chile relleno and got a jalapeño popper. Which isn't *wrong*, technically, but it's also really, really not right."

"I take it you liked your burrito?" The monk grinned at me, his teeth almost blinding white in the dawn sunshine.

"Aye, literally the best burrito I've had outside literal Mexico." I almost wanted to cry that it was gone.

Finn, who had just started eating his, was nodding in vehement agreement, though he had far better manners than I and wasn't trying to also speak.

Samuel just laughed, which deflated my burgeoning hopes and dreams. His next words returned some of my faith in humanity. "I am too busy to indulge in entrepreneurship, but if you like, I will teach you anything you'd like to know."

A ghost of pain followed over the older man's face.

I recognised that grief—and I recognised the meaning in the food he'd shared. It reminded me of how I felt working with animals. Because it reminded me of Mum and everything she'd taught me.

Despite wondering who had so lovingly taught Samuel to feed others, I didn't want to pry. Perhaps he would tell us someday.

"I'd be honoured to learn anything you'd care to share with us," I said at the same time Finn—somehow—gulped down his final bite of burrito and said, "Yes, *please*."

Samuel gave a small bow with his hand over his heart. "Perhaps you can teach me your Gaelic. I have long wanted to learn more than the few words I have explored in the abbey."

Wordlessly, Rhona went to him after dusting her flour-dotted hands on her trousers and gently kissed the old monk on his brown cheek. Her lips left a slight speckle of white, and she brushed it away with her knuckles.

With that, she went to the bow of the ship and started speaking to one of the sailors.

"What a sweet child," Samuel said, his hand going to his cheek.

Finn and I exchanged a look, and even though I'd seen Rhona in a *lot* of different contexts where that was the last word I'd apply to her, at the same time, I wasn't sure anyone else had looked at our young friend so clearly since the world had ended.

I thought of Alison and of Rhona risking her own sanity, safety, and life to be near what was very likely her first love.

"Aye," I said around the lump in my throat that had nowt to do with my breakfast burrito. "She is exactly that."

My vision flashed gold, and because I had nothing to do but wait, I glanced at the notification and had to shake my head ruefully.

*Through arcane exertion, you have gained a permanent +1 to Pathos. Please note that such increases have diminishing returns as your base statistics grow.*

Aye.

We might not have a bloody clue in hell what we were doing, but we *were* getting something right.

# FORTY-EIGHT

The final ionad-siubhail, thankfully, did not knock me on my arse.

Whether it was Samuel's magic burrito—get yer heid oot the gutter—or simply that I prudently selected something that wasn't billions of years old as an anchor, I wasn't sure, but by mid afternoon, we stood on one of Tiree's pristine beaches.

In an hour, we'd teleport back to Oban, but for the moment, my eyes drank in the topaz-blue water glimmering over white sand, and I thought I was the richest fucking man in Scotland.

Fuck it.

Finn and Rhona weren't far away, but I was sure they'd both seen worse than a peelly-wally Argyll elf druid running full Monty into the sea, so I stripped and waded right in.

Gaelic tradition said the seas turned warm at Latha Buidhe Bealltainn, but I think that was a long-running practical joke meant to take the piss out of visitors who might mistake our Caribbean-hued waters for the actual, literal Caribbean. Even with the Gulf Stream, the late May Minch was a balmy . . . eleven degrees Celsius.

And I was *made* for it.

"Looks like it's a full moon in June!" I heard Rhona crow behind me, and I flipped two fingers up over my shoulder, reaching thigh depth and plunged the rest of the way into the sea.

Burrito or no burrito, I was still tired after the ionad-siubhail, but the water rejuvenated me.

I dared opening my eyes, hoping ascension healing would save me the pain of brine to the retinas, and I was half right—it stung, but it was bearable in a way it wouldn't have been a few months ago.

When I surfaced, tasting salt on my lips as I shook water from my hair, I heard a gasp and a splash ten metres to my left and turned to see Rhona in her pants and a sports bra, spluttering as she stumbled off balance and pitched into a small incoming swell.

Finn's laughter burst through the air. Like me, he was no feart in his own skin, though I did suddenly realise Rhona might not have wanted to see our—ahem—lack of shyness.

As if in answer, she flailed back above the surface and was already rolling her eyes at me. "We're all adults, and I honestly do not care, so don't suddenly decide to be precious about skinny dipping. I'm only wearing this because I know I can make you Purifire it dry so I don't chafe when I get dressed again."

She didn't wait for me to ask how she'd known, only dived back under the waves, heading away from us.

Finn snorted. "Oh, for the confidence."

I raised an eyebrow at him. "You don't exactly seem to have a self-esteem problem, mate."

"I'm good at hiding it." Without further explanation, he copied Rhona's exit, just in the opposite direction.

Fair play—if a bloke who looked like a literal Adonis could still struggle with confidence issues, who was I to get on his case about it? Brains could be dicks.

I followed their lead, ducking back under the water to breast stroke out towards the open sea. I could see the sombrero-like silhouette of Bac Mòr to the east, and there was too much haze on the horizon today for me to make out more than the vague suggestion of Iona to the southeast. A pulse of Connection told me we were safe where we were, at least. Some fishes and early basking sharks—the latter a good distance away on the other side of the islands and out on the shallow shelf of sand they liked—but no kraken and no monstrously mutated moon jellies who wanted to blub-blub-blub over us till we drowned.

In all the tumult of the past few months, I couldn't remember the last time I was alone. Not that I was alone now, but with Finn and Rhona taking the time to themselves, I felt freer than I had in too many weeks to count.

For my introvert brain, the soft motion of the calm sea and the sound of wind and waves soothed me like a balm.

The waters here were crystal clear, the only obstruction where I kicked up some sand. Even the sight of the sun sparkling against silica and mica against that breathtaking teal backdrop was itself a mystical healer. The colour could take me over, fill my mind. It sparkled like jewels of the finest cut and clarity, threw back the light like a prism.

A long moment stretched out where I thought I might have never been happier—but for one thing.

I wanted Eilidh to be there with me.

She was still out of rockie-talkie range even if I had my communication crystal wedged between my arse cheeks instead of tucked into a pocket on the beach. I literally could not have reached her if I'd tried, but the urge was still there.

That said, I wasn't sure I wanted the first time she saw me fully naked for an extended time to be in pristinely clear, very cold water in the North Atlantic.

I considered that for a long moment as I came up for air, glancing down.

Aye, on second thought, today could just be for me.

Eilidh had not yet returned to Oban when we arrived an hour later, clothes dry but hair still damp.

I looked around for her in the gathered crowd, and with some worry, realised she still wasn't in rockie-talkie range. Even our new *extended* rockie-talkie range.

Someone would know where she was.

"Tiree and Coll?" I heard an anguished voice cut above the murmur of the throng and turned to see a middle-aged man with salt-and-pepper hair pushing towards the ionad-siubhail.

"Aye, you can get there now without going oversea," I told him.

He was tall and very skinny, to the point that he reminded me of Ronald. I suppressed that spike of sour spite in the face of this newcomer's obvious distress.

"We weren't able to—the kraken," he said, seeming to still struggle with the word. "My mother."

All at once, he seemed to remember something, and he went on in what hit me with a pang as Tiree Gaelic.

"Tha mo mhàthair a' fuireach ann. Chan fhaca mi i o thoiseach a' bhùraich seo."

The pure pain in his eyes hit me straight in the heart. Plenty of folk hadn't seen their mums since the start of this mess, as he hadn't, but plenty of folk also hadn't suddenly been given the option.

"Siuthadaibh," I said to him, pointing towards the ionad-siubhail. "Cha toir e ach mionaid, a charaid."

I could tell the man hadn't used it yet for the fear that sparked in his eye, but before I could reassure him, he was off like a shot, long legs taking him into the arch I'd just vacated.

He vanished in an instant.

Strange to think that my telling him it would only be a "minute" was actually far longer than it took.

I envied him for longer than his journey would have lasted —what a gift to be able to walk through a gateway and see someone you loved on the other end.

Assuming she'd survived this long. Tiree had suffered some heavy casualties in the early days, which made me worry all over again about the Outer Hebrides.

Worry would keep me from doing what I needed to do now, and that was get our plan rolling.

Now that we had instant communication between the mainland and four islands, news would spread fast.

For myself, I needed to find Catrìona.

It was late enough in the day that I didn't expect she'd be out fishing, not with the kraken currently unaccounted for, but even so, it took me longer to track her down than I thought it would.

I wanted to kick myself when I got to the Whyte house and found her in the lounge with her feet up on the settee. Catrìona hummed a jig as she read a battered and abused copy of C.L. Clark's *The Unbroken* for what must have been the hundredth time unless she'd purposely dropped it in the toilet and then run over it with her car before the ascension—and I knew Catrìona well enough to know that she would sooner die than do either of those things even to a book she hated.

Well, maybe if its author wrote a story set on a fishing boat and got everything wrong. I wouldn't put it past her to throw me in the toilet and run me over if she heard me attempt to talk about anything fishing related. Or boat related, to be honest. I liked boats; beyond knowing port from starboard and the keel from the stern, I was not going to cosplay a sailor.

Sailean perched on Catrìona's chest purring, so content that the wee wildcat didn't even notice me through our bond until I was practically beside the settee.

"What's the use of a rockie-talkie if you're no gonnae answer, a Chatrìona?" I asked with the exasperation I was only allowed due to our decades-long acquaintance.

Sailean bounced into the air like she'd been goosed, but Catrìona only looked at me with mild amusement. The cat clawed her way onto the back of the settee, earning a less-mild wince at the needle feet breaking the fabric of the sofa cushion.

"The crystal's in the other room, a ghràidh. I hated mobiles before the world ended, and I haven't changed my mind now that it's a shiny rock."

I rolled my eyes like I had as a teenager. It was surprisingly a stretch for whatever muscles had grown unused to expressing exasperation like that. Huh.

"Don't you roll your eyes at me," she said, but she sat up and moved her feet so I could sit down. "Why's your hair wet?"

"Went for a swim in Tiree," I said with as roguish a grin as I could muster.

Sailean let out a mew, and I plucked her from the settee back and put her in my lap, where she settled down with a sleepy yawn and resumed her purring.

"So the ionad-siubhail—" Catrìona broke off and crowed, weathered hand doing a wee fist pump. "Sin thu fhèin!"

"Have you heard from Eilidh?" I asked her. "She seems to be out of range of the rockie-talkies."

Iain's mother frowned. "No, but like I said, my communication crystal's been in the other room since I got off the boat today."

I felt my own forehead crease. "Did she go to Jura or something?"

"I don't know—we'll find out. I'm sure she's fine. Eilidh is perfectly capable of taking care of herself if anyone is." Despite the reassurance in Catrìona's words, her own brows had taken a small dive towards the middle of her forehead.

Blowing out a breath that ruffled the soft fur on the top of Sailean's head, I nodded. I'd have to trust that was true; it wasn't like I had much of another choice.

It didn't take long to walk Catrìona through the plan, which was simple. We would need her, however, and everyone in Oban used to sailing these waters. The kraken didn't move whilst it was dark, and the eagles couldn't track it, but it also gave us a safe—relatively safe—window to get our boats in position.

The only thing was that sailing at night, without pre-ascension technology for navigating all the mundane dangers that could hide beneath a deceptively smooth sea, was a whole other kind of risk.

We needed people who knew not only the sea, but each specific route between their boats' current berth and Oban. Some would come up from farther south on the mainland; others would sail in from the islands.

Everyone would have to do so with only the faint daylight of the early summer midnight, no cabin lights, and no hope of a rescue.

We'd start with smaller boats from Iona, Colonsay, Tiree, and Coll—those with the farthest to go and the fewest people. Our thought was if they left early as the kraken finished its day hunting trouble, they could slip through the Sound of Mull or past the Slate Islands safely.

The kraken hadn't ventured close to Oban since we'd almost boiled it alive; if we had any hope of luring it back, we had to have all of our ducks—or boats—in a row and far from sight.

Oban harbour was about to be very, very full.

# CHAPTER
# FORTY-NINE

*People plan, the universe laughs.*

An old adage, one I would remember for the rest of my days. That thought stuck in my mind like it had been nailed there as my communication crystal lit up with the setting sun.

It felt like a bad omen that no one had been able to get hold of Eilidh. She'd been expected back within a day—it had now been two with no sign of her.

As most of the eagles had come home to roost for the night, I scanned the skies for Scout until I found her soaring with the pair of white-tailed sea eagles at her flanks. Our bond was still tenuous, but familiarity made it easier to grasp now than it had been.

*Have you seen her?* I knew Scout recognised Eilidh; eagles mated for life, and more than once, I'd caught a sense of *home-mate-nest* from the golden eagle when she caught the edges of my thoughts about her. I'd taken that as a cultural mistranslation, to put it delicately, but now, Scout's spirit took hold of my distress, and our bond flared to life.

*Lismore. Kerrera. On the ship . . . Luing?*

So Eilidh had gone south, farther south anyway than she'd

originally meant to. Something had to have happened, and the kraken hadn't yet touched Jura, maybe because it was so sparsely populated. Iona was too, but the proximity to much-larger Mull made for more traffic.

None of that mattered now.

People surrounded me where I stood on the north pier near Ee-usk, but no one spoke to me. This coated me in the strangest sensation that I was invisible, alone in a crowd in spite of the hundreds of Oban folks who waited anxiously for the boats.

It was pointless to tell them to go home; everyone wanted to be ready. The night would be long, waiting for the boats to form a motley flotilla and hoping we didn't lose more than we could rebuild.

That and hoping the kraken didn't notice until we wanted it to.

The eagle, still enmeshed in my mind, tried to reassure me that the kraken had retreated southward, that it currently slept between Iona and the northern coast of Ireland. This was a good thing by all accounts; it hadn't gone all the way back to its lair, so it was still close enough to fall for our trap, and it wasn't exploring the coastlines through the night.

Ulva had lost a handful of other boats between it and Gometra, I'd heard from the Muilich, but the boats had been old, in disrepair even before the apocalypse. The owners didn't even live on the island, and they'd not yet been retrofitted with ascension upgrades.

As far as anything could go well, our quickly implemented plan was going well.

We had mages posted in Kerrera and on the mainland, at Clach a' Choin and even in Lismore.

So why couldn't I relax?

Probably the same reason no one else could, either.

The smell of a grill reached my nose from the pier, and it

swiftly gave way to the familiar scents of seafood. And some beef, which had become a rarity. The mages were becoming mad scientists with meat, trying to figure out if, like one of their clean water spells I'd not come across myself, they could somehow replicate or produce steak.

With the sun setting and my entire body trying to seize up with the tension of what-is-gonnae-happen anxiety, I'd half a mind to go lend my hand to anyone. I'd try to clone a mutated sheep faster than you could say "Hello, Dolly" if I thought it would buy me enough of a distraction.

Instead, I found myself caught in an eddy of Argyll natives from the mainland and the islands alike, and for maybe the first time since I'd set foot in Oban, no one was trying to flag me down to do something, answer something, craft something, fight something, or sing something.

The latter had become an unnervingly common occurrence.

No, I was here on one of the year's shortest nights that somehow threatened to stretch out longer than the average twenty-first of December when the sun hadn't shone in weeks. Meeksy was still in Kilmelford, Iain was with him, Rhona was running news between islands, and Catrìona was out on the boats. Sailean, bless her, was asleep at the house, and I didn't have the heart to wake her.

As much as I wanted to go through my notifications, aside from checking to see a few of my Stamina gains and Strength gains, along with another bigger boost to Spirit from all of my work with the ionadan-siubhail, there was nothing of note. No levels since I'd not been fighting and I guessed the ionadan-siubhail didn't really count as crafting.

"Penny for your thoughts." The voice belonged to Sammy, one of the . . . Glaswegian childfree swingers.

Just that she'd spoken to me somehow gave me a wash of relief, like she'd at least proven I wasn't invisible or dead. Also that the arrival of a gaggle of Glaswegian childfree swingers hadn't actually been a hallucination, just an example of reality being stranger than fiction.

"Reckon it'd take a lot of pennies," I said to Sammy wryly. "But the gist of it is that I hate waiting for other shoes to drop, and it's bad enough when we're talking about something that's only got two legs. This kraken chappie has—"

"Eight?"

"*Way* more than eight. So many more than eight." My tone grew even more wry, bordering on dry enough to dehydrate venison. "There are altogether too many other shoes that could fall on our heads."

Sammy nodded at that. "Not much we can do about that sometimes," she said after a moment, but she gestured around us at the burgeoning crowd. "You're certainly not the only one, pet. Everyone's here to stave off the fear."

Almost as if she'd summoned it, cacophony exploded in my ears. My pulse ratcheted up to a full-on march.

"Calum!" Eilidh's voice was sweet relief for all of half of a suddenly faster heartbeat—that relief turned brittle with her next words. "The kraken is chasing boats in from Colonsay and Iona! We've been tracking it off the Irish coastline because its movements were erratic. I saw—fuck, I'll tell you later. I couldn't tell you how it did it, but it was like something sounded an alarm. It was settling in a ways out to sea to hunt, and then it got alerted like my dad's old pointer, like it scented its quarry. The eagles went to warn the boats, but it might be too late for them."

"Sammy, find Angus or Eliza, fast as you can," I said to the Weegie woman, who bolted. "Eilidh, don't the boats have rockie-talkies?"

"No, there weren't enough, I guess. We've been expanding so fast that the crafters ran out yesterday."

"Fuck."

"Aye."

"Where are you?" My heart felt like it might break my ribs one by one.

Eilidh's silence was almost answer enough.

"You're not following it," I said.

After the heavy thuds in my chest, the skip made the silence louder than a snare drum could ever be. An echoing cavern that stretched out far too long and threatened to deafen me.

"We have to," Eilidh said finally. "Calum, those boats—we might not be able to save them, but we have to try. We only just heard about your plan an hour ago when we got back in range of the Jura contingent who have communication crystals. We were trying to get back to Oban when we realised the kraken was on the move. We can't not help them."

I closed my eyes.

"Làn-earbs agam annad," I said to her. "Till thugam fhathast."

"Tillidh mi," she replied softly.

Then she was gone.

Maybe in the films, I would have told her I loved her. Maybe she would have told me the same.

I couldn't. Not like this.

I hoped she would know that from me, *you have all my trust* was one and the same.

The *come back to me yet* was a request for a promise I knew damn well she couldn't make. All I wanted to hear was that she planned to—and she'd said she did.

There was no way—none—Eilidh *wouldn't* go after the Iona and Colonsay boats. And I wouldn't want her to turn away from them. *I* wouldn't turn away, and Eilidh knew that, too. She knew me as well as I knew her.

Eilidh was a paragon of doing the right goddamn thing. If

she thought she'd done something wrong, she would find a way to make it right, and if she let her own boat sail away from people who needed her right now because I said so, that would be the end of us. As it should be, because I would never ask her to betray her own code of rightness, her own virtue.

If anyone could help those unfortunate boats, it would be her. Eilidh MacIntosh was perhaps the only person I would trust to do the right thing no matter what it cost her. She'd given up her chance at love with me for the sake of her abusive friend who hurt her because she refused to hurt Susanna back. Eilidh would, without any doubt, lay down her life for the islanders on these boats who were just trying to do their bit to help.

It was why I loved her.

Shaking myself out of my sudden adjustment of reality, I gave myself three deep breaths to calm my speeding heart rate. No use.

What could I do from here?

Aside from ping-pong back and forth between the ionadan-siubhail in the islands, I wasn't sure there *was* anything.

This was worse than being aboard the schooner on the way to Iona—at least then, I was moving.

*Think, hamster.*

Sending a bunch more boats out there would be useless. We had some in the Kerrera marina just across from the Oban harbour, which was sheltered from any route the kraken could take into Oban that wasn't climbing directly over Kerrera's hills. But sending boats would be both too slow and pointless; it would just endanger everyone, and our plan to deal with the kraken depended on getting it *here*.

Around me, the nervous cooking and laughter had faded to a fretting frenzy. Worried faces looked around, filled with

uncertainty. I gave a reassuring—I hoped—smile in no particular direction, my mind churning through options.

With a pat of my rockie-talkie, I started praying to any gods
or monsters listening that someone was in range of Catrìona.

"Rabbie," I said to the Mull sailor, who miraculously was
within range now where he sailed from Salen in our direction.
"I need you to find out how much time we would need to get all
the boats here down the sound. How far are the ones farthest
out?"

"Gies a minute."

I didn't take his curt reply as anything offensive, only expe-
dient, but even so, waiting felt like ticks burrowing into my
skin.

When his response came, I almost jumped out of said skin.

"Farthest boats are in Tobermory—they're the ones from
Tiree and Coll. Tob's boats are already near Craignure."

"Thank you," I said fervently. "So a couple hours?"

"Aye, maybe faster. They're experimenting with using that
community skill to boost speed." Rabbie sounded unsure, and I
could almost hear his shrug through the rockie-talkie.

"Which one?" I asked, perplexed. I didn't think there was a
*boat go faster* skill in that tree.

"Cumantas," he answered. "The one where certain people
can use everyone's spirit. They're trying that with the force
spell, the what's-it-called one."

"Spèird." I closed my eyes, fighting the urge to do a fist
pump. "We won't get our hopes up too high, but thank you."

"You got an idea?"

"More like a really bad Hail Mary," I muttered. "Tell
everyone on the boats to be careful—we'll alert you if the
kraken gets past the boats from Colonsay and Iona."

"Do."

The moment the connection ended, I gritted my teeth and

flung out my spirit to Scout. She wasn't far away, thankfully. Close enough for me to hear her crowing cackle coast through the air when my harebrained plan filtered to her with our bond.

The eagles were the size of small crop-duster planes, so they were visible even in the twilight above us, and their reply cries made heads tilt upwards to look at them.

Asking them to fly at night was a risk, but not asking was worse.

With a little luck—and a lot of scales tipping in our favour—my idea would buy us time for the sun to come up.

It felt a bit asinine that I'd already done my part of this contingency plan, but when startled cries rose on the other side of the harbour at the south pier where the fishing boats berthed, I stifled a smile.

Eagles swooped down and winged into the sky again, seven of them including Scout.

Her own opinion of the idea was a bit bemused, but I supposed it was a sign of trust in me that she was going for it anyway.

Minutes ticked by as the eagles flew over Kerrera and out of sight.

People milled about nervously, a few people talking into communication crystals here and there, but most folk simply hovering in tension like water striders on the surface of a pond.

"Calum!" Eilidh's voice burst through the silence of my own rockie-talkie once more.

"Yes?" I tried to keep my tone neutral, but curiosity lit through me like fire touching tinder.

"Why the fuck are eagles dropping pig-sized *fish* on the bloody kraken?"

"What's the kraken doing?" I asked urgently, wishing Scout were closer so I could see through her eyes more clearly.

Silence stretched out, followed by a grunt and a burst of maniacal laughter that was *not* Eilidh's.

"It's feasting," she said grudgingly after a minute.

"The boats. Did it reach them?"

More silence. Then Eilidh's rueful laugh was a balm to my ears. "Nope. They're pulling away. They're not free and clear, but they're also not in pieces."

"So," I said casually, giddiness bubbling to the surface at my absolutely ridiculous plan working, "would you say the fish tipped the *scales* in our favour?"

From the immediate resounding groan through the crystal *and* from everyone within a ten-metre radius of my corporeal presence on the north pier in Oban, I thought the answer was yes.

# CHAPTER
# FIFTY

My thought had been as simple as anything—the kraken may have been a monster, but it was still an animal, and it did still need to eat. All the talk about boats as bait had subconsciously planted the idea, and if it hadn't worked, well, at worst we'd be out some fish and the kraken would be confused.

Any time we could buy the boats would get them closer to somewhere we could actively help.

The eagles began an airdrop caravan, heading back to the pier and then winging out to sea again.

Knowing Eilidh was still safe at least gave me some comfort. I only hoped the kraken wouldn't get any ridiculous buffs from eating a bunch of raw cod or whatever our winged takeaway service was flinging at its hungry maw.

I'd banked on something Eilidh had said in passing, that the kraken had been settling in to hunt—it seemed my gamble had paid off.

I looked up just in time to see Angus parting the crowd to reach me. The older man looked a bit like he was about to box my ears, but instead, he just shook his head as he approached.

"Fish," he said, shaking his head once more. "Bloody absurd that it worked. But also strangely practical."

"We know the kraken is intelligent, but it's also still acting instinctually," I said, sending a silent thank you to my mother for all of the implicit and explicit teachings of animal behaviour over the years. "Food is one of the most basic things for survival for anything alive. I just thought maybe it would be a good distraction—anyone who's ever tried to win over a feral cat can attest that food's pretty motivating."

"I won't congratulate you until we see those boats sailing into the harbour." Angus crossed his arms in front of his chest, but the twitch of his lip counteracted his closed-off body language with a hint of amusement. "Maybe not even then."

"Fair play." Just as I was about to say something else, three of the eagles veered off their course, Scout leading the way directly towards us.

Her mind held a mixture of self-satisfaction and wariness as she relayed what she'd seen.

As if I was in her head to watch her memories play out, I saw the shape of the kraken in the water, a pale smudge on the twilit waves. There was little swell, but the undulating tentacles made their own currents, frothing the water with fish guts and bubbles where the creature fed. It glutted itself on the fish, occasionally breaching the surface of the sea with its body or its long, sucker-and-spine-ridden appendages.

While I had little context for the creature's usual movement speed, to my eye, it seemed sluggish.

I quickly told Angus what I was seeing, and he gave a tight nod, though his mouth quirked to one side as if he were chewing on the inside of his lip.

"We still need it to come this way," he said. "If we want a real shot at it, it needs to actually follow the boats to the harbour mouth."

"I know," I said.

Everything else we'd sorted depended on that.

The waters were shallower at the harbour mouth. We had access to land at the harbour mouth. We had reliable reinforcements available at the harbour mouth.

If we couldn't get the kraken close enough to throw everything we had at it, it'd be like trying to bring down a bomber with a BB gun.

Eilidh's voice for the third time in a quarter of an hour made me jump. "We've got a problem."

"Another one?" Angus muttered, and I shot him a glare, which shut him up.

"What?" I braced myself for anything from anomalies to a freak hurricane.

"The kraken's moving back southwest. Slowly, but it's heading back my way."

That sucked the moisture right out of my tongue. "How close are you?"

"Well out of range, but that's not the point—if it goes back out to open sea, we've lost our chance. For today, at least."

With a tendril of thought, I sent Scout winging back out over Kerrera to check. I wished my brain would move as fast as her flapping. I felt indeed like a hamster spinning in a wheel.

I touched my communication crystal again, keying my spirit into Rabbie's signature. It was so second nature by now that it was like firing off a text message had been pre-ascension.

"Rabbie, how close are the boats in the Sound of Mull?"

"Jesus, son, you gave me the fear," came an explosively gruff reply. "Gies a sec."

"What are you doing?" Angus asked me suspiciously.

"I don't know," I told him. "Let me figure it out by doing it."

The look I received for that response was enough to separate my red blood cells from my plasma. I did my best to ignore it as stoically as possible to disguise the fact that this was yet another harebrained plot that could work or could prove that I'd used up all my good fortune on the flying fish extravaganza.

By now, a crowd had inched closer around us. No longer was I invisible amid the throngs of Obanites.

I tried to ignore that, too.

Rabbie's voice returned a moment later—and not a moment too soon. Claustrophobia crept up around my ears with every shuffling step that brought the gathered throng closer in their curiosity.

"Mull folk are approaching Lismore, Coll and Tiree at Craignure. Guess their magical experiment's working all right, the time they're making."

Rabbie gave a disturbingly wet hawking sound and spit—probably unwitting to the fact that he had an audience here in Oban. To my delight, the crowd recoiled ever so slightly, giving me a bit of breathing room.

"Tell the Muilich to stop where they are, close enough to Lismore that they can reach land in a pinch, but have them all block off the sound." Gods, I hoped I wasn't talking out my arse.

"Hope you know what you're doing, lad," said Rabbie, and his presence vanished.

I swore under my breath. *Me too, Rabbie. Me too.*

Glancing at the softly lit marina across the harbour in Kerrera, I met Angus's eyes, pretending there weren't three score people pressing in on me to see what I'd do.

"As fast as we can, let's get boats through the Sound of Kerrera," I said to Angus. "We got folk who can sail them?"

"Aye," he said carefully, then added a blunt, "Why?"

"Because he's blocking off the kraken's escape routes, Aonghais," came an irritated voice I knew all too well and welcomed with every fibre of my being. Ealasaid. She stumped through the gathered crowd, thwacking the end of a heavy oaken staff on the pier with every step until she reached us. People prudently skittered back from the impacts—I'd no doubt taking those thumps to the toes would leave folk in need of healing. "The thing's gorged itself, and now it's trying to roll itself to its watery bed. If we can roll it this way instead, maybe we can kill it while it's digesting and sleepy."

"Do krakens *get* sleepy?" The voice that asked that question also came from a familiar voice, albeit one much younger. Wee Cara.

I'd a vague memory of another wee girl, one obsessed with spiders. What was her name? Rachel—that was it. One of the Kilninver weans. Half of me wanted to find her and introduce her to Cara, and the other half wanted to make sure they never got near each other. Between Cara's interest in monsters and Rachel's tendency to find coo-sized centipedes *friend shaped*, I thought the two of them together might be ever so slightly terrifying.

"They do, m' eudail. It's a monster, but it's still a living creature that needs to rest and digest." Even weeks into the ascension, Ealasaid wore her enormous, thick spectacles on their chain around her neck—insurance in case her eyesight suddenly shit the bed again—and as she shifted her weight, her eyes narrowed speculatively. "It's not a bad plan, a Chaluim, but it's got a major flaw."

"Hit me with it—I think I already know." I really hoped she'd identified the same one I had, mostly because I hoped naively that it was the only major flaw. Then again, if there was another, it would be best to know now.

"The kraken looks as boats as things to smash, a ghràidh. Why would it think they were a block?"

I blew out a breath. "It wouldn't—but so far it hasn't

encountered any boats that actively attacked it." Glancing at Angus, who'd heard at least some of Rabbie's report, I went on. "The Muilich have figured out how to funnel spirit from multiple mages into Spèird to propel the boats, which means they can displace water. And if they can displace water . . ."

"They can attack with less resistance," Ealasaid finished for me. "Assuming they don't just shoot themselves backwards into a rock."

"I'll remind them of Newton's third law," I said dryly.

"You do that, a ghràidh." Ealasaid looked at Angus. "Well, Aonghais? You've got the length of the Sound of Kerrera to chat to the Muilich about their ascended propulsion and practice it before you start your new profession as a kraken herder."

I was itching to get on a boat myself.

The problem was, I didn't know where I'd be most useful, and while I couldn't have explained it to anyone, something stopped me from joining Angus—even though I knew he'd be rendezvousing with Eilidh.

Instead, I walked to the edge of the pier with Ealasaid, the old woman's presence a strange comfort despite my not seeing her much in the past few days. Or was it weeks?

The sky above us had darkened about as much as it would. Only a smattering of brighter stars and planets showed through, though I had a wee start when I realised that was significantly more than I would have seen pre-ascension. Our eyesight really had improved.

That comforting sense of Ealasaid by my side eluded me until another familiar presence arrived.

Rhona.

Like the shadowy wee banshee she was, she simply materialised between one breath and the next, appearing on the other side of Ealasaid's shoulder.

"Carson a tha sibh nur seasamh, is eile a' sabaid?" she asked bluntly.

I winced, because she'd voiced my own underlying fretting. Why *were* we just standing around when others were preparing to fight?

"Thig an t-àm," Ealasaid said, her voice distant.

*The time will come.*

The cailleach's shrewd eyes seemed to see through the veil of darkness between the arm of Kerrera that reached towards Clach a' Choin and the flickering arcane lights of Lismore beyond. The boats were keeping their own running lights off for now, but the people on land had no need to. Unless the kraken decided to take a midnight stroll.

Reflexively, I cast Connection as if it could tell me something—anything.

There were so many variables I couldn't control from where I stood: whether the kraken would doggedly plough through Eilidh's boat to reach the open sea, whether it would respond to attacks and how, whether it would give us the slip altogether by diving under everything, whether it'd reveal it could set off a nuclear bomb.

But Connection showed me something that had nothing to do with the kraken at all.

It wasn't even something I'd not seen before; I had.

Like I'd seen in Ee-usk that day at our Hebridean Council meeting, thin streams of spirit ran between me, Ealasaid, and Rhona. Beyond that, they stretched farther, more tenuous, out to sea.

Without any doubts, I knew where they led. Eilidh to the southwest, Samuel a bit north of her, Finn almost due west.

The six of us were linked somehow.

We'd all felt it, stronger and stronger as we slowly found each other. I thought of how quickly Ealasaid had joined us. The look of recognition on Finn's face when we met in Ulva Ferry. The bone-deep familiarity of Samuel and my instant willingness to trust him to shepherd my spirit in Iona.

I almost had to snort at that—I was not a religious man, and he was. If you'd told me a year ago I'd be trusting a literal monk to wield shared magic to light a *candle*, I'd have laughed myself silly till I boaked. Let alone to fight a kraken on the shores of Scotland's holiest island.

I cast Connection one more time in the stillness, allowing spirit to fill me, move through me. My awareness of it had grown with use. I hadn't been conscious of the bonds here when we had joined together to mourn the auld Scots pine that gave its life to our birlinn.

*The birlinn.*

Instinctively, I pulled on those delicate strands of spirit where they connected with me.

Like the silk of a spider's web, the action rippled through us. Rhona and Ealasaid both snapped their heads towards me as if I'd poked them, and though it took a heartbeat or two longer, I felt with absolute certainty as Eilidh, Finn, and Samuel all looked towards Oban.

"A charaidean," I said faintly to the young woman and her much older counterpart, "an seòl sinn anns a' bhirlinn a-rithist?"

*Will we set sail in the birlinn again?*

I didn't need to hear their chorused affirmative "Seòlaidh!"

This was what had drawn me to the edge of the pier—this was what we needed.

One more boat against the kraken.

Just one.

Not even a big boat. No motors, nothing but oars and spirit to propel it.

But it was the work of our hands and the sacrifice of a centuries' old tree. We'd keened it into being together to create a community.

Now it would bear us into battle.

CHAPTER
# FIFTY-ONE

My words hadn't gone unnoticed.

Although the three of us had moved a short distance away from the crowds gathered at and around Ee-usk, people in an ascended world had more than just improved eyesight. They could hear better, too.

And Gaelic, well. It was foolish even pre-ascension to assume the people around you wouldn't understand you if you were slagging them off in the language of the Gaels. Now, it was better to assume everyone—everyone who wasn't Ronald, at least, bastard—could at least be arsed to walk up to Craobh an Òbain to learn it for themselves in five minutes. Put the green owl's time scale to shame, but I reckoned he'd be proud to be out of a job.

We'd barely made it two steps before voices started calling out behind us, asking if they could come.

Most were fighters I recognised from that fateful trek from Bawbag's corral, including that one painfully good-looking couple whose teeth still unnerved me with their whiteness. Their smiles practically glowed in the dark as if someone was shining a black light on their incandescence.

"You know we're about to take a rowboat to a kraken fight, yeah?" I said to the gaggle of people who had pushed their way to the front of the group.

"Aye!" came a few voices, along with a smattering of chuckles and one person who gave me a bombastic side eye and slipped away like what I'd said was somehow a surprise.

As they trooped down the wharf to the birlinn, I cast Keen Eye on the boat.

*Birlinn an t-Seann Ghuithais*

*This traditional birlinn arose from a community ascension. Begun by an ancient Scots pine willingly sacrificing its life to create this boat, its gift and generosity were funnelled through the hands and spirit of a fledgeling community in the early days of the ascension.*

*A mythic item due to the deep cooperation, symbolic sacrifice, and communalist intent, this birlinn may not be a living thing, but it has been imbued with a fierce spirit of protection and cannot be capsized.*

*Other properties discoverable.*

On one hand, taking a rowboat to a kraken battle was far more palatable when said rowboat could not be capsized. On the other, if a kraken tentacle were to wrap around it, would snapping the birlinn in half count as capsizing? I wasn't sure any of us wanted to find out through trial and error.

Especially when "error" came with the oh-so-dangerous bonus of the kraken's brutal venom.

Ealasaid and Rhona both watched our comrades clamber into the birlinn. I sent them over what I'd seen with Keen Eye— even though I thought Ealasaid had the ability, I didn't want to assume she'd used it already.

They both gave me a startled glance after they read it.

"I hope one of the other discoverable properties is a spirit laser beam that disintegrates krakens," Rhona murmured under her breath.

"You and me both," I agreed.

With everyone else now in the birlinn, the three of us joined them. Rhona and I took the foremost seats at the prow, and Ealasaid kept to the rear of the birlinn. I was suddenly that much more grateful I'd taken to doing pushups; even with arcane assistance, rowing required strength.

I informed Angus where we were going with the rockie-talkie as we unmoored the birlinn and rowed into the harbour.

As Rabbie and Eilidh and Catrìona—who herself was now back in communication crystal range—updated me on their positions, a map took shape in my mind.

Angus's gaggle of boats were making excellent time down the Sound of Kerrera, and Eilidh seemed to have pulled out all the stops on her class abilities to threaten the kraken enough to get it moving towards Oban. She walked—or sailed—a fine line between harrying the creature and provoking deadly retalia-tion. Right that moment, it had passed the inlet of Loch Spelve in Mull, a sea loch cradled by two arms of the Ross of Mull. The kraken moved sluggishly indeed, irritated by the boat chasing it but too full of fish to outright engage.

Catrìona and Rabbie had formed their flotilla between Duart Castle in Mull and the southwestern tip of Lismore, where the lighthouse blazed on its rocky islet, visible from where we rowed.

I could picture where everyone was, splayed out on a familiar map of these waters. What I couldn't picture was what would happen once the kraken realised we'd surrounded it.

One boat was ignorable, like a single midge zooming about the edge of your awareness.

Midgies were far, far more noticeable when they swarmed.

I counted the passage of time with each stroke of the oars.

As far as I could sense, none of us were using Spèird to boost our speed, but the birlinn skimmed across the night-still surface of the harbour's waters as if we'd an outboard motor propelling us out to sea.

Pulsing Connection now rewarded me with an up-to-date accounting of everyone's positions.

Everyone except one crucial player.

The fucking kraken.

I couldn't see it.

Minutes had slipped by and turned into hours.

The sky had reached its peak level of early-summer darkness and begun to lighten again on the northeastern horizon, though sunrise was still a couple hours away.

All around us where we'd stopped the birlinn to wait, the sea was calm and glassy. Light haze surrounded us, blending the desaturated hue of the nighttime waters with the predawn twilight of the skies until it felt as if we were in a globe of gradient blue.

Still, we waited.

The eagles, after a short reprieve, had taken up their patrols again, and Scout remained close enough in range that her unease provided an anxiety-boosting backdrop for our current holding pattern.

By all appearances, the kraken had fucking ceased to exist.

The waters here were not so deep it could have hidden unless it had tunnelled into the ocean floor, and even then, with ascension-enabled abilities like Connection and others, we had magical sonar.

Nothing was there.

Nothing we could see, nothing we could sense, and nothing we could kill.

Whatever advantage we'd had against an overstuffed kraken rolly-poly with raining cod seemed to have evaporated.

The sky lightened, imperceptibly to those watching intently but in leaps and bounds when I came up for metaphorical air between deep dives of Connection.

Now that I was aware of the tenuous threads that ran between me, Eilidh, Rhona, Ealasaid, Samuel, and Finn, that awareness wove through the eagle anxiety, the unnerving waiting, and fear. Because we were all nervous.

Angus and the boats from the Kerrera marina had long since moved into place. In theory, we now had the kraken completely surrounded. Boats from Connel and Loch Etive blocked the route north towards Appin; the kraken had no escape through the Sound of Mull or any other direction unless it took a walk.

It was only natural that when it came, it came like a tsunami.

Connection gave me a single glimmer of warning; that's how fast it happened.

The equivalent of a glimpse of bubbles on the bottom of a pot of water, a single swirl.

The sea erupted.

Dimly, I was aware of the birlinn *soaring* to port and hitting the water like a skimming stone. It was only the mythic boat's intrinsic ability to stay upright that kept us from getting thrown through the air arse over tit.

As it was, the impact still sent a jolt through the pine and into my tailbone, and ascension agility and strength alone kept people from spilling overboard—if only barely.

The woman in the impossibly beautiful couple was one of them. Flung into the air, she somehow caught the oar loop closest to her like a gymnast on the rings and with every ounce as much grace. The momentum of her body arrested when the birlinn hit the water, and she flew upwards only to loose a small blast of Spèird that propelled her back into the birlinn.

Her landing was less graceful; she pitched head first into her partner's stomach, where he caught her armour by a leather strap and held on tight.

The previously still sea roiled as if coming to a churning boil.

I pulled Brac-Meanmna out of inventory, feeling the living weapon's eagerness to get into the fray.

The problem was that I couldn't even see where to aim.

Bolts of Purifire and lightning and other spells I couldn't recognise flew through the air towards the raging maelstrom that had spun itself into being in the deepest section of the sea, but nothing struck anything solid that I could identify.

Connection still returned nothing about the kraken, nothing to pinpoint a target.

We'd have to rely on something else to clear the path if we had any hope of killing this thing.

A resounding crack met my ears.

Through the froth and wild water, an impossibly long tentacle had caught hold of one of the smaller boats that seemed to have been pulled towards the maelstrom as the kraken's enormous body displaced water flowing back towards its bulk.

Screams pierced the air.

They melded with the cries of the eagles above us, their grating screeches sounding far more enraged than I'd ever heard them.

Though my go-to spell had been rendered useless for the kraken itself, it *did* show me that no one was sitting on their heels. Trails of white headed by sparkling blue like comets showed up in the blue water in the pre-dawn light as from every direction, mages created chutes of Spèird through which to fire missiles of Purifire.

Where they struck the kraken—and they did—black blood darkened the water.

It may not have truly been black, but desaturated with the unlight of morning, it looked like ink.

Ink.

Fuck.

I'd no evidence but my own experience and intuition, but if *I* were an enormous mutated squid creature in a magical apoca-lypse, my primary defence mechanism levelling up to include an anti-surveillance shroud would certainly feel logical.

While what spilled into the sea must have been blood, I suddenly had no doubt whatsoever that it was the kraken's ink that had kept it hidden from us until it digested its meal enough to attack.

It may still be acting on instinct, but it was also shrewder than we'd credited.

"Keep hitting it!" I yelled, following my own advice even as I sent my voice through the rockie-talkie to all who were listening.

No sooner had the words left my mouth and my Purifire harpoon dipped into my spirit than the kraken's head breached the surface of the tumultuous maelstrom.

One flash of an eye, so quick I wasn't even sure I'd seen it, and high above our heads, Scout screamed.

I'd underestimated the eagle's rage.

While her first encounter with the kraken had ended igno-miniously with friendly fire, and while she didn't blame Rhona for that, Scout *did* blame the monster.

It was as if she'd somehow channelled the teenage banshee's keening wail.

In the movies, sound producers usually cheated with eagles.

Their natural calls weren't as dramatic as the red-tailed hawks' screeches producers usurped to make eagles sound more majestic. But Scout's grating cry became a palpable sonic boom that thundered through the water and sent waves of brine cascading outward from where it impacted the kraken's face.

As close as the kraken *had* to a face, anyway.

The creature recoiled, the five or so visible tentacles above the water surface spasming as if Scout had hooked it up to a live wire the size of an oil pipeline.

She'd hurt it.

*She'd hurt it.*

My burgeoning joy vanished as the kraken retaliated.

All of the kraken's tentacles seemed to contract at once. They curled inward, leaving splinters of the destroyed boat swirling in the churning water.

I caught one glance of what looked like thousands of bristling hairs puffing out of the tentacles and screamed "Shields!"

It was the only thing I had time to say, and I didn't know if it would be enough.

That deadly, deadly venom exploded from the kraken's tentacles like a mushroom cloud.

Our birlinn may not have been able to capsize, but from the screams and creaking wood, everyone aboard every other boat was employing every spell and trick of spirit they could to keep their own upright.

Droplets of venom rained down on us amid screams from those who'd not managed a forcefield of Spèird or the safety of Dìon-Slàinte, and blasts of Purifire continued to vaporise that hellish mist.

Yet our noose tightened, despite everything, around our enemy.

I couldn't see Samuel or Finn or Eilidh, but I felt their

bedrock determination through our strange connection. Chatter ricocheted through the communication crystal as the boats coordinated, and the rowers behind me did the same, propelling us closer to the nest of danger.

Firing off spells from a moving boat in a seething froth of water took all my concentration. In all the din, slowly the other boats came into clear view.

*Eilidh* came into clear view.

She stood with legs braced at the prow of a schooner. Her claymore may have been sheathed between her shoulders, but there was no mistaking that she was battle ready.

I felt her grit through the strands of spirit, sensed her spell as it built even as she took on an unearthly golden glow as if she herself were the oncoming dawn.

I wasn't sure I'd ever seen this spell before, and when she loosed it, I heard a collective gasp—not just from the people in my boat but through the communication crystal.

It was as if pure sunlight exploded from her chest, a ray of brilliance that lit up the morning's haze with prismatic glory.

We speak of the sun as if it's warm and comforting.

We so often forget that it's a blazing ball of unimaginable heat and fire.

It cut through the air with an audible sizzle. The remaining venom that the kraken had blasted out in every direction must have rocketed a hundred metres into the sky for how long it was taking to come back to the surface of the water. Eilidh's beam devoured it in a metres-wide radius—such was the intensity of heat from her weaponised spirit.

The molten light also flash boiled the seawater when it struck.

Eilidh's nuke hit the kraken with a sharp hiss like pouring out a bucket of water on a red-hot griddle.

It hit.

Oh, gods, it hit.

But the kraken spun with impossible agility, its myriad tentacles a propeller it could wield with breathtaking precision.

It bore the brunt of Eilidh's strike on its trunk—had it been a split second slower, I was certain the blow would have blasted straight through its eyeball and slain the kraken in one vicious torrent of flame.

Even as it was, the spell tore through the kraken's trunk and almost sawed it in twain.

I aimed a Purifire harpoon at the wound and loosed it, feeling a host of others do the same, but only a handful of our strikes hit home.

The kraken was *fast*. Heavens above, it was fast.

It reacted with preternatural reflexes.

It launched itself at Eilidh.

The entire prow of her boat exploded from beneath like a wrecking ball hitting a matchstick house.

## CHAPTER
# FIFTY-TWO

I felt my own scream of rage and terror before I heard it. My throat shredded itself with the noise, and across the water in Oban, the intensity of pathos jerked poor wee Sailean from her nap with a screech.

My mind noted that only dimly; the kitten was safe.

The sound of other screams—people, eagles, wood tearing apart at the grain—laid waste to any remaining peace of the morning. Somewhere in the distance, I heard a howl on the wind. Maybe it was the wind responding to our plight as the movement of the kraken's enormous girth tossed us about on the surface of the sea.

*Eilidh.*

All I could think of was Eilidh.

Dimly, I was aware of Ealasaid and Rhona yelling beside and behind me, their back-and-forth words incompressible to me as I desperately scanned the chaos for a golden glow, a splash of auburn hair, anything.

Then something caught me by the upper arms and jerked me into the air.

My throat already raw from my rage, I could barely make a

hoarse croak as a massive, forearm-length talon poked dangerously into my armour.

It wasn't Scout.

Powerful wings beat upwards, and then I did see Scout. She circled below, the sea far beneath us churning with the tumult of battle and death. Her head tilted enough to see me, and I felt a wave of emotion from her as she sent one single sensation through our bond: *trust.*

The eagle that held me let go.

My vocal cords grated soundlessly together as I plunged downwards, and with some absurd presence of mind, I shoved Brac-Meanmna into my inventory even as Scout's feathered back flew up to meet me.

The impact was not soft—her feathers, at that size, were rigid and more like scales. Built to withstand fierce dives and high winds, I hit with a *whumph* that almost stole my breath.

Something caught me as I almost slid off her back—spirit.

Not mine.

Scout's.

The fucking eagle kept me glued to her back of her own accord, and for the first time since we'd met, I felt her make a demand.

*Bond-help-partner.*

At first, I thought she meant Eilidh. We circled above the battle, the view over Scout's shoulder a surreal sensation of watching a fireworks display from the top down. With the coming dawn, it was easier to see, and what I saw was carnage.

*Bond-help-partner!*

Oh.

*Oh.*

I knew what Scout meant. Despite the tumult in my mind, I reached for the spell.

I cast Tàthadh.

Tendrils of spirit reached out to the enormous eagle beneath me, and she seized them without a moment's hesitation.

Where before, I'd been able to catch glimpses of what she saw, now I *felt* her. Felt her elation at being aloft on the wind, the precise and perfect adjustments of wings and tail that steered us through the air.

And I felt what she was trying to tell me.

I wasn't the only elf on an eagle's back.

Closest to me was Finn, looking all the more like a golden god on the back of a white-tailed sea eagle. He had taken to his sudden flight like he'd been born for it, and spirit poured from his outstretched hands, soaring downwards to hit the kraken.

As we banked towards him, I heard something cutting above the wind.

Finn was *singing*.

Am Bàrd Muileach, a' seinn.

Samuel, clinging to a golden eagle. Rhona on the other white-tail. Ealasaid I couldn't see, but I could feel her.

Eilidh.

*Home-love-nest.*

Pride exploded through the bond I shared with Scout, and I saw why she'd veered so suddenly through the air.

Eilidh.

She swayed where the golden eagle's spirit kept her from falling off, her eyes frantically darting back and forth as she tried to take in what was happening.

And then she saw me.

I knew the precise instant she registered the sight of me, because all the terror drained from her face.

Before I could react, Scout tugged at our bond a split second before someone—Samuel—did the same thing I had done on the pier.

He took hold of those strands of spirit between us and *yanked*.

In unison, six eagles cried out in fierce triumph as if they were the ones orchestrating this. Hell, maybe they were.

I cast about with spirit. My well was depleted from the use of Tàthadh, but I strangely felt that was moot.

All I needed to do was catch hold of whatever it was tying the six of us together.

And I did.

My spirit met theirs and I sent out my own resonance through that web. Power came rolling back, sparking down those threads like signals along telegraph wires.

Rhona.

Ealasaid.

Finn.

Eilidh.

As we all became conscious of the web, it flared to life.

My mind . . . expanded.

The eagles flew in a wide circle, dipping lower, lower.

They flew low enough that I thought the kraken could have reached up and grabbed one of the eagles' talons, but despite the wreckage of boats littering the water below, the kraken was far too distracted to look up.

Spirit strikes still rained down upon the beast.

*Calum.*

I felt more than heard Samuel's soft voice.

I knew what to do.

I thought of the hare in Salen, the threads of spirit I sensed grasping from Alison.

Everything that had happened in the past few days had shown me.

Connection was such a basic spell, but it was also perhaps the most profound.

It showed me how everything fit together.

And when our strange circle of eagles and elves lent me their spirit, I looked to the heavens, and I reached out with every thread of connection I held to my own abilities, to the land, to the sea, to the community below.

I reached out through the connection I felt to the birlinn, the fierce protectiveness of that ancient pine.

For a heartbeat, all that existed was the sound of wings, the rush of air as we circled.

Then, like the kraken had churned a maelstrom from the sea beneath us, spirit swirled above like a tempest.

It blended together Ealasaid's passion, Eilidh's justice, Rhona's ferocity, Finn's strength.

It took my own essence as a draoidh.

And it wrapped it all in the mercy of a monk.

I cast Tairm.

From the centre of that raging storm emerged a column of wild magic more precise than a sniper's aim and stronger than a fork of lightning wielded by Zeus himself.

It smote the kraken with a bolt fuelled by all of us, every soul present, and it speared all the way through the beast's enormous body and into the ocean floor.

A wave of water erupted outwards from that epicentre, and before it rushed back in to cover the suddenly exposed sand, the sun broke over the eastern hills and for a single moment, it flashed against a perfect circle of spirit-infused glass.

One blink, and it was gone, relegated to the bottom of the sea.

Slowly, ever so slowly, the waters grew smooth, leaving only wreckage of boats and the enormous, bloated body of the dead kraken.

*You have killed a kraken.*

*Caught in a wave of spirit upon Earth's ascension, this kraken mutated far faster than can normally be expected for a creature of its complexity, spurred on by the trauma of having watched its mate caught in a boat's propeller at the moment Earth ascended.*

*Such creatures frequently contain common crafting materials such as: kraken meat, kraken beak, kraken ink, kraken ink sac, kraken ink gland.*

*Do you wish to harvest this kraken?*

It was with relief I hit the *yes* and shuddered at the wave of spirit, pathos, and will that suffused me.

We had all helped here, and because of that, the gains didn't blow me away, but I didn't care.

It was done.

The kraken was dead.

The moment it was harvested, the rescue work began.

Between the lookouts stationed in Kerrera and Lismore and the relays of communication crystals, it wasn't long before more boats poured out of Oban harbour to retrieve the wounded and the dead.

I couldn't bring myself to look at faces, not yet.

As much as I wanted to ask Scout to fly me directly to land with Eilidh, I couldn't. Yet again, we would put off our own needs to see things through here.

The sun had crept high into the sky by the time we reached Oban again, and as I slid from Scout's back onto the sparring circle near the old CalMac ferry terminal, I could feel the quivering in her feathers that told me she'd pushed herself nearly to death.

"Gabh fois, a charaid," I said to her, encompassing the other eagles in my order to rest.

It was a mark of her exhaustion that she didn't even attempt to make it to the roosts we'd built, which were just over the railroad tracks at the Tesco carpark. Scout simply shuddered and collapsed onto the sparring ring, her eyes already closed.

I sent a ripple of healing through her, but that kind of tired wasn't something healing would really fix.

Whatever threads of spirit had connected me to the other elves—when had I fully stopped thinking of us as humans?—remained. The sensation was mildly uncanny valley, yet another sense to add to the pile. I could feel Eilidh and Ealasaid in the Tesco carpark where their eagle companions had flown with them. Scout must have truly been ready to lose consciousness.

When she woke, I'd have to ask her to be more careful next time.

Gods, I hoped there wasn't a next time.

Rhona and Finn and Samuel were all at the north pier. Eating, I thought.

Knowing what they were doing and where they were felt unnervingly right more than it felt wrong. I hoped there were ways to maintain some privacy, since I'd no illusions that they were also just as aware of me, and there were certain activities I did not think any of us cared to share with the whole class.

That was a bridge we could jump off when we came to it.

Even as I thought it, a wave of fatigue hit me. It wouldn't hurt to just sit down with Scout for a moment or three, would it?

I decided to do just that. My notifications flashed gold around me, and I figured I ought to probably go through them.

*You have reached Level 25! You have two attribute points and three skill points to distribute.*

*Through diligent use, you have increased the level of your skills: Tairm (Level 5), Connection (Level 13), Spèird (Level 7).*

*Through arcane exertion, you have gained a permanent +11 to Spirit, +3 to Pathos, and +5 to Will. Please note that such increases have diminishing returns as your base statistics grow.*

*Through physical exertion, you have gained a permanent +2 to Strength, +3 to Agility, +7 to Mind, and +5 to Stamina. Please note that such increases have diminishing returns as your base statistics grow.*

*You have increased your affinities: Healing (Level 8), Nature (Level 21), Synthesis (Level 14)*

*You have increased your specialised affinity: Wild (Level 17), Coimhearsnachd (Level 8).*

I honestly wasn't sure where my attribute points would be of best use—two per level now felt pitifully small—so I chucked them both into Mind, where at least they'd increase my spirit well. A pittance, maybe, but every little bit counted.

My skill points could wait until I had more than fluff for brains. I pulled up my stat sheet, noting with some excitement that I was now only two levels away from my next class specialisation. Also, the spirit harvest from the kraken had boosted those attributes a wee bit. The near miss on an extra permanent point of Will left me feeling slightly surly, however.

I still wanted the time to really explore what all these stats *did* and what I could accomplish with levelling up my skills. That was a project to concentrate on, maybe, now that the kraken was dead and we could turn our focus to the anomalies.

Hell, it was a project we *should* concentrate on. I'd . . . make a note of that for the next meeting of the Hebridean Council.

Until then, I would just vibe to the small joy of *numbers go up*.

Name: Calum Green

Age: 36

Level: 25

Class: Draoidh (Further class specialisation at: Level 27)

Affinities: Nature (Level 21), Healing (Level 8), Synthesis (Level 14), Staves (Level 20)

Specialised Affinities: Wild (Level 17), Coimhearsnachd (Level 8), Justice (Level 2)

Marks of Esteem: Life, Connection, Justice, Passage

Alteration:
    Strength: 46
    Dexterity: 55
    Agility: 63
    Mind: 127

Regeneration:
    Constitution: 44
    Stamina: 82

Manipulation:
    Spirit: 127 (+237 for 24 hours)
    Pathos: 50 (+111 for 24 hours)
    Will: 54 (+89 for 24 hours)

Boons:
    Blessings
    Làmh na Glaistige
    Glòir a' Ghiuthais
    Blàr Ghaineamhain

As I closed out of my stats, I felt another bond flare to life—one I had last felt in a moment of distress.

I winced as a little furry comet flew across the sparring ground and landed with a thump against my chest.

Sailean's relief suffused our bond to the extent that it filtered through to Scout, who stirred in her sleep with a small chirrup.

"Hey, you," I said to the kitten, who purred even louder. "You were asleep when we left. We should have just sicced you on the kraken."

The wave of indignation was short lived. Sailean settled into the crook of my arm where I sat resting against the arch of Scout's shoulder in the crook of her chest.

"Guess this means we're staying here for a wee while," I said to the kitten with a yawn.

She mewed in response, but it wasn't the sound that made me look up.

Eilidh emerged from behind an outbuilding, and I scrambled to my feet, depositing Sailean on Scout's shoulder.

A small sob escaped Eilidh's throat as we closed the distance to each other, and I swept her up in my arms.

I had to hold myself back from crushing her; I wanted to hug her tight, not turn her into paste. Even so, she still had the higher Strength stat, and after a moment, I had to gasp out an "Air!"

Breath filled my lungs as she loosened her grip, pulling back only far enough to plant her lips against mine.

The kiss was not a soft one; it was a reassuring-yourself-your-partner's-no-deid kiss.

I wasn't sure which of us was more in need of reassurance.

A long while passed with our lips pressed up against one another, and a longer while passed when we gave up on kissing and simply held each other close.

When we finally pulled apart, both of us sank to the strangely springy sparring floor, hearing the whistling snore from Scout along with Sailean's rattly purr where she slept, still atop the enormous eagle's shoulder.

"One problem down," Eilidh said softly, snuggling into my shoulder.

I adjusted my arm to make it easier for her, for some reason unable to find any other words than "Aye, we did."

"Reckon we can take a wee mini break?"

Her question drew a small guffaw from me. My voice had mostly healed from screaming my throat raw in battle, but it still had the tiniest hint of rasp to it when I replied, "We absolutely can. Want to bugger off to Tiree? Let the Hebridean Council deal with the aftermath of all this?"

At Eilidh's explosive sigh, I almost laughed again.

"Absolutely," she said with a groan, then turned her head until her nose was almost in my armpit, which spoke to the fact that the battle might have addled her wits considering I hadn't yet bathed.

I was about to say something to that effect, but she sighed, a shockingly contented sound, and I couldn't bring myself to crack a joke about my body odour.

No, for now, I would let her drift off as we leaned against a giant eagle after killing a kraken.

I'd let the warmth of her presence wash away the remainder of the fear I'd felt when I thought I'd lost her.

I hadn't.

And I wouldn't.

Leaning my head against Eilidh's, I let Scout's soft snores lull my own eyes closed.

# EPILOGUE

"I cannae believe we missed the fucking Cunty MacKraken battle," Iain burst out for what had to be the fifteenth time since I'd shown up in Kilmelford.

With an irritated sigh, I spiralled my finger around in the air. We stood by the ionad-siubhail, where I had engaged the rowan's help once more in protecting the people who worked most closely with the anomalies.

Rhona was with Alison now, though she'd been much less inclined to visit now that her rowan chain revealed the pull she'd felt as unnatural, a product of the grasping filaments that accompanied the anomalies. I'd already covered Meeksy—right then, he stood with his back up against the wall of the house a short distance away. He shook his head fondly at me as if to say, "You can tell him *again* if you want to."

"What?" Iain asked me blankly, looking back and forth between my face and my gesturing hand.

"Turn around, wanker. I need to put this thing on you."

"Oh." Without protest, Iain spun, and he waited with remarkable patience for me to clasp the rowan chain at his neck.

When I was done, he grunted and stood back, poking at the thing. "It's weirdly warm."

"It's not metal," I said.

"Pfft, obviously—I just mean it's different."

Meeksy pushed away from the wall and came over to us. "Thank you for these, Calum. I hadn't realised the effect the anomalies were having on me until I put it on."

"I just wish we could explain it better," I said with a shudder. "For now, I'll settle for lassoing Ronald with one as soon as we track him down."

"After you get back from Tiree, right?" Meeksy gave me a knowing grin and slapped me on the back.

My face suddenly grew warm, and it had nothing to do with Ronald.

"Aye, after I get back from Tiree."

Iain waggled his eyebrows at me lasciviously, which did not look at all sexy—it just looked like he was trying to dislodge a bee that had landed there.

"I'll see yous when we get back," I said, clearing my throat. "Take care of Sailean?"

"Pfft, obviously," Iain said again.

I gave the lads a brief hug, waiting for them to turn back up towards the compound before I aimed myself at the ionad-siubhail.

In all the crafting of the necklaces, I'd gained another level, which was a small comfort. I'd craft them all day long if it would get me to level twenty-seven and the promised further specialisation.

I think we were all a bit unnerved that the kraken hadn't actually given us more than experience and crafting materials. I still had the bulk of that in my inventory, though I'd given some samples of the ink to mages who had practically drooled at the prospect of analysing it and checking out its properties.

There was one thing that had happened in that battle that had oddly taken a day or so to ping, and I wasn't ready to think about that yet.

*You have unlocked the specialised affinity: Pantheon.*

*To access, craft the Resplendent Throne.*

Aye, naw, wisnae ready tae fuck wi' that.

I stepped into the ionad-siubhail.

Well. I wasn't ready to think about how the word *pantheon* pertained to me personally.

I was, however, quite keen to make my date with my god of justice.

I'd been right the first time.

The only thing that could have possibly improved upon the perfect waters of the Tiree beach was Eilidh's presence.

We both floated in the sunset-touched waves, the golden-hour rays touching her water-darkened hair with ruby.

I'd never seen anything so beautiful.

Even though she was currently gnawing on her lip as if she were afraid to say something.

It was our third day in Tiree. Three days of perfect sunny weather, three nights of . . . well.

Heat.

My face warmed at the thought of it, and even the chill of the water couldn't quite disguise my body's other reactions to the memories. Eilidh, though, looked less thirsty and more nervous. Even though we were both in the buff—skinny dipping was apparently my new hobby—I couldn't have her feeling anxious, now, could I?

"All right, there?" I asked her, taking her hands in mine and lowering my feet to stand in the waist-deep waves.

For a moment, I thought she might dissemble. A few times in the past couple days, I'd caught her looking at me out of the corner of my eye like she wanted to say something but was too scared.

"I need to know what we are," Eilidh blurted out before I could think of a way to gently prod her into speaking. "I didn't think I did, but I do, and I just—I need to know that I'm not alone out on this limb. Before it breaks."

My heart gave a *crunch*, but before I could answer, she went on all in a rush.

"It's not that I'm not happy with whatever that is—it's just that I—I'm." Eilidh stopped then, looking lost.

"Will you tell me what you want us to be?" I asked carefully. "If I promise the limb won't break?"

Silence spread between us, touched only by the muted lapping of the sea against our torsos.

"*Can* you promise that?" Eilidh's voice suddenly sounded very small.

The urge to laugh competed with the sudden military tattoo beating out a rat-a-tat-tat in my chest. This woman could say she wanted to marry me in an hour and I'd ask her if she wanted me to put on clothes first.

But I couldn't make myself say that—not after years of thinking she hated me, however untrue that had proven to be. That'd be coming on just a wee bit too strong.

Instead, all I said was a fervent "*Yes*."

Her sudden outburst had fizzled, and though her eyes were wide with my single-syllable answer to her question, her mouth just opened and shut a couple times.

Was I really going to make her be the vulnerable one here? After she worked up the courage to raise the subject even though she was clearly terrified of rejection? Hell, that she was still so afraid of me rejecting her after we'd spent the past few days bouncing back and forth between bed and the sea, barely putting on clothes at all, well. She must have been in tumult.

I'd only *thought* she hated me all that time with Susanna, and I'd been an absolute tit.

No, this was my job.

Without another thought, I closed the remaining distance between us, pulling her up against me until even the water couldn't quite edge between the skin of our stomachs.

"Tha gaol agam ort," I said to her. It felt right to say it in Gaelic, where love is something that covers people with its warmth. "Tha mo ghaol-sa ort."

Eilidh's hands were so cold in mine, her fingers so still as if she hadn't quite processed what I'd said.

Honestly, I hadn't quite processed it either. I'd started with the simple version of *I love you* and then anted up with a much more emphatic *My love is yours.*

It was apparently my turn to blurt things out.

"You have always seen me in ways no one else did," I said, my voice so hushed it hardly stirred the air between us. Eilidh couldn't seem to meet my eyes, so I held her hands tighter in my own, feeling my own warmth slowly thawing her chilled skin. "Even when I thought you hated me, I respected you. Your courage and your strength, your way of thinking and the ferocity with which you protect everyone you love. I should have realised sooner that you showed that same ferocity protecting me."

At that, her blue eyes met mine, pupils dilated and expression ever so slightly dazed.

"What grew here was respect and *trust*, Eilidh, and it grew so naturally that we were standing in a forest before I realised we'd planted trees. So no, that branch won't break. What I feel for you is not fragile."

Once the words were out of my mouth, they seemed to hang

there between us, and I got a taste of how she'd felt only a few moments before. What if *I* was the one alone here? What if that had gone too far?

But what I saw in her eyes was not fear.

Something in her relaxed, and what bloomed in those clear, blue depths was more akin to wonder.

"Is tusa mo ghaol," she said. Eilidh pulled one hand from mine and raised it, trembling, to touch my cheek.

When her lips touched mine, her words singing in my soul —you are my love—it felt as if the heavens opened above us, like something vast and at once infinitesimal clicked into place.

Gone were worries about what might come next, what meaning the word *pantheon* held for us and the way I could now see Rhona, Eilidh, and Ealasaid in my mind's eye like the maiden, mother, and crone of old.

That was part of it, part of us, as were Finn and Samuel.

But right here, this was what mattered most to my heart.

It was a feeling I'd chased my whole life that had somehow eluded me, and now, in an apocalypse with magic surging between us, it washed over us both as I lowered my lips to hers and she met them with a fevered sweetness.

*Home.*

We were home.

We would face whatever came next together.

# Afterword

Thank you so much for reading *The Resplendent Throne*!

I've had a hell of a year here in bonny Glesga, which began before the New Year when a cold snap burst a pipe above my flat just before Christmas (whee!) and proceeded with pneumonia, a pinched nerve in one shoulder, a pulled muscle in the other shoulder (ironically, this happened at my final physio appointment for the pinched nerve), and a litany of other disasters that kept me from being able to write this book as fast as I meant to. Turns out when your shoulders are buggered, it's pretty much the worst possible thing you can do to sit at a computer with your arms out in front of you.

Thank you hugely for your patience and for your kind messages and support for this series. It makes my curmudgeonly Gaelic heart sigh with joy. I hope you've enjoyed this instalment. As a wee bug-fix notice, I realised very late that I'd changed Calum's age in my head and in the narrative . . . but left it as-is in his stat sheets. My dyscalculia makes numbers an arch-nemesis anyway, so I literally didn't even see it. D'oh! It's now fixed across all three books—you can update your Kindle versions if you want—but sorry for the inconsistencies—he should be 36, not 30.

I've commissioned the next three covers from my artist, and I cannae wait to keep bringing this series to life. Whilst I wait on art, you can expect two more smaller books in the *Terra Incognita* mini-series. Aye, that's right! Will and Trudy return—those covers are already burning a hole in my hard drive, so you won't have horribly long to wait to get your ascension fix.

If you're new to LitRPG, there are some great places for you to get your groove on! Try the LitRPG Books group on Facebook to chat with fellow readers and authors!

I've had an absolute blast writing in this world, and I really wanted to bring LitRPG to my homeland. Figured it'd be good craic, and I think that proves true. Calum isn't so much a pathetic hamster now, I reckon—I'm champing at the bit to see where he goes from here.

If you've not yet read it, I wrote a wee book for the Inkfort Press Publishing Derby last year that was a concurrent prequel to *The Transcendent Green*. That book is called *Terra Incognita*, and you can find it right here.

I'm hard at work on getting new books out to you. If you want to get first crack at them, find me over on Patreon! I'm an absolute chaos gremlin and can't commit to a regular posting schedule for neurodivergent brain reasons. If you don't care about my wild inconsistency and want to really gie it laldy and support me anyway, I truly appreciate my patrons putting up with my all-over-the-place yeeting of chapters!

One last thing: if the Gaelic has you floundering at all or you're just burning with curiosity about how things sound, check out LearnGaelic. Their dictionary has over seventy thousand sound files, and whilst you may not find everything due to me taking a fluent-if-not-native speaker's licence to play with things for alliterative purposes (or, in Brac-Meanmna's case, to make up a word), you'll find most of it.

If you fancy going all out and *learning* our language, some fantastic folk (including an Oban lad!) worked their tails off to get it on Duolingo, where you can learn exciting and useful phrases like "Tha mo thòn dìreach àlainn" (my arse is just gorgeous) and "An aithne dhut Iain Rùisgte?" (Do you know Naked Iain?) and "Obh obh, thusa a-rithist!" (Oh, no, you again —AKA what people say when I walk into the room).

Great craic. And contrary to popular paranoia when people see our spellings, Gaelic is worlds more regular than English once you learn the rules. I believe in you! Siuthadaibh!

Or, did ye ken, you can also just go learn all the words to "Sìne Bhàn" yourself and then sing it eighteen times in a night until everyone weeps from the sheer glory. (That will definitely be why they're weeping if you've sung it eighteen times drunk. The glory. Aye, the glory.)

Despite my fond jokes, it's a lovely song and a staple of the Gaelic massed choirs on a end-of-Mòd Saturday morning. Written by Islay man Donnchadh MacIain, whose contributions to Gaelic song are still sung far and wide even beyond Fair Sìne, it's a pure classic.

Anyhoo, go forth and get learning! Suas leis a' Ghàidhlig!

# CALUM'S STATS AND SPELLS

Calum's Stats

**Name:** Calum Green

    **Age:** 36

    **Level:** 26

    **Class:** Draoidh (Further class specialisation at: Level 27)

    **Affinities:** Nature (Level 21), Healing (Level 8), Synthesis (Level 14), Staves (Level 20)

    **Specialised Affinities:** Wild (Level 17), Coimhearsnachd (Level 8), Justice (Level 2)

    **Marks of Esteem:** Life, Connection, Justice, Passage

**Alteration:**

    **Strength:** 47

    **Dexterity:** 56

    **Agility:** 65

    Mind: 137

**Regeneration:**

    **Constitution:** 44

**Stamina:** 82

**Manipulation:**
**Spirit:** 133
**Pathos:** 51
**Will:** 55

**Boons:**
Blessings
Làmh na Glaistige
Glòir a' Ghiuthais
Blàr Ghaineamhain

## Calum's Spells and Skills

### Bas-Ogham *(Passive)*

*Ogham is a form of writing that, much like the runes of the Nordic peoples, was also used for divination. Its letters correspond to the trees of the Gaelic alphabet. Bas-Ogham is the art of divining with small rods of wood into which the letters of the ogham are carved.*

*The writing can be found carved into stone, though wood carvings would have also proliferated at the time of its peak usage. Those have largely been lost to time.*

*Regain the knowledge of those who came before. In an ascended world, your connection to your ancestors is as real as that to those who walk and breathe beside you on your path.*

*The uses of ogham are limited only by your imagination—and your will. They can be formed into sacred trees, etched into weapons, tattooed into skin. Be mindful of what you create. Allow Bas-Ogham to guide you.*

*Bas-Ogham as a skill will improve with each tree attunement you cultivate.*

*Your current attunements:*
*Darach*

**Beannachd Shlàinte** *(Level 3)—This skill can be used once per day to heal a severe injury of tissue trauma and infection. You gain an increased affinity for Healing, allowing you to intuit what is necessary to save lives of humans and animals alike.*

*Increased use of this skill allows for more complex healing, including but not limited to: internal haemorrhaging, progressive disease, antivenin formulation, purging toxins, and limb regrowth. Additionally, greater knowledge of the body's anatomy and physiology makes you more effective in combat.*

*Through your growing Synthesis affinity, you have combined this spell with others to great effect, and your increasing understanding has cut the cooldown time by 50%.*

*Affinity: Healing*
*Skill Tree: Slàinte*

**Caidreabhas**—*This skill is a foundational one in the Tàthadh tree, but it is not one to be used lightly. Caidreabhas, like Tàth, forms a consensual bond with an animal companion, but unlike Tàth, this bond is permanent and will persist until your death or that of your companion.*

*Many animals in an ascended world stretch past their previous limits, often ranging from sentience to outright sapience, in time. Caidreabhas encourages such growth in your companion, bolstering the animal's natural strength and adaptability as well as their intelligence.*

*Unlike most active skills, Caidreabhas will not level, as for it to* do so would cause first bonds to eventually lose their appeal with the ability to form more complex bonds. Instead, Caidreabhas evolves—with each animal you bond, your relationship with your companion will shift depending entirely upon what you invest in it.

Your current abilities allow you: 1 companion

Affinity: Nature

Skill Tree: Tàthadh

·ᴄ ᴄᴋ-ᴅꜱ ᴊ·

**Connection** (Level 15)—You gain a deeper affinity to the earth and its needs, and it whispers to you. With this skill, you are able to see how things around you interact, be it the tracks of a deer hunted by paw prints of a stalking cat or the passing of a band of hunters.

Increased use of this skill enables you to take in an entire scene at a glance and appropriately assess its secrets. Additionally, the skill will allow you to ascertain the needs of the natural world, giving you the power to aid creatures and plants that may one day return the favour.

Your use has granted you a bonus to clarity. Your ability to see and identify patterns has increased, and you are now 12% more likely to spot items of import, foes in stealth, and escape routes.

Affinity: Nature

Skill Tree: Nature

·ᴄ ᴄᴋ-ᴅꜱ ᴊ·

**Cumhachd** (Level 3)—This spell is one of the most versatile in the hedge witch's arsenal. By tapping into the ambient spirit that surrounds you to augment your own, you are able to form missiles based upon your environment. Not only does this spell shift dramatically from mage to mage, but it also enhances your acquisition of points in Spirit. This ability is bolstered by and best used within your existing affinities, but it also rewards creativity.

Continued use may unlock additional benefits and upgrades. As with all things in an ascended world, the limits are your own imagination. (ch23)

Affinity: Synthesis, Nature

Skill Tree: Arcane

**Darach** (Passive)—Some believe that the word for druid, and thus all magic, originated from the word for oak. This word in the old language was dair, and whether or not the etymology proves true, it is undeniable that the oak is a symbol of magic and protective power even now.

As a Draoidh, you will slowly begin to demonstrate a Draoidh's connection to the power of trees. The first of these is always the oak, for it is within the stalwart oak your power finds its roots.

Darach allows the Draoidh to draw consciously from this power, which grows stronger when using staves of oak or when in contact with living oak.

While Darach will not increase in levels as active spells will, your understanding of magic will, on occasion, trigger evolution.

You have already demonstrated your connection to the oak, both in your creation of the living weapon Brac-Meamna and with your spontaneous cultivation of an oak tree in Kilninver. Evolution of Darach: Imminent.

**Dubh** (Level 2)—The Draoidh knows there is nowt to fear in darkness.

To the contrary, darkness is the source of all things, including light. It is from darkness the universe was born, and in that darkness is the potential of all creation.

Dubh allows you to tap into the creative power. Coupled with Bas-Ogham, it can be used to write ogham into your skin. In the heat of battle, the Draoidh can use Dubh to obscure an enemy's sight. While it will only work upon a foe who lacks the Draoidh's understanding of the true nature of darkness, on a fearful opponent who relies fully upon sight and light, it is a powerful weapon.

The skill taps into our most ancient connections to a time before time itself, before light, when all was one in the womb of the endless void. Dubh does not ascribe fear to this void; for the Draoidh, it is a source of comfort and solace. In returning to Dubh, the Draoidh finds the will to write reality into existence.

Affinity: Draoidh, Wild

Skill Tree: Draoidh

**Faicte 's Neo-Fhaicte** (Passive)

The Gaels have long known that there are more worlds beyond the physical, worlds into which people sometimes slipped, unseen or unheard or both. On occasion, they reemerged with tales of delight or horror or a mingling of the two.

Food so delicate and sweet all else would taste forever of ash. Beauty so rare and tantalising one could weep—but denying it would bring swift and brutal death.

The fuath, the glaistig, the beithir—all of these are creatures of your world and always have been. Now, though, they slink through the veil.

Faicte 's Neo-Fhaicte alerts you to the presence of the otherworlds and may, for the canny, provide insight into its inner workings and motivations.

Affinity: Draoidh, Nature, Wild

*Skill Tree: Draoidh*

· ( ⟨⟨ ⟩⟩ ) ·

**Fuaran**—*Like its name, Fuaran is a skill that brings with it a wellspring of refreshment. This skill increases your spirit regeneration by a base of 20% for 3 minutes, and if comrades are within 10 meters of you, it will also do the same for them.*

*Increased use of this skill will increase its efficacy and area of effect and may also bestow other boons that can benefit you and your party.*

Affinity: Arcane

Skill Tree: Arcane

· ( ⟨⟨ ⟩⟩ ) ·

**Gu h-Àrd** *(Passive)*—*You gain an understanding of all things above the earth: the currents of the air, the patterns of the clouds, and those that make their home therein. You receive an immediate +2 to Mind and a bonus to calling upon the powers of weather, wind, and creatures of the heavens. With experience, you may also summon the storm.*

*While Gu h-Àrd will not increase in levels as active spells will, your understanding of magic will, on occasion, trigger evolution.*

*Affinity: Nature, Synthesis*

*Skill Tree: Nature*

· ( ⟨⟨ ⟩⟩ ) ·

**Gu h-Ìosal** *(Passive)*—*You gain an understanding of all things below the earth: the waters that flow, the roots that grow, and those that make their home therein. You receive an immediate +2 to Mind and a bonus to calling on the powers of flora and earth-bound* *fauna. With experience, you may also free the forest to do your bidding.*

*While Gu h-Ìosal will not increase in levels as active spells will, your understanding of magic will, on occasion, trigger evolution.*

*Affinity: Nature, Synthesis*

*Skill Tree: Nature*

· ( ꙮ ) ·

**Keen Eye** *(Level 5)—This ability allows you to examine an item, foe, or location, and in conjunction with Connection, it can reveal secrets or vital clues that will push you towards helpful information. Keen Eye comes with a one-time bonus to Mind of +1.*

*Continued usage will improve the complexity and usefulness of the information Keen Eye provides. As your knowledge of its uses has grown, you have discovered the boons to this subtle skill. As with many worthwhile things, you get out of it what you put into it.*

*Affinity: Synthesis*

*Skill Tree: Arcane*

· ( ꙮ ) ·

**Liminality (Passive)**—*The Gaels and the Celts both venerated liminal spaces—the place where land meets water, dusk and dawn, and the traditional markings of the year for equinoxes as much as solstices. There is power to the between-places, where the world becomes veiled. Neither shore nor sea, yet both at once.*

*Liminality increases all Nature and Wild affinity abilities based on the following temporal-spatial locations: dawn, dusk, Imbolc, Samhain, Beltane, Lughnasadh, equinoxes, being within nine metres of a body of water, and being in places that house the dead.*

*Your magic shall respond with alacrity in these times and spaces, and you gain a 10% chance to bend others' magic to your own will to disarm it if it seeks to harm.*

*Any permanently bonded animal companions immediately unlock this passive skill.*

*As the bridge between the physical and the spiritual world, the Draoidh draws power from both.*

*This spell cannot be increased with skill points after unlocking, but mastery of its ways may trigger evolution.*

*Affinities: Synthesis, Wild*

*Skill Tree: Draoidh*

· · ⟨⟨ ⟩⟩ · ·

**Mac-Talla**—*Like Tursa allows you to connect with the turning of the earth and the constancy of the stars above in the present, Mac-Talla opens you to echoes of the past.*

*When you use Mac-Talla, you gain insight into what has come before to better prepare you for what is ahead. Your Earth philosopher George Santayana once said that "those who cannot remember the past are condemned to repeat it"—the Draoidhean live by this understanding. It is also said that a smart person learns from their own mistakes, but a wise person learns from the mistakes of others. Listen to the echoes. Learn from them. Use them to chart a stronger future.*

*Affinities: Wild, Arcane*

*Skill Tree: Draoidh*

· · ⟨⟨ ⟩⟩ · ·

**Òran na Cloiche**—*When the Draoidhean speak, the people listen. And when the Draoidhean sing, the people weep. With this passive skill close to your heart, your words will reach receptive ears. Once per week, you may also find inspiration to weave words into song,* and those songs will ring out through your lands to touch all those who hear them. Friend or foe, the listener will not remain unmoved —for better or for worse.

*Affinities: Wild, Synthesis*

*Skill Tree: Draoidh*

·‹ ⸱⸱ ›·

**Purifire** (Level 11)—*This skill is most used in combat, instilling basic fire with the power of the arcane, making it burn hotter and brighter than typical flame—and all within the mage's control. This fire is not friendly fire in more than one way. Magic is will and intent, and it will strike only your foes. While a staff is needed for advanced use, this skill can be wielded without need for a weapon.*

*Increased use of Purifire allows for more complex use. Many mages utilise it with metal weapons to great effect, adding burning damage and spirit damage to physical. Others prefer a staff's elegance and the advanced precision a mage finds therein. At its heart, this skill moulds itself to its wielder, and only the mage can decide its limits.*

*You have discovered the utility of this offensive skill in using it not only against your opponents but also to control your environment. As such, you have gained the upgrade Ring of Fire, which you can use to encircle your foes.*

*You have utilised Purifire in myriad ways with efficiency and cunning. In combat, you have often used it in combination with Spèird to great efficacy. As such, you have gained the upgrade Fist of Flame, which you can use to pack an even greater punch.*

*Increased use of Purifire allows for more complex use. Your use of it has been diverse, from illumination to cleansing to combat, and you are only scratching the surface of its potential. At its heart, this skill moulds itself to its wielder, and only the mage can decide its limits.*

*(upgrades: Ring of Fire, Fist of Flame)*
*Affinity: Nature, Staves*
*Skill Tree: Arcane*

‚‚ ⷜ⸬ ⸬⸬

**Slànaich** *(Level 5)—A basic healing spell, Slànaich provides a general increase to inherent healing in both speed and duration. While it will not stave off death in the event of a mortal wound, it will both refresh tired muscles and soothe smaller injuries, which may make the difference between life and death even if it feels less dramatic.*
*Affinity: Healing*
*Skill Tree: Slàinte*

‚‚ ⷜ⸬ ⸬⸬

**Spèird** *(Level 7)—Often the first spell a mage learns, Spèird is a blast of force that can be used to fling projectiles and foes alike to buy the wielder precious time or space to manoeuvre.*

*Increased use of this skill allows for more targeted applications and, with the power of a true proficient, can be as lethal as a martial arts' master's fists.*
*Affinity: Staves*
*Skill Tree: Arcane*

‚‚ ⷜ⸬ ⸬⸬

**Tairm** *(Level 5)—This spell calls upon the land around you to respond, which it will, based on your affinities and your own intent. As this is wild magic, the results are difficult to anticipate for the caster, though if that is true, it is all the more confounding for the targets.*

*Be clear in your need, and nature will respond to your call.*
*Affinity: Wild (Special)*
*Skill Tree: Wild*

· ( ⟨⟨⟨⟩⟩⟩ ) ·

**Taobh a-Staigh** *(Passive)—You gain an understanding of the intrinsic qualities of all life and its relationship to spirit. Rooted in Connection, this skill grants a permanent +1 to Mind and +1 to Pathos, and you receive a bonus to all spells and skills that deal with things internal: healing, buffs, and your understanding of your own spirit.*

*While Taobh a-Staigh will not increase in levels as active spells will, your understanding of magic will, on occasion, trigger evolution.*

*Affinity: Nature, Synthesis*
*Skill Tree: Nature*

· ( ⟨⟨⟨⟩⟩⟩ ) ·

**Taobh a-Muigh** *(Passive)—You gain an understanding of the relational qualities of all life and ecosystems as well as their place in the web of spirit. Rooted in Connection, this skill grants a permanent +1 to Mind and +1 to Will, and you receive a bonus to all spells and skills that deal with things external: bonds, brawls, and anything that acts upon the outside world.*

*While Taobh a-Muigh will not increase in levels as active spells will, your understanding of magic will, on occasion, trigger evolution.*

*Affinity: Nature, Synthesis*
*Skill Tree: Nature*

· ( ⟨⟨⟨⟩⟩⟩ ) ·

**Tàth** *(Level 2)—This ability allows you to form a consensual bond with an animal, giving you the power to see through the animal's eyes and guide the creature's movements where necessary. These bonds, once created, will bring a consistent drain on spirit until released, but the benefits far outweigh the sacrifice. Tàth comes with a one-time bonus of +1 to Pathos.*

*Continued usage will improve the usefulness of these bonds, providing a symbiotic balance for both you and your companion. You gain eyes and ears and mobility—they gain intelligence, protection, and, in rare cases, special abilities. (Ch 18)*

*Affinity: Nature, Synthesis*
*Skill Tree: Tàthadh*

**Tuairmse** *(Passive)—Whilst most flounder with patterns in the wilds of nature, you thrive riding the waves of weather and land-scape alike. Tuairmse is like a volcano; it may lie subtly dormant for a time, but when it wakes, the results can be course altering.*

*Tuairmse works best in tandem with the Nature tree's root-level passives: Gu h-Ìosal, Gu h-Àrd, Taobh a-Muigh, and Taobh a-Staigh. It is recommended to learn those skills prior to learning Tuairmse.*

*Once all of these are unlocked, however, your innate under-standing of nature increases tenfold. You will not only be able to sense the turning of the seasons like the woodchuck who builds a thicker-walled den before an intense winter, but you will also judge the tides, the whip-quick shifts in weather, and most importantly, how to use those things to your advantage.*

*Affinity: Nature, Synthesis*
*Skill Tree: Draoidh*

**Tursa** *(Level 3)—The ancients moved twenty-tonne slabs of rock hundreds of miles to build their monoliths. From this we have gleaned not only their technological capabilities but also their astronomical understanding. Many of these ancient monoliths were built with an intimate knowledge of the stars in the sky and the movements of the sun's path.*

*This skill is the bedrock upon which the Draoidh builds their power. In unlocking it, you will gain an instinctual knowledge of astronomy and its relationship to you. While this many not seem like much, it will root you in time, in the seasons, and upon the surface of the earth itself. For what is more constant than the stars for navigation? To get anywhere, you need to know where you are.*

*Both a passive and an active skill, Tursa will allow you to carry an instinct of time and the turning of the wheel, but upon casting, it will give you an innate understanding of your environment, a precious glimpse that can allow you to strategise in the heat of battle or work your way out of natural obstacles when you can see no escape.*

*Affinity: Nature, Synthesis*
*Skill Tree: Draoidh*

# LOVE LITRPG?

To learn more about LitRPG, talk to authors including myself, and just have an awesome time, please join the LitRPG Group!

# ABOUT THE AUTHOR

Mati Ocha is a Scottish author of LitRPG and progression fantasy. He likes scrambling up mountains, jumping in cold lochs, and generally making mayhem in Gaelic and English. When he's not being chaotic in the wilds, he can usually be found ruining his characters' days or grinding yet another seasonal character in Diablo III.

His social media game is less than ideal, but you can follow him if you really want to on Twitter, Reddit, or Patreon, and if you want to support his Patreon, you can get first crack at new stories!

If you're looking for more LitRPG gremlins like me and you, check out the LitRPG Books group on Facebook!

# More from Robot Dinosaur

**Mati Ocha's Ascension World Stories:**

*(ApocaLitRPG Progression Fantasy)*

*Terra Miniseries (Concurrent Prequel to The Transcendent Green)*

Terra Incognita

Terra Nova

Terra Infinita

***The Transcendent Green:***

The Transcendent Green

The Ascendent Sky

The Resplendent Throne

Books 1-3 Omnibus

The Reverent Creed

The Penitent's Cry

**Death Spiral:**

Death Spiral 1 (Prologue)

Death Spiral 2

Death Spiral 3

* * *

**R.J. Theodore's Peridot Shift:**

*(Swashbuckling Science Fantasy)*

Flotsam

Salvage

Cast-Off

* * *

**Aurora's Rift: A Progression Fantasy Romance by Emmie Mears**

Riftsworn

Beacon

Reborn

* * *

**The Worlds of Novae Caelum:**

Magnificent (A Superhero Novella)

The Throne of Eleven (Epic Fantasy)

The Truthspoken Heir (Epic Space Fantasy)

* * *

**The Many Marvels of Merc Fenn Wolfmoor:**

Wolf Among the Wild Hunt

Friends for Robots

These Imperfect Reflections

Monster Girls Don't Cry

Robot Dinosaur Press
robotdinosaurpress.com